A Question of Fate

A Novel

Stephany Cavalier Houghton

This book is a work of fiction. The characters, conversations, and events in the novel are the products of the author's imagination, and no resemblance to any actual conduct of real-life persons, or to actual events, is intended. Although certain public figures do make incidental appearances, their interactions with the characters are wholly the author's creation.

For Amelia, whose query in Berlin got the ball rolling.

Chapter 1

July 1999

The man with the bright blond hair should have taken note of the two men hunkered low in the front seat of the parked box van facing him at the curb. The street was empty of all but a few parked cars. Even at this distance the seated young woman recognized him immediately. His hair was even more unruly than she remembered from the night before, his fast gait far more distracted. *What were the chances?* The smile on her face faded quickly as she glanced back at the van.

She had awakened suddenly this Sunday morning at dawn, far too early, time to kill. After a quick stretch, she set out on a run and then a fast walk down dimly lit, silent streets. She kept walking even after she grew tired, her eyes carefully searching the sides of the streets and the few passing cars for signs of trouble. She looked at her watch. She must be most of the way back to the yacht harbor where she had started. Almost an hour and a half had passed. The humid summer air in New York City was beginning to heat up.

Her steps slowed when she spotted the men in the van, ominous and out of place. Taking off her runner's backpack, she finished her water bottle and stood in thought for a moment. Then she took a seat on a shadowy bench across the street to observe. Her damp, dark brown hair fell across her muscular shoulders and sweat dripped down her forehead, but she didn't dare move to wipe it away. She couldn't be sure the men in the van hadn't yet noticed her.

As she watched The Blond approach, she thought again how he seemed to have a strange, serene grace about him, an attractive gentleness, despite his solemn expression. She found his face handsome in an ageless sort of way, dark-toned from the sun but unlined, youthful even. He looked Slavic, perhaps Russian, with high cheekbones, but she couldn't say if he was forty or fifty. Average height, five feet ten at most, built like a gymnast, narrow-waisted and broad-shouldered, though it had been his head of sun-colored, slightly curly hair that caught her eye, earning him the private nickname.

He was wearing the same clothes as when she'd first seen him the night before: nondescript tan shirt with sleeves buttoned at the cuffs despite the heat, now soaked through as if he'd been up all night and then worked out hard in it, rumpled khakis, worn work boots. Not a man who cared much about his outward appearance. She thought momentarily about calling out to him, but what would she say? Maybe nothing would happen at all and he would pass safely.

As he walked past the van, the front doors flew open. The curbside door slammed into him as the men scrambled out. The closer one pummeled him over the door while the second rounded the front of the van and grabbed him around the throat with a beefy arm. She was off the bench and on top of them in a second. Even odds, piece of cake. Hands on shoulders, vicious knee to center of back, hard leg-swing sweeping the attacker off his feet, the blond man free to take on the first assailant while she got in a good kick to the groin to the one on the ground. Gathering his wits, The Blond ducked behind the van door and heaved it shut, trapping his attacker. Then he swung around the door to reach for a wrist, bending it sharply backward, and landed a fist in the attacker's throat. She met his eyes for a moment – saw triumph, surprise, curiosity. But the moment was all they had.

The back doors of the van burst open and four more men spilled out, three of them joining the fray and the fourth standing back, positioning himself it seemed. The new assailants were younger, more adept fighters, but her skills were more than a match for them. The Blond was defending himself with ferocity and martial arts expertise. She threw one man hard to the ground, kicked his head and spun around to help the blond man when she saw the assailant by the van raise his arm. A dart gun... Too late. She saw the dart strike the man in the neck and he crumpled to his knees. A searing pain from a blow to the back of her head brought her down as well. Her last sight was of The Blond motionless on the ground, the recovered assailants reaching to lift him.

She awoke in near total darkness, head reeling. She ignored the pain to take stock. Unbound, lying flat, van in motion. She sat up slowly, hands at the back of her throbbing head. A sticky, good-sized bump but no real damage – thought process and memory were clear. Reaching out cautiously to explore, she discovered a prone figure beside her, unresponsive, one blanket, two heavy, empty buckets, and

the inside walls of a cargo van, surely the same one. She tried the rear doors. Locked, of course. The road was smooth, probably a highway from her sense of their speed, the noise, and the quiet ride. There were two small windows in the back doors, but they'd been painted over almost completely. The only light came from a few scratches in the paint. Her unfailing sense of time told her it was late morning the same day.

Her hands explored the body next to her. From the damp mop of hair, the blond man. His head felt feverish. Fully dressed, also unbound, which surprised her. This was not a quick rescue, this was a disaster. She forced herself to stay calm, focused, as she had been taught. Both of their lives were in danger now, and with the condition of her fellow captive, escape was going to be up to her. She quickly analyzed her mistakes. There were far too many. She had been too soft, not treated this like a life or death situation. She should have recognized the man standing by the van for the threat that he was, thrown off her second attacker and taken him down first. She should have dealt the assailants broken arms, heads, put them in intensive care for a week. She had been trained how, she'd just never done it. And she should never have been so distracted that one of them was able to hit her from behind. The Blond had been too soft, too. A harder throat punch would have crushed his attacker's trachea.

She didn't know the man's name. He had spoken anonymously at the Global Human Rights Conference last night in New York, a long, impassioned, eloquent speech on the horrors of human trafficking in Southeast Asia where he worked, doing what, she wasn't sure, but it sounded dangerous and violent. His accent was slightly Australian, though he'd tried to disguise it. She had an excellent ear for languages.

Her first sight of him had been at the back of the auditorium; he looked hesitant, as if about to bolt. An earnest-looking young man in a blazer and blue tie was talking in his ear, cajoling, calming, convincing. While she watched, the man seemed to come around, donning a pair of dark sunglasses. He pulled a black watch cap down low over his blond hair and strode purposefully to the podium. His electrifying speech was unlike anything she had ever heard, spoken from years – decades even – of personal experience fighting on the front lines of a war on humanity. How old *was* he, she wondered. He enumerated a multitude of approaches and plans for countering the epidemic as he called it and received a standing ovation from the

3

assembled crowd of international human rights commissioners, ministers, workers, and journalists. No wonder someone high up in that business wanted him taken out. But then why not just kill him?

His pockets were empty – no passport, wallet, keys, or cell phone – all taken, as hers must have been. She didn't feel her runner's backpack anywhere. Her watch was gone. Holding onto one wall, she attempted to stand. There was plenty of head clearance, even for her five-foot eight frame. She continued to grope around the inside of the darkened cargo hold, trying the door handles. Another blacked out window, this one barred, at the front of the compartment, communicating with the cabin. There was nothing more. Rapping hard on the window, she tried giving a loud shout to see what would happen.

"The van is soundproofed. Shut up and enjoy the ride while you can. It's going to get a lot worse," a rough voice called out faintly, followed by raucous laughter.

New York accent, Bronx. She stayed silent, hoping to hear more. Placing her ear against the barred window, she could hear a murmur of discussion, but couldn't make out what they were saying. An argument from the tone. *Good*, she thought, *I can use that*. She was sure they were the same two men who had been waiting in the parked van, late-thirties, white, dim-witted thugs. She wondered why such men had been chosen for this assignment. Local talent, most likely, perhaps unfamiliar to a non-resident employer. She could use that too. They had not been especially good fighters, but then they hadn't needed to be. She hoped the other four assailants weren't following in a second car. And what did he mean by a lot worse?

Within the hour she knew. Her fellow prisoner sat up suddenly and began to retch violently, his entire body in spasms. She held one of the buckets to his face, then turned him on his side. The air in the van was stifling in the heat of the day, and the smell soon made it nearly unbearable. She waited for symptoms of her own to begin, but nothing happened. Then she remembered the dart. Was this a reaction to the drug, or had he been poisoned as well? His range of symptoms made her think maybe both. She decided there must have been a special combination of drugs in the dart, for the variety of symptoms: his immediate unconsciousness, the retching, the fever.

As the temperature rose inside the van, she took off his boots and socks and his now bespattered outer clothing and tossed them to the

4

furthest corner. She added her own sweatshirt, leggings, socks, and running shoes, leaving only her t-shirt and underwear.

He retched and heaved for what seemed like hours, until he fell, finally, into an exhausted sleep. There was no water for hydration or to cool his fever, no relief from the sweltering heat, so she forced herself to empty her mind and close off her senses. This man was now her patient and her job was to get him through this.

Sleep must have overtaken her as well, for she slowly became conscious of a low constant moan that evolved into a rasping voice calling out first in German, then Russian, then Mandarin Chinese – just a word or short phrase in between groans and long spells of silence. She understood them all. She held him tighter, but he resisted, writhing, speaking clearly now in Vietnamese. He was hallucinating, carrying on an agitated one-sided conversation with someone. "You came back … too late… a boy. Where is our son? You know I will never stop loving you …" It was a woman. She answered for his unseen subject in Vietnamese, "I am here. Calm yourself. I am here for you."

She lowered him back down and lay close to his half-naked body, touching him gently with her hands. She started to hum, then broke into a Vietnamese song that her grandmother had sung to her long ago. He seemed to settle and slept once more. She knew she shouldn't, but she couldn't resist exploring his arms and upper torso, her fingers discovering the raised fine lines of multiple scars on his chest and back, sensing a pattern, along with a number of more random scars, some that could have been bullet holes. She wished she could see him, marveling at his athletic build, his rock-hard muscles, feeling an inexplicable closeness with this stranger.

Many more hours must have passed. The day was cooling, and the cargo hold felt less stifling, though the reeking air was still hard to breathe. It was well past sunset. She had seen no car lights behind them for quite a while, so she was sure there was no second car filled with the other four assailants following them. She had only the two men in the cabin to deal with. The van had stopped once, possibly for a fill-up and a switch of drivers. She had pounded on the wall of the van the entire stop, but the only response had been a single thump in return. From the angle of the light earlier, she was sure they were now headed west, still on a freeway. Suddenly her hand was wrenched away from his chest and gripped with a power she didn't expect from a man in his weakened state.

"Who are you?" he demanded in a hoarse angry tone, this time in English.

She debated which of her many Truths to answer. After a long silence, she responded simply.

"My name is Katya."

Chapter 2

The man's grip on her hand did not lessen. He propped himself up on one elbow, pushing himself away from her body.

"No one touches me," he growled.

"I've been touching you for hours," Katya answered, just to gauge his reaction. To her astonishment, he lay back down abruptly, releasing his iron grip on her wrist.

"That's not possible," he moaned.

Katya wished she could see his face. He sounded overwhelmed.

"You've been ill. I've been helping best I could," she said softly.

"That smell? I've never been sick like that. Ever."

"You were extremely sick, retching, feverish. But now you remember nothing? The attack?"

"I remember everything," he protested, then hesitated. "It's foggy, but yes."

"How about the year? What year is it?"

"Still 1999, I hope."

"Good. It's the same day, approaching our first night. I'd say seven o'clock. We're heading due West, apparently nonstop. My wild guess is towards California. That gives us perhaps three days at this rate to get out of this mess or we'll surely find ourselves in a worse one. Whatever boss man there hates you, he wants you to suffer along the way to whatever comes next, and I don't think we'll like the reception party he has planned. So now that we're talking, I gave you my name – who are you?"

He remained silent for a long time. So long, Katya thought he might have passed out again.

"Sasha. It's Sasha," he finally said. "And I can guess why I'm here, but why are you? Why were you near this van, at that moment? Why did you try to help me? Who are you?"

Katya sighed. So many questions. So many possibilities. She noted that both of their names contained the same pair of 'ah' sounds. That had to mean something, didn't it, she thought wryly.

"Pure coincidence. I couldn't sleep, was out running. Stopped to rest on a bench and the fighting started. I thought I could help." Katya paused, then added, "I'm nobody special."

"Bull. I don't believe in coincidences. You know martial arts, you know how to fight dirty. You know the time and where we're going and seem to know why. And you speak Vietnamese."

Katya was taken aback. Did he remember what she'd answered, that she'd sung to him while he was delirious? She decided to go further, why not.

"I speak six languages fluently, plus a number of dialects. Spanish, Mandarin Chinese, Vietnamese, and a couple more. My grandmother was ethnic Chinese, born in Vietnam. She taught me both languages. I'm a great impersonator of voices and accents, too," she said, trying to sound light. "Love that touch of Australian in your speech. You tried hard to hide it. Now I hear it plain as day. As to your other questions, I'm just good at figuring out things."

"Again bull. Who sent you?"

"You just don't let yourself swear, do you? Maybe I'm not at liberty to answer. Maybe you should just be glad that they did. Though I can't say I helped much back in New York City. Sorry, but I pictured quite a different outcome when I thought I was coming to your rescue. Thought maybe we could have breakfast together when you were free."

"How can you be so flippant? You must know I have no sense of humor. Nothing about this mess is remotely amusing." Sasha stopped, as if trying to regain control of himself, to put his thoughts together. "I can't trust you if you can't tell me the truth," he continued, in a calmer voice.

"The fact is I'm the only one you can trust, I'm the only one here. You trusted Mr. Blue Tie at the conference and he betrayed you to these goons."

Sasha didn't reply for a long time. She could tell he was in great pain and admired how hard he was trying to hide it.

"I'd figured that out for myself," he said finally. "But that doesn't tell me how you knew about Derek."

"Derek, is it? Ah, there's your problem. Never trust anyone named Derek. I suppose he's also the one who talked you into coming to this country, into giving a speech, kept you up all night talking at his apartment, sent you out walking back to your digs after your morning workout. He knew the way he sent you would take you past a certain parked van. Derek, the close, trusted contact would not betray you without good cause, so the men behind your abduction must have taken his wife or sister."

"No. Yes. How could you know all this… That has to be why. I'm not used to being wrong about people. Derek is a good man, he was…"

Katya placed a hand on his shoulder. He did not pull away.

"I can answer some questions, but you're going to have to trust me on the rest. I don't know who you are either, but I trust what I see and hear. We're not going to die here, at least you aren't, I won't let you. Here's what I do know. I was at the Global Human Rights Conference, I observed you and this Derek together. You're dressed in the same clothes as yesterday, but much worse for wear, soaked with sweat. I surmised the rest. I told you, I'm good at it. Great speech, but no, you shouldn't have put yourself out there. You pissed off someone in the human trafficking business, and I bet there are quite a few choices.

"This van, how many men and women victims of trafficking have suffered or died in a hot closed van while under transport? And California, well, it's just a guess, really. But we are heading west; we need another coastal state. His human trafficking business didn't go through New York or he would have taken care of you there. And three or so days suffering, the way these drivers are traveling non-stop, maybe you have an answer for that, maybe he's just that pissed or crazy. No food, no water, your illness some nasty combination of drugs injected into you. He knows a lot about you. You told me you've never been sick and he made you violently ill. Are you feeling any other symptoms?"

In the faint light, Katya could sense that Sasha was holding his hands in front of his face.

"My extremities. I can move my fingers, but I can't feel them. Almost no fine motor control. And my feet and legs are numb up past my knees."

"That will make escape fun. And the significance with the numb fingers?"

Sasha sighed. "I'm also a musician, among other things," he said quietly.

Katya took up both his hands in hers. Again, he did not pull away.

"We'll trust that this is a temporary side effect. Anything else?"

9

"My brain feels totally wooly. My thoughts are slow, muddled. It's hard to think clearly."

"I'm sure that will pass too. You've been drugged. Your tormenter wants you to panic."

"You don't understand. My brain... my brain is never, has never been slow like this in my life... I can't believe... I can't believe that you don't know who I am."

Chapter 3

"Enlighten me. Who are you?" Katya asked petulantly, but she immediately regretted her tone.

Sasha pulled his hands away and lay flat. He would not answer her. There was too much to say. Maybe this woman didn't know who he was. Maybe she had just been sent to watch over him. Katya lay still also. He rolled over, signaling an end to conversation, and withdrew into his own physical and psychological anguish. He would not admit the pain was unremitting, his gut roiling, his head feverish and pounding, his heart racing. He could not admit he was overcome with fear that the loss of sensation in his hands was permanent, that it was worsening, that he might never again play any instrument, let alone his violin. And was she still safe in the small sleeping quarters of the boat he'd rented in that New York City harbor, his Artemisia, the incomparable and irreplaceable violin that had accompanied him from the horror of his early childhood every day of his life until this very day?

"Katya," he finally whispered, hoping she was still awake, rethinking whether to confide in her, but she had fallen asleep.

Who am I? A musician, first and foremost. Only by playing music was he able to silence the horrible visions and memories in his head. Only by playing music did he feel centered and calm. Music was his lifeblood.

Who was this woman next to him? He could feel her heat, hear the steady rhythm of her breathing as she slept. He had so wanted to ask her to touch his body again, but he hadn't known how and now she was asleep. Why couldn't he remember what she looked like? He was incapable of forgetting. He had stared into her eyes for that one moment, now he couldn't picture her face, had only a vague memory of someone Asian... or part-Asian.

Katya stirred and Sasha rolled back over to her. He was sweating profusely, head and gut more painful than before. She had said to trust her. He doubted that her name was really Katya. She had deliberated far too long before revealing it, and it seemed too theatrical, too

Russian for someone who was obviously not, though she had pronounced it the Russian way. He wondered, was she a plant, the abduction and drugging a ruse to enlist his trust? An innocent bystander playing the good Samaritan as she first claimed? A trained bodyguard sent by someone to protect him? The latter seemed most likely.

Nobody special, she'd insisted. She was anything but a nobody. Her skills were too strong, her intuition and decisiveness too practiced. She spoke Vietnamese, multiple languages, she said. Had she really sung to him, in Vietnamese? The voice he thought he'd heard had been magical. Her sense of humor, despite the danger they faced, amazed him. Nothing seemed to faze her, although he suspected her bravado was a cover for concern, if not fear. How could even a professional not be afraid? He decided her motives didn't matter right now. If she was there to save him, all the better. She had certainly tried her best. He would follow whatever plan she came up with. But first, he would get her to touch him again.

Hesitantly, Sasha slid a hand up and down her arm. His fingers were still numb. He wished he could feel her skin, but the sensation was still thrilling. He had just spent most of a day next to a woman whose touch he could tolerate, who he wanted to touch. He could tell by the change in her breathing that she was awake. She sat straight up and placed her hand on his forehead, then behind his neck. Sasha leaned into her touch.

"You're burning up!" Katya's voice rose with her alarm. "Listen, you need water immediately. I'm going to tell them you're about to die – shhh, I know you're not – that we need water, electrolytes. Their boss must want you alive at the end of this bus ride to hell. They know he won't be happy with a dead cargo!"

Katya crawled her way to the front of the van and pounded on the wall. She hoped the drivers hadn't stopped for gas recently. She needed them to be willing to stop again soon. Katya breathed a sigh of relief when she heard arguments flying between the two drivers. She didn't hear any cell phone calls being made, so now she was fairly certain they were on their own, radio silence from California. That might also mean California had no idea Sasha was not alone in the van.

12

She tried to put a bit more panic in her voice as she shouted and pounded again. "We're dying back here! We need water!"

Within the hour the van slowed, then stopped. Gas, change of drivers, hopefully a purchase at the station store. There was still a bit of late daylight showing through the scratches in the back windows, and lights from the gas station. Maybe she could get help. Katya pulled her clothes and shoes back on and positioned herself by the back doors. There would be just one chance to get this right and she doubted the men would be stupid enough not to expect an attack. They would both be there, perhaps weapons ready. She was expendable.

But the doors stayed closed. Instead, the small window in the front slid open and one plastic bottle after another was pushed through the bars. Katya sat down in frustration, then jumped up and started shouting for help, pounding on the side wall. Maybe someone outside could hear her with the glass window open and perhaps a van door as well. The van took off with a squealing of tires and a roar of laughter from the front seats. The window was pulled firmly shut and latched.

Katya collected the bottles, groping around the floor for where they'd been sent rolling. They had gained four water bottles and what appeared to be two Gatorades, but not their freedom.

"Sorry." Katya tried to put on the bravest front possible. "I'll keep trying to get them to open those back doors. Start drinking. Eventually I'm going to need you to pretend to get a lot sicker. When you're ready, we're going to get you back in your clothes. If you want to live, you're going to have to be able to walk. I'm stronger than I look and I can help you move around, but I don't want to have to throw you over my shoulder like a sack of potatoes when we make a run for it."

Sasha was impressed how quickly she moved on from the setback at the convenience store. This was how he would have handled the situation with his crew. He was the man in charge, the man who feared nothing, the man who made others unafraid. First rule of planning an attack – be ready to make a new plan. He was also relieved she hadn't had to go through with it. Odds of success were against them and he might have been making the rest of the trip with her corpse and even less chance of escape. He drank down one water and what Katya told him was a Gatorade, full of electrolytes. It tasted vile and full of sugar.

He noticed that Katya drank none of the water herself. She was the captain, he the wounded crew member whose needs came first. He

13

didn't enjoy the role reversal, but he knew his brain was not up to the task of survival, and that hers most decidedly was. Still, it was difficult for him to feel so helpless. Her irreverence was actually welcome. No one in a thousand missions had ever accused him of irreverence, of any humor at all.

"Thank you," Sasha said as he lay back down, wrapping the blanket tighter around himself. "You may well have saved my life already with these drinks."

"I should never have allowed us to get into this mess. I'm not going to let you die while I'm figuring out how to get us out of it. That would be very bad form."

"You haven't told me who sent you. Where did you come from?"

"And you haven't told me who you are. So, I guess we're at an impasse."

"I'll tell you one thing about me," Sasha said. This woman was a stranger. He knew his body must smell as rank as the air in the van. "I have what is called haphephobia. I know what it stems from, but I won't talk about it, with you, with anyone. Only one other person has ever been able to touch me. That was why I was so astounded that we could have physical contact without my having a violent reaction."

"And you would like me to touch you again?"

"Yes, I would, if you can stand to. Just my head. Please."

Katya sighed. Such a simple request, but so difficult for him to ask. She couldn't begin to imagine a lifetime with little or no human touch. Without saying a word, she reached out to him in the darkness and stroked his face, his wet hair. His head felt somewhat less hot; his fever was abating, she thought. Katya could feel his body relax, and she carefully, slowly, moved her body closer to his. Rolling on his side, Sasha faced away from her, and she continued stroking his face and head with one hand as she molded her body into the curve of his. They stayed this way until she fell asleep with her arm wrapped over his shoulder. One night gone.

The second day passed much as the first, the heat hovering near unbearable at times. They shared one of the water bottles. Katya intermittently dozed and moved around in the near darkness, Sasha only occasionally awake for short periods. Neither could get the other to talk about anything personal or revealing, so they hardly talked at

14

all. She slept better when the van was cool, after again stroking this strange man's head, running her fingers through his hair, massaging his scalp.

Sasha lay awake most of the second night, reveling in her touch, then in the weight of her arm. The pain had subsided a little, and his thoughts returned to her question. *Who am I?* I am a survivor, he could have answered. Just as he could not recall her face, he reflected on other faces he could not remember, like the face of a parent, or anyone at all from his very early youth. He would never forget the faces from the camp… Sasha forced himself to stop there. He would not let his feverish brain dredge up the horror of his early childhood, not now, though those experiences had shaped and distorted his life. Perhaps his drugged and disordered mind was making it difficult to concentrate on the present moment. Perhaps he was trying to avoid thinking about the sleeping young woman next to him with her arm across his shoulder.

Chapter 4

Katya was first to awaken. It took her a moment to realize where she was, to remember the danger she was in, who the man was she had wrapped her body around. Two nights now they'd slept together, two days in the dark. Slowly sliding backwards away from him, she sat up. She could tell that it was well past dawn from the light coming through scratches in the paint on the window. The air in the van was still cool, but fetid. She fumbled to relieve herself in one of the foul buckets. She thought how embarrassed the man had seemed every time he'd had to ask her to bring him a bucket. Sitting against the front wall of the van, as far away from the buckets as she could get, she worked out a survival plan. First on her list was to try harder to stifle her fears. She remembered what she had been taught. Never picture failure.

She would start by stretching and exercising. There would be much to do getting Sasha on his feet again and ready to escape. She had no way to be certain how much time they had left before the back doors would open. She was disappointed he wouldn't tell her anything more about who he was, falling silent each time she tried to get him to talk, but she was encouraged that he'd confessed his touch phobia. That was a start. How was it that she was able to touch him? She and only one other person. She was sure that person was the Vietnamese woman, the mother of his son, the woman he had spoken to in his hallucination. Perhaps his wife. Since he was so desperate for her touch, perhaps a wife no longer living. She heard Sasha stirring and crawled back towards him. She placed a hand gently on his shoulder and then against his forehead.

"How are you feeling? You're still warm, but much cooler than yesterday."

Sasha remained silent for a long time. She knew he was awake. Perhaps he too needed time to remember where he was, what had happened.

"Everything still hurts," Sasha finally answered.

"I have a plan for getting us out of here. But you're going to have to work at regaining your strength. Once you're dressed, we'll start you moving again. Maybe we'll start with back flips."

"Katya, what? Please, I can hardly sit up," Sasha moaned, then belatedly realized she wasn't serious. "Oh, you're making a joke. Stop trying so hard to be witty. My head is throbbing… could we start there again?"

Katya understood, and the next hour was a pleasurable relief from the pain for him, even better than the day before. His body began to tremble, he could not hold back contented sighs. She massaged his head, shoulders, his scarred chest and back, then skipped to his feet and lower legs and back to his hands.

Katya felt around for Sasha's clothes. They reeked, but then so did her own clothes. She imagined the two buckets were already each about half full. She carefully helped him dress in everything but his socks and boots. He would feel less helpless now. She had him practice sitting up and laying back down a number of times before she pulled him slowly to his feet, bracing him carefully. She helped him move around until he seemed steadier, more confident. Arm and neck exercises followed, slow stretches with lots of rest breaks.

"How are the fingers now?" she asked.

"They're still numb to the tips. My hands work, but they feel disconnected somehow."

"And your feet?"

"Also improving. The movement is helping. They're a little numb but I can move them. Knees, too."

The air in the van became hotter and riper as the afternoon passed. Katya continued her own exercise routine each time Sasha took a break. But now it was time to raise hell if her plan was to stand a chance. She helped him to his feet, and this time he took the few steps to the front of the van with minimal assistance. As he was coached to do, Sasha got close to the front window, groaning loudly and shouting nonsense while Katya pounded on the wall, screaming for help.

As soon as they heard the window start to slide open, Sasha collapsed onto the floor. A powerful flashlight lit up the cargo hold through the bars, revealing Sasha writhing and thrashing, Katya doubled up in apparent agony. One of the drivers shouted out to shut up, but they noticed the van speed up considerably, which was her goal. Sasha stopped thrashing while Katya continued her histrionics.

The light vanished, the window closed, and a shouting match ensued between the two drivers. Katya smiled.

"So that went well," Katya whispered. "Wherever it is they're taking us, we'll get there a little faster, maybe arrive unexpectedly. Anything to throw off their game."

"I hope it works. If the drugs don't kill me, this smell will." Sasha stood up, steadying himself with one hand on the van wall.

"You're not joking," Katya groaned.

"I never do," Sasha answered, lying back down. He was frustrated that he felt so exhausted from his brief exercise and activity. His head and body still ached.

"So I get that you're not the life of the party. What else don't I know about you?"

Sasha sighed. "I don't remember the last time I laughed. Or even smiled, for that matter."

"You really can't even smile? I find that quite sad."

"I don't need your pity."

"That's not how I meant it. I'm sorry. I can't seem to stop embarrassing you, or maybe I'm embarrassing myself this time."

"Honestly? I find myself enjoying your wit, most of the time. But I'm still in a lot of pain. I can't think straight, and I feel weak."

Katya was surprised at how much Sasha was beginning to trust her. She felt a little guilty that she would not be as open with him.

"It's starting to get cooler," Katya said. "I'm going to take a rest. Here's the last of the Gatorade, so drink up. We'll share the last water tonight and tomorrow. At the speed we're traveling, my hope is we'll cross into California by late night or very early morning." Katya knew she was taking another wild guess, but Sasha seemed like he needed some hope. "Try to get a little sleep. Maybe a head and neck rub would help you feel better?"

"Yes, please," Sasha answered quickly, grateful he didn't have to ask. He imagined he should tell her how much he appreciated everything she was doing for him, but he couldn't seem to find the right words. "I'm sorry I'm not much help," he managed to say, as he melted into the warmth of her hands kneading the top of his shoulders.

Katya worked the muscles of his neck and gently massaged his head until she grew tired. Her hands slid back down towards his shoulders and he could feel her quiet, rhythmic breathing against his back. He was growing quite attached to this self-confident young woman whom he could inexplicably allow to touch him.

Sasha felt Katya stirring, but she did not awaken. He turned and ran his fingers across her damp hair, let them trail lightly down her back. She was lying on her side and his hand followed the curve of her body to her hips. It's been so long, he thought. Katya stirred again, and he snatched his hand from her hip. He lay down on his back and tried to think about something, anything. Music. He played a short solo violin work in his head, then part of a concerto. The music made him miss his violin all the more.

But then the music in his head was not enough to keep the dreaded images from returning, not enough to keep his body from sweating. The memories appeared as always, on the screen of his inner eyelids. Only actually playing the violin had ever stopped the torrent of images. Then, there was music and only music. Now all he could see were piles of corpses everywhere, two, three meters high, starving adults and children lying on the bare ground, hardly distinguishable from the dead, a multitude of hollow, gray faces, the mountain of dead prisoners' shoes, gaunt bodies in scraps of clothing draped on barbed wire and hung from poles. The same sounds and smells always followed the images. He could hear gunfire, ferocious barking of dogs, the laughter of the officers as they held him down, feel the touch of the hated hands, the pain of yet another beating, and then he could smell the rotting bodies, the burning bodies, the stench of excrement, typhus and death, far worse than the smell in the van.

And then there was the guilt, overwhelming guilt, for what, he was never sure. Perhaps just for surviving when so many had not. Desperate, he pounded out a musical rhythm on his thighs until they ached, but the memories took a long time to fade without his violin. They would be back. They always came back. It seemed like hours had passed, but he knew it had only been a quarter of an hour.

Katya awoke to Sasha's shudders and his loud gasp. Another nightmare. Her fingers ran through his hair, and she was surprised to find it wet with sweat. She rubbed his damp shoulders and back and felt him relax under her hands. She knew she hadn't been asleep for very long.

"Sasha, are you awake? You must have been dreaming."

19

"I wish," he answered enigmatically. He hesitated. "I was remembering things I don't wish to remember but have no choice. I've been incapable of forgetting anything except for now in my drugged state. I have to confess, here in darkness, I can't even remember what you look like."

"That's understandable. Our eyes only met for a brief moment before you were hit," Katya consoled him.

"Normally, a moment would have been long enough."

"We'll be back in daylight before long. Fresh air. Clean clothes. Your right mind."

"You sound confident."

"I have no choice," she replied. "I was taught never to picture failure."

"Who taught you?"

Katya smiled in the darkness but didn't answer. "Do you feel ready to stretch and exercise again?"

"Yes, I'm ready."

"I remember very well what *you* look like," she said. "You must work out constantly."

Katya didn't know how to politely tell him he was the most handsome and fit man she'd ever seen, at any age. She didn't often hold her tongue. For once, she was glad she'd managed to keep her thoughts to herself.

"These are the only mornings in the last several decades I haven't woken up at dawn to work out." How could he tell her his build was due more to his strange hypertrophic musculature than to his workout routine. He'd had adult-like muscles apparently since birth. His childhood curse, the cause of much pointing and laughing at the Displacement Camp and growing up in Australia, had developed into a more than decent adult body shape. He could not help who or what he was.

"Since you can't see me, I'll let you feel my arms. I do a pretty mean workout routine myself," Katya said. God, I'm right back to talking without thinking, she admonished herself.

Sasha hesitantly reached out his hands to locate her and felt her arms. He was impressed by the shape and hardness of her muscles, the breadth of her shoulders. This time there was no numbness in his fingers. A second chance to touch her, and with permission, he

20

marveled. He was surprised and embarrassed by how much he suddenly wanted to take her in his arms, how aroused he was becoming, glad of the darkness. How could he have come so close to behaving so inappropriately, he wondered. And what was he to do with these unaccustomed emotions?

He pushed himself up and carefully moved away, groping around to make sure the area was clear of buckets. He started a workout and pushed himself as hard as he dared for as long as he could. It was still nowhere near as intense as his usual routine, but it was a huge improvement over his first pathetic attempt. He could hear Katya working out near him, just far enough away that they wouldn't accidently bump into each other. They both rested for an hour, then started in again. That night he and Katya curled around each other again, for warmth he told himself, and slept soundly. The day had been a big push to get himself back on his feet, and it had indeed gone well.

Chapter 5

Sasha was the first to awaken. It was still dark. This could all be over soon if they were lucky. But even if they gained their freedom, they almost certainly would be pursued. Sasha had to get word to his people immediately if they escaped. He would still have to get to safety. He stopped himself. Katya would have said "*when* we escaped."

He thought he'd arranged his adventure so well that no one would have missed him yet. Who had sent Katya? If his handlers had discovered his subterfuge, they would have sent a small army after him. He'd lied to everyone, and yet he dared to speak to Katya of trust. Lying, at fifty-nine, just to get to the U.S., his first ever "vacation," secretly invited to speak at the Global Human Rights Conference. He'd been flattered, excited. Foolish. Of course it was a trap. How had someone guessed how hungry he was for any sort of recognition? He hadn't really admitted it, even to himself. But he'd fallen for it. When he'd arrived in Sydney, he'd loaded his staff with enough new projects to keep them busy all month. He'd have his laptop with him to answer any questions. Perfectly encrypted, impossible to trace its location, technology he hadn't shared with his handlers.

Ah Derek, his long-time trusted collaborator on human rights issues. Derek had flown to Thailand looking for him, had found a way to talk to him privately on his boat, his only home, had signaled that they couldn't be overheard by his crewmates. Derek wouldn't have known of Sasha's leash and collar, as Sasha called them. The sensitive GPS tracker and voice communicator that connected him to the government agency that protected him, owned him.

Sasha had brought out his laptop and they communicated back and forth while making small talk, typing and deleting each line afterwards. An extra measure of caution. No one but Sasha could access his laptop. Derek had made the whole trip to New York sound like a game changer, not just an adventure. Sasha's speech, even given anonymously, would be a wake-up call for action, would inspire agencies and nations to take up arms against the scourge of human trafficking. And he knew his speech had been just that. Once he started speaking, his excitement only grew. He could still hear the applause, feel the crowd's approval and appreciation. He could do this. He had loved every minute of it. Had developed a manic high that kept him up all night talking in Derek's tiny apartment. Now Sasha was as sure as Katya that Derek had been sent, pressured by threats against a kidnapped family member. But by whom? The criminal organization, human traffickers most likely, awaiting him at the end of this van ride, as Katya had surmised?

Sasha had never been to New York City, but then he refused to fly. One of many such idiosyncrasies, he thought sadly. His list was still a long one: severe touch phobia, not able to smile, cry, laugh or understand humor, a man who had great difficulty dealing with emotions, haunted by a past he would discuss with no one. His personality traits when he was young made an equally grim list: rigid, overly logical, obsessive, annoyingly literal, even arrogant at times. That was all behind him, well, most of it. Why was he being so hard on himself, he wondered. He was also passionate about what he did, about music. He couldn't help who he was, what he was…

And yet he'd used his shore leave for this escape, this adventure, well-deserved he thought. For the first time in three decades, he'd taken off his audio-equipped tracker, had managed to put it on his crewman Sonthi's back without his knowledge. They were to attend a Zen Buddhist silent meditation center in Sonthi's native Thailand together; no one would be expecting to hear Sasha's voice. At the last minute, Sasha wrote Sonthi he'd changed his mind, would be staying with Dima in Sydney instead, that his handlers had been informed. He hoped Sonthi would forgive him. Sonthi would be grilled mercilessly when Sasha's disappearance was discovered. There was no way Sasha would still be able to sneak back to Sydney. Right now, he would be satisfied with surviving.

Derek's offer touched a nerve. Sasha had felt the need to be truly alone for a while. The long journey to New York would give him that time. Just his violin and the open ocean, a faceless worker on his own freighter, a black watch cap over his blond hair, fake name, fake passport. What chaos would have broken out if he'd been recognized. Leaving everyone behind. Ten crew members, all close colleagues and musical partners, friends, responsible for him even on shore leave, watching his every move, keeping him safe and sane with all his eccentricities, in their work and in this dangerous job he had insisted on undertaking. His handlers listening in 24/7. Handlers,

24

crewmembers, all believing he couldn't last a day without their assistance. Well, so far, he hadn't proved them wrong.

His work throughout Southeast Asia should have been enough for him. It would have been if these same simple coastal people he served weren't being preyed upon ruthlessly by human traffickers and other criminal elements. He found the chase exhilarating, needed the thrill of it. Maybe he also liked frightening his handlers, the government agency that had tried to control him since he was seventeen years old. Not maybe. He knew very well why he had named his boat the *Trib*. Short for Retribution. Retribution for how he thought his government had been exploiting him all these decades. His handlers hated his shipboard life, his insistence on chasing traffickers, feared losing him. He had given them no choice after his wife's death, when they finally caught up with him after he'd disappeared for an entire year. Nearly starving, still deeply depressed, alone. Hence the leash and collar ever since.

Sasha felt cold. He wrapped the blanket tighter around himself, disregarding the smell, wishing for light, any light. He was frustrated that his thoughts were so jumbled, out of order, flying back and forth between past and present. He queried each memory as it came to him, looking for its importance. Maybe there was something his brain was trying to tell him. Or maybe it was just the effects of the drugs.

Who am I, he asked himself yet again. Was he the sum total of all that had happened to him, what he had accomplished? He was only certain that he wanted to share none of this with Katya. If she really didn't know who he was, whatever else he did, he wasn't going to tell her. For now, he wanted to be just an ordinary man.

When Katya awoke, she felt Sasha exercising next to her. She stretched and put her eye to the largest paint scratch, seeking light, a view, anything new or helpful, but it was barely dawn. They had to be getting close to their destination. The drivers were still spelling each other, driving pretty much non-stop, continuing at their new faster speed, but arguing, checking constantly if everyone was still alive in back. Katya was happy to keep their anxiety levels high. Three nights down, it was morning of the fourth day. She stretched and joined Sasha in exercising. They rested for a few minutes before working out for another half-hour. Then they found their footwear and finished dressing.

"No matter what happens today, it has been an honor sleeping next to you," she told the dark shape moving beside her.

"I look forward to seeing your face," Sasha answered.

Katya shared the rest of the details of her plan as they moved the items they needed into position. They sat in silence as the minutes slipped by, lost in their own thoughts. The van had turned onto side roads, bumpy and curvy, up and down steep hills. Then, finally, it slowed to a crawl, stopped momentarily, starting up again on gravel. A gate, she thought, on a private drive. Katya took note of how long each section of road was taking. A second stop, a second gate. They prepared themselves for what they had to do next.

The van stopped. They waited to see if the doors would open immediately. There would be no reinforcements if the drivers panicked as planned and were stupid enough. This time luck was with them. When the doors opened, Katya and Sasha threw the contents of the two stinking buckets into the drivers' faces, then smashed the buckets against their guns. Katya jumped out first and pummeled each gasping driver into unconsciousness with a bucket and powerful kicks. She did a quick search of their pockets and found wallets, but nothing of hers or Sasha's. Grabbing the wallets, she ran to the front of the van to make sure the keys were still in the ignition, then helped Sasha, dressed but wrapped in the foul blanket, out of the van and into the passenger seat. A hulking modern house of concrete stood silent before them. No sprinting assailants, no firing guns. She climbed into the driver's seat, floored the accelerator, and, hesitating just a moment, smashed through the first wooden gate, then the second. She was soon exhilarated by the open road, fresh air, and the blue, blue California sky.

Chapter 6

"I know where we are! Definitely California, Sonoma County. I know this road. We'll soon get you to San Francisco. Check the glove compartment for our wallets and things." Sasha searched thoroughly, including under his seat, but he found only maps, the flashlight, a plethora of empty food wrappers and bottles, matches, and a switchblade. "Give me the switchblade and matches. Damn, wish there was more."

As the van raced on, Katya stole a glance from the hilly, curvy road at Sasha, slumped against the passenger door. His eyes were a dazzling dark gray. He was staring at her, and he quickly tilted his head away. *God, I must be utterly disgusting looking*, she thought, reaching up a hand to touch her matted, filthy hair.

"My kingdom for a shower. And food. And a cold drink," she said. "My brain tells me it's seven thirty. Time to find breakfast."

She worried that the rush had been too much for him in his weakened state. She needed to find safety and nutrition for him fast. Their escape would soon be discovered and who knew what hellhounds would be on their trail. The van was low on gas but there would be a small town soon among these steep brown hills. Sasha hadn't said a word since the van doors had opened.

"I think you're beautiful. And impossibly young," Sasha said at last, certain now of his feelings towards her and equally certain he could not share them.

Katya was taken aback. No one sober had called her such things in a long time. But then she hadn't dated anyone in years.

"I'm twenty-nine. Not that young. I don't suppose you'd tell me how old you are."

"No, you're right, I won't," he said wistfully, and left it at that. Katya looked much younger than twenty-nine to him, and she did look beautiful, in all the right ways. He looked past the tangles and dirt, to the dark brown, sun-bleached hair, the unusual, deeply tanned face. Certainly, what she had said about her grandmother was true, but she looked half Asian, not quarter. Sasha appreciated the Asian features in her face and her dark eyes, though he couldn't tell their actual color.

Medium brown, perhaps. He'd felt the hard muscles of her arms and broad shoulders and could now see the athletic shape of her legs. The thin shapeless sweatshirt did little to hide her figure.

He had only known one woman intimately in his entire life, his Le, far more beautiful, but also lithe and athletic. He had never looked at a woman this way before or after her. He had considered himself a totally asexual being. That first accidental touching of their hands so many years ago had awakened something tragically missing in him, a bolt of electricity wired directly to his soul. The surprise, and dare he say, joy, that Le could touch him, that he could not only accept her touch but feel such a frisson of pleasure had been overwhelming.

And now another young woman, this Katya, was able to touch him as well, and he'd felt that same frisson, both in touching her and being touched. But what did he know about her? Whatever her motives, however she had come to be near this van that morning in New York, she had to be an angel of mercy, like his Le a good person, selfless, amazingly clever. She was also a fearless and well-taught fighter. He knew he was a man with no sense of humor, who never smiled, so how is it he found himself attracted to her light-heartedness? He was sure she'd made up her name and she'd told him no more about herself than he'd told her about his own life. How could anyone but a professional fight like that... if he created a different backstory for himself, and she did the same, where did that leave them? And if she had been sent to watch over him and really did know who he was, would she laugh at his lies? When did he start caring what another person thought of him, anyway? He knew that if he'd been in his right mind, had not felt so completely addled by drugs, he would have had an answer. Was this how it was to be an ordinary man? Be careful what you wish for.

"So silent," Katya broke in on his thoughts. "Let's play a guessing game. I'll say a number for your age and you tell me higher or lower." Katya stole another glance at him. "Not a grey hair, no balding, no wrinkles or age spots. Prime of life, built like a weight lifter, gymnast, a ballet dancer, all rolled into one. I'm going to start with forty-two."

"Forty-two will do nicely. I don't play games." Sasha smiled inwardly.

"So now that we're free, introduce yourself to me. What do you do, besides give speeches you don't want to give, get in trouble with traffickers, and play a musical instrument? What do you play?"

28

"Violin mostly, also cello and piano. Music is my passion."

"Are you a professional? Do you concertize?"

"No and never. But I hear I'm quite good."

"I'll bet that's an understatement. I'm also a musician, my passion, not my profession. Guitar, mandolin, lute, zithers, ethnic instruments. Piano, but as accompanist mostly. What do you do?"

"You could say I'm sometimes a policeman these days."

"Hardly a beat cop on the street in Australia. I don't see it."

"I do work in Sydney part of the year."

"So, the rest of the year you hunt down human traffickers?"

"Some of the time."

"You're enjoying this, I can tell. 'How little can I say that only covers a small part of what I do or who I am.' Are you married, children?" Katya worried that her question might be cruel since she had surmised the answer, but she wanted to know for sure.

Sasha didn't reply, but his face darkened. He turned to the window. Only an occasional green oak broke the monotony of the seared brown landscape stretching into the far distance. But there, down the road, he could see the trees multiplying into groves flanked by tawny grass slopes, and taller hills bathed in a bluish haze.

"Sorry, very sorry Sasha. I have also lost a love. I have lost a great number of people I loved. Let's start again."

At that moment, the van gave a shudder and lurched forward.

"Shit, shit, sorry don't mean to swear," Katya groaned. The gas gauge had dropped to near zero. She raced the van to the top of the next high hill and stopped. Jumping out, she scanned the curving road behind and in front of them. Behind them by perhaps fifteen minutes was a bus headed their way. Racing far behind the bus were three black dots. Ahead where the road flattened out was a small bus shelter. And there was someone sitting in it.

"They're coming!" she shouted as she slid back into the driver's seat. "New plan, brace yourself."

Katya threw the van into reverse, backed five meters, and then flew forward at the aged wooden guardrail.

"What are you doing?" shouted Sasha, as he was thrown backwards and forwards like a rag doll.

"Just hold on!" Katya shouted.

She backed up again, this time further, gravel from the side of the road flying, and rammed the guardrail again, bashing through it, brakes squealing as she stopped the van just inches from the edge of a steep drop off. She backed quickly away from the tangle of splinters onto the road again and raced down the hill.

"Just listen! I have not gone mad, just looks like it! Or maybe I have. I had to know if this would work. There's a bus shelter up ahead. You're getting off there and you're going to get on that bus, with or without me. It's almost here. I'm going back to push the van over the cliff, then I'm going to run like hell to join you. If I don't make it, I'll be hiding in the hills while they think we're dead in the wreck. Got it?"

Sasha nodded, although it all seemed too preposterous to work. Katya slammed on the brakes in front of the shelter and ran around the van to help Sasha out. She sat him on the end of the bench, still wrapped in the reeking blanket, and rushed back to the van. Calculating the chances of any of this working, she raced back up the hill. The odds were pretty miserable. But maybe she could succeed in getting Sasha to safety.

Katya drove through the shattered guardrail and stopped the van right at the edge, leaving the motor running. She popped open the hood and used the switchblade to slice the gas line, hoping there would be enough gas left to do the trick. She lit a match and threw it in, then ran to the back of the van and pushed as hard as she could. The van teetered over the edge, then plummeted. She was already running back down the road before the van landed at the bottom of the steep hill with an extremely satisfying explosion and fireball. The bus passed her before she was halfway to the shelter, but she found a last reserve of energy to run faster. She apologized to the State of California for the quite probable grass fire that was to come. But a bonus of a fire would be that their pursuers would not be able to get close to the van to examine it for quite a while.

ॐ

Sasha leaned on his elbows at the bus shelter. Everything hurt, but he was definitely improving. He watched the van race away and, grasping her plan, admired Katya's ingenuity. Stumbling through the barren hills with no food or water was not what he wanted to be doing right now. He would not let the bus leave without her. Beside him sat a middle-aged Hispanic woman, dressed for menial work in the city, clutching a lunch box. She looked over at him with revulsion, wrinkling her nose as she scooted as far away as she could get on the bench. He asked her in Spanish where the bus was headed, and she stammered back "Santa Rosa." He then asked her if she had a cell phone and she looked even more frightened as she shook her head vigorously. He wanted to ask if she would share her lunch, but he was sure she would hit him with the lunchbox if he did. He would have to think of some story to tell or he would not be allowed to get on this bus. He watched the road for Katya's return, catching sight of her just as the fireball erupted, smoke billowing up above the hill. The woman gasped and crossed herself. The bus swept into view, but he knew that Katya would make it.

As the bus came to a stop, Sasha could hear the pandemonium inside. Several passengers were already standing, looking back at the smoke, some shouting at the driver, one with cell phone in hand, punching in numbers. The Hispanic woman was screaming at the driver that he could not let "this stinking creature" on board. Sasha pushed passed her and addressed the driver in a pleading croak.

"Help me, please!" He turned to the passengers and held up both hands for quiet. All eyes turned to him. "My name is Fred Baxter and my associate and I have just escaped from kidnappers. I know I smell, but we've been held underground in a bunker for three days without food or water. That's my associate, Maria Lopez, running towards us. We got away in their van and they're after us. Maria put it over the cliff to slow them down. You cannot believe how happy we are that you are here to save us!" A few heads were nodding. He repeated his words in purposefully poor Spanish.

The atmosphere in the bus changed completely. Thermoses of soup and bottles of water and juice came tumbling out of lunch boxes along with bottles of hand sanitizer and wipes as Sasha collapsed onto an empty seat. The man with the cell phone asked him who he could call for him but Sasha asked for the phone so he could call the FBI himself. By the time two passengers helped pull a heaving Katya onto the bus, a celebration was in full swing.

"Driver, please take off! There were three cars following us and we may not be safe yet!" Sasha had to shout over the noisy crowd. He'd made them all feel like heroes and they were happily talking to each other. Katya smiled over at him. His voice was perfectly flat, without a trace of an accent. Katya moved around the bus, sliding into empty seats and telling the story over and over to the delighted passengers of how she crashed the van. Sasha dialed and spoke quietly, then looking disappointed, placed a second, longer call before handing the phone back to its owner. He stood up again and the crowd became silent.

"Please don't talk to anyone else about us until you hear on the news that we are safe. I've just talked to the FBI and they want your help in catching these monsters. Put away your phones. Hopefully your first calls will bring out the police and fire department to the crash in time to catch the kidnappers there!"

As Katya translated his words into Spanish, a cheer went up from the passengers, everyone nodding with enthusiasm. Katya and Sasha kept repeating to their saviors that the FBI had insisted they not talk about themselves or the kidnapping. They hungrily ate and drank as much of the eagerly proffered lunches as they dared. Katya noted that Sasha asked about the contents of the lunches, quickly passing on anything that contained meat. She decided to follow his example and only ate what he ate.

"Did they just call you Fred Baxter?" Katya whispered, smiling.

"Most benign American name I could think of."

Katya looked back at the now distant cloud of smoke. A single black car emerged into view, traveling fast. She put her hand on Sasha's shoulder and he turned to look. Sasha stood up again and hushed the passengers.

"One of the kidnappers' cars is going to pass us. It is worth all our lives that you don't give them a reason to suspect we are on this bus. Please act normally and do not look at them as they pass. Can you do that for us? Turn your heads away or pretend to be asleep. One suspicious look and they might stop the bus. Ok, Now!"

Again, Katya repeated his words in Spanish sentence by sentence and a hush fell over the passengers. Sasha and Katya hunkered low over each other in their seats on the right side of the bus. The sleek black car slowed in passing, kept even with the bus for a minute, then swung past them and sped away.

Chapter 7

When the bus arrived in Santa Rosa, Sasha and Katya asked to be let out in front of the police station. They waved at the happy passengers until the bus was out of sight, then headed to a part of town that Katya knew to have cheap hotels. Katya helped Sasha walk, but he was already much steadier on his feet. The reeking blanket was carefully stuffed into the first dumpster they passed. They had no intention of trying to explain themselves to the police, and no guarantee their whereabouts wouldn't quickly be discovered. They hoped to stay "dead" until Sasha's reliable people could reach them. The credit cards in the abductors' wallets were useless, but there was a fair amount of cash.

Sasha had a better idea than cash. He picked a seedy looking three-story hotel with a back staircase that had a one-way locking door opening to the street and jimmied the lock quickly and expertly. Katya wondered where he'd learned to do that. They went up the stairs, checking each floor. The top floor hallway contained a ladder and several unopened cans of paint, all deeply covered in dust. Thick dust lay on the hallway floor. No one would be disturbing them, no nosy neighbors and no bribable desk clerk to know they were there. He jimmied the door at the end that would have a view of two streets. Katya was overjoyed that there were sheets on the bed and towels in the bathroom, however dusty and dubious their cleanliness. The water taps worked and there was even hot water, though no soap or shampoo.

"I don't understand why we have to wait until morning to be picked up," Katya complained in as quiet a voice as she could manage. "You don't have people in San Francisco you can trust?"

She had people that close. She could be back with them in less than two hours. Neither Sasha nor the abductors knew who she was. She had rescued this man, job finished. Then she remembered. The other attackers, the ones who had thankfully not followed them, must have her cell phone, wallet, identification, address… but maybe they didn't. She'd left her runner's backpack on the bench when she ran to join the fight. How long would a backpack last on a bench in New

York City? But if the attackers had found it, she couldn't go back until this was ended.

"I told you, my one contact in San Francisco was not there when I called, he's in Australia. Everything will happen in a hurry when he gets the message. There will be a firestorm. And my American contact is in Washington D.C. and can't get here with an extraction team until tomorrow morning. I know it sounds like bull, but he thinks it would be safer to lay low overnight. We'll be out of here in the morning."

"I'd feel safer in the police drunk tank."

"We will be safe."

"Then I would like to meet this extraction team looking like a human being. I'm going to take a five-hour shower, even without soap and shampoo, and sleep on a bed."

"Just wait an hour or two. I'm going out and I'll be back with supplies and a change of clothes for you. You have to promise me not to leave, make noise, or even be seen looking out a window."

He turned his filthy shirt inside out, ripped off the bottom of his pant legs, took one of the towels and rubbed it in the dusty corners of the room until it was gray, then threw it over his head like a hood. He demonstrated a shuffling, bent over gait and started muttering to himself. Katya was too worried to laugh, or even wonder at Sasha's unexpected attempt at humor, but she knew he would be unrecognizable on the street. After he left, she scrubbed herself under the soap-less shower for a half hour, amazed that the hot water lasted that long.

The first homeless man Sasha met pointed him in the direction of the men's shelter but advised him it would not open for sleeping until seven. Sasha nodded thanks and shuffled onward. When he arrived, volunteers were sorting donated clothing. He picked through the piles and collected clothes and hats for himself and for Katya. The volunteers took one whiff and escorted him quickly into the shower area, brought him shaving gear, and asked what else they could do for him. He asked the time, and begged for a hairbrush, some miniature bottles of shampoo and a bar of soap for the road. Clean and refreshed, he made a bundle of the extra clothes and toiletries and used some of the abductors' cash to buy food and drink at a corner grocery. He pulled his new watch cap low over his hair and shuffled to the location he'd been given.

Sasha spotted the waiting car right away. He was relieved to see his CIA contact had chosen a nondescript brown Chevy. The FBI would probably have arrived in a black Lincoln Navigator bristling with antennae. The back door opened, and Sasha slipped into the car. Brian Mason had assisted his operations against traffickers and gunrunners several times, and he trusted him as much as he trusted any American, which wasn't much, but he liked the man. He looked better than when Sasha had last seen him, exhausted from a long jungle stakeout.

Mason, he'd always called him. Mason was now in his late forties, a non-descript man of average size and looks. A man who could blend in, not be noticed. At least outside an Southeast Asian jungle. Sasha gave him another glance. Mason's short brown hair should have been turning gray, but wasn't. The brown over his temples was a slightly different shade. Since when did he notice such things?

The second number Sasha had dialed from memory back in the bus was a Washington, D.C. number, but it had been routed to Mason in San Francisco. Sasha hadn't expected Mason to be able to come himself, thought he would send trusted local people. Sasha regretted not having a number to call S-Branch directly; they'd always been listening. He hadn't known what to do when he'd learned his contact at the Australian Consulate in San Francisco was in Sydney. It was unlikely anyone else there would know who he was.

Mason greeted him like a long-lost friend, but was careful not to touch him. "My God, Sasha, it's good to see you alive and well! What an ordeal! How the hell did you get to New York?"

"Took a freighter. Signed on as a deckhand. Used a fake name and passport, even a fake security clearance. My government must know where I am by now. If they weren't so desperate to keep me alive, they'd kill me for disappearing like this."

"I've been in contact and you're damned right they're mad. Once they believed me! Your government had no idea you were even missing. Your tracker showed you at a Buddhist silent retreat in Thailand! Clever choice, by the way. And not exactly a place where people answer the phone. Your government was only somewhat reassured knowing you were going to be under my capable protection. I know what they think of us Yanks."

Sasha only grunted. "I'm sure the man who invited me to New York is the one who betrayed me. His name is Derek Adams, one of the organizers of the Global Human Rights Conference. But I'm also sure he was coerced. See if any of his close relatives went missing."

"I'll get someone on it."

"Were your people able to pick up my violin and computer from the rental boat in New York? I don't care about the duffel."

"All three safe and sound. They'll be hand-delivered to San Francisco. I understand my people were quite in awe of the small size of your computer – any new technology your government cares to share with us?"

"Sorry, I understand you'll have to wait a decade. They had better not be trying to snoop inside."

"Wouldn't dream of it," Mason answered with a grin.

"Your CIA won't be successful, so don't get cocky, Mason."

"You're looking at an Interpol agent now, Sasha. Working my way slowly to the top, too slowly for my taste. Left the CIA behind four years ago. Going by my real name, Allen Lane, but I was always fond of Mason. You know how we spooks are with our noms de guerre. I'm working a case with a team of FBI agents right now, but you can keep calling me Mason unless they're around."

Mason introduced the two men in the front seat, the scowling driver in a black cap as Bill and the second man, a head shorter and baby-faced with glasses, as Jake. Sasha was sure that whatever their names were, they weren't Bill and Jake. They had the unmistakable look of ex intelligence officers and he wondered why they were working with Mason. They were both dressed casually in contrast to Mason's dark suit and tie.

"From your description of the concrete house, it was Markus Cutter and his gang who abducted you," Mason continued. "I've been in San Francisco preparing an assault on that compound in Sonoma you were almost a guest at. You would have begged to be back in the van. Since you're alive and here with us, I want you to be a part of our team. No one has had more experience dealing with the Cutters than you, and there's no one better in a firefight. And maybe you'd like a little vengeance after what you've been through."

Sasha could well believe his tormentor was one of the Cutters. Four brothers with criminal enterprises spread throughout Southeast Asia and the West Coast, all famously overweight and each one vying with the others for who was the deadliest. Human trafficking, drugs, and arms dealing were their primary occupations. No one really knew where they were from, but Sasha had always suspected they were Californians. Their real names didn't matter. The name Cutter was their calling card – torture with sharp instruments and dismemberment their specialty.

"You know I'm in. My people can just have another aneurism." Sasha stopped to consider the situation more clearly and regretted his words. He must still be under the influence of Cutter's drugs, he thought. The timing of Mason's raid was far too suspicious, as well as his presence in California. Sasha didn't believe in coincidences, or in fate. And how could he imagine going right back to that house of concrete he had just escaped from? Only torture and death had awaited him there.

Mason should be evacuating him to the Australian Consulate in San Francisco, even with the Consul-General away. At least he'd thought to leave his name when he called the Consulate first. If he hadn't reached Mason, how long would it have taken for – what was it Mason used to say – the shit to hit the fan? His literal mind had always been dismayed by that image... Why hadn't he asked for help? He was an Australian citizen in trouble – that might have been enough for the Consulate, but he would have had to figure out how to get there, without getting caught again by Cutter.

He should have learned never to trust an American after Derek's betrayal. But then Katya was an American. Or was she. He was no longer certain of anything about her except that he trusted her. He could see Mason was staring at him, waiting for a response. He would play along for now, but he had to be cautious. He'd get the subject back to his mysterious rescuer. He wanted to know who she was more than ever. "But what did you find out about this Katya?" he asked. "She knows this part of California well, that's for sure."

"A total mystery. We couldn't find anyone by that name, description, or reputation in the profession. I know you said you like and trust her, and that's really big coming from you, but we need to know more. Listen, I know you won't like this, but I want you to put an audio tracker on her and set her loose. We'll have a team on her, see where she goes, who she meets."

"But Cutter's people will be looking for her. They'll figure out soon we're not dead in the burned van." Sasha was feeling guiltier by the minute. She had saved his life. If she was paid to save people, where was the harm? Why did he care so much who she really was?

"I promise we'll watch over her carefully. I know what she's done for you and she sounds like someone I'd prefer to have on my team, not in opposition. She was brilliant! The fact that she can touch you… that's extraordinary. And have you been listening to yourself? I don't know a more reserved and literal man than you. Something tells me this Katya's been having an effect on you."

"I have no idea what you're talking about," Sasha replied.

" 'They'd kill me for this?' 'have another aneurism'? You're making me laugh, Sasha." Mason looked over at him and his expression turned serious. "I don't know exactly what it is you do for your government, but I know how wild they are to get you back in one piece. Katya is a part of this, and I have to figure out how she's involved. We'll keep a full team on you, too, until this is accomplished."

Mason reached into his jacket pocket and pulled out a tiny device. Sasha frowned – it was one of his own inventions, identical to the one he'd taken off his own back and put on Sonthi's. His leash and collar. How many other agencies and governments were being sold his technology, he wondered. The tracking device was a radio transmitter as well and would allow Mason's team to hear everything said within a seven-meter radius. It attached nearly invisibly and unnoticeably to the skin at the center of one's back. Sasha deactivated the device. He would decide if and when to activate it.

"I want until tomorrow morning with her," Sasha said. "And I don't promise, but I'll think about it. She may just open up to me."

And maybe I will open up to her, Sasha considered. He didn't think he could walk away from her. There was something real between them, and not just his gratitude.

Chapter 8

Sasha returned to the hotel room about three hours after he'd left, wearing his clean but worn clothes and carrying the bundle. He felt a new man, showered and shaved. Ready to confront his feelings head on. He folded the dirty towel he'd borrowed to cover his head on the way out and placed it on the bureau.

"I can't promise you'll love my clothing selection for you, but I couldn't quite ransack the women's shelter too," he said, handing her the bundle. Katya was wrapped in a sheet, worn like a toga. Sasha admonished himself for letting his imagination run wild. "Try these."

"These are fine. I love wearing men's ugly ancient clothing. At least they're clean and don't stink. And you brought food! Juice!"

Her eyes widened at the soap, shampoo and hairbrush. She grabbed them and ran into the bathroom, closing the door behind her. He lay on the bed listening to the sound of the shower. He felt so guilty about the decision he had to make he couldn't rest. *We will both talk openly and honestly when she's finished*, he thought.

An hour later, she opened the door carefully. He rolled over at the sound and could not stop looking at her. She was dressed in nothing but a small towel. Her body was muscular, hard. An athlete's body. Her face glowed, her hair glistened and was even darker wet. She had a warm, natural beauty, her mixed Chinese ancestry even more evident. And she looked so young.

"I forgot my new clothes," she said simply.

He looked away as she glided in to grab the clothes and disappeared back into the bathroom. This was all wrong, totally illogical. He would have to reassert control over himself. He was thirty years her senior, more than twice her age, and didn't remember anything about love. She knew how to laugh and smile, be outrageous. He knew how to be logical and humorless. How could she possibly be interested in him in that way? He had insisted on this extra day and night before leaving, but now deeply regretted it. He would have only needed a few minutes with her to plant the tracker. He knew he might never see her again after this night. Maybe he would never know who she was. He would pretend that it didn't matter anymore to him. When this was finally over, he would be returning to Sydney, then his boat, sailing back to the South China Sea. There would be no extraction team coming for her.

They ate in silence, parceling out the food to last through the day and into the morning. Sasha looked uncomfortable as she put the top sheet back on the bed. Katya was perplexed. He was acting so differently towards her, cold.

"Katya, I'm sorry," he said at last. "I am just more exhausted than I thought. You have been so wonderful to me. I cannot thank you enough for saving my life. But listen. You may not understand what I'm telling you or why, but you will. From now on, be careful what you say and where you say it."

Katya nodded warily, but she didn't understand his words or his changed behavior. He moved away when she came close. Katya paused, hurt, then finally spoke up.

"So talk to me, please. It looks like you're getting ready to go your separate way tomorrow when the extraction team gets us to safety. I just don't understand why we have to part like this after all we've been through together. And don't tell me again how exhausted you are. I don't believe you. Is it because you don't know who I am?"

"No, no, there's something else, though maybe that's part of it. I don't want to have to explain myself."

"That's not good enough. I care about you, Sasha."

"You care about me," Sasha repeated, a quiet sadness in his voice. "Then tell me who sent you to protect me."

"I can't do that."

"You don't want to, or you're not allowed to?"

Katya didn't answer and turned away. This was the time for honesty, but she couldn't bring herself to say the words. Maybe if Sasha wasn't being so cold. Maybe in the morning when they'd both had much needed sleep in a bed. And what about the bed? It was a single, not much room to avoid touching each other.

"Well, I'm not going to sleep on the floor and I won't let you, either," Katya said, with more confidence than she felt. "Since this isn't a very big bed, let's just make the best of it. We're going to be up early, so you let me know when you're ready to sleep and I'll give you a last long massage. Something to remember me by."

40

Sasha looked dubious, then nodded. Why is he so reluctant, Katya wondered, what had changed in such a short time? He had been so desperate for her touch in the van. They alternated resting on the bed or exercising until dark. Both of them were already barefoot to keep noise to a minimum. Katya couldn't take her eyes off him each time he worked out, astounded by his grace and masculine beauty. Sasha was clearly not doing his usual routine, but one he had tailored to his still weakened state and the need for quiet. He glided in absolute silence, in what Katya saw as a combination of martial arts, ballet, and Tai Chi. In her eyes, his exercise became a breathtaking modern dance performance. Sasha seemed unaware of her watching him, in contrast to her self-consciousness when it was her turn. She moved with her back to him, but she could feel his eyes following her. She had no clue what he was thinking.

Katya turned out the light as soon as evening began to fall, and the darkness in the room reminded her all too much of their time in the van. Sasha finally crawled into bed fully-dressed, hesitated, then pulled off his shirt. She returned from checking both windows for any suspicious movement and joined him under the scant covers. He turned his back to her and she rubbed her hands together to warm them. She started to massage his tense shoulders. How much more pleasurable an experience this was compared to the first time she massaged him in the van, she mused. Clean bodies, clean hair, comfortable temperature, a real bed, only a slight odor of dust and mildew in her nostrils. She worked her way over almost every inch of his body, kneeling over him at times, wondering again at the lines of scars on his torso she still had not seen. She felt him begin to relax, and again she felt the slight trembling. Eventually he started making his contented sighs, then they began to increase in volume.

Katya realized with a start that Sasha's shudders and gasps were almost orgasmic. He seemed quite unaware. She was arousing him with just her touch and she was becoming aroused herself. She quickly moved her hands back to his shoulders and started massaging them with renewed vigor to distract them both, scooting her body further away from his. *I'm just as desperate for touch as he is*, she mused. She had not allowed herself to date anyone in years, had felt nothing but the casual touch of friends, the kicks and punches of her martial arts partners. She had told herself there was just no time, no place in

41

her world for a relationship, although she knew the real reason. What would she have done if he had turned to her and expected sex?

She didn't really know this man, and he did not know her. She really didn't know men at all. Could a man get aroused with a non-sexual touch? Had she accidently touched him through his clothing while massaging him? She'd tried to be careful. She attempted to think of an English word for a man's privates that she didn't find ridiculous and gave up. She had never touched a man's private parts, even those of her one and only love. They had never done more than kiss and caress each other, naïve as she was then, and as conservative as he was. Sex was for marriage, he'd said. Sex, she thought, followed real love. How could she have once imagined renouncing her Judaism and converting in order to marry him, and what, live in his small village the rest of her life? Her well-meaning naiveté and her big mouth had gotten him killed, his whole village butchered. Oh God, there's a memory to end arousal, she thought. She'd never imagined such evil could exist. The kind of evil Sasha evidently fought against regularly. Worse. How many times on the gun range, in her imagination, had she shot at the image of the colonel... She felt she could never atone enough for what she had caused to happen.

Tears flowed silently down her face. She had saved Sasha and he could return to his life, saving other victims of human trafficking. What she was doing now in her world, as good and well intentioned as it was, seemed inadequate by comparison. Maybe Sasha would let her come with him, let her join him in his work. He needed protecting, he needed her touch, she needed to be doing so much more. Although she had failed to prevent his abduction, she had gotten him free. She would not fail him again. Maybe she was just being naïve again. Maybe her false bravado was just a cover for her guilt, her constant self-recrimination, her self-doubt. Maybe she could never feel at peace again. She kept on massaging Sasha's now totally relaxed back until, miserable and exhausted, she fell asleep.

∽

When Sasha awoke at dawn, Katya was wrapped tightly around him, sleeping. He disentangled himself carefully and, lifting her shirt, placed the activated tracker on her back where it appeared to absorb under her skin, matching her skin tone almost perfectly. Sasha sat on a chair across from the bed and quietly put on his clothes, watch cap, socks and work boots. He sat watching her sleep for a long time before he left the room. Walking quickly, he returned to a park he'd passed the day before. A grove of trees offered a place for him to do his exercises out of sight of any road, of Cutter's searchers. He had an hour and a half before he was to be picked up by Mason, although he spied one of Mason's men watching him. He threw as much energy as he could into his workout, but he could not block the last image of Katya alone in the bed.

؎

When Katya awoke, it was already mid-morning. She sensed Sasha's absence before she looked around. If she'd told him who she really was, he might have been ready to listen, she thought sadly. They had a connection they both could feel, she was sure of it. She began to be concerned that he had not just walked out of her life, but back into danger. The sense of impending peril grew stronger as she jumped out of bed. She readied herself quickly, slipped down the stairs and out the door. She asked after him at the men's shelter and all of the small grocery stores and scoured the cafes. She thought she was being careful, pulling down her hat, her form disguised by the men's clothing she was wearing.

A passing car slowed behind her. The driver, one of the men from the van, desperate to get back in the good graces of Cutter, was elated by his good fortune. There she was out on the street, he was certain. He was sorely tempted to run her down, but Cutter had been adamant that he wanted her alive and relatively unharmed. The man made a quick phone call, parked the car and followed her on foot.

Katya returned to the hotel room several times over the course of the morning in hope that Sasha had returned. As noon approached, she decided to return to the room for one more night. If Sasha was not there in the morning, she would find a taxi and return to her life. Sasha had kept all the money, but her people would gladly pay at the other end. She took note of a new car parked a half block away from the back entrance to the hotel. She waited in the shadows near the door for a long time, but the man in the driver's seat appeared to be asleep, head tilted back on the headrest. Since she had left the back door cracked open, she was able to slip quickly into the dimly lit stairwell.

An immediate punch to her gut sent her reeling back against the door. An unseen arm grabbed her around the neck and she began to lose consciousness. She summoned all of her energy, ran up on the wall and flipped over her assailant's back, releasing his grip. But then

43

another pair of arms grabbed her, and a second punch landed in her diaphragm, leaving her gasping for breath. One of the assailants pinned her legs, and the other grabbed her throat with his arm again, holding tighter and longer. This time she succumbed to the lack of oxygen, falling limp into her attacker's arms.

∽

Mason's car had just reached their staging area after a long talk at breakfast when Sasha called out for them to stop. A sense of foreboding had overtaken him, and he could not shake it off.

"Check the tracker on Katya. Something's wrong." When the three men just looked at him, he glared back. "Do it now!"

"My man watching the hotel has the reader. He would have contacted us if there were a problem," Mason maintained, sounding unconcerned. "I haven't heard from him in about an hour."

"There should be multiple readers! That's how it's designed!" Sasha fumed back. "Contact him."

When there was no answer, Mason's concern matched Sasha's and the car turned back towards Santa Rosa. Even if they rushed at top speed, Sasha knew it was already too late.

The parked car sat just where it had been down the street from the hotel. Sasha suspected the small bullet hole through the front windshield before he saw it. A second small hole could be seen at the hairline of Mason's agent sitting in the car. Sasha spied the tracking reader still sitting in his lap, half hidden under the newspaper he had been pretending to read, dropped there as he died. The assailants had not discovered the device.

Sasha was furious. "You are idiots," he said under his breath.

He pulled open the car door and retrieved the tracking reader, pausing only a moment out of respect for an unknown man's life, no time for a Buddhist prayer. The tracking reader showed Katya already half way back to the house of concrete in Marin. There was no conversation in the car she was in, only the sound of the road under its wheels and silence.

Chapter 9

This time when Katya awoke, she found herself naked in a luxurious king-sized bed. She rubbed her sore stomach and sat up, taking in her new surroundings. The décor was in elegant and expensive taste, abstract paintings on the walls. A huge closet, doors wide open and filled with colorful clothes, took up most of one wall. A digital clock informed her it was already 6 p.m. – she had been out for hours. There was a vanity in the room, covered with perfume bottles and make-up kits, and another open door led to a huge marble bathroom. The walls of the room were concrete. She had to admit she preferred this reception to the one she had imagined when she was in the van.

Katya did a quick self-examination and determined she hadn't been abused while unconscious. Someone must have gotten their jollies examining her for tracking bugs or transmitters, she thought. She spent the next few minutes examining herself with a mirror from the vanity but could see nothing that might have been missed. She prayed something was hidden on her anyhow. Realizing she was still naked and probably being watched, she began searching the extensive closet for appropriate clothes. Pull out drawers afforded her a selection of silk bras and panties, so she started there.

Sitting on the bed in her new underwear, she pondered what her next move would be. What was the motivation for keeping her alive, in treating her like an honored guest? Was she bait to catch Sasha? If so, she would more likely be festering in chains somewhere in the cellar. The mastermind behind all this wanted something from her, or else thought she was something she wasn't. She knew now for certain that the attackers from the van hadn't found her wallet or she would be dead already. Her identity was safe. Katya knew she had to set aside her terrifying self-doubts. She would have to come on strong and be ready to improvise fast.

She examined the clothes in the closet. There were many sizes and styles, probably intended for the boss's Girlfriend of the Week. All the clothing was high fashion and looked incredibly expensive, and included a variety of cocktail dresses, evening gowns and dressy shoes. No jeans, no t-shirts here. She needed clothes she could run and kick in, so she finally chose a power-red jumpsuit in a clingy, stretchy material that was low cut and, in her mind, disgustingly sexy. Shoes were the next problem. She would be helpless staggering around in spiked heels. Katya found a pair of bejeweled low wedge sandals that would at least stay on her feet. She laid the clothes out on the bed and took a first-class shower, styled her hair as best she could, and put on a modicum of make-up.

She suddenly remembered Sasha's last words to her. He had left a message: be careful what you say and where you say it. She felt the memory of the touch of his hand on her back, the almost supernatural connection between them. There could be no doubt. There had to be some kind of listening device on her back that could not be easily discovered and if so, she could communicate with him. And if there was such a device, Sasha had to have gotten his hands on it during the one time he'd left the room. Which meant he'd met with some kind of law enforcement. Which meant backup, hopefully an army. If Sasha was making plans to storm this castle, she wanted to be in a position to talk him in.

Katya took one last look at herself in the full-length mirror. She had never seen herself as a glamorous woman, and hardly recognized the image staring back at her. Now she had to imagine herself as perhaps a cold-blooded killer and steeled herself to romance and bamboozle whatever monster was waiting for her outside the bedroom door. She had no idea if she could successfully pull this off, but she had no choice but to try.

Katya expected to find a guard outside the door, but the hallway was empty. She forced herself to walk resolutely down the grand concrete staircase to the first floor. She made a mental note of the layout, starting with a front hallway/living room with a reinforced front door that looked like it belonged on a bank vault. A single guard was posted there. An open side door led into a room that looked like a bunker, with monitors lining one wall, four guards on chairs chatting, and two more nearly out of sight, sitting on a small balcony, and a similarly reinforced door from the bunker to the outside. A kill zone. The guards noticed her right away, stared but did not move. She followed the sound of voices through the front room to closed double doors opposite the bunker. She opened one and entered a study furnished with several heavy oak tables and a desk. Here the concrete walls had been plastered over and painted white. An inviting,

46

comfortable room in contrast to the rest of the house. A narrow balcony ran along the right wall, with floor to ceiling bookshelves and two wooden doors leading to the second floor. She didn't see any stairway to reach it.

In the center of the room stood eight powerful and dangerous looking men, three of them ethnic Chinese, the rest Caucasian or mixed race. The two New York drivers were not among them. Talking ceased as she entered, and all eyes turned to her. Made a good first impression, she thought, as she quickly tried to distinguish their leader. Her eyes focused on a tall, well-dressed gray-haired man, heavyset, very nearly fat, but with a handsome face, who, as soon as their eyes met, flashed a smile and came to meet her.

"Welcome, welcome, my dear," he said, as he reached for her hand and gave it a lingering, stagey kiss. "My name is Markus Cutter. These are my best men, my soldiers. Please consider yourself a guest in my home. I have become a great admirer."

"A simple invitation was all I needed," Katya replied icily, in what she hoped was a mysterious and slightly Eastern European accent. It was immediately clear to Katya what he thought she was, and she would play the role. "My job here was finished, and I have other clients awaiting me. If you care to issue an apology for my rough treatment, I might consider forgiving you. I will not apologize for removing your victim from your clutches. That was what I was paid to do."

"My dear, of course, I've been boorishly rude," he said, bowing low. "Please forgive the manner in which you were brought here. And for the days in the van, they must have been horrid. Please believe that I did not know about your existence until we got the story from the New York drivers. What a scene! I must admit I had to laugh at them."

Katya glared at him as long as she dared, then smiled.

"My name is Katya. And I forgive you, if only because you are so handsome and charming. But since I did not receive a formal invitation, I do not know why I am here."

"Katya. That is a beautiful name for a beautiful woman. I have brought you here because I want to know more about you. You're obviously working for someone now, and I would like to know who paid you to guard Sasha."

"Well, Markus, that is certainly blunt. I never reveal the names of my employers. I would not live long if I did. I am loyal to the death."

"To the death." Markus chortled. "What a lovely turn of phrase. Then perhaps you can tell me what it is that you do and what your motivation is?"

"I do what is asked of me. Kill, blackmail, guard, rescue, it is all the same to me. And what better motivation is there than money? This past year I have concluded five contract kills. Some are easy, a few days, finished. Some take months of careful planning. Guarding is usually very much easier than this one was."

Katya prayed that Sasha would see through her game if he was listening. Would the other law enforcement agents? It was time to get them to pay attention to her usefulness.

"I still want to know about Sasha's protector. You are not in a position to say no."

Katya could detect no threat in Markus's voice. It sounded like just a statement of fact.

"And I thought you were falling in love with me," Katya said seductively, as she traced her finger down Markus's chin. "You seem to run a good business here, lots of good strong muscle. You know how to protect yourself. Your seven soldiers I see here look intelligent, loyal. Maybe not that tall one on the right, who looks so stupid. I do not like his face. I am trying to decide whether to break one of his arms or both."

The man bristled, and Markus and the other men laughed.

"Gunner!" Markus called out. "Our distinguished guest doesn't like you!"

Katya had thought the huge man looked the most loyal, the most dangerous, and made a plan to take him out first. Gunner was tall and heavily muscled, a vicious looking Scandinavian. His t-shirt stretched across a massive chest, baring powerful thick forearms. She could not let herself fail this time. The threat of a painful death is also a strong motivator.

"You are as amusing as you are beautiful," Markus snickered. "And clever. I was impressed how you pulled that stunt with the crash. We wasted so much time getting down the hill, fighting the fire, searching those hills. A stunt like that takes planning and amazing strength, not to mention guts. You had no time and no help. Simply amazing."

"I thank you for the compliment. You are clever yourself. Your house is a fortress. It would take a tank to blow in your front door. No

48

wonder you need just one guard. Of course, you know an attack would come from the side, and you have such a lovely kill zone set up. But your six guards look very, very bored. I should go in there and entertain them."

"I would rather you entertained me."

Good. Markus was starting to sound smitten, she thought. She steadied herself to continue. She pretended she was in a play without a script and improvising her way through. Her training had prepared her for such an eventuality.

"Then I will indeed entertain you. I have a proposition you will love. I do not like to work for many employers. I would like to work for just you. But first, I would like to play a game. I would like to choose one of your men to fight. The tall one there I don't like will do. I have decided – I do want to break both his arms. Let him keep his gun. I will not give him a chance to use it. I want you to take your gun and place it on this small table in front of me. You decide if you want to leave the bullets in it or take them out. I will not look. If you leave them in, I might just shoot you all in the head, though, so think carefully. Then your friend here, what is his name again, the one I do not like, the one who looks stupid and disloyal?"

Katya could tell Markus was entranced. If she could pull this off, he would do anything for her. The tall man was seething, as she knew he would be, as she wanted and needed him to be. He would make mistakes if he was in a rage. The other men were already teasing him.

"Gunner is my trusted right-hand man. If you lose I hope you will apologize to him."

"Oh, I never lose, and I never apologize. So, Gunner and I will fight. The gun will be right here. One of us must hold this gun to the other's head for the count of five for the game to be over. Pulling of trigger or not is up to winner. It might go bang, it might just go click. Only you, Markus, will know which it will do. And Markus, this you will like very much. If I win, which I will, I will work for you, but I will not tell you who paid me to guard Sasha. If Gunner wins, he will get to keep his arms unbroken, and I will still work for you, but I will have to tell you."

The room was silent. Katya could feel the anticipation and excitement growing as Markus and his men processed her words.

"Only one small thing." Katya sighed loudly. "I am very, very hungry and I will not fight until I receive a very, very nice dinner with you, Markus. And I want you to give me a tour of your house. I want to know all about you and your business. Four hours from right now, eleven o'clock this evening, I will fight Gunner and you will be proud of me."

Katya held her breath and watched Markus' face. She took both his hands in hers. There was no doubt in her mind what he was thinking. She had already won.

Chapter 10

The meal Markus's chef prepared for them was delicious, with multiple courses. Katya ate slowly, stretching the dinner out over hours. She flirted outrageously with Markus, flattering his ego and frequently touching his hand. She regaled him with made-up tales of her many contract kills, pulling from memories of unsolved celebrity and political assassinations in the news.

"Show me everything," she purred after the final course. "I know a man like you has powerful secrets. Show me your most powerful one."

Markus pulled out her chair and held her elbow as she stood up.

"Do you know much about computers?" he asked.

"My only contact with my employers is through computers. Much of my business is done on them," she answered. "Research into my subjects' lives, hacking emails, planting false information, well, I don't need to tell you what you can do with a computer."

Katya could tell how much this pleased Markus. They walked through several hallways to a metal door. As Markus placed his hand on the security reader next to the door, she placed her hand over his and smiled up at him. The door swung open into a room full of computers and equipment. He ordered the man working there to leave and ushered her in.

"All of my work around the world is here. My lucrative trafficking networks in humans, drugs, and weapons," he boasted. "And no one in the world has assembled a greater collection of data. I have information on everyone I deem important, every wrong deed, every falsehood, every breach of trust I could manipulate to my advantage. I have plans to hack into many of the banks and police stations in this country. There's no limit to the power my investment in all this information will give me."

"And I had thought you a simple trafficker in human lives," murmured Katya. *Now he's exaggerating, just trying to impress me,* she thought. "Perhaps you will accomplish this hacking capability, perhaps not. But your data files, they interest me. Tell me, you must have searched. Did you find me in your computer? By my description, by my methods? I use many names."

"You know very well that we didn't."

"That proves how good I am. I know how to hide in the system and I can show you how to find other people who are hiding. But how do you protect all this? What would happen to you if the American government were to get their hands on your nice little computer lab and find out about all the bad little things you're doing and planning?"

"One little button on my desk and it all goes away, erased in a huge explosion. With a time delay, of course."

"All that hard work, and you would let it all go, just like that?"

"It would be the last thing I did before escaping."

"Oh, you are being more dramatic than me," Katya pouted. "I won't have it. And just how much time are you giving your time delay? Where is this little button?"

"Now you are asking too, too many questions, my dear," Markus said. He looked carefully at her face, concern and doubt clearly etched on his own.

"Suspect me of what?" Katya answered, keeping her smile steady. "Falling in love with your computers instead of with you? I am hoping to be much more than just another employee for you." She moved closer to him, touching her body against his and lowered her voice. "I just do not want to lean on your little button by accident and make it all go 'poof.' I do love your computers and I do want to know more about what you have and how it works. And I want to know more about you."

"Then name me one thing you want to see," Markus laughed, caught again in her web.

"Convince me how complete and accurate your data files are. Can I choose one name to explore?"

"You seem difficult to impress, my dear. But I'm quite certain you will be impressed with this. Let me show you how to enter your request. What name would you like?"

"Let me just think. Ah, let's try Sasha's. My last employer had given me a particularly extensive file. I wish to see if yours is so very much better as you claim."

"I promise you it will be so very much better," he said, smiling. Katya smiled back. She could tell he was charmed by her language.

Katya watched as Markus entered the name Alexander 'Sasha' Borodin and a few code words into the computer and awaited the result with bated breath. Alexander Borodin. How did Sasha get the name of a 19th century Russian composer, she wondered? One who was also a chemistry professor, physician, and researcher? The file opened. Katya sat down at the computer and started reading.

The first lines Katya read on the screen made her mind reel. She had to concentrate not to let her astonishment show.

Alexander Borodin, goes by single name Sasha, general surgeon and neurosurgeon, medical researcher, inventor. Undoubtedly among the most intelligent men living, a genius in the fields of medicine, biochemistry, chemistry, physics, robotics, artificial intelligence, nanoscience, computer science, mechanical and bioengineering. Has been able to remain a complete unknown outside his localized medical career, his privacy, person and extent of his genius protected by secret branch of the Australian government, S-Branch, aka SB, created to exploit his genius. Uncredited creator of all successful commercial products, inventions and innovations of Australogic Laboratories in Sydney, including prosthetic devices, medicines, alternative energy systems and top-secret advanced weapons and defense systems, computer technology, and spyware. Estimated current business value over fifty-eight billion Australian dollars. Refuses income from laboratories, has no savings we have been able to discover and no possessions of importance. Serves as Captain, accepting modest salary, and lives on sailboat/ hospital boat named the *Retribution*, aka the *Trib*, provided and provisioned by S-Branch. Crew of ten, mostly doctors, trained in combat as well as medicine. Runs free clinics, medical practice and surgery from boat along rivers and coasts throughout Southeast Asia, maintains strong connection with local hospitals. Pursues missions against drug smugglers, pirates, slavers, gunrunners, and human traffickers. Ongoing disruption of our operations. Twenty-four/seven security including, we believe, via satellite, and high esteem among local populations create major

53

problems for us getting close enough to eliminate him. Attempts to destroy boat have failed. Strongly suspect boat has high-tech defensive and offensive systems. Both he and fiercely loyal crew have been determined, after many efforts, to be incorruptible. The man is a saint and well-protected.

A saint, Katya thought. Saint Sasha had a nice ring to it. She'd have to tease him. Then again, maybe not. But was this a joke? Who the hell was this man? Saint Sasha indeed. Was such genius in so many fields even possible? She knew he fought against human traffickers, but the rest was just too much to comprehend. She'd had no clue he was a doctor, a neurosurgeon no less. She could imagine a doctor developing medicines maybe, but weapons systems? This description did not fit with the considerate, vulnerable man she knew. Markus was testing her. She forced herself to keep her expression unchanged as she looked up at him. His proud air told her he thought this information was true.

Sasha had told her he was incapable of forgetting anything, that his brain never slowed, and he had been surprised that she, his would-be rescuer, didn't know who he was. Is this what he meant? Sasha, surgeon and inventor, one of the most brilliant men alive, under the protection of an entire governmental organization. Why then had he been left completely unguarded and alone in New York? Maybe he would still need her protection long after this business with Markus Cutter was resolved.

She continued to read the report on Markus's computer screen, a long list of Sasha's achievements and discoveries, a surprising number of which she recognized, including dozens of popular household products and medicines, new treatments and even a couple of cures for a variety of tropical diseases. Key among his creations was the One Pill, which had become commercially available twelve years ago. Katya reflected on how the wildly popular One Pill had changed women's lives around the world, a second sexual revolutions, decreasing the birth rate and virtually eliminating sexually transmitted diseases at the same time. His work had tremendous impact on clean water and waste management systems, helping to slow disease outbreaks in the developing world, helping solve water shortages. His innovations in solar energy were curbing the use of fossil fuels. The description of the prostheses and neural implants to operate them he'd developed took her breath away. He had even developed a hydrogen fuel cell that would have eliminated the need for oil and gas altogether, but the report noted that it had mysteriously disappeared from the news and was never marketed.

Screen after screen of details followed. Katya read quickly since she didn't know how much time Markus would allow her. Certain facts jumped out at her, some of which she already knew. Eccentric, severe touch phobia, does not travel by air or alone. Knowledge of dozens of languages. What do they meant by *dozens*, she wondered. Parentage, country and date of birth unknown. Given birthdate January 1, 1940, in Celle, Germany. Katya was astounded that Sasha could be fifty-nine years old, he looked so much younger. Adopted around age five or six by professor and inventor Harrison Mandelbrot in Sydney. Medical degree at nineteen. Surgeon and neurosurgeon by twenty-five, a neurosurgeon with the University of Sydney, in their prosthetics department. Volunteered for Australian Army Medical Corps as surgeon in Vietnam in 1965. Met and married Tran Thi Le in June of same year, daughter of General Tran Huy An of North Vietnam. Devastated after wife's death in December of 1966. End of public medical career, was fugitive from SB for a year. Began life-long search for missing son. Why would his son be missing, perhaps since he was an infant? His son would be older than she was. Cutter's men now also searching, as capture of son would be useful in gaining control or in drawing Sasha out in the open.

There were just a few labeled pictures in the report: an oddly adult-muscled, solemn blond child of about six with his adoptive parents, the woman in a wheelchair, the man a haughty looking professorial type; a group graduation picture from medical school; an informal wedding picture of a young-looking Sasha in uniform with his beautiful, raven-haired Vietnamese bride, Le; lots of pictures of the boat; more recent long-range surveillance photos of him and his current crew. Such a sleek looking boat, ninety-nine feet from the description, berths for eleven, a small but complete high-tech hospital. A twin-masted sailboat, although the photos showed the boat with one or no masts as well. Sasha supposedly designed the boat himself.

Bare facts, so much story left untold, Katya thought. A Vietnam War veteran from Australia, tormented widower with a missing child. Both wife and son lost thirty-three years ago, married only a year and

55

a half. Had he really not been touched, not had a romantic relationship in thirty-three years? Had she begun to develop feelings for him, Katya wondered, and if so, were they entirely misplaced? Protecting him did not require her to love him. Besides, he seemed totally disinterested, other than craving her touch.

Katya forced herself to quickly read on. She read how Cutter's organization had hacked the Australian government's files to discover this information, and the details about the government's creation of S-Branch in 1957 to handle Sasha as an asset, to keep him to themselves. Sasha would have been seventeen, a teenager. God, that was years before she was born. He was thirty years older, the same age as her late father, she thought with a start. There was information about their creation of Australogic Laboratories and his continuous work for them, even in Vietnam, and the reason for their procurement of Sasha's specialized, high-tech sailboat, the names and backgrounds of the crew Sasha brought in to work with him over the years, the current crew.

Katya couldn't continue to doubt the accuracy of this astounding report. She knew there was nothing more to decide. Fate had made the decision for her. Sasha needed her more than he could possibly imagine, and she needed him. Sasha had only told her he was sort of a policeman. And a musician. There was not one mention of music.

"All much too basic." Katya tried to keep her face calm as she turned back to Markus. "Background. I know his enemies, friends, routines, loves, hates. You have nothing of the person, his daily schedule, his life. If I must guard or destroy someone, this is the kind of information I must have. Let me help you build your files to be more useful."

"You have yourself a partnership, Katya." Markus tried to take her hand, but she pushed him gently away with a palm to his chest.

"But now I must prepare myself to fight Gunner. Tell the boys to place their bets, but you had better bet on me if you want to win big. I will not disappoint."

Chapter 11

Sasha and Mason sat on hard benches in the staging area, transfixed, listening to Katya's transmission. Mason was alarmed, Sasha amused. Sasha had to spend an inordinate amount of time convincing Mason of the value of the information Katya was getting across and of the certainty that she was putting on a successful act.

"She has no accent, Mason. She's doing a near perfect imitation of a Slovakian," Sasha summed up. "And now we know about the computer room. She has given us everything, from the details of their defenses to their manpower to the exact time we should strike. She'll have every eye in the building glued on her with this Gunner fight. My concern is that she doesn't know what she's getting into. She could be killed."

And if not, she knew too much secret information about his life, if Cutter's computer files were anything like what he claimed. He was a mystery to her no longer, no chance of remaining an ordinary man in her eyes. No chance of hiding his age. He was back to being a freak of nature, an inaccessible genius, guarded and forced to wear a tracker like an extremely valuable pet. An asset. A moneymaker. Even Le had never known the full extent of his abilities. But having Katya on the inside gave him hope that their raid might have a chance of success. Mason's initial plans had been flimsy and surely doomed to fail. Sasha couldn't bail now, with Katya in such danger. For him, the raid was now a rescue.

"But how did she know we could hear her?" Mason protested. "You must have told her."

"She may have inferred it from something I said." It was meant to be a warning about Mason, Sasha thought. "I told you I feel a connection with her. And perhaps she discovered the device on her back after all. I wouldn't put it past her."

There was now only the sound of opening and closing doors and footsteps coming from the device, so Mason and Sasha joined the other men. Sasha knew there was no love lost between the CIA and the FBI, so Mason wouldn't have mentioned his background. Mason had assembled a crack team of FBI agents from several Western states, and they had been preparing for days. Mason introduced Sasha as Ian Dirkson, a computer expert also with Interpol, just arrived from Australia. A lean, buzz-cut Californian by the name of Dan Schultz introduced himself as their leader and made the rest of the introductions. Based on Katya's information, the team added greater firepower to their arsenal, including tank-busting missiles capable of quickly taking out the fortified doors. Ambulances would be standing by. Mason told the team that Ian's technical wizardry would disable all security screens and alarms before the attack. Hopefully no one would be watching them at that moment anyhow. Their eyes would be on the fight.

Mason had to convince Sasha to wear the same armored vest with the letters FBI written large on the front and back as the others. The men would be wearing helmets as well.

"I know it bothers you, but do you really want one of us Yanks shooting you in the back by mistake?" Mason said. Sasha could see his point.

The team was in position just out of sight of the concrete house a half-hour before the eleven o'clock fight was scheduled to begin. There were fifteen of them, including Mason and Sasha. Sasha would have preferred a larger team, but the men – no women, he noted – were well-trained field agents who had all seen plenty of action and were superbly armed. They had the element of surprise, and Katya on the inside. They would move forward under cover of darkness and wait for whatever signal they could glean from Katya's tracker. For Sasha, this was just another mission against armed and dangerous men. He had spent the last thirty-four years in one sort of a war or another.

Sasha thought back to the last fight he'd engaged in, just two months ago. This would be a messier, much deadlier affair. That fight had been off the coast of Vietnam. Sasha received word that a group of pirates had been terrorizing the coastal area, robbing passing boats and killing passengers. The *Trib* had been refitted and disguised as a falling-apart Vietnamese junk, a new high cabin built over the pilothouse, her twin masts each equipped with a single indigenous orange sail, fake diesel smoke billowing out her engines, her sides covered in a veneer of old wood with green peeling paint. His men planted rumors among the villages along the coast that the ship had been smuggling drugs to Ho Chi Minh City and would return with a large amount of cash. They didn't have to travel far before three motorboats approached from the shelter of the coastal rocks, quickly surrounding the junk. Their leader, a small, wiry man with a shock of black hair and many missing teeth, shouted out in Vietnamese that they would be boarding. Anyone resisting would be shot. There was no reply from the junk and no movement on board.

The boats pulled alongside, and seven of the ten pirates, heavily armed, clambered over the sides. From the safety of the high cabin, Sasha watched their frustration as they could find no way to enter the hatch or portholes, now covered with steel panels. Several began to climb the steps to the high cabin. Three powerful shots rang out from the junk. The three small boats exploded into the air then sank, their waiting drivers thrown out into the choppy water. The pirates began wildly firing at the high cabin, but their bullets bounced off the reinforced sides. One by one, the pirates were taken down by shots from above. Sasha and Hiro, his best marksman, managed all the shots themselves, carefully aiming the dart-firing rifles, dropping each man where he stood.

When all was still, the hatch door opened, and the rest of Sasha's crew exited cautiously. Aashir, Chen, and Hau lowered a Zodiac to pick up the three men in the water while Tuan and Kiko collected weapons, and Maxim, Sonthi, Dima, and Keung attended to the unconscious men, binding their wrists behind their backs and carrying them down the hatch to the cells. After the prisoners awakened, Sasha offered them the chance of rehabilitation at his Vietnamese refugee center. Anyone who refused, or who failed his lengthy interrogation for suitability, would be handed over to local police and would face lengthy incarceration. It was the rare prisoner who rejected this offer, and none of these men wished to languish in a fetid cell.

Not every takedown was as low-risk as this one. But surprise firefights were uncommon, and Sasha and his crew hadn't been forced to kill many men in the last several years. Some men were just past redemption, he reflected. Sasha took few chances with his crew's lives. Every man was too valuable as a healer, as a friend, and as a fellow musician. He only wished that there wasn't a never-ending supply of desperate men willing to kill for money.

59

Chapter 12

Katya was ready. She'd spent the last half-hour in her room, carefully planning each move, remembering the layout of the study precisely. She prayed Markus wouldn't choose to change the venue.

"I will take him down in two minutes," she repeated over and over out loud, as if psyching herself for the fight. She still suspected Sasha was not the only one listening to her, and she didn't want the men attacking the building to assume this was going to be a long, drawn-out competition. Gunner was much larger and stronger than she was, and raging or not, he would be too much of an opponent if she didn't make short work of him. And if she was completely wrong and there were no forces aligned outside of this building, she wanted to survive long enough to make a new plan.

She practiced a few kicks in the bejeweled sandals. The cork soles would cushion the blows too much; she would have to do this barefoot. She could hear the growing murmur of excited voices even through the closed door. She took off her sandals and shook out her limbs. She didn't look at the clock in the room, but she knew it was almost eleven. It was time.

As she hoped, all the guards from the back and front doors were standing in the hallway, backs to their stations, watching her as she stepped down the stairs. The double doors of the study had been thrown wide open so there was a clear view across the hall and open living room from where they stood.

"You boys have got yourselves a good vantage point. Do not look away, because Gunner is going down fast. You will be seeing a lot more of me around here," Katya cooed.

Some of the men laughed; a couple even cheered. She was sure Gunner was not very popular. She swayed her hips a little as she sauntered on through the front room and then stood in the study doorway. She could feel the eyes of all seven men behind her as she faced the men in the study.

"Ah, precisely on time, my dear Katya," said Markus, smiling broadly. He sat behind a wide antique oak desk, leaning back in a tall black leather chair. The rest of the men stood in a semicircle behind him. They appeared to have arranged themselves into two camps, the four closest to Markus joining their boss's side in supporting Katya, currying favor but against their better judgment, she was sure. The other two stood with Gunner, patting him on the back and making encouraging remarks. Gunner glared at her, but he seemed confident and fearless. After all, she was only a woman, and not a very big one, dressed for a cocktail party, and barefoot at that. She would have to rile him up again.

"Only two supporters I see, Mr. Gunner. Your friends know who pays their bills, who they owe their loyalty to. They will be very sorry they chose you over me. If they have any smarts at all, they have both placed side bets against you." She forced herself to laugh out loud when the two men looked sheepish. Gunner noticed as well and was turning red. "Just try not to cry when you get crushed by a mere girl."

Gunner's friends had to hold him back. *Gunner's a goner*, she thought to herself to keep her adrenaline flowing. Casually looking around, she sized up the room once again. To her left stood the thick oak table with the delicately carved legs, flush against the wall. Katya turned to Markus.

"Well, shall we dance? Do you have the gun?"

"Right here, my dear Katya." He held an antique Colt 45 six-shooter up in the air for all to see, then held it below the desk while he either emptied or filled the chambers and clicked it shut. Ah, Katya thought, he's not going to take any chances with a high-powered weapon after my teasing warning. Katya listened carefully but she already knew what he would choose. She would know when it was in her hand in any case. Markus gave the gun to the man beside him and nodded at the small wooden table that now stood alone in the center of the room. The man stepped around and placed the gun on the table, then walked back to his place. The room grew quiet but for the sound of Gunner's angry breathing. She could sense the held breath of everyone else.

Katya stayed close to the doorway, hands on hips. With a sudden flash of movement, she jumped and whirled around, hitting the right leg of the huge oak table full force with one foot. The leg cracked at the tabletop and slid out at an angle but did not break off. The table sagged an inch but held. The surprise and seeming pointlessness of her move paralyzed Gunner. He remained standing where he was, waiting for the fight to begin. Katya whirled twice and flew at the table again, striking the now stressed left leg with her foot nearer the bottom.

"Now!" she shouted. The leg broke off and landed on the tile floor with a loud crack as the table crashed onto its side, the reverberation rocking the room. Gunner turned to Markus and his mates, shrugging his shoulders as if to ask – What the hell! Katya only needed a fraction of a second to dive for the table leg and swing it full force against the back of Gunner's head. As his body swung around, she threw the leg aside and grabbed his right arm in both of hers and cracked it like a nut over her raised leg, then twirled once dramatically, repeating the devastating crack with his left arm. Gunner fell to his knees, only half conscious from the blow to his head, staring at his arms. Bloody bones projected from both of them. Katya picked up the gun and held it to Gunner's head. She knew she might not have time to count to five. She pulled the trigger and they all heard the click just before the explosion hit them. Smoke and dust blew through the room like a tornado.

Chapter 13

A gaping hole showed daylight where the fortified side door had been. All of the guards ran to the hole with guns drawn and four of Markus's remaining soldiers drew their guns as well, rushing towards the study doors. Two stayed to push Markus under his desk and stand guard. Katya grabbed the gun out of Gunner's shoulder holster and dove for cover behind the oak table. How could they have not understood her? Anyone entering through that hole would be slaughtered. Thick smoke was still billowing in the hallway, rendering the front door invisible. Seconds passed and no shots were fired.

"Drop your weapons! FBI!" a loud voice called out of the smoke.

Katya heard shouts from the hallway and the sudden burst of automatic gunfire. No one was surrendering. Markus's men had just reached the hallway and rushed back towards the study, searching for cover. She dared a peek and saw men in FBI flak jackets pulling off gas masks as they sought shelter themselves in the front room, firing at Cutter's retreating soldiers in both directions. Katya now knew what they had done. The front and side doors had been blown simultaneously and the hole in the front hidden in smoke clouds. She recognized Sasha among the entering assault team and he saw her as well. A sudden movement behind her caught her eye. One of the soldiers guarding Markus had raised his gun to fire at Sasha's head. She aimed her gun and fired. The man flew backwards. As Katya threw herself back behind the table, a burst of gunfire from the second soldier sprayed the table and wall behind her, knocking the gun from her hand. It spun in fast circles and stopped a few feet away. She had never shot a man before, but her years of target practice visualizing the face of that certain monstrous colonel had prepared her for this moment. She could shoot the right hand off the paper target and put the last bullet between the eyes every time.

The gunfire ceased as quickly as it had begun. Katya could hear shouts and movement in the other rooms. She stayed behind the table but risked another look. Six men in their FBI flak jackets stood near her in the study with guns raised, Sasha among them. Markus was standing up slowly from under his desk, a lowered small machine gun in his hand. His one remaining soldier also held his gun low and still. The rest of Markus's men in the room were down.

"Mason." Markus said his name scornfully.

"Markus, it's over. Drop your guns," Mason demanded.

"Sasha and I have unfinished business. I want him to watch his little woman die."

"No more deaths today, Markus, unless you want to die. There are six guns on you and your man. Move a finger and I won't have to bother with taking you in."

"Watch her die slowly first, cut to ribbons. Then all of you. Then he can meet the fate I brought him here for."

"There are many more of us outside this room. We've only lost two wounded. You've lost all but this one."

"You may think so," Markus smirked.

The two doors flew open between the bookshelves in the narrow strip of balcony. The space filled quickly with six men, each pointing a gun at a different head.

"I will be taking you instead. My seven hostages, including Katya, for our freedom."

This time Mason, Sasha, and the four agents lowered their weapons but did not drop them. No one noticed Katya creeping forward, reaching for the gun on the floor. Until Markus did. He sprayed a long burst of fire her direction and turned back to his captives. The oak table was ripped full of bullet holes, the plaster wall pulverized, plaster dust mixed with blood spread out the open end of the table shelter. But the gun was gone.

"So maybe it will be six hostages without Katya. Drop your weapons or I will make it five hostages."

The splintered table flew forwards into the room and Katya stood, aimed and pulled the trigger six times, hitting six hands on six guns belonging to the men on the balcony. Furious, Markus fired a continuous stream of bullets in her direction. But Katya was not to be seen. Sasha didn't know if she had dropped down in time or been shot. Mason was the first to fire back, emptying his gun into Markus and his last man. Markus fell backwards over his desk but managed to roll over and reach for something on it before he lay still.

Everyone moved at once. Mason pointed to the balcony and the four agents sprinted to find the stairs to capture the six men who were writhing against the bookshelves. Then he ran to check if Markus and

66

his man were dead. Sasha had already rushed to the splintered oak table. At first there was no one visible behind it, just a deep pile of plaster dust. He scrabbled through the mess until he found her body and pulled it carefully to the surface. She was completely white with dust, but as he wiped her face, the skin showed through. She was smiling.

"Bet you didn't see that one coming," she was able to mumble through her dust-filled mouth. "Is there anyone else left out there?"

"We're all here. Markus is gone, all his men dead or captured. Don't move yet. There was a lot of blood and I want to see where it's coming from."

Sasha gently swept more of the dust off of her and found two red soaked areas on either side of her left upper arm. Two bullet holes, looking like they passed through. Sasha was relieved to see both bullets appeared to have missed her humerus, were maybe just flesh wounds. Katya tried unsuccessfully to get up.

"Where is Markus?" she demanded.

Across the room, Mason shook his head. He was attempting to move Markus off the desk and onto the floor.

"Markus is dead," Sasha told her. "The ambulances are almost here. Katya, you did it again. I am losing count of how many times you've saved my life."

"No! I mean where is his body!"

"Mason just rolled him onto the floor from his desk."

"His desk! See if there's a button of some sort he may have pushed!"

Mason checked the desktop and found a small box with a red button wired into the desk. Markus had been lying on top of it.

"There's a box emitting a faint beeping alarm, and numbers counting down, showing twenty minutes. What does that mean?" Mason asked anxiously. "Don't tell me Cyrus was serious!"

"I have no doubt. It means evacuate the building – the computer lab is set to self-destruct. Sasha, help me up. I'm going to get what I can before it's gone."

"You're getting to an ambulance. You've been shot and you're in shock," Sasha argued.

"Mason, do you want his files or not? You two drag Markus out of here and follow me."

"What the hell do you mean, drag Markus? Sasha, she's clearly in shock."

"Just do it!" Katya shouted. "We need his hand to get past his security system!"

Katya got to her feet and shook the plaster off her head. Before either could stop her, she was off and running down the hallways she had walked earlier that day with Markus. Sasha and Mason exchanged a glance, lifted Markus' dead weight, and carried him between them, hurrying after Katya as best they could. She was leaning on the computer room door when they caught up with her, brushing herself off and breathing hard.

"You must evacuate. I know what do to. Sasha, I've worked too hard keeping you alive to risk losing you now!"

Sasha swung the dead man's hand up and placed it on the sensor.

"I'm not leaving you, mate," he said.

Katya slipped through the open door and quickly closed and locked it behind her before Sasha or Mason could react. She grabbed a thumb drive and fired up a computer, calculating quickly where she should start and end her search. There wouldn't be time to copy all of its contents. She didn't want the Americans to have the data on Sasha, but they might need more information to take down the rest of Cutter's organization, so she began an alphabetical total download starting with the letter C. Was Sasha really named Alexander Borodin? She would have to stop long before she got to S. Katya had an uneasy feeling about this Mason, something in the way he and Markus had looked at each other, then Mason shooting him when he could have captured him. But she was unsure if Mason was his first name or last and would just have to hope his data would be included in her grab.

She looked carefully around the room for any sense of her remaining time. To her great relief, she found a small box on the main desk with numbers racing downwards. There were less than twelve minutes remaining. Katya searched in vain for any computers small enough to take with her, then grabbed up files and charts that looked even vaguely important. Her time was down to four minutes when she pulled out the thumb drive. The search had ended at the name Kanter. She ran to the door with her arms full and stumbled through, relieved that Sasha was not still standing there, and rushed back through the deserted house and out the gigantic hole where the front door had

been. She had not gone thirty steps before a massive explosion sounded behind her, blowing her
off her feet. She lay with her face in the papers until she no longer felt pelted with debris, then turned back to look at the concrete shell wreathed in billowing smoke.

Chapter 14

Sasha reached her first. He ran his hands expertly over her plaster and debris-covered body and ascertained no new injuries. He picked her up and carried her forty meters to the waiting crowd of agents and set her down gently next to an ambulance. Tall floodlights had been set up and Katya woozily imagined a night construction site. She looked at the anxious faces and realized they thought she might be dead or dying.

She handed her mashed pile of papers to Mason and gave a thumbs up signal with her uninjured hand. The agents and medical personnel cheered and started high-fiving each other. Sasha tried to keep them back, but the agents streamed by to offer best wishes for a speedy recovery and to congratulate her on making the assault a success. She watched Mason's face as she handed the lead FBI agent the thumb drive and explained its contents. Mason's immediate look of concern confirmed her suspicions about him – he had much to hide, even if it was in the past. She worried that he might yet lay claim to the thumb drive, not knowing if his name was included or not. Maybe she should have made the transfer in private. Would Mason be suspicious of her now?

The medical personnel were doing their best to clean Katya's left arm so they could examine and treat her bullet wounds. Sasha explained that he was a doctor and examined the wounds as well.

"What is your pain level, from one to ten?" asked one of the paramedics.

"A moment ago, it was a one but we're moving up on eleven. I think my adrenaline rush has finally worn off after five days. Can you get addicted to adrenaline?"

"We'll give you something strong for the pain right now," he said. "Just hang on until it kicks in. It won't be long."

Katya was more concerned about being admitted to a hospital. It would all have to come out in the open. Name. Real identity. What would Sasha think of her then? Would he walk away? The more she thought about what she'd read in Cutter's files, the more she felt deeply moved by the man Sasha was. She believed what she had read was true. He must feel desperately alone, misunderstood, taken advantage of. A man with the intellect to change the world. He had already changed the world for the better. She wanted nothing more than to be able to stay by his side, to work with him, protect him. He needed her touch. He needed *her*.

The solution came unexpectedly. Mason had pulled Sasha aside and they remained in deep conversation, and then a long, heated argument ensued. She sensed her fate was being decided but she was allowed no input. Sasha asked one of the medical personnel to join in the discussion. She could see the man shaking his head.

"Hey," Katya shouted. "You are talking about me and I'm right here."

The three men returned to her side. Sasha squatted down on the gravel drive next to her.

"Katya, listen. Mason wants to take you with us back to San Francisco. He doesn't want you to go to the hospital. He thinks I can take care of you although the EMT and I disagree. You have been through so much. You belong in a hospital."

"Do I need surgery?"

"No, both bullets passed through the flesh of your upper arm, although you should have an X-ray. You're lucky that they missed arteries and nerves, didn't smash into your humerus. But that gives you four wounds that need to heal, along with injured muscles. Your whole body has had one shock after another."

"One shock after another sounds like your life. I've been through this much before. I will be fine with painkillers and your help."

"What are you saying?"

"I'm not going to the hospital. I want to get cleaned up here. I will walk to a car with you and whoever you are, Mason. For some reason we've failed to have a proper introduction."

All three men stared at her.

"Allen Lane, Interpol. Calling me Mason is an old joke between me and my friend Ian here," Mason said nodding at the medical and FBI personnel standing around them. Katya tried to remember if she had called Sasha by name since the assault began. She still didn't know if this was Mason's real name, or whether there would be incriminating information on the thumb drive. Now, avoiding the hospital, it appeared she would have time to find out, even though it would keep her in danger. But she would be able to stay close to Sasha. She couldn't lose sight of him, not now.

"Then Allen, Ian, please remove yourselves and give me privacy so this nice young man can get me cleaned up, bandaged, and shot up with some more of that great painkiller. It's doing a fabulous job, but I might not be making much sense in another couple of minutes. And find me some shoes."

Chapter 15

Hours later. Sasha assisted Katya to Mason's car. Bill and Jake had reappeared with a black Navigator and vehicles were moved to allow them to park as close as possible. Sasha didn't imagine the thin hospital style slippers from the ambulance did much to cushion her feet from the rough gravel, but Katya seemed beyond caring. He was not pleased that Mason had been given a dozen doses of morphine to take along for Katya, along with syringes, antibiotics, antiseptic swabs, and extra bandages. He had developed much safer and more effective painkillers, but they were not yet on the U.S. market and certainly unavailable to him here.

Katya slept on the leather back seat, her dirty rag of a formerly glamorous jumpsuit exchanged for a simple cloth hospital gown, her head on Sasha's lap, her heavily bandaged arm in a sling strapped to her waist. Her hair was still full of plaster dust. Sasha found himself nodding off for moments at a time. It was now past 3:30 in the morning. It startled Sasha to think that he and Katya had slept next to each other every night for the last five. He was beginning to distrust Mason's motives for taking her along with them. Something was not right here but he trusted himself to ferret it out, despite still feeling drug-addled himself. And he would stay close to Katya.

"Where exactly are you taking us?" Sasha asked. A hotel in San Francisco was all Mason had told him. Didn't Mason have a safe house? Why not the Australian Consulate?

"The St. Francis. Posher than you're used to, but I've arranged a four-bedroom suite that will accommodate all of us. The staff there is very discreet. We'll get room service for our meals. Katya will be able to recover in luxury. Hell if she doesn't deserve it. She saved all our asses more than once today."

"And you're still determined to find out who she is?" Mason's real motive, Sasha thought, along with finding out what she knew and didn't know about him.

"Hell, yes. I've already run her fingerprints through our system, no matches. Nothing on facial recognition. No one I know shoots like she did, and I mean no one. Where did she learn to shoot like that? I have to know. And the description of her fight with Gunner from one of our arrestees – I'd pay a lot to have that on video. Who fights like that? You saw the bones sticking out of his arms. Christ, keep me on her good side."

"And what makes you think she'll tell you anything about herself? After all our time in the van, I know next to nothing about who she really is."

"I think she's ready to talk to you. Tell me what you know."

"We both know she's familiar with this part of Northern California, at least Sonoma County," Sasha replied. "She said she was also a musician. Mentioned guitar, mandolin, lute, ethnic instruments, by which I'd imagine dombra, balalaika and such, plus piano, mostly as an accompanist. Too strangely specific for her to have been making it up."

"What else?"

"Also said she'd lost someone she loved, had lost lots of people she loved. Maybe she's a refugee from a violent country, but her English is perfect. You can see she's part Asian, said her grandmother was an ethnic Chinese from Vietnam, also strangely specific. Seems to speak Vietnamese, said she spoke six languages. I'm sure Chinese is one of them, definitely Spanish. Her martial arts are phenomenal, and her gun skills …"

"I think we may have found her home turf," Mason said, "even if not current. We could show her photo in local guitar shops, check the Asian communities, gun clubs, martial arts studios in San Francisco. We'll play the missing person card, family worried."

"I do want to talk with her. But no more morphine."

"We'll see. We're just about to the hotel. I've pre-arranged a wheelchair. Jake will run in and get it. Jake, ask for a blanket to cover her with, too. We don't want anyone to see her bandages, all that plaster dust. We're claiming that my niece broke a foot. Such a shame on vacation."

The move into the suite went smoothly. The hotel staff was accommodating, despite the late hour, and from the large bills Sasha saw Mason handing out, they would be more than discreet. Katya, Sasha, and Mason had their own bedrooms. Bill and Jake would share a twin-bedded fourth room. Each room had its own bathroom. A large living room with huge overstuffed chairs and two sofas facing each other and a small but well-equipped kitchen with dining area

76

completed the suite. Katya was lifted into her bed, sleeping soundly. Mason, Sasha, and Jake went to their rooms to catch some sleep while Bill settled on a sofa with coffee from the kitchen.

The quiet was soon shattered by a loud cry from Katya's room. All four men rushed in. Katya was tossing back and forth on the bed, crying out in pain. She begged for more of the pain killer. Mason stuck a prepared syringe in her arm before Sasha saw what he was doing. Sasha was angry enough to hit him but held back. Then he caught Katya's look.

"Where did you get your medical training? I'm the doctor here and she's in my care, not yours. If she needs the morphine for pain, from now on I'm giving it, and not without an alcohol swab first. Everyone, back to bed! I'm staying here for a while."

Mason retreated, but not before nodding to Bill to stay. Bill settled in a chair in the corner while Sasha glared at him. Mason and Jake returned to their rooms. When they came back in a few hours later, they discovered Sasha asleep on Katya's bed and Bill nursing yet another coffee in the same chair.

"Wake up, mate, we all have work to do." Mason knew he couldn't put his hand on Sasha's shoulder, so he fairly shouted in his ear. "Bill's going to get Katya cleaned up some more in the bathroom so we can take some photos."

Sasha woke up with a start and looked embarrassed. He didn't remember untucking and unbuttoning his shirt. The thought of Bill in the bathroom with Katya repulsed him. As Sasha began to protest, Katya stirred. "It's okay, Sasha. Just help me to the bathroom," she said groggily.

"How are you feeling?"

She grunted. To his practiced eye she looked too drugged from the morphine, too weak to be standing, but he gently helped her to her feet, supporting her as she walked, Bill close behind. When she reached the bathroom door, she gave Sasha a big push into Bill and slammed the door on both of them. They heard the click as she turned the lock.

"See you in an hour. Have that morphine ready," she called through the door and they heard water taps being turned on.

"My God, that's my kind of woman!" Mason laughed.

Sasha said nothing. They all returned to their rooms to get ready. Sasha stopped by the kitchen on his way and left a glass of water by

Katya's bed. Over an hour and a half passed before her bathroom door opened again. She had somehow managed to take a bath and shampoo her hair without wetting her bandages or sling. She wore a white St. Francis robe over her hospital gown, her feet were bare. She looked reasonably good under the circumstances, Sasha thought. He had used the time to complete his morning workout in his room and had showered as well. He still felt sluggish compared to his usual level of activity, his mind dulled, but he felt capable.

"They even have a toothbrush and toothpaste here," Katya said, smiling, "What have we got to eat?"

Mason shook his head in wonder and picked up the phone to order room service breakfasts for everyone. Sasha watched Katya carefully. He would follow her lead with the morphine, but he already knew what he had to do next.

Katya asked about the wheelchair by the door and said she was okay with playing the niece with the broken foot. She settled on a sofa with her legs stretched out and let Sasha cover them with a blanket. Mason took the photos he wanted. She knew she'd have to run soon now. She seemed to doze off after breakfast as the men discussed their plans. Sasha insisted, over Mason's strenuous protest, that he was going to get some new clothes, and did not need to be shadowed by Bill or Jake.

"You know I could shake either one of them, mate. You take your photos around town and I'll be back here by four o'clock. I need to make some phone calls back home. I need to explain myself to my crew. And when are my violin and computer going to arrive?"

He'd been out of touch with the lab for days and was eager to get his hands on his beloved instrument. The idea that his ability to play had been robbed from him forever by Cutter's drugs still obsessed him.

"I'm so sorry Sasha," Mason answered. "There was a dust-up in New York over jurisdiction. Your Aussies came in and took off with both of them, duffel too, sent them to Sydney. They thought you'd be back home in a couple of days and would want them there."

"Why am I not surprised?" Sasha replied sadly.

Chapter 16

Katya pretended to sleep until shortly before Sasha's departure. She couldn't risk being knocked out again by the morphine. Mason was not going to let her be alone with Sasha, not when he didn't know for certain that she had nothing but her suspicions to share. She might have learned something about him from her computer search. But she now felt confident that Sasha was onto her game, at least as much as he could guess of it. She wasn't ready to run yet; she felt she needed one more day to recover. Tomorrow morning. She'd overheard that Mason would be showing her photo around San Francisco. Wrong city, but he could luck onto a connection, especially within the martial arts world. No one in the Chinese community would give her up to Mason no matter what his story, not to a ghost with the look of the immigration police.

Katya could no longer deny the intense connection she felt with Sasha and had ample proof now that he felt the same connection with her. She still worried that Mason's suspicions about her could be endangering him. She would have to dream up a plan to get him in the clear. From the sofa, she stared out the window across Union Square, trying to think of something that would keep her and Sasha together. A billboard on the far side of the square caught her attention. She had her answer.

It was show time again. Katya started tossing back and forth where she lay, moaning for a good ten minutes. Then she sat bolt upright on the sofa and started shouting, taking hold of her bandaged arm. She wrenched off her sling.

"God, the pain! Please, please, I can't take it! You promised me more morphine, I need it now!"

Sasha rushed to her first and tried to quiet her, stroking her head.

"It's too soon after the last dose. Just calm yourself. Stop shouting," he soothed.

"Just give it to me!" she yelled and swung at Sasha's head with her uninjured arm.

He grabbed it and held her down. "I told you the morphine was a bad idea, Mason."

"Just give her a dose and shut her up. I can't be dealing with hotel management."

"It's against my better judgment, but I'll do it. Bring me a swab and the syringe."

Mason brought Sasha what he needed and watched as he prepared the dose. Sasha cleaned her arm with his back turned to Mason, blocking his view. Out of sight, he slid the sponge he'd taken from the kitchen into a small plastic bag, emptied the syringe into it, and dabbed a cloth over the expected injection site as if mopping up a drop of blood. He expertly palmed bag and sponge back into his pocket when he was through. Katya continued to act wild and restless for another couple of minutes until she drew a deep breath and lay still.

"I have seen cases like this before," Sasha said, shaking his head as he turned back to Mason. "She's developed an immediate addiction to the morphine. Something in her physiology. She's either going to be sleeping or just drugged out for the rest of the day. Under no circumstances can she have another dose until I return. Do I make myself clear?"

Mason reluctantly agreed. Sasha decided it was safe enough for him to leave the suite. As he exited the hotel, Sasha wondered what end he was helping her to achieve. It was clear to him Katya was planning to escape from Mason, but where was she going to go? If he didn't go with her, would he ever see her again? She was by no means ready to be out on the street. But if he were in her position, he would run first and ask questions later, bullet wounds or no. He had escaped with worse injuries more than once. He wanted to know what Mason needed from her. It had to be something Katya had learned about him in Cutter's computer lab. Or might have learned. Had Mason had dealings with Cutter before, looked the other way, taken bribes? Dead men don't talk, and Mason had filled Cutter full of bullets. He had nearly done so himself, for what he thought Cutter had done to Katya, and that was just the excuse that Mason had used. And how could Mason afford this suite? This kind of expense would not be authorized by Interpol, he was sure. Where were the answers? Sasha was sick of his new, hopefully temporary, "ordinary" brain. But if he could not be who he really was, he would just have to reinvent himself.

Stepping into an empty elevator, he contemplated his next steps. The elevator opened on each floor and hotel patrons crowded in, heading for the lobby. With a growing sense of panic, Sasha moved

80

to the back corner. He shouted out for no more passengers to be let in, causing all heads to swivel in his direction. Escaping the elevator, Sasha stopped by the front desk to pick up a street map of San Francisco, then stood in the doorway, trying not to panic at the crowds jostling each other on the sidewalks. He never thought he would miss having a wingman to protect him from accidental contact. A packed cable car clanged by. *There's one San Francisco experience I'll never have*, he noted to himself.

His first stop was the department store on the square that he'd seen out the hotel window. He wandered among the myriad displays looking for what he needed, appalled by the sheer volume and variety of clothing, purses, and beauty products, amused that the men's department was practically deserted in contrast to the women's. A veritable temple of consumerism. Nothing made of bamboo fibers anywhere; he and the crew mostly wore loose, finely-made bamboo fabric clothing manufactured in one of his four refugee and rehabilitation centers. Earth shades of sand and off-whites – none of these garish prints. Cotton would have to do.

But maybe he could branch out a little, look at other colors... He'd retained one of the New York thugs' wallets, and used some of their money to buy a pair of comfortable black shoes, socks and underclothes, belt, black trousers, and a dark blue shirt, after carefully checking their labels, and wore them out the door. He decided to keep nothing but his worn work boots, carried in a separate bag from the old clothes he'd arrived in. Sasha wondered how the store or its customers would react if they knew how many of the clothes on the racks were made by slaves in sweatshops around the world. He'd seen these sweatshops firsthand in Southeast Asia, had rescued women and children from many of them.

Sasha returned to a leather goods store he'd passed and used most of the rest of the money to purchase a used-leather-look dark brown bomber jacket he'd seen in the window. He needed the warmth, surprised by how cold San Francisco was in the summer. It was colder than Sydney this time of year, but there it was the middle of winter. He preferred hot, humid Southeast Asia.

He hardly recognized himself in the mirror. He'd never dressed like this in his life. The jacket would have cost him all of his spending money for a month. He debated whether to try to buy clothes for Katya, but decided she had her own plans. Maybe he could slip her a pair of shoes, but he didn't know her size. He asked for the store's bathroom and once there, pulled two trackers out of his wallet. One he had quietly slipped off Katya's back, one he had discovered on his own back and had removed with a wooden spatula from the kitchen. He had no idea when it had been placed on him. He had to have been in a deep sleep. He dropped Katya's down the toilet, flushed, and left the store. His own he stuck onto the arm of a tourist walking hurriedly in the opposite direction. He lost Bill before he left Union Square.

Sasha handed his bag containing the old clothes from the shelter to the first homeless man he saw. What a needless tragedy, he thought. There was no excuse in this affluent country not to take care of those in need. He kept only his worn work boots. He passed what looked like a pharmacy and decided to buy more bandages and a better antiseptic cleanser for Katya with his remaining money.

The store was larger than he imagined and seemed to be selling a bit of everything. Checking the displays, Sasha noticed some of the products he'd developed through his own laboratories on the shelves, including the One Pill. He never paid much attention to most of his inventions and commercial ideas once they reached production stage, but he had pushed for the One Pill to be nonprescription, available free of charge in clinics around the world to those who could not pay its nominal cost. One month of birth control per pill. Effective up to four days after intercourse if a woman wasn't already on it. Virtually no side effects. No more unwanted children, no more abortions wherever it was in use. And then, there was its effectiveness in preventing STDs, even HIV. The disease-preventing version he'd created for men was there, too.

Discovering a box of his self-adhesive water shields, he purchased those as well to keep Katya's bandages dry when she bathed or showered. How had she managed that first time? He then made his way on foot to the address he had long ago memorized and rang the bell. Within minutes he was inside being greeted by the ecstatic Australian Consul-General.

Chapter 17

Mason spent his day alone, playing the private detective searching for a missing young woman. He'd made the mistake of starting in Chinatown, where he was met with stony silence or in one case, a hard swat out the door with a broom. The cell phone message from Bill about losing Sasha put him in a dark mood. Jake and a chagrinned Bill were waiting in the suite, sitting next to Katya who was slumped over on the sofa. She was awake and babbling incoherently about spiders in the bathroom, but at least she wasn't complaining about pain.

"We've been hoping she'd say something useful, but she's been talking gibberish for the last hour," Jake informed him.

"Enough already. It's time to move this along," grumbled Mason. He knelt down in front of her and took her face in his hands. "Katya, can you hear me?"

Katya appeared to focus and stopped mumbling.

"Katya, I need you to tell me who you are. Your full name, where you come from, who sent you to Sasha. This is what Sasha wants you to do."

"Sasha does?" Katya's voice sounded far away. "Sasha?"

"Keep listening to my voice. Tell me who you are."

"I'm, I'm…"

Mason held her face more firmly. If he could get her talking, she might spill everything in her state.

"I'm... the one... who's not telling you... anything." She slowed her speech, slurring it like a drunk, then laughed.

Mason grabbed her upper arm and squeezed hard over the bandages, digging in his thumb.

Katya cried out in real pain. Mason squeezed again. She cried out louder and tried to hit him in the throat with her other hand, but Bill grabbed on and twisted her arm backwards. Mason placed his other fingers around her throat threateningly as he jammed a knee against her, pinning her to the sofa.

"Don't even think about screaming. Tell me what I want to hear and the pain will stop."

In response, Katya tried to scratch at his face. Mason tightened his grip on her arm. Jake looked alarmed by the sudden violence, but grabbed her fingers and forcefully pushed her wrist back. She was trapped, helpless against the three of them.

Mason was not going to stop until he got what he wanted. The pain became nearly unbearable as Mason's pressure increased. She had to make it end. Catching her breath, Katya pulled deep into herself and pretended to pass out. Mason stared at her inert form for a full minute before he relaxed his grip. He nodded to Bill and Jake to release her. Jake jumped up but another long moment passed before Bill reluctantly let go.

A sharp knock sounded at the door. Glancing at Mason, Bill walked over to look through the spyhole and let Sasha in. Mason quickly pushed off of Katya. It only took a moment for Sasha to see what had been going on. He'd felt a strange tug of alarm as he stood outside the door. Mason was still standing over Katya. Jake stared at the floor and wouldn't look at him.

Sasha's voice was cold and steady. His eyes flashed with anger.

"All of you, leave the room. I don't care where you go."

Jake and Mason moved away from Katya. When Sasha glared at them, they retreated to their rooms. Bill stood his ground for a moment but he followed Jake when Sasha strode towards him. Sasha closed their doors after them. Walking over to Katya, he sat his bags on the floor and took her pulse. His anger increased when he saw the bandages were turning red. He took his bags into the kitchen, took off his new jacket and draped it across the back of a chair, scrubbed his hands, and returned with clean towels, an empty bowl and one with soapy water, the new antiseptic, and a roll of bandages. Katya shuddered, opened her eyes, and began to breathe heavily as he sat next to her. He unwrapped the bloody bandages and dropped them in the bowl. After a careful examination and cleaning, he started rewrapping her arm. As he leaned over her, Katya whispered in his ear. She had to concentrate to keep her voice from trembling. Her arm throbbed, the pain continuing.

"It's the thumb drive he's worried about. I don't know if his name and information are on it. I ran my grab alphabetically and the last name on the captured data was Kanter. I don't know anything about Mason and Cutter but what you and I can guess. Mason's rotten, I feel it. He's sure I know more than I do and wants to keep me from sharing with you. I'm going to have to give him my story to get you clear of this. Forgive me for not being what you may think. And if I get away, I'll be back, I promise." Katya hesitated, then dared to add, even more quietly, "Come find me. I don't want to live without you."

Sasha bowed his head close as he listened, trying to make sense of her words. Then he tried to make sense of how he felt about them. One problem at a time, he thought. He whispered back.

"Your search didn't catch him then. Lane is his real name, Mason was his last name when I knew him."

When the bandaging was done, Sasha regarded Katya. She smiled up at him wanly.

"Did you really just fake passing out?" he asked her.

"I wanted to make him stop. No guarantee but worth a try. Am surprised myself that it worked."

"But through such pain..."

"Pain is all in the head. You should know that as a brain surgeon."

Sasha regarded her again. "I'm appalled Mason and his men resorted to torture. I shouldn't have left you. Would you like me to kill them for you?"

Katya's smile broadened. "That won't be necessary. But thanks for the humor. You're learning... At least I think you're joking." Her smile faded as a wave of pain washed over her. "On second thought..."

"I have a different idea," Sasha told her, as he picked up the room phone and made a call.

Katya listened in and nodded. Sasha then rose and whispered for her to lay back and close her eyes again. He carried the bowls and other items to the kitchen, cleaned up, washed his hands, then knocked on the closed bedroom doors and asked the men to return to the living room. They walked past him cautiously, wary of the fury in his eyes, his outward calm belying the potential for violence.

Katya lay quietly for a while before she stirred, pretending to wake up. Bill and Jake sat on the chairs and Mason on the sofa across from her. Sasha returned to sit next to Katya. She sat up slowly and leaned heavily on him. The pain in her arm was worse than when Mason was squeezing it. She didn't have to do any exaggerating to convince them she was really hurting.

"Katya, we are out of time. Tell me who you are and you can do as you wish." Sasha spoke softly, as if they were alone. He put his arm gently around her shoulders.

85

"Will you give me more morphine if I do?" she begged.

"Are you in that much pain?"

"Excruciating. Truly."

"I will. You need to sleep as much as possible."

"Then I will tell you," she said, groaning with the pain. "Short version. My name is Amy Townsend. I was born June 9, 1964 in New York City. Yes, I'm thirty-five. My parents divorced when I was seven – I never saw my father again. I spent summers with my grandmother, my mother's widowed Chinese mother, in San Francisco, where I studied Kung Fu and other martial arts. Went to college at New York University, where my left leanings turned radical. I spent my Junior Year Abroad in Berlin, where I was recruited by the East Germans as a spy.

"I returned to Europe after graduation and business school and spent the next several years training, and then working in espionage, while working a day job in international banking as cover, living in Switzerland, Luxembourg, Germany, France, and then England. Got caught by the British in 1989, when the Wall fell and Stasi records were opened to the public. The British liked my unusual skill set too much to throw me in jail. Been working for Mi6 since then. They use me for special jobs that require some... shall we say, finesse.

"You were a special job, Sasha. Protecting you. You were recognized in New York, where I was temporarily stationed, by a former S-Branch agent who now worked for Mi6. I had no idea what S-Branch was or why you were so important to them, and I wasn't informed. They didn't even give me your full name. I now think my agency wanted to show off to S-Branch, be able to call and tell them they'd found you off on your own, unguarded. I was ordered to make sure you stayed safe... and to bring you in. We weren't going to kidnap you off the street – you were a free man, in the company of a trustworthy human rights worker, Derek, and in no apparent danger.

"I followed you to the Global Human Rights Conference and on to Derek's apartment. One of our men kept guard outside all night, informed me when you left. I waited on the bench, ready to confront you. I'll never forgive myself for underestimating the threat of the men in the van, for failing to stop your abduction. I wasn't certain what they were up to, then when the fighting started, I thought I could handle them myself. God knows what Mi6 thought when we both disappeared... or why they didn't then contact S-Branch. I assumed, incorrectly, that they had done so. Maybe they were embarrassed to have lost you. After Cutter was eliminated, I knew who you were and saw no reason to inform my bosses, and thus this S-Branch, of your location. You seemed to want to stay with Mason and Interpol. But I didn't consider my job to be over – I had to stick with you, look out for new threats... best I could, with these bullet holes in my arm, and this unexpected morphine addiction."

Mason stared at her for a long moment when she was through, then opened his cell phone and walked into the kitchen. Sasha stared at her also. He queried her for further details in French and German, and Katya answered fluently in both languages.

"But don't expect me to speak Luxembourgish," she said, starting to sound out of it again. "I would have really stood out too much. No one but the Luxembourgers speak Luxembourgish. Now my arm is killing me. I want to eat some dinner before you load me up with more morphine. I've given you what you wanted to know and now I'm done."

"And what about your Vietnamese?" Sasha questioned.

"My grandmother's good friend was a Vietnamese widow, lived in the next apartment with her son and his family, kids about my age. I had Chinese, Vietnamese, and very bad English all around me every summer growing up."

Sasha had no idea if she was telling the truth or not. Was it really possible Katya had been an East German spy, then a British one? His anger had abated; he asked Jake to order room service. Mason returned from the kitchen when the food arrived, after turning in her story to Interpol. They all stayed in the living room to eat, although they couldn't get Katya/Amy to answer any more questions. No one had anything much to say. The ringing of the room phone broke the silence. Bill answered it and handed the phone to Mason, whose face brightened considerably as he listened. He was smiling as he finished eating.

"That was Dan Schultz from the FBI. He asked how you were doing, Katya, or I guess I have to start calling you Amy."

"Anything else?" Sasha asked.

"That was all. Just singing her praises on and on."

Sasha knew more had been said. His own call earlier had been to Schultz, asking him to give the man they knew as Allen Lane an update on the contents of the thumb drive, and to emphasize that the data was alphabetical, ending with the letter K. Sasha had been relieved to learn that the data had also been encrypted – it had taken the FBI this long to start decoding it. Sasha had asked Schultz for this information to be passed on to Lane as well. Mason would know that there would have been no way for Katya to read any information on him without Cutter having overridden the encryption, as he must have done when she searched for Sasha's name. Sasha was still convinced Mason had much to hide, but all things considered, he and Katya should remain safe.

"Nice someone appreciates me," Katya said weakly. "I feel awful and I want that dose now. I'm going to bed."

Sasha started to help her get off the sofa when Mason's cell phone rang. This time his look was pure rage as he listened.

"Sit down! Amy Townsend, international banker, is enjoying her vacation in Prague. My contact there has verified it. Your story was true, just not any of the spy bits or the very big fact that she is not you. You have wasted my time and the resources of my agency! Who the hell are you really?"

Sasha and Katya sat back down, but he did not release his grip on her elbow. What was she playing at, he wondered? Did he really feel some relief that her story wasn't true? Who did he want her to be?

"So why Amy Townsend?" Sasha had to ask.

"She is a friend from my past. We bonded over our physical similarities and the fact that we both had Chinese grandmothers. We still write to each other. Now I'm starting to get desperate for that morphine, so let me have it and get me to bed."

"How long did you think it would take us to figure out it was all lies!" demanded Mason.

"I'll admit, I'm impressed," Katya sighed. "You work fast. Maybe if Amy had written me she was vacationing in the Himalayas, and not in Prague, I'd have gotten some drugged sleep."

"You'll get your morphine when we get the truth," Mason growled.

Sasha moved his arm to engulf her shoulders protectively. Mason looked more than capable of resorting to torture again, if he could only get past Sasha...

"Morphine first. I'll tell you after I sleep."

"Nothing until you talk. No more wild stories. The quicker you tell us and we can confirm it, the sooner you'll get your dose. So go ahead then!" Mason could contain himself no longer. Despite his fear of Sasha, he stood up and moved closer.

"I have committed no crime, Mason. I'm supposed to be here recovering. I got shot saving your life, and Sasha's. Why do you care so much who I am?"

"You didn't just appear out of nowhere," Mason snarled. "Someone sent you and it's vital we know who it was and why. No morphine!"

"You win! Oh God, I have to have it. No more lies. My name, my true name, is Adah Halevy. I'm an agent of Mossad."

Chapter 18

"At least I have been for the last twelve years. Mossad and I have not seen eye to eye lately. My story is a complicated one, so I'm going to have to go back a long ways," Katya said, her face taking on a sorrowful expression. "My grandfather, David Kohen, and his young bride, my grandmother, made it to Shanghai from Austria as the Nazis came to power, joining 23,000 other Jewish refugees. They spent years there. My grandfather made a living dealing in Chinese and Vietnamese antiques, and learned both languages, eventually teaching them to me.

"When the Japanese moved everyone into a ghetto, my grandparents tried to flee to Israel. My grandmother was raped by Chinese thugs during their escape. She died during childbirth in Tel Aviv, but by that time my grandfather, now David Kahan, had made himself so useful to his new country that his child, my mother, was accepted without question of her Eurasian looks. She married Ori Halevy, a successful businessman, and I was born in Tel Aviv on March 12, 1967.

"I followed in my grandfather's footsteps, however. He was now high up in Mossad. I excelled in martial arts, especially Krav Maga, firearms, and languages, so there was never any doubt about my joining Mossad after I finished my IDF service. I have served my country well for years, helping to catch or kill our enemies. I have been responsible for many deaths, but I had not yet had to pull the trigger or wield a knife myself. I was often present at the kill though, and the faces of these men and women haunt me still."

Katya leaned back heavily onto the sofa, holding her arm. Mason had sat back down, scowling, arms crossed, as soon as she'd started her story. The men waited for her to continue. Sasha thought she looked upset at the memory. Or she could be putting on an act.

"My worst experience was in 1990, in the last violent year of the Lebanese civil war. Due to my fluent Arabic, I was assigned to gather intelligence for the Israeli Defense Force. I was posing as a temporary schoolteacher in a small Christian village outside East Beirut. I made the unforgivable error of falling in love with a fellow villager. I was still young and naïve, but there was no excuse. Mossad suspected, but had no proof. I told them I was only acting. I got carried away with my love of this man and his villagers and tried to organize them in defense against continued threats by the Shia Muslim Hezbollah and other factions. I did weapons training with them, helped them erect barricades around the village, put the word out we weren't to be trifled with, made stupid boasts..."

Katya/Adah hesitated, looking pained, then continued in a softer voice. All four men listened intently.

"Occupying Syrian forces, encouraged by the U.S. to take down General Aoun and his government, mistook our defenses and big talk as provocation. One of their colonels led his soldiers into the village and slaughtered every man, woman, and child, all forty-seven of them. Wounded and left for dead, I witnessed it all. The colonel was standing no farther away from me than you are, Mason. I saw the glint in his eye, the disgust on his face as blood splattered his uniform... I helplessly watched him give the coup de grâce to wounded friends all around me. God knows how he missed me. At the time, I wished he hadn't. I tried so hard to move my right hand to shoot him, but I couldn't move. I could not move." Katya took another moment to compose herself, then continued in Hebrew. "I feel all of their deaths are on me. I have not been able to forgive myself."

Sasha saw a single tear slide down her cheek as she stared off blankly. He wondered why she'd mentioned her right hand when it was clear she was right-handed. But even he could tell the difference in emotion between a memory and a fiction. He was sure Katya was in genuine emotional pain.

"I know about this slaughter," Mason said. "But as I recall, Hezbollah was blamed and there were no survivors."

"My last desperate transmission was to Mossad but help arrived too late. It all happened so fast. They found me still alive and carried me out before the deaths were discovered by anyone else. The Syrians planted evidence to implicate Hezbollah. As soon as I recovered, Mossad put me right back on another assignment. I went on spying and betraying, watching our enemies die.

"And then it got to be just too much... I was assigned to get close to a Palestinian doctor and so I volunteered in a refugee camp with him for nine weeks. The more I learned about him, the more I knew he was a good man, an innocent caught up in an impossible situation.

But my superiors would not listen. I was ordered to assassinate him. Instead, I helped him fake a new identity and flee to the United States. I was lucky I was not terminated. A colleague I knew and trusted later told me my death sentence had been hotly debated; my grandfather's legacy helped protect me. I moved to New York, and last week Mossad reached out to me with a way to redeem myself."

Katya paused and looked straight into Sasha's eyes.

"Your friend Derek had a change of heart and contacted us. He thought if Sasha was rescued as if by chance at the last minute, Cutter would believe Derek had played his part and release his sister. Derek didn't give us a name or who you really were, just what you looked like and where to find you. But I knew what kind of person you were," she said in Hebrew, placing her hand on Sasha's, "when I heard you speak at the human rights conference."

"So you did hear me speak," Sasha replied, also in Hebrew.

"A magnificent speech. Your standing ovation was well earned."

"And the Palestinian doctor? What was his name?" Sasha asked in Arabic.

"I cannot divulge that information, for his own safety. Mossad is still looking for him," Katya replied in Arabic as well.

"And how did you learn your American English?" Mason inquired, still looking skeptical, but impressed by her language skills.

"Along with my music. I'm a gifted guitarist and play other instruments as well. That I did not lie about. When I was growing up, my parents sent me to music camps in Michigan, New York, and California. I lived in San Francisco two entire summers, enrolled at the music conservancy. I still have friends in the city. And Mossad contacts."

"That makes eight," Sasha said.

"Eight what?"

"Eight languages, including the Spanish you spoke so fluently when we were on the bus.. You said you spoke six."

"Well, I've said and not said many things. This is the truth. This is who I am."

Mason looked frustrated. He snapped his cell phone open and shut repeatedly. Bill and Jake stared at her with renewed interest.

"I'm sure you know your story is going to be extremely difficult to verify. Mossad does not share information about their agents with us," Mason said frowning.

"That is your problem, not mine. I want the morphine and I want to sleep."

"Go ahead, Sasha, give it to her, let her go to bed," Mason said, relenting. "Bill, come with me. We're going out. I need a more secure line and lots more manpower. Jake, get some rest, but stay sharp. Let them have some privacy."

Sasha sat on Katya's bed, Katya propped up on pillows, thinking how much had changed since he'd fallen asleep next to her the previous night. He now believed he knew who she was. It would make no sense for her to keep on making up one complete fabrication after another. There was no logic in doing so.

"Katya... should I call you Adah?"

"Katya will do. I've used many names over the last twelve years."

"All right. Why didn't you tell me who you were in the van?"

"Why would I? I tell no one who I really am. I wish I'd been able to tell only you now, and not this Mason and his thugs. This will scarcely help me get out of trouble with Mossad, especially when Mason goes snooping."

Sasha looked at her for a long time, thinking. He found himself wanting to tell her about himself. He had spoken to no one about his history, not in over five decades of torment. Katya was someone who might begin to understand him.

"I hadn't thought you were Jewish," he said at last.

"And you?"

"I've always imagined that I was by birth. I was raised Jewish by my adoptive parents."

"Cutter's files stated that you were born in Celle, Germany, in 1940, but that the real date and place of birth are unknown."

"The Mandelbrots invented that, for something to put on the adoption paperwork. You must have figured out what that signifies."

"I didn't have time to think about it then, but I have since. That was near the location of the Bergen-Belsen concentration camp."

"I've never spoken of it. But somehow with you I feel I can begin to."

"Your waking nightmare in the van, were you back in Bergen-Belsen? You had to have been such a small child, Sasha." Katya ran the fingers of her hand along the back of his neck. He melted into her touch.

94

"From about age three and a half, I was told, to just before six. I didn't live in any of the compounds beyond the barbed wire."

"What do you mean?"

"I mean I was pulled out of the line of arriving prisoners, taken out of the arms of the woman who'd been holding me in the cattle car. I did not know her. It was like my memory had been erased, I knew nothing of my past, just some German. Not even my name, my language. Nothing of my parents. A Nazi SS officer had chosen me for my blond hair, my strangely muscled body. He must have thought I looked like a perfect little Aryan... I had these hypertrophic muscles... I must have been born with them... I looked strong even though I was starving. I can't bring myself to say much more, but he enslaved me, made me his pet, enjoyed tormenting me..." Sasha's voice trailed off.

He couldn't imagine telling her about the overwhelming sense of guilt that washed over him during his memory attacks, the nameless guilt that seemed to always be in the back of his mind. How he remained a prisoner.

"Sasha..."

"The memory of the camp haunts me, what he did to me haunts me. You felt how I shuddered and sweated in the van. I can't believe I've told you this much. Let's stop there."

"I feel honored that you confided in me. Don't say any more than you are ready to. I'm here for you."

Sasha thought she looked even more miserable than he felt.

"The man you killed saving my life during the Cutter assault... he was your first?" he asked, touching her face.

"It was terrible. I shook under that table for a long time."

"An amazing shot, directly between the eyes."

"I don't want to think about it. I did what I had to do. You know I would do anything to keep you safe, and not just for Mossad. But I cannot forget what I did."

"There was a time many years ago when I had never killed," Sasha said, attempting to console her. "You must have read that I was a surgeon with the Australian forces in Vietnam. My job was saving lives, not taking them. But early into my time there, our jungle medical unit was overrun by North Vietnamese soldiers, well-armed, experienced fighting men. They'd thought an American general was visiting, but he'd canceled last minute. It was clear we would all

95

perish. I had a trick I knew – a whole other story for another day – of being able to climb a tall pole. I could fling myself off and land safely in a series of somersaults. I didn't think twice. I slung two rifles over my shoulder and flew up the flagpole. I became a sniper, legs wrapped around the pole at the top, the flag tied tight around me, picking off soldiers. From that height, I could see an ammunition truck, surrounded by soldiers and I blew it up with one shot. It all happened so fast, not a bullet even whizzed by me. The enemy retreated, our soldiers finished the job, and our unit was saved. I spent the entire day, night, and next day stitching up men and nurses.

"One of the enemy soldiers, an officer, was discovered alive, but barely. I remembered with horror having had him in my sights before I pulled the trigger. I demanded to treat him, tired as I was, and exhausted myself in the effort, but he could not be saved. I killed twenty-four men that day, but his particular death became personal. I will see his face until the day I die. I offered Buddhist prayers for all the men I had killed, but especially for this officer's soul. I found a way to have his body delivered to his family at my own expense and made sure the other bodies were returned to the enemy as well. The entire camp thought I had lost my mind, kneeling and bowing my head to the ground before candles for hours. My government attempted to award me a medal for saving the unit, but I told my commanding officer I would ram it down his throat if he followed through, and that's the last I heard of it."

"Sasha, I don't know what to say," Katya said, her eyes glistening. "Thank you for sharing your story. It helps."

"Let me give you some painkillers and a glass of water. You look like you're hurting again. I picked up a bottle of my Australogic specials at the Consulate. One of the staff brought two bottles back with her from Australia. Non-addictive, don't worry. You'll feel much better in a few minutes. I'm sorry I didn't think to give them to you earlier. I'm still not thinking clearly."

"Please. I'm just about ready to go back to the morphine. My arm has hurt so much worse since Mason's thumb played around with it. And his goons were part of it." She gratefully swallowed down the pills and emptied the glass Sasha brought her.

"Bill is a psychopath, but Jake at least seems to have a conscience," Sasha growled. "Mason only cares about himself."

Sasha suddenly sat upright, rigid. He turned Katya toward him and looked into her face.

"Mason was standing over you when I arrived back at the St. Francis. He looked like he'd just gotten off of you. Did he also sexually assault you?"

Katya was shocked by his conjecture and his bluntness.

"No! Nothing like that, Sasha, I swear! Pressing on my wounds was bad enough. He'd held me down with his knee. The other two were keeping me from hitting and scratching him. The whole episode lasted barely three minutes."

Calming down, Sasha shook his head. "I really would have killed them if you'd been sexually assaulted. Mason for his actions, Bill and Jake for allowing it to happen, for watching."

Katya shivered. She had little doubt he was serious this time. What a study in contrasting moods, from his last story to this... the inner conflict he must suffer from – the saintly healer, the reluctant and remorseful taker of lives and then the angry would-be killer, fearlessly contemplating murder, against three armed men. She was certain he wasn't armed, although he'd been gone a long time; his attractive new clothes hid no weapons. Where else had he gone? Had he killed other times since Vietnam? He implied that he had. She thought of the violence he must have witnessed, and participated in, chasing human traffickers and their ilk... Such a complicated personality, with its roots in his horrific Bergen-Belsen childhood. She didn't want to imagine what he'd seen there, the kind of abuse he said he'd experienced.

"Do you mind telling me more about Vietnam?" Katya asked, eager to change the subject. "What did you do afterwards?"

"It's all right. I'd rather talk about Vietnam than Bergen-Belsen. Or killing... Everyone called me the Monk after that, even the Yanks. They thought me strange, a conceited, eccentric prude who couldn't stand to be touched, never swore, with no interest in women, a boring non-drinker. I'd already gotten into trouble with American troops shortly after I arrived in Vietnam..."

Beads of sweat began to appear on Sasha's brow. He was touching on a terrible memory he clearly did not want to recall. Katya reached out her right hand and stroked his face, massaged his shoulder. Sasha leaned into her hand, quieting, and was able to continue.

"I moved out of my quarters and onto an old boat moored on the Mekong River outside of Saigon's city center. I did surgery in our improvised field hospital with my unit when there was action and held an on-going free medical clinic for the villagers on the boat, with my government's encouragement. We Aussies did a much better job winning hearts and minds than the Americans. I also put in a few hours every day in the laboratories, which had been moved to Saigon by then. I'm sure you read about my laboratories in Cutter's files or I wouldn't be able to mention them. My other life. I made evening surgical rounds and played my violin for myself.

"I still didn't feel like I had atoned for all the deaths I'd been responsible for. Sometimes I ran rescue missions at night in disguise, recovering captured soldiers or South Vietnamese officials, evading the guards the Australian government put in place to try and keep me alive. I could hear them patrolling the jungle and riverbanks. They were more in danger than I was. My clinic was making me popular with the locals even in Saigon, and I felt well-protected already.

"Then everything changed for me. A young woman brought me a small basket of native medicinal herbs during clinic hours on my boat. She said she was a student at the university in Saigon, an undergraduate with the goal of becoming a doctor herself. I hardly looked at her as I reached for the basket, but then... but then our fingers touched accidently. I saw her as if she had just materialized. I was struck silent and held onto her fingers for such a long time, there were titters of quiet laughter among the people crowded around us on the boat, and one by one they departed, leaving us alone. She was the first, and until you, the only person who could touch me."

"Lê," Katya said quietly.

"Yes, Lê, that was her name. You and I have no trouble with its pronunciation, but she called herself 'Lee,' not 'Lay,' which would have been closer, around English speakers so much we grew to jokingly prefer it, and she wrote it as Le. She told me later she had at first been embarrassed, but then as thrilled with our connection as I obviously was. I was in love for the first time in my life and Lê loved me back. My government 'handlers' as I thought of them did everything they could to end the relationship, even tried to convince me that she was a Northern spy. Lê told me why she was in Saigon – she had fled her autocratic father, a North Vietnamese general, who had wanted her to marry one of his elderly colleagues. I knew that what she told me was true. We married in a small Buddhist ceremony. Lê continued her studies, while living and working with me on my boat. When she became pregnant, we bought a small house on the riverbank. I had never been happier in my life. We had friends – her fellow students, my doctors and nurses. I had musical partners... But that is all I will tell you. It is far too painful to go on."

"I do know about Lê, Sasha, you don't have to say more. I'm so sorry," Katya said, stroking his hair. "But I can't leave you so sad. You are going to have to tell me why you liked to somersault off flagpoles. If I never see you again, I will wonder about that for the rest of my life."

"That's an even longer story. I'm quite sure Cutter's data files had nothing on it."

"Tonight, we have time."

"You might think differently about me. I was an outrageous fifteen-year-old."

"I can handle it."

"It starts with my adoptive mother's death, from complications of her multiple sclerosis."

"Hey, I was trying to cheer you up!"

"Let me continue!" Sasha snapped. "I was angry. To take my mind off her death, my adoptive father took me to a Gypsy, that is, a Romani, circus that had escaped to Australia during the war. I went crazy for the horses. Stood in the corrals touching them, feeling their breath on my neck. They could touch me with their noses... Two Romani boys confronted me. I knew some of their Romani language – from the camp – and they liked how well the horses reacted to me. I was so enamored of the horses I wanted to run away with the circus to be near them. Those boys offered to smuggle me out of the country. They told me they'd see to it I would get a job caring for the horses. When the circus departed by ship for Europe two weeks later, I was with them."

"Where were you in your schooling?"

"I was taught at home. I never attended a school until college. And I'd just graduated."

"At fifteen. And you ran off with a Romani circus."

"I told you you'd think differently about me."

"Go on. I'm trying not to laugh. Why did you really leave?"

"I wanted to get to Europe to track down my identity, perhaps find my family, although I had no idea where to start. The Roma were very helpful in teaching me how to break into records offices and government files, though I found nothing. And they helped me to avoid all the searchers my adoptive father had sent after me. I cut my hair short and kept it dyed black, and wore this wig of very long black curls, shoulder length, and a fake moustache for the shows. There were crowds of girls trying to get my attention wherever we went."

"I'm really having a hard time visualizing you. So back to the flagpole…"

"Eventually I became a performer as well when I wasn't playing the violin – purposefully badly – with our little Romani band, doing gymnastics on horseback and somersaulting off the tent pole. The pole routine was the grand finale. There was actually a running plot around the acts, with an envious suitor chasing me up the pole, shooting at me, and me somersaulting to the ground as if shot, standing up to cheers, scooping up the girl and riding off, the girl backwards on the horse, waving to the crowd."

"No way. That can't be all you did, for what, a year?"

"The Romani circus is also where I got interested in becoming a doctor. My first job was carving up dead stock to feed our old lions. Spent hours laying out the entire nervous, skeletal and other systems of the carcasses. I also assisted in treating the circus animals, and my reputation grew so that local vets began asking me to assist them. The Roma, being Roma, rented me out to them. When one of the acrobats dislocated her shoulder and I pulled it back into place, the Roma thought I had special healing powers for people as well, and everyone sick or injured began coming to see me. I was rented out to help local doctors, who gave me medical texts to read, which I consumed avidly. I thought I knew more than they did by the end of the year, egotistical teenager that I was."

"Stop, my head is spinning. I don't believe any of this, Sasha. I didn't think you knew how to play a joke, but you must be joking now."

"All of it is true, and much more. I haven't even gotten to where I snuck into the Soviet Union. The only clues I might be Russian came from my tormenter at Bergen-Belsen naming me Alexander Borodin and calling me his little Russian Doll. And my looks. I came to search

100

for records on my existence but found nothing. But, while there, I managed to meet up with Dmitri Shostakovich."

"You did not!"

"Broke into his apartment, had my violin with me. Even with Stalin dead, I thought he might be under watch and I didn't want to be seen. Once he got over the scare, we had the most amazing discussion about music. He had me play a movement of his as yet unperformed violin concerto, the one David Oistrakh would premiere in Leningrad later that year in October. You'll find a hand-written dedication to me on his personal copy of that 1955 first violin concerto, 'For my mysterious Sasha.' Musicologists have debated who this Sasha was for years."

Katya shook her head but said nothing. She pulled Sasha down onto the bed beside her. He pulled off his shoes and curled up with her. She lay quietly next to him, entwining her hand in his. Katya knew there had to be many more painful truths and wild stories. She hoped she would have a lifetime with him to hear them all. She knew now for certain she had to become a part of his life.

"Sasha, are you all right with me being a Mossad agent? I've done terrible things in the name of my country. I'm trained as a killer, and if I go back home, I will surely become one again. I lie and betray for Israel, that's all I've been taught to do."

"I'm sorry, I have to admit I find it difficult to reconcile the person I thought you were with who you really are. There is a, well, a normalcy, an innocence, as you said of your Palestinian doctor, that I appreciate. Do you want to return to Israel after this?"

"I have another idea what I want to do. But it is not just up to me. I'm working on it is all I can say. Thank you for the pain medicine, Sasha. I think I can get to sleep now," she murmured, then after a pause she spoke again, very quietly. "One last question. Since you don't fly, how did you get to New York?"

Something close to, but not quite a smile flickered across Sasha's face. A near smile, she named it.

"I took a freighter."

"That would have taken you weeks, even over a month, Sasha!"

"I had just one month while my boat was in dry dock, my crew and I on shore leave. I took one of my laboratory's top-secret small freighters. You know now I'm an inventor, cursed with too many ideas in my head. The freighters were built using my own hydrogen-

101

powered motors and a special design. Incredibly high-speed, just a few short stops, from Sydney to New York in ten days. I used a false identity and got a job on it as a deck hand, loading and unloading. I lied to my handlers and to my crew about which crewmember I would be with. I arranged it so no one would know I was missing, so no one would be looking for me... I had done the scheduling myself from the laboratory, was planning to take the same freighter back again before Fate intervened."

"I didn't think you believed in Fate."

"A figure of speech, just for you, Katya."

"I think I'm becoming a believer in Fate, even if you aren't."

Sasha didn't reply. He was deep in thought, troubled. She kept quiet too, letting him work out whatever was on his mind. When he spoke again, she was surprised by the tenderness in his voice.

"Would you mind, Katya... if I slept here again? This may be the last time we get to hold each other. I cannot describe the depth of my need for you to touch me. It's been so many years."

Katya wrapped her injured arm lightly around him, able to caress his face and chest with her right hand. Sasha's pills were doing wonders. Sasha hesitated, then encircled her in his arms. She began moving her hand gently around his neck, back, shoulders, arms. The sensation was immensely pleasurable to Katya. She could only imagine how it felt to Sasha; she detected the slight trembling of his body, heard his contented sighs as she continued her caresses. *I'm falling in love with this man*, she thought. They lay together that way for a long time, breathing each other's breath, before they both fell asleep.

Chapter 19

Morning arrived crisp and foggy, a typical San Francisco summer day ahead. Sasha and Katya were awakened by angry voices, and the room door slammed open. Mason stormed up to the bed, his face livid.

"Lies, more lies," he raged. "Not of word of what she told us is true. She's no more a Mossad agent than I am! Get out of that bed, Sasha, she's poison!"

Mason practically spat the words. Jake stood in the doorway, looking confused.

"What the hell is wrong with you!" added Bill, looking ragged and unslept. "You're a sick fuck!"

"Language, language. I hurt far too much for you to be yelling at me," Katya protested. "I just want another dose of morphine for breakfast," she said calmly, yawning and sitting up, nursing her arm.

"Maybe it was the morphine talking last night," Sasha ventured, getting out of bed, grabbing his shoes, and stumbling to a chair. He didn't want to admit how stunned he was, and he needed to diffuse the situation quickly. Mason looked like he was going to strike her. Once again, her new elaborate history was a sham. Her innocent Palestinian doctor, the village in Lebanon, Mossad, her grandparents in China – an entire fabricated life…

"Morphine my ass. She's playing with us and I'm sick of it!" Mason shouted.

"Shush, shush, don't forget hotel management," Katya teased.

"Why, Katya, why do you keep making up these stories?" Sasha didn't expect a straight answer, but he had to ask. He put on his shoes and ran a hand over his wrinkled shirt, through his wild hair. His mind was a blur. Was he still under the effects of Cutter's drugs, he wondered...

"I have my reasons," was all she replied.

Mason ran towards her and Sasha jumped up to hold him back. It took both Sasha and Jake to get Mason out of the room. Bill glared at her one more time, then followed.

"Close the door!" Katya called out, but the door stayed open.

"Get up. I want you out of here in five minutes!" shouted Mason.

"An hour if you're lucky. And you'd better have that morphine ready for me," Katya called out the door. "I promise I'll start screaming bloody murder if you don't."

The four men sat down silently in the living room, Mason still fuming. There were so many thoughts going through Sasha's head he wasn't sure where to begin. He still didn't want to believe that Katya had been lying yet again. He'd grabbed his shoes when he left the bedroom and bent to put them on; he'd slept in his clothes and had nothing to change into.

"Are you certain Mossad wasn't just protecting their agent?" Sasha asked.

"I'm damned sure," Mason snapped. "Nothing was true. I called in a lifetime of favors just to get laughed at."

"Did you check out her story with Derek?" Sasha asked.

"Derek disappeared the day of your abduction. I learned last night that his body and the body of his sister were just recovered from a construction site in New York. Seems Gunner was very talkative in custody."

Poor Derek, Sasha thought, just a hapless pawn. And his sister, an innocent victim. Sasha said a silent Buddhist prayer for both their souls, then returned his thoughts to Katya. He could only imagine Katya's plan. It was time for her to run and he needed to let her go, help her go. And didn't she say she'd be back, but also "come find me?" It was confusing, it wasn't logical, but he felt the tug of their strange and somehow wonderful connection. She knew what she was doing, even if he didn't.

"Just let me get my hands on her again," Mason growled.

"Mason, calm down," Sasha said firmly. "I'm as angry about her lies as you are. She's the only reason I'm still here. I want to know who she is as badly as you do. You look like you've been up all night. Why don't you and I and one of your men get away from here for a short while, mate. Coffee, tea downstairs. Talk rationally about our next step. You know I'm not going to let you beat it out of her. Remember she saved your life, too."

"You're right, I do want to beat it out of her. And you're right, I need to calm down. Jake, you're with us. Bill, I know you're exhausted, but keep a sharp eye on her."

"Let me give her a light dose of morphine and she'll be out long enough for us to talk and Bill can get some rest."

"Not Bill, Jake!" Katya was standing in her doorway, hair a mess, flimsy gown sliding off a shoulder, eyes blazing. "And I'm serious about screaming if I don't get my morphine! Jake, or I scream. Morphine or I scream."

"What the hell!" Mason exclaimed, stepping back a pace.

"It's the morphine addiction. She's over the edge," said Sasha, as he reached to prepare a syringe.

"She's fucking crazy is what she is."

"Calm down, Mason. I'd like something better than tea from one of these tea bags and Bill could use a good, strong coffee. I want to hear what he has to say, since he worked with you last night. Let Jake stay," Sasha said quietly.

Sasha stepped towards Katya and escorted her back into her room, closing the door behind them. She put out her hand for the syringe and nodded, mouthing a thank you. She smiled at him and put a hand on his chest, then gently pushed him backward towards the door. He was now sure that she was leaving.

As soon as the three men were out the door of the suite, Jake shut it behind them. When he turned, he was surprised to see Katya standing right in front of him. Katya punched him hard in the solar plexus, then chopped down on the back of his head with the side of her hand as he doubled over. She wrapped her right arm around his neck and squeezed until he passed out. It felt good to be on the other side of a throat choke for once, she thought. She lowered him quietly to the floor and began going through his pockets. She found his wallet and took out all the cash, throwing the wallet on the floor. She was disappointed she didn't find a room card. Then she began removing his clothes, leaving only his underwear. She'd picked Jake because he was closer to her size than the much taller Bill, although she would have preferred to be humiliating Bill right now.

She dressed herself in Jake's clothes, and stuck the syringe in his arm, pressing down all the way. At the last minute, she decided to put the despised hospital gown on him, then used tape from the kitchen to bind his hands and ankles and tape his mouth. She put the cash in a pocket, grabbed Bill's cap he'd left behind and stuffed her hair under it. The shoes were too big, but they would do. An extra pair of socks rummaged from Jake's room helped. She decided to load a bottle of hotel shampoo into a pocket, then she was out the door, noting the room number.

Her first stop was to locate a bellboy. She asked if she could leave a message for Suite 3202, to be delivered in precisely three hours, handing him a small slip of paper and a twenty-dollar bill, and asked for a number she could call him at for another big favor. He was happy to oblige. Katya then slipped through a side exit of the hotel, avoiding the lobby café, and stepped out onto the cool and misty street.

She dodged a cable car as she crossed the street to look up at the billboard she had seen from the suite one more time, then headed to the Powell Street BART train station. She had a lot to accomplish in just a few hours. Katya ran through the list in her mind. Buy burner cell phone on way to station. Call David – she would need him at the house. If he could pick her up at the station, she could save a cab ride and stay off the radar. That would also give her more time to explain everything to him. He would cooperate. David would do anything for her.

She needed to shower, change clothes, pack her passport and what clothes she needed, and stuff in Jake's clothes. Move trunk to David's room, but leave traces. Set up postcard on desk, along with her composition with Terry's note. Those three things will pique his interest. On to the bank when it opens, empty all accounts – everything would have to be in cash – then to travel agency, dump Jake's clothes, to hairdresser for darker tint to get rid of sun bleaching, new cut, quick shop in that store with the beautiful, unusual silk jacket she'd seen, other clothes as well for the trip, her wardrobe was pretty awful. Ah, Fate: she remembered dresses of the right style and ethnicity. It would be hot. She hadn't owned a dress since her trips to Hawaii with her father... Call Vladimir, ask for a big favor, back on BART with rolling suitcase in tow. Or should she take a taxi this time? Another traveler arriving in style at the St. Francis. Ask to have them hold suitcase, call bellhop, back to suite well before five o'clock, deep breath. A calculated risk takes a lot of calculating.

Sasha would come to the house, she was as sure as she had been about anything in her life. She had set up too great a mystery about who she was for him to resist. She was convinced the reality of her reasonably ordinary life would now stand up favorably to that of the spies, agents, and killers she had invented. Sasha knew what he didn't want. She had to convince him she was what he *did* want, an innocent, a normal person as he put it. Someone who shared his passion for music. Someone with the skills to share his life. Someone like his first wife.

Katya was deeply in love, despite love not being part of her plan. She hadn't known this kind of love before, not for Paulo. This was a selfless devotion quite apart from how Sasha might feel about her. She honestly doubted if Sasha could love her back, if he was capable of romantic love, despite the tenderness he'd shown her last night. But it didn't matter. She wouldn't be like her friend David, who had loved her all these years, with an unrequited, hopeless love. It must have been excruciating for him living in the same house, watching her with others, forced to share in her happiness. Enduring her only great love, for Paulo, even when he was so far away, and then her despair at his death, the misery of her guilt. This would be different, better. She would be Sasha's shadow, his protector, his partner. That would be more than enough. Or so she told herself.

There could be no guarantees any of this would work. Just her strong sense of their connection, the unseen bond she felt for Sasha and she was sure he felt for her. She would know soon enough. In just a few hours, her St. Francis bellboy would deliver her message to Suite 3202. It would read simply:

Katherine Zhang Kaplan
Will phone suite at 17:00

Her actual name, although she couldn't resist adding her mother's and grandmother's last name in the middle for effect. Kat, as everyone called her. It should take only a short while for Mason to find DMV records, date of birth – February 4, 1970. Twenty-nine years old. Five feet eight, 125 pounds, brown eyes. Place of employment, graduate student status, home address. They would all come to Berkeley.

Chapter 20

Sasha tried to talk Mason into staying behind while he traveled with Bill and Jake to the address they'd discovered, but there was no holding him back. Sasha insisted on completing his hour and a half workout, then showering, and Mason was already furious at the delay, was pacing around the suite. He seemed to have discovered additional information that had unnerved him, that he didn't share with Sasha. Slipping on his leather jacket, Sasha finally allowed Mason to usher him out the door.

The three-story gray house in Berkeley stood near the top of a hill, a steep series of steps leading up to it. The house was a handsome older building, well-maintained, modest, but Mason knew the high value of homes in this area, especially this close to the UC Berkeley campus. The view over the city and the bay would be stunning. Katherine Kaplan was listed as the sole owner. The DMV photo was clearly of Katya. Records listed her as a graduate student in multiple language departments at the University of California, Berkeley and as an instructor at the Dragon Fist Martial Arts Academy in the same city. Sasha tried to imagine it was all an elaborate cover for whoever she really was.

The front door was opened by an unassuming man in his early thirties with lank brown hair, glasses, soft brown eyes and a worried look. He was just above average height and weight and had a pleasant but not quite handsome face. He wore a Cal Berkeley sweatshirt and clean, pressed blue jeans.

"Kat called me and told me to let you in and answer your questions," the man said. He stared at each of them in turn and made no move to make them welcome. Reluctantly, he stepped aside and closed the door behind them. "I don't know why, you don't look like friends of hers. There are three other people who live here, so don't go throwing things around or getting into their stuff. Her bedroom is at the top of the stairs to the right."

"And who are you?" Mason asked, looking around.

"Oh, my name is David. I live here too. We're all five renters. Where is Kat anyway? Today was the first I've heard from her in a week. She was supposed to be back two days ago. Missed work, her sifu has been calling."

Bill and Jake explored the kitchen and the living room, opening doors and cupboards, then headed up to Katya's bedroom. They seemed to want to be far from Sasha.

"Where did she go?' Mason asked.

"New York City. She wanted to write about a Global Human Rights conference for her newspaper and we got concerned when we didn't hear from her."

"She's a journalist?"

"Sort of. Writes occasional articles for the college rag. It's unpaid."

"Does she travel a lot?"

"This was her first trip in five years. She's always here in town, seven days a week."

"And she teaches martial arts?"

"Yeah, she's fabulous. You should see her compete. There's a wall of trophies at her studio. She practically runs the place with her sifu."

Sasha had been absorbed examining the door and windows, then he wandered through the living room. A seven-foot grand piano, a fine old Steinway, filled much of the space, along with a charmingly hand-painted harpsichord. Built-in shelves filled with books, LPs, CDs, and sheet music lined the walls on either side of a stone fireplace whose hearth was decorated with well-used candles, an old brass menorah on the mantle. Against the heavily curtained front windows, a worn, comfortable-looking sofa and two mismatched stuffed chairs faced the piano across a plain coffee table covered with political and literary magazines. On the opposite wall, a long, low oak hutch held a high-end stereo system and record player. Two large JBL speakers stood on either side.

Eye-catching original artwork hung on the walls, perhaps works by local students. Sasha didn't know much about contemporary art, but he was drawn to these pieces. There was a beautiful Persian rug on the floor. Sasha bent down to feel it. It was genuine and decidedly expensive. Two guitar cases sat on their sides next to a wooden chair along with a collapsible metal footrest and a music stand under a floor lamp. To Sasha, the room looked inviting, a room full of musical life. Sasha was relieved that Katya's professed passion for music was real, at least. He examined the music on the piano, harpsichord, and music stand while he continued to listen to Mason and David conversing.

"How long have you lived here?" Mason asked.

"About ten years. As long as I've known Kat. We met here at this house."

"Is Kat your girlfriend?"

"God no, she's my best friend though. She's not dating anyone now, not for years actually."

"You say you're all renters, David?" asked Mason.

"Yeah. Kat acts as house manager, collects rents, which are unbelievably cheap, let me tell you. Everyone wants to live here."

"So it would surprise you to learn that Kat, as you call her, owns this house outright? No mortgage?"

David looked taken aback. "You've got that wrong. She deals with the owner for us, gets things fixed."

"Okay… And what do you do, David?"

"Whatever this is, it isn't about me. I'm a computer programmer, I work for the university. Who are you people?"

"We may not look like friends of Kat's, but we are. We're also worried about where she's been this last week. We want to help her."

"Bullshit. Kat is fine. She called me."

"And asked you to let us in, answer questions. That's all we're doing."

"Well, I've done that. Look around if you must."

David studied Sasha, then walked over to him while Mason called up to Jake and Bill and headed upstairs. Sasha could tell David wanted to talk to him, so he reluctantly left the piano and headed through the kitchen to the backyard, David following. His fingers ached to touch the keys. Maybe he would feel less concerned about whether his hands would be able to play his violin if he could test them at the piano. The backyard was rather large and flat for such a hilly neighborhood, filled with flowers, fruit trees, and vegetable plots. The space was completely private, tall shrubs shielding it from view. Sasha noted a scent of moist earth and some unknown fragrant flower in the air. A blooming hedge the length of the property grew about a meter from the fence on the right side of the yard, forming an enclosed space with its own metal gate. David opened the gate for a small, mixed-breed brown dog to join them.

"That's Cesar Chavez, the house's latest rescue. He belongs to all of us. We all take care of him."

Cesar licked Sasha's shoes, wagging his tail, then trotted into the house. Sasha didn't like dogs, but he had good reasons. All he could think about were his experiences in the camp, the vicious German Shepherds. But this one seemed to be all right, didn't trigger his usual violent, fearful reaction.

"Who designed the yard? It's pleasing."

"Oh, that's Kat's doing. We grow enough produce to share with the Food Bank."

"My name is Sasha, David. I appreciate your time. I'm trying to get to know who Kat is. She has been more than helpful to me. Do you mind if I ask you some questions too?"

"Go ahead. Kat told me to try and talk with you. She said you're not like the others."

"No, we have little in common. Who are the other renters?"

"We're all employees or students at the university. Kat tries to rent to musicians, so we've got a piano student, Carlos, and a flautist, Sonya – she's studying social work – plus another computer nerd like me, Yan, who also plays guitar. His room is the only one downstairs."

"No violinists then."

"Sorry. Do you play?

"Yes. My violin is far away and I miss it. Why did she say she wanted to travel to New York for this conference, since she hasn't otherwise been traveling?"

"She said she'd never seen the sights, that it was time. Kat has a major interest in human rights issues and told her paper she could make a great story out of it, though she had to pay for the trip herself."

If this was true and Katya had not been sent by an unknown power, he might have to readjust his opinion about coincidences. Or Fate.

They walked back across the patio, past outdoor chairs and tables, a barbecue and glider, and through the kitchen. Sasha noted baskets of produce crowding the counters. The smell of ripe tomatoes wafted through the air. The kitchen was as orderly and welcoming as the yard, with a long farmhouse table and ten chairs in various styles.

"Would you show me her room please, David?"

"Follow me upstairs. Her room overlooks the garden."

Despite the search by Jake and Bill, Katya's room looked relatively undisturbed. Sasha was surprised at the smallness of the

112

room. A single bed with an Indian print cover, a dresser, desk with a recent model computer and a wooden chair, small closet, one window. The entire wall around the entrance was built-in with bookshelves, crowded with books and notebooks, even above the door. But every open space on the other three walls held musical instruments on hooks, none of them in cases. Sasha recognized a lute and a mandolin, as well as a balalaika, a dombra, a Turkish Qanun zither, a Vietnamese traditional zither – a dàn tranh, a Japanese koto, and a Chinese lute-like pipa. Taking a deep breath, he was certain Katya had been in this room recently. He could smell the hotel shampoo. He examined the desk and made a few keystrokes on her computer. The password had been changed not two hours before. A postcard caught his eye – a striking image of Tahiti, a large sailboat in a blue bay with sharp emerald mountains. He turned the card over. Bora Bora. Handwritten on the card were the words "come with me." Sasha held the card in his hand for a long time.

There was also a stack of handwritten sheet music on the desk. A sonata for piano and violin, with Kat Kaplan the composer. Sasha looked closer at a note affixed to the top sheet which read:

> Thanks, but much too difficult for me.
> Good luck finding a violinist who can
> do this justice!   Terry

Sasha sight-read through the first several pages; although derivative, it wasn't bad. A strong influence of Prokofiev.

"Does Kat perform publicly?" Sasha asked, already suspecting the answer.

"She runs a chamber music series called First Tuesdays during the school year down at the Julia Morgan Theater, plays piano or brings her harpsichord – they do a lot of Bach and Telemann. Local musicians mostly, but she gets a few San Francisco Symphony players. Oh, she's subbed on guitar and mandolin with the San Francisco Symphony a couple of times, played piano in the Shostakovich quintet at one of their chamber concerts."

Sasha hadn't thought Katya could keep surprising him. He noted there was no jewelry on the dresser, no perfumes, just two family pictures in plain frames. One was of Katya with a handsome, dark haired man in his early forties on a sailboat. Certainly her father. There

113

he was again in a bat mitzvah group picture, Katya a self-confident looking thirteen-year-old, and her grandmother, a tough looking Chinese lady with an arm lovingly around her. The grandmother had short grey hair and was also wearing a prayer shawl. So, a convert, Sasha thought. No mother. Sasha had been about the same age as her father when these pictures were taken.

He looked through her closet. Ordinary clothes, a multitude of well-worn running shoes, two pairs of black flat-heeled shoes. A more formal black top and trousers suitable for wearing while performing. Not a single dress. Le had loved dresses, as well as jewelry and perfume. He had never understood their appeal, preferred her natural and unadorned, although he'd loved the red and gold elaborately embroidered silk wedding gown she'd worn... Two fifteen-pound weights and, over a hook, an exercise stretch band. An empty space the size of two suitcases on a top shelf. And a large empty space on the floor, dust free, with drag marks through the dust in front.

"Where is her trunk?" he asked David.

"God, how did you know she had one?"

"Can I see it, please?"

David hesitated, then led him into his room. Next to the bed stood a small metal footlocker. It was unlocked. Sasha opened it up and carefully sorted through its contents. There was a strange, old-fashioned looking dress that smelled of mildew, beads, worn tall boots, a floppy hat, dark sunglasses, and a long, messy, dark blond wig.

"Um, Kat's alter ego," David said. "She sings ballads and folksongs in a café sometimes, with her guitar. She gets a kick out of it, I don't know why. I go to hear her sing. Her voice is terrific. She mimics all the old favorites, Joan Baez, Joni Mitchell, Judy Collins. She does their voices perfectly."

"I don't know who they are."

"Well, you're not an American, that's for sure. Is that an Aussie accent?"

Sasha didn't answer. More surprises. Sasha looked further into the trunk. The only other item of interest was a photo album. It looked like it hadn't been opened for a long time. A village somewhere in South or Central America, lots of smiling people. Katya helping to construct a simple building, Katya with her arms embracing a

114

handsome young man with a moustache, Katya surrounded by children, and dozens of other photographs.

"Where and when was this, David?"

"Guatemala. She went there three summers in a row, until five years ago. She was pretty destroyed by her dad's sudden death, was looking for distraction. Joined a language emersion program, got involved with the village she was sent to. Spent money I didn't know she had helping the villagers make improvements, building a school and clinic, hiring a traveling teacher and a visiting nurse. That's Paulo in the picture. They planned to get married someday. She'd never been in love before and was quite out of her mind about him, but she laughed that they'd never done much more than kiss."

"What happened five years ago?"

David's demeanor changed completely. A heavy sadness came over him as he stroked a photo of a smiling Katya.

"It was a total disaster, a horror. Some colonel tried to squeeze the villagers off their land, ordering his soldiers to harass them. Kat set up a resistance, got everyone armed and trained, including herself. Thought they could scare him off. Made the terrible mistake of actually confronting him. Told him she'd cut off her right hand before she let him take their land." David stopped and hung his head. "Kat the hero. Kat the naïve."

"Continue please, David." Sasha had a bad feeling about what might have happened, remembering her story about the village in Lebanon, her lost love. It sounded like she hadn't ventured far from the truth.

"In the fall, right as university classes started up again, Kat got a visit here at the house from two men. They didn't identify the organization they were with, but I got the feeling they were spooks, CIA. They wanted to know about her connection with the village. I stayed in the room with her because I didn't trust them. They brought pictures with them. Horrible, horrible pictures. I thought Kat was going to tear her hair out. The pictures... the pictures were of a pile of hands, and bodies spread out all over. Even the livestock was dead with missing feet. There had been one survivor, a child who had somehow managed to hide, who had seen it all. The colonel and his soldiers had come back after Kat returned to Berkeley... and shot her villagers – forty-seven of them – then butchered them... cut off all of their right hands."

David had to stop and compose himself. Sasha was stunned. Katya had also experienced the kind of loss and horror that he had witnessed too many times in his life. And she must be blaming herself. So much explained about Katya, so much yet unanswered. Sasha noticed how David was nervously massaging his right hand. The memory of the photos, the horror of the colonel's act, must be exceedingly painful for him to recall. Sasha remembered that Katya had inserted a reference to her right hand in her fabricated story. Maybe it had been subconscious and not deliberate. He nodded to David to continue, and when he didn't react, placed a hand gently on his shoulder.

"Kat would tell them nothing but what they already knew," David continued, pulling himself together. "The men wanted assurances from her that she was not going to go public or seek revenge. They were supporting this monster. There was a war going on, a rebellion. Our government was supporting a man who would do such things... They said Kat would be stopped if she tried to return to Guatemala, even for the funerals. They implied, but never actually stated, that she would not survive if she did. They were really nasty, telling her that her leftist revolutionary ideas had been to blame. She didn't talk to anyone for days after they departed, just stayed in her room. Carlos and I finally shouldered the door open and got her some help. Not long afterwards she went back to Hong Kong with her sifu – she'd been there the year before at a Kung Fu tournament – and she seemed okay after that, though she came back with a broken arm." David sighed. He stared out his bedroom window until Sasha asked him another question.

"What about her family? Were they able to help?"

"She has no family left, all gone. As I said, her dad was dead, had an unexpected heart attack at work eight years ago. She'd been very tight with him, and her mom died of brain cancer when she was twelve, dead in three weeks from a belated diagnosis, but they were never close. No brothers or sisters, no aunts or uncles, no cousins. Her Dad's parents died in a car accident when she was six, drunk driver hit them. Ironic that they were the only two from their families to escape Austria, all the rest of their families died in Auschwitz. Came here as newlyweds, Kat told me, in 1936. Her mom's dad died just before Kat was born. Kat took her grandmother's death the hardest. Wonderful, feisty Chinese lady, I loved her. She passed away just before Katya's last summer in Guatemala, before the horror, so it was

116

a double blow for Kat. The grandmother is the one who pretty much raised Kat since she was born. Her mom had a busy career with the university."

Sasha remained still for a while, watching David's face.

"You're in love with her," he said.

"How could I not be?" David replied, with a sad, resigned look.

"It's hard to love someone when it may not be possible for that love to be returned," Sasha said quietly. He was beginning to think this could be true for all three of them.

Chapter 21

"Sasha, come here. You need to see this."

Mason was calling from the hallway. Sasha replaced the album, closed the trunk, and put his finger to his lips. He and David found Mason standing in front of a hall closet. The coats had been pushed aside, revealing a secret staircase to the third floor.

"Bill noticed right away that the regular stairs only led to one room, that there had to be more up here under the dormers. We did a bit of snooping and found this. Take a look."

"Hey, are you immigration police?" David asked, his voice sounding alarmed.

"Why would you ask that?" Mason taunted as they climbed the stairs.

They entered a large bright room with a low ceiling. The view out the dormer windows stretched over the city to the bay. There were five single beds and a crib, toys and stuffed animals, a sofa, small table and chairs, bookshelves, a long desk with two computers and two wood chairs, and closets full of clothes for men, women, and children in a variety of sizes. Sasha examined the books – English language primers and workbooks, several Spanish-English dictionaries, employment guides, books of fiction in English and Spanish, and dual-language pamphlets on how to apply for asylum.

Mason glared. "Care to explain, David?"

"We have a lot of guests," David replied, stone-faced.

"Let's try that again," Mason demanded.

"It's all right, David." Sasha's voice was calm. "These people aren't with immigration and won't be reporting to them. We're here to understand who Kat is and what she's been doing. Just explain her connection to this and what kind of people you were helping."

"Okay, okay. Kat said I could believe you. We belong to an organization that helps refugees from Central America. There are boys who are being pressed into gangs, witnesses to horrific crime and corruption, women fleeing prostitution or dangerous marriages, people fleeing for their lives or from crushing poverty. Sometimes we're able to free people from traffickers and we have to hide them."

"I noted heavy, state-of-the-art security on your doors and windows. Have you been threatened?" Sasha questioned.

"So far just a precaution. Kat also took us to a gun range and taught us all how to shoot, even me. God, she's an amazing shot. She goes regularly. We all know where the gun is kept in the house."

"You're going to show it to us," Mason demanded.

"Why not? I have no desire to touch it again."

"How long do your guests stay?" Sasha inquired, changing the subject.

"Usually from two to five weeks, then they move on. Kat got us involved. Everyone who lives here helps. Our guests have the run of the house and yard. Cesar has been a great therapy dog, especially for traumatized children, and Kat uses gardening for therapy too. One of us, Carlos, is from Venezuela, Katya speaks Spanish fluently, and the rest of us have learned quite a bit. We haven't had any guests since Kat left, but now she told me she doesn't know when she'll be back, and that we have new guests arriving next week, a family of four, with boys ten and twelve. We're committed whether she's here or not."

"Very noble of you all," Mason sneered.

"We're a sanctuary in a sanctuary city," David replied, defiant.

"We're done here, everyone back downstairs." Sasha motioned for David to go first.

"Show us where you keep the gun," Mason ordered.

They all returned to the kitchen. David reached high into a cabinet, pulled out a heavy black metal box, and punched in a code to open it. The box was empty.

"Damn it!" shouted Mason. "She's been here, hasn't she!"

"I told you, she called me," David answered, remaining cool. "If she's been here, I haven't seen her."

"Thank you, that's all we need." Sasha threw a warning glare at Mason. "Would you let us talk among ourselves for a while, David? We have no more questions. I hope Kat contacts you again soon. I can assure you she's all right."

Mason was going to lose control and Sasha had his own issues with him now. As soon as David was outside, Sasha turned on Mason.

"When were you going to tell me about Guatemala?" Sasha asked angrily.

"How did you know I found out about what happened there..."

"I didn't know. You just told me. Your CIA would have killed her five years ago. We're through. You now know who our Katya is, where she lives, how she lives, and that she's no threat to anyone. You can go look for her on your own. I have no doubt whatsoever that she will call or knock on the door at the St. Francis at five o'clock like she wrote, and if she wants to arm herself to keep you from shooting her, well, I think I understand. I'm going to the university and her martial arts studio because I like this Kat as much as I liked Katya and want to know more. I'll be back to the suite before five."

"So you really think she just happened onto your abduction in New York?" Mason asked, still skeptical.

"Perhaps she did."

"And the fact that she owns the house... that she just keeps coming into piles of money."

"Her parents and grandparents have all passed away. Perhaps she inherited it."

"And you think you're safe on your own! I'm under obligation to your government to watch over you."

"I've already slipped your man once. If you think sitting outside watching the door at my next two stops is worth your time, go ahead, I can't stop you."

"That's what we're going to have to do. We'll be parked outside the studio to take you back to the city." With a noticeable effort, Mason made his voice more civil. "Can we at least give you a ride to the university?"

"I've had enough of all of you. I would much rather walk. Now get out of this house."

Sasha looked around the living room one more time after Mason, Bill, and Jake left. He felt strangely at home here and found himself hoping he would be able to return. He could picture Katya at the piano, accompanying him as he played his violin. His music on the boat was limited to the violins, violas, and cellos played by his crew. He'd always imagined playing piano with a chamber ensemble but had stubbornly kept his piano playing to himself all these years. He regretted never inviting any of his crew into Mandelbrot House during their dry dock month; he'd never even considered it. He closed the front door behind him and noted the quiet and lushness of the neighborhood. The day had warmed to around 70 degrees Fahrenheit and he carried his coat over his arm. The views were impressive as he headed down the steep sidewalk towards the bay, looking for the famous campanile of the university. It would be a long walk but this last week had been far too sedentary.

The secretary at the office of East Asian Languages and Cultures was delighted at the mention of Kat Kaplan's name and informed Sasha that he was in luck – one of Kat's favorite professors had a summer course and was in his office. Sasha bowed instead of offering a handshake, and it was returned by the professor, a short, fit-looking Japanese man of about sixty by the name of Fujio Takahashi. Sasha decided on a Danish persona for the interview.

"Thank you for your time, Professor Takahashi. My name is Rasmus Johannsen and I'm interviewing a candidate that I like for a position in an international aid organization I'm a part of. I'm afraid that I am not at liberty to give you its name. I hope that is not uncomfortable for you. I understand you know Kat Kaplan well and I would like to have your opinion of her language skills, integrity, and most importantly, her character."

"Ah, Mr. Johannsen, you have found yourself a gem. Several departments here have been trying in vain to get her to do a doctorate and apply for a professorship, or to work here in any capacity. I have not had a brighter or more capable student than Kat, even though she does things her own way. She's been taking at least two courses a semester for years since she finished her undergraduate studies. She must have three Master's Degrees by now. Her papers are brilliant, simply brilliant. By my last count she speaks and writes twelve languages and her Mandarin Chinese is flawless, plus she speaks Cantonese."

"Twelve? I was only aware of eight, including English. If you have a record there, could you please tell me what they are?"

"Oh my, has our Kat been too modest?"

The professor consulted his computer and wrote down a list on a piece of paper for Sasha. The additional languages included Japanese, Russian, Filipino/Tagalog, and Thai.

"Thank you, Professor. She has indeed been too modest. What else can you tell me about Ms. Kaplan's character?"

"Honest. Honorable. Empathetic. Someone who would jump to the aid of a person in trouble or just needing help. Let me tell you my favorite story about Kat. Last year our department joined the South and Southeast Asian Studies department in hosting a visiting Thai professor at a local Thai restaurant. When we arrived, we found our table for twelve waiting for us, but the restaurant was packed and a server had not shown up for work. The owner was in a panic; she could barely take care of the rest of the tables by herself. I noticed Kat at a table eating dinner alone and gave her a nod. She nodded back, then I saw her size up the situation. She pulled her hair into a ponytail, grabbed up her dishes, whispered to the owner, then hurried to the kitchen, returning with a server's outfit on, drying her hands. She got us seated and took our orders, and as soon as we had our drinks and appetizers, took care of a few other tables, bussing dishes in between. She charmed our Thai professor in his own language and helped make the dinner an enjoyable celebration. We stayed past closing time, and I saw her eating her belated meal in the kitchen as she laughed and chatted in Thai with the staff. I knew for a fact she had never waitressed before. That's the kind of person Kat is."

"I have indeed found her to be more than willing to help even a stranger in need," Sasha replied, in purposefully stilted English. A pretend waitress, Sasha mused. What would this professor think of her being a pretend seductive contract killer, a pretend spy, a pretend Mossad agent?

"Full disclosure, Mr. Johannsen. I have known Kat all her life. She is a child of the university, and that's why she can take classes as she pleases. Her father, Gabriel, was a renowned professor of mathematics here at Berkeley and a close friend of mine. Gabriel came from a family of professors stretching back to Europe, and her mother was a physicist and then a researcher at the new Berkeley Nanoscience Lab. And *her* father, Kat's grandfather, was a professor of Chinese Studies here at Berkeley, Heinrich Hartmann. No one is as surprised as I am that Kat seems content teaching martial arts, though she does excel there, too. I went with her father to several of her tournaments. And you do know that she is a musician as well? I attend her chamber music series regularly."

Nanoengineering was one of Sasha's main focuses: he could hardly believe the coincidence. He wondered if he knew the mother's work. Nanoengineering was a small world. She would have been working in the forefront of the field.

"What about her IQ? Is that part of the record you can share with me? I mean, is there a reason she didn't feel she could finish a doctorate?"

"I'm going to go out on a limb here..." The professor stopped when Sasha looked confused. "I'm sorry, it's an English idiom. I mean I shouldn't be telling you this, but I can see where you might think Kat is not capable of higher-level work. She has an IQ of well over 150, that's all I can tell you. She doesn't even know that. Her father insisted I never tell her.

Another genius. Sasha felt that explained a lot about her abilities. How he envied her never being told, able to lead a normal life, not have expectations put on her, on herself.

"Did you know her grandmother as well, her Chinese one?"

"Oh yes, Jiang Mai Zhang. Did Kat tell you Jiang was born in Vietnam, parents moved to China when she was six? The grandmother raised her. Kat grew up speaking Mandarin and Vietnamese before she could speak English. No wonder she has such a gift for languages. Jiang was a doctor in China. I never learned why she gave it up, or how she met Kat's grandfather, who was quite a bit older. Gabriel said she wouldn't talk about her past. Kat was devastated when she passed away."

"Is Ms. Kaplan religious at all?"

"She and her father attended a Reform temple together until his death. I was at her bat mitzvah. She has a beautiful voice. I know she took voice lessons for years. She stopped attending services after her father died and seemed more interested in Buddhism. I may have been responsible for that. But I know she considers herself Jewish."

Another parallel, thought Sasha. He remembered the bat mitzvah photo he'd seen in Katya's room. At least Katya had been truthful about being Jewish. He'd only done his bar mitzvah for his adoptive mother Maddy. Had given himself one week to prepare, instead of the usual year, then had no use for any of it afterwards. But Judaism would always be a part of him. Who could have imagined she would have an interest in Buddhism as well. And her music... she'd been truthful there, too. She'd sung to him in the van. In Vietnamese. He remembered that beautiful voice... This Kat was more and more fascinating.

"Tell me more about Ms. Kaplan, Professor Takahashi, since you know her so well. I know she gardens, but all that time in classes and with music... I can't see her tan and physique a result of gardening and indoor martial arts alone."

The professor laughed. "Our Kat bikes, swims, and runs! She rides that bike of hers up and down that steep hill to her house, to work, to the BART station. Runs and hikes all over our local hills, swims at the University athletic facility."

"A triathlete? She has the look of one."

"That she is! She doesn't go in much for events, but she's very competitive, as in her martial arts. A superb soccer player, too, a forward. Took her team to State Championships in High School –they came in second – continued in college, graduate school. Only stopped playing when her grandmother got sick, oh, five years ago. Kat nursed her through her last months, then left for Guatemala for the summer after her funeral."

Sasha nodded. "Guatemala. Do you know anything about her time there?"

"Just that she was helping a village there every summer after her father's death. She did a language residency and got into a romance. Seems the romance must have gone sour because she stopped going at the end of that summer. Young people!"

"Yes, young people," Sasha agreed, for an entirely different reason.

She hadn't told him much during their time in the van, but everything she had said, even if understated, was the truth.

Chapter 22

Sasha bowed and thanked the professor for his time and valuable input. He asked for directions to Kat's martial arts studio and set off again on foot, passing Mason's car parked inconspicuously on a side street. He took note of a car he'd seen earlier, parked on the next block, then another similar car two blocks later, three men sitting in each. *Of course.*

The puzzle pieces of Katya's life he was putting together were starting to make sense. A young woman with a sense of justice and a driving need to atone, alone in a strange city, leaps into a fight to aid a stranger, but not heedlessly – a young woman who feels she has the skills to succeed. A young woman with romantic notions who decides to reinvent herself when the truth is not believed. A young woman searching for ways to save the world, if just one person at a time. Both he and Katya had experienced great loss and found ways to deal with trauma by dedicating their lives to helping others, living simply, their only pleasure in playing music, with like-minded people in a world of their own making. And she could touch him, he desired her touch. No, he would not be capable of walking away from her forever.

Yet all at once the full weight of his fifty-nine years descended on his shoulders. Never had Sasha so wished for a possible insight to be wrong. He selfishly hoped Katya wasn't looking for him to replace her father. Another reason not to tell her how he felt about her.

It was just past one when Sasha reached the studio on a busy downtown street. Giant windows gave view into a large, well-lighted room, its floor covered with mats, its walls with mirrors. A trophy case stood against one wall, crowded with framed photographs. In one corner stood a small Buddhist shrine. Friday afternoon was obviously a quiet time of day and there were no students. Sasha knew the sifu's name was Ai Yeung, but he would use his title of master/teacher only. Sasha entered and the sifu, a hard-bodied Chinese man dressed in a gi, came out of a back room and looked him over, clearly making a quick assessment. The sifu was on the short side of average with salt and pepper hair, was perhaps sixty-five. They bowed to each other, and the man motioned to Sasha to enter the back room. There were two desks, one orderly and one piled with papers, and two hard chairs. Photographs of the sifu as a much younger man with groups of students, and of Katya, in a gi, in several mid-leap kick poses, cluttered the walls.

"You have come about Kat. I most anxious to hear what you have to say," the man stated without preamble in a strong Chinese accent.

The man was as intuitive as Katya. "Please call me Sasha, sifu."

"Can you explain to me what has happened to her? Is she well?"

"She was injured saving my life, sifu. She is recovering but I don't know when she might be able to return. Things have gotten complicated."

"Complicated, I see."

"She has not been able to call you or she would have. She sends her deepest regrets for worrying you and for not being here for her classes."

"Where is she now?"

"She has just arrived back in the Bay Area and is, as I said, still recovering."

"And she injured herself how?"

"She was shot, twice, in her left arm. She has been in a lot of pain."

"I see... Pain and injury would not have stopped her from teaching. I have watched her win a fight, teach classes, with broken arm."

"Sifu, I assure you she had no choice. She was abducted, we both were, and it is thanks to her and her alone that we are free and that I am alive."

"And who are you?"

"I was only a stranger she stopped to help. She didn't know I was someone worth saving. And now I think Kat is someone worth knowing much better. I find her an exceptional young woman."

"I see. What you want to know about her that you don't already know?"

"How she fights in tournament style, how you've taught her to think on her feet, how she knows how to street fight. And how she won that fight with a broken arm."

"She street fights good, as good as me. I grew up street fighting in Hong Kong, and Kat wanted to be able to defend herself in all situations. I oblige. We also work on getting out of bindings, even handcuffs. Want to know how to fight with no rules, if attacked, not just in tournament. I must admit she scare even me with her drive."

128

"And did you teach her to never picture failure?"

The sifu laughed. "She learned that lesson well. I also teach her to observe. How to see, how to size up situation, get in mind of opponent. She got good at guessing. Better than guess. She pay attention, she knows.

"I know there's more you taught her."

"We do role play. She calls it Brain Game. I give her story plot, I sometimes villain, sometimes other. I give her character to be. At beginning she has one week, then just one hour to research, become that character, work her way out of situation I make up, convince me. Then no time, improvise."

"Was one of these characters a Mossad agent?"

"Ah, she tried that on you. That was good one, no?" he asked, following his head shake with a belly laugh. "She had whole week for that one. Even spent five days with ex Mossad agent, learned some Krav Maga, tried it out on me. Very effective method."

Sasha hesitated before moving into shadier territory. "What about your two trips to Hong Kong with her? Did she fight outside the tournaments?"

The sifu eyed Sasha a long while before answering.

"Kat wanted more money for that village of hers in Guatemala. She spent most of money she had from family on schooling, to live on, and now on that village, and not that much begin with. Berkeley very expensive place to live. But she still had money from grandmother. She want to save it for something special. After tournament we went to fight club, very dangerous, but Kat willing. She fought and won, I bet and won, we came home with tens of thousands of dollars."

"And the second trip? After she knew what happened in Guatemala?"

"Ah, you know about that. She was angry, depressed. Wanted to buy her house, had plans for it she did not share. There was no tournament. We did several small fight clubs, we win big. But she wanted more. I take her to biggest illegal fight club, but worse, more dangerous than I thought, I want to leave. Dark, smoky, loud, crowd really rough, spotlights on ring with cage around it. She stay, sign up. Wore black and red mask make-up, like she sees on other fighters, looks very scary. Tells me to bet everything we have. Big woman comes out for no rules fight, mixed martial arts, Kat thrown all over

129

but gets up again and again. I know Kat better, she trying to look weak. Waiting for her moment, for opponent to make mistake.

"But opponent stomp hard on arm, I hear it break, she hide it well. She sway over to me, she must be in agony but she does not let on. Tells me to move. Stand in front of two huge mean-looking thugs at ring-side, and when she motion, I am to make meanest glare I can at her opponent. I do not know what she doing, but I agree. Kat goes back in ring with swagger, walks around this monster girl, kicks her hard in knee, gets her real mad. Girl throws her and pins her neck with arm. I see Kat talking to her, pointing at me. I make mean face. Girl looks scared, loosens grip. Kat throws her with one arm, and pounds her head hard against floor, one pound, she out. Crowd goes crazy, Kat standing there holding her one arm high in air in victory. We win very big, but she never does fight club again."

Sasha could hear the roar, see Katya's victorious gesture. "So what did she say to that other fighter?"

"She say 'You see my boss there, with his guards? He biggest crime lord in Hong Kong, in disguise. Every bone of mine you break, he break ten. Then he kill you. Let me win and I let you live.' The sifu laughed another long belly laugh. "Me, old sifu, crime lord. Kat pass out on way to hospital, but when she wake up, she not angry anymore."

"I have seen Kat fight like that. I can picture this scene all too well... Did you teach her how to break a man's arms?"

A shadow of concern passed over the sifu's face. "Ah, she in trouble for that? She want to know how, I teach her. Practiced on pair of strong sticks."

"No, she's not in trouble. She was using her wits again and saved many lives. Would you show me what she knows, how she fights in a tournament, her style?"

"You want to spar? Jiu-Jitsu? Karate? Kung Fu? Judo? Aikido?"

"Yes, all, one after the other, sifu, but no broken bones, please."

"No broken bones, promise," he said, smiling and grabbing a gi from a shelf. "You look like you know how. I like your build. Put on gi. I have twenty minutes until afternoon class."

Sasha waited for Ai Yeung to leave the small office space, but the sifu stood with arms crossed at the closed door, watching him, no longer smiling. Sasha struggled to read the man's emotional state. He felt he was being sized-up. Judged. The sifu stared at his sculpted muscles, then at his scars when he stripped off his undershirt, but made no comment. Sasha kept the inside of his left arm from the man's view. Was it possible this man was also in love with Katya? Or was he just concerned he was about to lose his best instructor, his much appreciated partner... Sasha suspected this martial arts demonstration was going to be a competition instead.

The two men bowed and began sparring. As they flowed from one martial art form to the next, Sasha noted that the sifu had a fluidity and grace that was not dissimilar to his own. Both men had been training since childhood and had been masters for decades. Sasha felt they were fairly equally matched, but he held back, almost letting himself be thrown twice, but expertly blocking most of the blows and kicks, careful not to throw the sifu too hard. He was sorry when the twenty minutes were up. The room had begun to fill with arriving school children and parents. Everyone clapped when the two men stopped and bowed to each other.

"You did not need to protect me. I bow to your superior skills," the sifu said as they toweled off.

"I wanted you to look good to your students," Sasha replied quietly. "Thank you for the opportunity to spar. I didn't get to see Kat use all the skills you have taught her, and I know now that you have taught her well."

"She as good as me. Take care of my Kat, Sasha. Tell her I will miss her."

Sasha bowed again in reply and strode to the back room to dress. It was clear from his words the sifu knew Katya might never be returning to work at the studio.

Chapter 23

At precisely four o'clock, Katya called the number the St. Francis bellboy had given her. He hurried to check if Suite 3202 was empty and phoned her that it was, waiting by the door for her as she'd instructed. She'd decided to take a taxi back to San Francisco after all and left her suitcase at the bell desk. She didn't think Mason or his men could recognize her, but she still checked carefully before walking through the crowded lobby and entering an elevator. She flashed the bellboy a smile and handed him another twenty as he opened the door to the suite for her. Katya enjoyed the stunned expression on his face. Her looks had certainly improved since he'd seen her in Jake's clothes.

"Remember, one more job. Call the suite phone at five o'clock and hang up when someone answers. Oh, and text me if you see any of my friends heading to the elevator."

"Yes, ma'am! I know what they look like and I won't forget," he replied, returning her smile.

Katya reentered the suite she had fled that morning. She checked herself in the bathroom mirror, opened the floor-length curtains to the view across Union Square, and practiced concealing herself. The curtains would do nicely. The glare from the window would help. She knew she couldn't get too comfortable in the room. Her bellboy accomplice might miss the men's arrival and not be able to warn her. She'd accomplished everything she'd wanted to and was more than pleased with the results. A calculated risk takes a lot of calculations, she repeated to herself. But what if Sasha were to react differently than she hoped? Jake might be mad enough to try to punch her, Bill was unpredictable, and Mason... Mason was a loose cannon. Not to mention that all three were armed. Well, now they'd think she was armed, too. It would give them pause.

Katya moved quietly and just a little nervously around the room until she felt the buzz of her phone. Her bellboy had come through again. All four men were coming up the elevator together. She silenced the phone, double-checked that everything was in position, and stepped behind the curtains to wait. It was only 4:45. She had to be still until it was time.

She heard the men enter and move around the rooms. Bill was probably getting a beer from the fridge. Someone sat down on the sofa right in front of her. Then a second person. Their backs would be to her. Mason was the first to speak.

"If she does call, and I still doubt that she will, I bet she'll be calling from a thousand miles from here. She emptied her bank accounts."

"I don't understand how you can think she's somebody's agent after all we've seen and heard. She has a full life here. She almost makes my life look sedate by comparison. You need to listen to what she has to say, then leave her alone." Sasha's voice sounded tired, and annoyed. Mason was proving that he could try the patience of a saint, Katya mused to herself.

"Well perhaps she's been in a sleeper cell, waiting for her next assignment, which was you."

"A sleeper cell of do-gooders for five long years. Listen to yourself."

"And now she's armed."

"She might be armed when she comes back," Sasha said. "Or she might not. You haven't proven to be any sort of friend."

The two men glared at each other, then looked away. There was just no convincing him, Sasha thought. He then noted that the curtains were open and he looked out the window at the view. He knew the curtains had been closed before they left. Maybe the cleaning staff had opened them. He took in a deep breath and again smelled the strong scent of the St. Francis shampoo. They were all using it, so maybe he was wrong. Not stopping to take off his jacket, he started walking around the rooms just as Bill came to join Mason and Jake by the phone. He took a seat across from them.

Katya had placed the phone at the edge of the coffee table close to one of the sofas to encourage the men to sit near it. She hoped they were all looking at it, as people do expecting a ring at a specific time. She was hidden not one meter behind a sofa. At five o'clock, the awaited call came. The ring was loud in the quiet suite. Mason picked up the phone on the second ring and held it to his ear for a long moment before he heard the click of disconnection at the other end.

"Damn it, she hung up," he growled.

134

"Because I'm not a thousand miles away," came a voice right behind him.

He saw Sasha staring from across the room, and he jumped up and turned at the same time as Jake. There stood Katya, her right arm held out in front of her, the end of what looked like a gun hidden in the depths of the long flowing sleeves of her jacket, pointing right at Mason's heart. But Bill had scrambled to his feet with his gun drawn and pointed at Katya.

"Well done, Bill," Katya said calmly, without taking her eyes off Mason, but this was not what she'd planned for. New plan. "This doesn't need to get messy. I'll put mine down if you put your gun down first. No other moves. We all need to talk."

"Bill, lower your weapon!" Sasha called out, now truly alarmed.

"I don't think we have anything more to say," Mason snarled, keeping his eyes on Katya's. "There's another way this could go. Bill shoots you, we claim you were going to shoot Sasha. We're the heroes."

Mason was acting way too cool, she thought. She raised her arm and aimed between his eyes.

"Your skull may be too thick to understand me, but it won't stop a bullet. You're not wearing a vest between your eyes, Mason. And what are you going to do with Sasha after you shoot me? Think he'll play along? Will you have to shoot him too?"

Mason's smile faded. Katya could sense Bill wavering. For all the danger she'd faced this past week, this was the closest she felt to possibly dying.

"Mason, Bill, listen to me carefully," Sasha called out. "I'm wearing a listening device, a tracker. We're being heard by my people from the Consulate. That's where I went when I lost Bill. We've got five men in the building. They've tailed us all day. Lower your weapon, Bill, now, and we can call this a misunderstanding."

"All of you, weapons on the table, including that ankle revolver, Bill," Katya said. "Sasha, take their guns and put them in the freezer."

Katya didn't move her arm until the guns were out of sight. She sighed with relief and walked around the end of the sofa, her arm lowered. Sasha was astounded by how different she appeared. Her hair was darker and cut in a shorter, angular style that made her look decidedly Asian, a style that recalled Le's, he thought, catching his breath. Her eyes seemed a darker brown as well, perhaps because of

135

the darker hair. No jewelry, just a plain watch. His eye was drawn to the loose jacket she wore: a striking iridescent peacock blue silk with an elaborately embroidered Chinese pattern, along with black tight-fitted trousers and short low-heeled black boots. She had gone from unusual and attractive to sensational, even to a man who never looked at women.

"Now that the games are over, please let me say what I came here to say." Katya held up her arm again and shook back the sleeve. There was no gun, only a long, tight roll of paper. Mason, Bill, and Jake looked upset that they'd been taken in. Katya held out the paper to Sasha. Her eyes were locked on his.

"Come with me," she said.

Sasha suddenly remembered the rooftop billboard on Union Square he'd been looking at for the past two days and had just viewed again. The words over the image of a beautiful Tahitian woman, sharp emerald mountains and sparkling blue water behind her. An airline advertisement for travel to Tahiti. Katya's postcard on her desk. And now the papers he'd taken in his hand. Two airline tickets for the next day at 7:30 p.m. and a voucher for a private resort on Bora Bora.

"There are two beds," Katya said quietly. "I'll be your bodyguard and your friend and ask nothing more. We can relax, recover on Bora Bora, Tahiti. You can have your crew bring the *Trib* to meet us there. But I won't take a freighter, no matter how fast. You're going to fly for the first time in your life."

Katya held her breath. This was the moment. She felt everything she'd done in her life, her music, her martial arts, her gift with languages, her refugee work, had prepared her to work with this extraordinary man, this brilliant, selfless, humanitarian doctor. A quiet hero. Saint Sasha. She couldn't read his reaction. Had she overdone it with the hair, the jacket? She'd only seen the one photograph of Le, on their wedding day... Sasha was still staring at the papers in his hand, thinking, deciding. He finally looked up and nodded yes. He placed the papers carefully in the inside pocket of his leather jacket and held out his hand. Katya walked forward, took the offered hand, and felt him pull her to him. He put both arms around her and hugged her close. She couldn't have been more surprised if he had kissed her.

Mason stared, then sat down hard on the sofa. Jake and Bill sat down as well. Katya didn't mind at all that they must be panicking, thinking back to what they had said to Sasha, to each other, that had been overheard.

"Katya, you know I would never have let Bill shoot you," Mason said, attempting a soothing tone. "I just needed to get you to put your gun down. I know you're mad about what the CIA was doing in Guatemala, but we were as horrified as you were at what happened. I read the whole file and you were not to blame. It was a land grab, plain and simple."

Katya turned to glare at him. She nestled her back against Sasha.

"Plain and simple. You dare use those words? A murdered village! And I thought you were with Interpol. I didn't know you were with the CIA before. I didn't come with a gun. You were never in any danger."

Katya enjoyed the look on Mason's face when he realized the number of mistakes he'd just made. She hoped she would never have to see him again after this day.

"But Tahiti! Sasha, you can't do this," Mason protested. "Your government won't let you do this. They're going to want you back in Sydney. And she expects your crew to sail to Tahiti? This is madness!"

Sasha liked feeling Katya press against him. He was done with Mason as well and ready to leave this room forever. The more he thought about his crew sailing to join them, the more he knew it was the right choice. How could his men not like Katya as much as he did? His crew would have been informed he was in the States, that he'd almost been killed, had gone missing again. S-Branch would have brought them all in from leave. He owed them this trip; he owed them so much. He had never been east of New Zealand, never had reason to explore French Polynesia. He saw Katya's postcard in his mind's eye, could visualize the *Trib* as the sailboat in the harbor. He and Katya would still have one more night and day, more than twenty-four hours, in San Francisco together. He hadn't gotten to see the sights in New York, so he would explore this city instead. And he would conquer his refusal to fly, for her.

"Yes, Mason, Tahiti. Bora Bora," he said at last.

"Then you'll still need someone besides Katya to watch your back. I'll send one of my men with you," Mason insisted.

"Never. I have no doubt I'll be well guarded," Sasha growled.

Shaking her head, Katya for once agreed with Mason. "No, let's take him up on his offer. As long as this extra guard watches from far away and leaves us alone."

Katya looked over at the three men on the sofa. Only one of them would possibly do.

"Jake, you haven't said a word to me since I met you, and I appreciate that. You haven't stuck your thumb in my wound or put a gun in my face. I owe you for the beating and humiliation I caused you when I left. If Mason will pay for the ticket and lodgings, you have just won a trip to Bora Bora tomorrow night. But I warn you Mason, it's exceedingly expensive. It's going to cost you," Katya said with a straight face. She couldn't imagine that Mason was charging the hotel suite or anything else to his Interpol account. Hopefully it was his own dirty money. She was happy to deprive him of some more of it.

Jake looked astounded, but nodded his head. Bill and Mason shared a defeated glance.

Sasha picked up his paper bag containing all that he possessed – a worn pair of work boots – and added the jar he'd brought from the Consulate and medical supplies for Katya. If only his beloved violin wasn't in Sydney... if only he knew he could still play her...

"I'm sure your spooks or whoever can figure out our flight information and the name of the resort," Katya continued. "I'm not going to help you there. What Sasha and I are going to do is walk out that door together."

Without another word, Katya and Sasha left the room and did not look back.

Chapter 24

"**I**'m taking you out for sushi!" Katya said, as they reached the lobby. "I have a suitcase here with the bell captain. We'll need to stop by and pick it up later."

"You were so sure I'd come with you?"

"I was going with or without you. I spent all my money on this trip, I emptied my accounts! But since you're coming, we'd better get you a new passport."

"I took care of that at the Consulate already."

"Good! So where are all your Aussie men? I'd like to meet these hunks," Katya asked, looking around.

"Hunks of what?" asked Sasha, puzzled.

"I mean the five men sent to guard you at the hotel."

"I lied. I've been taking lessons from you. The Consulate may have sent someone, I don't know. It wasn't discussed. There were two cars following me in Berkeley, though."

"But what about the listening device?"

"That at least was true. And I have living proof right here." Sasha nodded at a tall, sandy-haired, distinguished looking man of about fifty in an elegant pin-striped gray suit who was walking rapidly in their direction, removing an earpiece.

"Sasha!" he called out loudly. "I thought we were going to lose both of you for a moment! You and Katya could talk your way out of anything!"

"Katya, this is Peter Hammond, our Consul-General for San Francisco, and the man who had my back for many years in Australia." Sasha looked around, then lowered his voice before continuing. "Peter's been Consul-General here for the last two years, since '97. Now that you know about S-Branch, I can tell you Peter was my handler, then liaison between S-Branch and the Prime Minister. I couldn't have asked for a better mate," Sasha said, his Australian accent reasserting itself. "Peter, you're the only handler I ever liked!"

"My very great pleasure," Peter boomed out in his even stronger Aussie twang, grabbing her hand. "Please call me Peter. One never leaves S-Branch, much as I tried! My country and I owe you a tremendous debt of gratitude. You have no idea how important a man Sasha is to us."

"Thank you, Peter. It's a pleasure to meet you. But I *do* know how valuable Sasha is. I'm afraid I know most of his secrets now. I assure you both his secrets and his person could not be in safer hands."

"Well! You have proven yourself again and again. Tough and clever. And a real Scheherazade! I enjoyed listening to your wild stories, but I think I like the real Katya even better. Sasha, you didn't tell me your Katya was as beautiful as she is intelligent."

"I thank you again for the compliment, Peter. We are off to our first dinner in a restaurant together, then I want to show him San Francisco before we leave. We're coming back here for my suitcase, but I need a recommendation for a place to stay tonight, far from this hotel."

"Please let me be your guide! I have a limo and driver waiting outside. Go get your suitcase and we'll give Sasha a personal tour tonight and all day tomorrow. I insist you two be my guests at the Consulate tonight. We'll drop you off at a great sushi place I know, then pick you up afterwards. Leave your bags in the car. Sasha, is that all you have? And there is something more. I found the seats you booked, in coach. I'm calling the airlines and upgrading you both to first class. If Sasha is going to fly for the first time on such a long flight, I don't want the experience in coach to terrorize him! He would never fly again!" The Consul-General laughed loudly.

"We cannot thank you enough. That is amazingly kind and generous." Katya remembered that Peter had been listening to them through Sasha's tracker. He'd had a way to instantly look up her airline booking. That meant he'd heard everything Sasha had learned about her in Berkeley and trusted her. "Maybe I can get him to sleep the entire flight and he won't even notice he's in the air."

The Consul-General laughed again. The suitcase was recovered, and they moved out into the cool, damp late afternoon air to Peter's limo. Katya noted four men following close behind them. Four security personnel, not the five Sasha had made up, she mused. Not much of an exaggeration. Sasha's government wasn't taking any chances on losing him again. A second car and driver waited behind theirs; the four men piled in. Peter turned to speak to Katya as they took off.

"You can't begin to imagine how relieved I was when Sasha showed up at the Consulate yesterday. He hadn't slipped his leash like that in decades, disappearing to New York, of all places! The call from Interpol came in first – S-Branch didn't believe them. Since he's never flown, someone thought to check security tapes at the freighter docks, and recognized him under a black watch cap, just as an all-too-casual phone call came in from my Consulate that a Sasha Borodin was in town and looking for me. Taken by a Cutter! Three days in a dark van! You'd be a dead man, Sasha, chopped up alive for chum to be eaten by seagulls, except for your Katya here!

"Then my horror when he described what he'd been up to since you rescued him. We had no idea this Allen Lane, or Mason as you call him, was going to raid Cutter's compound and we sure as hell wouldn't have thought Sasha would be part of it. We thought Sasha was in safe hands with Interpol and then we heard nothing for two days. I'd rushed back from Sydney with four guards in tow, and everyone was breathing down my neck. Since I was based in San Francisco, S-Branch put me back in charge of him. Listening device and tracker or no, I didn't want to let Sasha out of my sight when he showed up at the Consulate. But I bet you know already how immensely stubborn he can be. He just had to know, well..."

"Who I was?" Katya finished his thought. "What Mason was really up to? One answer out of two isn't bad. He joined the raid to make sure I survived, and for that I'm thankful."

"I think I've counted four times now you've kept him alive for us, five if you count Mason's threat just now. I was terrified we'd lose him right there in the St. Francis, shot right after you, Katya!"

"You know I put my life on the line constantly, Peter," Sasha said quietly.

"Just not on my watch lately! For two blessed years I haven't had to worry about you getting yourself killed. The PM gave me this peaceful, cushy job in thanks for putting up with you for a decade. I've been enjoying marketing your Australogic products instead. I'm trying to say, I'm glad you're alive and I think you're going to enjoy the peace and safety of Tahiti. You both deserve it. Your crew will love it too."

Sasha knew Peter and S-Branch too well to think there wouldn't be numerous safeguards put in place on Bora Bora. Peter's reference to Sasha's leash was a long-standing joke of his. Sasha knew Peter had no idea how much it always galled him to have it be a joke. Sasha had since begun to refer in his own mind to his tracker and listening device as his leash and collar, but they stood for much more. He'd been under his government's tight control almost continuously since he was seventeen, his adoptive father's before that. As he'd once been under the even tighter control of the Nazi monster Krüger as a small child. With a real leash and collar.

He was surprised Peter hadn't raised a dozen objections to the trip. He would surely have been yanked back to Sydney but for Katya. Jake and Katya would have already been thoroughly vetted. Whatever Mason had been up to, Jake wasn't a part of it. Maybe, just maybe, Peter liked what he'd learned about Katya and in so quickly getting S-Branch's permission to allow their trip to Tahiti, was placing Sasha's interests ahead of his country's. Peter had always supported him. Sasha had few friends outside his crew, but he considered Peter foremost among them. He stayed quiet and let Peter get to know the "real" Katya.

"Peter, I'm hoping you can do one more thing for us," Katya said, turning on her charm. "I would very much like Sasha to hear our symphony orchestra tonight, especially the last piece on the program. Would it be possible for you to get us two tickets?"

"Absolutely! We'll drop you off at Davies Hall after dinner, then we'll pick you up afterwards and see the city by night. I have fond memories of escorting Sasha to concerts at the Sydney Opera House. We'd attend almost every one each July he was in town."

"Please give me your number so I can call you when we're ready. We may be a while after the performance," Katya said, already forgetting Sasha's tracker.

"I'm not a man who goes to bed early, not in this fabulous city! But you won't need to call. I'm afraid we'll be listening in and we'll know when it's time."

"Peter, you can imagine what information Markus Cutter had on Sasha," Katya began, unsure how to ask. "I'm still trying to process it all. My question is, *why* is Sasha kept a secret from the world? Why did he have to risk his life to achieve some alone time, to speak at that conference in New York? You listen in to his life with an audio tracker, like now, he gets no acknowledgement of anything he does. Sasha, is this how you want to continue to live your life?"

Sasha remained quiet. He looked out the limo window, giving Peter free rein to answer for him. Katya's understanding of him was uncanny. He could barely admit to himself how unhappy he'd been with the status quo for a long time. It was unclear in his own mind why he could never break away, be his own man.

"I'll put this as bluntly as I can, Katya," Peter answered, looking uncomfortable. "Publicity would destroy who he is. This is the way Sasha has lived most of his life. We try to keep him safe, allow him his freedom with his medical boat, give him the space he needs to create. His crew members know about his genius, his work for Australogic, but they're fiercely loyal to him, not to the Australian government. They follow his lead, no matter where it takes them. We hate that his work hunting traffickers has made him enemies like Markus Cutter, puts him in danger. Look what nearly happened to him! If not for you…"

"But some of his inventions, especially the prostheses and neural implants – that miniscule computer he implants in the brain! Surely you could let him take credit for those."

"Katya, I don't think you grasp how difficult it would be for Sasha to live in society if the true extent of his genius was known, even without enemies. You have no idea what stunning masterpieces his prostheses are. They're at least forty years ahead of the rest of science! Someone would snoop further, discover what a genius he is – an incomparable genius! He would be famous, overwhelmed by the media. Since, miraculously I might say, you can have physical contact with him, you must not know he has haphephobia."

"I do know, and what of it?"

"He told you? Do you know what happens if he has a severe attack?"

"Peter, don't," Sasha pleaded. He sank a little lower in his seat. He felt enough of a freak already. He'd wanted as much normalcy in his relationship with Katya as possible, and now Peter wanted to lay all the sordid details on the table.

"All right, Sasha. But she'll have to know sometime if she's going to be your minder. What about your deep depressions, your silent spells. Followed by your manic obsessiveness! I could never keep up with your changing moods! What about your fits, when you have to play the violin to quell some horrendous vision?"

"I know about those too, and they are hardly fits," Katya replied. She could sense Sasha seething beside her. "It sounds like you don't even know what's going on in his head when those happen. And you are never to call me his 'minder,' ever. That's not what we are to each other."

"I must say I'm impressed with how well you've gotten to know him in just a few days, how much he's told you. And now we at S-Branch know a bit of his history at the camp – he's never said a word about what he went through. And that Gypsy story! Playing for Shostakovich! But the answer is, Sasha's abilities must stay unknown to the world at large for his own sake. Enjoy your time together here in San Francisco, enjoy Bora Bora. Keep him safe. Then we'll see what happens next."

Katya abruptly changed the subject. Sasha was still angry. She noted how Sasha had recoiled at the word "Gypsy." He'd called them Roma. She asked Peter questions about his job as Consul-General the rest of the way and the tension lifted. Sasha appeared to be enjoying the conversation by the time they arrived. His rapid mood swings and deeply depressive episodes were going to be as interesting to deal with as his haphephobia, she mused. He'd seemed fairly even-keeled to her these last few days. Subdued. When he wasn't threatening to kill Mason and his men... ah yes, or recalling the past. He also seemed to look younger since his visit to the Consulate, the skin on his face and hands smoother.

At the restaurant, Sasha and Katya chose to sit at the counter to watch the master sushi chef prepare their dishes. Katya noted how Sasha ate well, but methodically and unenthusiastically.

"Thank you for choosing sushi," Sasha said. "I don't know what I would have eaten if you'd picked a steak house. The potato and a salad, I guess."

"I noticed you didn't eat meat. But you eat seafood. A vegetarian who eats fish."

"I'm a pescatarian. If I was a vegetarian, I wouldn't eat fish either. That's what nearly forty years of living on boats will do for you." Sasha didn't add that he'd refused to eat meat as long as he could remember, even as a child in Sydney, and at the displaced persons camp, that he didn't know why. Yet another repressed memory.

144

"A new word for me, thank you. I'm a pescatarian, too, just didn't have the right name for it. We'll find plenty of meatless choices here!" Katya was glad she hadn't asked for bacon with the St. Francis breakfast or a meat dish for dinner. Now she remembered that Mason and his men hadn't either. Could no one even eat meat in his presence? She would be whatever Sasha needed her to be.

The sushi was the best Katya had ever tasted, and the most expensive. She laughed to herself that she would be out of money before they even arrived in Tahiti. The small resort was all-inclusive, but there were always additional costs. She couldn't help herself and chatted amicably with the chef in Japanese, with Sasha joining in. She wasn't surprised that Sasha's Japanese was as good as hers. She laughed off the chef's question about her ancestry. He'd assumed she was part Japanese and seemed unconvinced when she told him she was part Chinese instead.

"This is one of the ways I've been practicing my language skills over the years," she told Sasha. "There are restaurants of every ethnicity in the Bay Area. I can order and at least greet people in fifteen languages in addition to the ones I speak. I know, it hardly compares to your knowledge of languages, but it's pretty good for a mere mortal."

"I'll try not to be offended by that," Sasha replied. "I've felt as mortal as one gets this past week. How is your arm feeling? You haven't mentioned it once."

"Your painkillers are doing a good job. The pain is down to a dull roar. I don't talk about it because there's no point."

"Please tell me if it gets worse. You know, Katya, I can't remember the last time I ate in a restaurant with just one other person. It does make me feel like a mere mortal. I think I may be experiencing something you mortals call pleasure."

"Sasha, listen to yourself. You may be experiencing something like a sense of humor. I can tell I'm being a very bad influence on you."

"Please don't stop. I like this influence very much," Sasha replied with his near smile. "You must have had other ways to practice your language skills, Katya. Did you travel much?" Sasha thought with regret how much his refusal to fly had limited his own travel options. He didn't have a flight phobia. He'd just been stubborn, claimed he preferred boats.

145

"Berkeley is an international campus. I converse regularly with friends in all the languages I speak. I started out with three since childhood, plus Japanese with Fujio and Umi, took every language offered at my high school. I've been taking language courses at the University for over a decade, used their language labs. My father and I traveled together every summer and holiday since I was a child. We covered most of North and South America, lots of trips to Hawaii, then Israel and Jordan when I was thirteen, after my bat mitzvah, two-month-long grand tours of Europe after high school and college graduations, the three big game parks in Tanzania, the Soviet Union before the fall of Communism.

"My father encouraged me to speak with the locals, seemed to love watching me interact. My mother never left Berkeley. My grandmother didn't want to travel. I kept planning trips to China and Southeast Asia with her, but she would make excuses, and then my involvement with Guatemala happened, filling up my summers, and we ran out of time. She was vehemently opposed to my relationship with Paulo and the village, thought she'd lose me forever, and then I lost her, lost everything."

"I'm very sorry, Katya. I would have liked to have met your grandmother."

"Jiang Mai Zhang Hartman. She was fierce, let me tell you, but loving. Made me study hard, got me to all my music and voice lessons, martial arts classes, soccer games, made sure I practiced. A Tiger Grandmother to be sure. Grandmother spoke only Mandarin or Vietnamese with me, although her English was excellent. She was reticent about her life in China, would only say that my grandfather had saved her life. Nothing ever about her career as a doctor. She never traveled farther than to visit her women friends in San Francisco but seemed satisfied with her life in Berkeley. You would have liked my parents, too, although they were polar opposites. Since you talked with Professor Takahashi, you know that my father, Gabriel, was a mathematician, a kind and generous man who enjoyed life to the fullest, an avid sailor. My mother was equally brilliant, but humorless and always distracted. I didn't see that much of her... Nothing mattered but her work."

"I know she worked in physics and then nanotechnology. What name did she use?" Sasha asked.

146

"Mai Zhang. Never used a middle name, nor my father's last name, Kaplan, nor her father's name, Hartmann, just her mother's name, although that seemed to anger my grandmother, I don't know why. They didn't get along, to put it mildly... My mother was quite the researcher."

"I do know her research, Katya. Mai Zhang made some very important early discoveries in the field."

Sasha found himself enjoying talking with this young woman more and more. Katya had come from a remarkably intellectual and capable family. Now would have been the time to talk about Harrison and Maddy, but all he could think about was the sad fact that he knew nothing of his own birth family, nothing of what had become of his son. Not a day went by when he didn't think about him, wonder why he couldn't find him, despite his good relations with the Vietnamese government. Sasha decided some personal   secrets would remain unspoken. He had already revealed more to her than to anyone in his life, including Le. Katya's life was now an open book. Unfortunately, that also meant S-Branch had heard everything he'd told her since his trip to the Consulate, as Peter pointed out... But there was one question still nagging at his brain's logic centers.

"Katya, New York is such a big city. How did we manage to cross paths twice if you weren't sent to protect me?"

"I really don't know. I was so surprised to see you again. I must admit I was quite taken with you at the Global Human Rights Conference. I'm usually a late sleeper but that morning I woke up at dawn, couldn't get back to sleep, and eventually started a run, fast walking at times."

Dawn, Sasha repeated in his head. Katya had awakened around the same time he woke up to exercise. He mulled over the thought then dismissed the idea of a connection. Things like that just weren't possible.

"Where were you staying?" he asked.

"I wanted some open scenery and fresh air, so I found a place overlooking the North Cove Yacht Harbor, not too far from a subway station. I told you my dad loved to sail. He and I used to go sailing often with a good friend who kept a sailboat on the bay, and I love the sound of halyards clanking on the masts. You won't believe this, but I thought I also heard the faint sound of a violin late Friday night as I

147

was unpacking. I'll have to ask Peter if he can get my suitcase collected, if it's still there. I'd forgotten all about it."

More strange twists of fate, Sasha thought. Maybe, just maybe, the connection he imagined with her was more real than he could logically understand.

"But there you were on the bench across from the van," he said, still unwilling to believe.

"I spied the men in the van on my run and they worried me, so I waited around. When I saw you, I was even more concerned someone might be after you, because of your speech."

Sasha nodded, but his brain was reeling from the many coincidences. Derek had helped him find a rental boat to sleep on in that harbor because it was less than a half-hour's walk from his small apartment. Could it really be just a question of fate that he was alive because of her decisions to travel to New York, to go for a run at that particular time and on that particular route? That they had arrived in the same city on the same day, and were staying so close to each other, so close she could hear his violin? That he was experiencing such a strange emotional and, dare he say, psychic connection to this fascinating young woman who could touch him, who wanted to be with him, who had used all the money she had to arrange this trip to Bora Bora with him? He hesitated sharing his discovery with her, then decided he must. He didn't have any answers, but it was time to stop questioning and to just pretend that Fate, if it existed, was for once being inexplicably kind.

Presented with the check, Katya was afraid to look at it. She was surprised and relieved to see that the bill had been paid by Peter. She thanked him again profusely as they were whisked over to Davies Hall. Their seats were in the ninth row, center section, and Katya gave Sasha the aisle seat so he could avoid accidental contact. They waited until the row was filled to sit down. To further protect him, she stood talking with him until nearly everyone had taken their seats. Sasha kept his leather jacket on; he'd never felt such self-consciousness about his appearance before. His new shirt was wrinkled and sweated through.

"Peter found us amazing seats. This performance was supposed to be sold out. I wonder if he gave us his own tickets. The Symphony season hasn't started – this is a special fundraising concert, and exceedingly expensive. I usually sit in the nosebleed section."

"Where?"

"The much cheaper seats at the very back of the top balcony."

"Why would your nose bleed at the symphony?"

"Because the seats are up so high – oh never mind," Katya said, smiling at him. Had Sasha really been this literal all the time when he was younger? "Look at your program. I just had to bring you here when I heard what they were performing."

The first half of the program included Britton's Four Sea Interludes and Prokofiev's Symphony Number Five, two of his favorite pieces. The second half was Dmitri Shostakovich's Violin Concerto Number One, featuring Itzhak Perlman as soloist. Another inexplicable twist of fate, Sasha thought. Sasha placed his hand over hers and wished he was capable of showing her just how much this meant to him.

The performances were nothing less than stellar. Sasha hadn't attended a symphony performance in over two years and he'd never heard the entire Shostakovich concerto live. Perlman gave the audience an exquisite encore, "Variations on a Theme by Corelli" by Fritz Kreisler. Both Sasha and Katya felt themselves transported back to the world of music they both belonged to and had sorely missed this past week.

When the symphony was over, Katya took Sasha by the hand and practically pulled him – carefully through gaps in the departing crowd – out the door, and around to the musician's entrance at the opposite side of the building. She gave her name to the laid-back guard, signed in, and accepted the two visitor stickers. They entered a back hallway, lined with framed, autographed photographs of musical celebrities. She stopped by a group of three symphony players still holding their violins while they laughed and chatted.

"Vladimir! Wonderful performances, everyone! This is my friend I called you about who has been separated from his violin by a nasty quirk of fate. Thank you for agreeing to meet with us. This is Sasha. Sasha, Vladimir. Vladimir often plays with my chamber group."

Sasha gave a short bow and the two men discussed the evening's music and Vladimir's violin in Russian for several minutes, Katya joining in at times. She marveled at his command of Russian, as fluent as his Japanese. Then Vladimir held out his violin to Sasha. It was the oldest violin in play in the orchestra, Vladimir told him. Katya knew

149

it to be a fine and prized instrument, belonging to the conductor, who insisted that Vladimir play it instead of his own far inferior instrument.

Sasha was surprised, then overwhelmed. Without a thought to his worn and wrinkled shirt, he took off his leather jacket and handed it to Katya before he reached for the instrument. He held the violin carefully in front of him, examining it, fearing yet again that his fingers would not be able to play. After some hesitation, he adjusted the bow, checked the tuning, lifted the violin to his shoulder, and began playing.

The moment was sheer magic. Sasha launched directly into the rhapsodic opening measures of the Barber concerto, then moved on to most of the Chaconne from Bach's Partita Number Two, then the first cadenza from the Beethoven concerto, a solo segment of the Prokofiev's second violin concerto, then moments from the glorious Brahms and the Sibelius violin concertos, followed by the first movement of the Shostakovich that Perlman had just performed. Katya stood back, transported, the room dissolving around her. She found Sasha's tone sumptuous, his playing masterful. The sound was pure, powerful and full of passion, the most brilliant playing Katya had ever heard, furious but perfectly controlled, bold, completely unsentimental. Then Sasha stole a quick glance at Katya and played the violin line of her own composition. He lowered the violin and gave a deep sigh of relief and joy. Vladimir and the two other violinists were stunned. A small crowd of curious departing musicians had formed around them. Katya had stopped two musicians from recording or taking pictures with their cell phones while Sasha played.

A single pair of hands began clapping from somewhere behind them. Katya and Sasha turned to see Itzhak Perlman himself, still applauding, seated on a chair, his two special crutches laying on the floor. Next to him stood the conductor, beaming.

"Bravo! Vladimir, won't you introduce us?" the maestro asked.

"Maestro, Mr. Perlman, this is Sasha, a friend of Kat Kaplan's? You remember she played one of the mandolins in Prokofiev's *Romeo and Juliet* last year? And guitar before that? She runs First Tuesdays in Berkeley, plays piano and harpsichord? Played piano in the Shostakovich Quintet with me for one of the Symphony's chamber concerts?"

"I do remember you, Ms. Kaplan," said the maestro. "But you look very different from what I recall. I would have hardly recognized you tonight. And that is a stunningly beautiful jacket, may I say."

"We are astounded by your playing, Sasha. You are truly a virtuoso. Where are you visiting from?" queried Mr. Perlman.

"It is a great honor to meet you both," Sasha answered, bowing. "Mr. Perlman, I have long been an admirer. I'm on my way back to Australia via a stay in Bora Bora, Tahiti. My violin has tragically managed to get home before me. Kat surprised me by finding a violin for me to play. This is a superb instrument," he said, as he reluctantly returned the violin and bow to Vladimir.

"Do you concertize outside of Australia?" asked the maestro.

"I have never performed publicly."

"But why?" asked Mr. Perlman. "You have an amazing gift to share."

"I am a very private person. And alas, I have a full-time profession and am more than a bit of an eccentric. But music has always been my passion. I have a group I play chamber music with just about daily, all strings."

"What was that last piece you played? Was it a Prokofiev student work?" Mr. Perlman asked.

"That was the first pages of a contemporary sonata for violin and piano, a sort of thank you to the composer," Sasha answered, giving Katya his near smile.

"I enjoyed your interpretation of the Shostakovich. Much more melancholy than mine," Mr. Perlman said, sitting forward eagerly on his chair.

"That is how Dmitri asked me to play it. I played that movement for him in his apartment five months before Oistrakh was finally able to give its premier in Leningrad. I have not played it since."

"But that was in 1955! You don't look old enough!" exclaimed Mr. Perlman. "And you remembered every note!"

"I just heard you play it. And I was an eccentric child prodigy, an extremely stubborn one."

Everyone laughed, especially Katya. She liked this version of his story. She would never have thought he could be so imaginative.

"You must be the 'mysterious Sasha' I've read about!" Vladimir exclaimed, amazed. "Maestro, Dmitri Shostakovich wrote 'for my mysterious Sasha' across the top of his personal copy of his concerto!"

No one in the orchestra was more of a Shostakovich scholar than Vladimir. Katya could hardly believe what she was hearing. Sasha's wild tales of his time in Europe could all be true.

"I confess. But other than learning it is indeed my name on the concerto score, you will not be solving the mystery of who I really am. I've taken up enough of your valuable time. Kat and I must take our leave. This has been an extraordinary experience. This week has been both horrific and wonderful for me. I've had much time to contemplate and reevaluate my life, to think about my past and what I might have done differently. For one, I deeply regret never having played a concerto with an orchestra, despite several opportunities. Mr. Perlman, thank you for your inspiring work. Maestro, you have a truly fine orchestra. I hope to hear them perform again. I think I may have found a second home here in the Bay Area and I look forward to returning someday."

Sasha gave another short bow to each of them and reached to take his leather jacket from Katya. She was excited by his suggestion of wanting to return. Could he really envision spending a part of each year as a guest in her home? Mr. Perlman leaned in to talk to the maestro, who bent over to listen, nodding his head.

"Sasha," the maestro called out, "Mr. Perlman has given me an intriguing idea. If you give us some way to contact you, I may have a way of fulfilling that desire. I could arrange to have you stand in for the soloist at a special rehearsal of a concerto, before the performance date. We could decide when and what between us, according to your travel schedule. There would be no audience, no outsiders if you so wished."

Sasha was astonished. His world really was changing rapidly.

"Maestro, Mr. Perlman, thank you. That is an exceedingly generous offer that I could not possibly refuse. I hope we can make this possible. You can contact Peter Hammond, the Australian Consul-General. He will be here shortly to pick us up. He's giving us a tour of the city and we'll be staying at the Consulate tonight."

"I know Peter well! We're going to have a very interesting conversation about you," the maestro said with a smile.

"Maestro, Mr. Perlman, I thank you from the bottom of my heart as well on behalf of Sasha," Katya added. "The first live concert I remember my father taking me to was one of your solo recitals, Mr.

Perlman. I can always tell when you are the soloist when I listen to the radio. You have inspired my music-making all my life."

Mr. Perlman gave a deep nod to her in response.

"If you don't mind my asking, Sasha, Ms. Kaplan, how did you two meet?" asked the maestro.

"It was pure chance. Ms. Kaplan was there at the right time to help a stranger in need," Sasha answered.

"It was Fate," countered Katya.

Chapter 25

Peter Hammond was all smiles in the limo. There was an additional man in the front seat next to the driver, but Peter didn't introduce him. The new man had the unmistakable look of a security guard, a communication device in one ear. Katya noted the same car following them as well. Katya and Sasha had no idea where Peter might take them first. They were still excited by the music and anything but tired.

"Well played, Sasha, in every sense of the word!" Peter said with another booming laugh. "You said just enough to carry some truth but didn't give them any clue who you are."

"He's had a lot of practice with me." Katya was also smiling.

"I'm about done playing our government's games, Peter," Sasha growled in a surprisingly angry tone. "It's time for me to be honest about who I am, what I do."

Katya wondered why Sasha felt so emboldened. It must have been the frustration of having to remain a cipher back in Davies Hall, or maybe he was responding to her questions earlier in the limo.

"There goes any sort of a private life if you do," Peter stated, looking startled. "You will be hounded by reporters and people who want things from you night and day. Not to mention abductors and vengeful criminals who will know where to find you at any time."

"I don't have to reveal all my secrets to the world. I want my name back. I want a public persona. Why can't I publicly be Dr. Sasha Borodin, physician and surgeon, again? My work with robotics and prosthetics alone sounds like a full-time profession. I could rejoin the University Prosthetics Department. If I can get myself on that flight tomorrow, I will be able to fly the world demonstrating my medical inventions, training surgeons and neuroscientists, helping thousands of people regain eyesight, use of hands, mobility."

"Making the blind see, the lame walk."

"Don't be facetious, Peter, and don't be blasphemous. I know I'm not God. I'm completely serious about taking back my identity. The government can't stop me. My medical degree is part of the public record. I was well known at the University of Sydney. I just need to pick up where I left off."

"That was thirty-five years ago!" Peter pointed out, sounding even more alarmed.

"I was a legend. Legends don't die. There will be plenty of people who remember me."

"You weren't exactly popular, as I recall."

"I admit I was a more than a bit conceited then. The University is brimming with surgeons who are full of themselves, who are unpopular like I was. If S-Branch can't come up with a backstory to cover my last thirty-five years, I certainly can. I'm not the only veteran who got lost in the Vietnam War. My floating free clinic and surgery are known throughout Southeast Asia; we can build on that. I want to come back to the University, part time, of course. I would still live on the *Trib* most of the year."

Peter shook his head. "You would put yourself in danger, the rest of your work in other fields in jeopardy. Too many people would start asking questions. And what about your memory attacks, your phobias, Sasha! You'd be overwhelmed. Your level of genius is just not comprehensible to the world at large. You can never tell anyone the prostheses are your developments. And now the Americans have Markus Cutter's entire file on you. S-Branch has no idea where that's going to lead, but no place good."

"Oh God, Peter, I never had a chance to tell anyone," Katya called out. "I purposefully started the alphabetical data dump with the letter C so Sasha's file would be destroyed if it was under either Alexander or Borodin. Since you were listening in already, you know the data dump ended long before S for Sasha, too. The Americans have nothing."

Peter looked ecstatic. "You, Katya, are amazing! I could just kiss you!"

"Tempting as that is, I'll pass. And I think Sasha is completely within his rights. He is not your government's property. He is going to be Dr. Sasha Borodin, vacationing surgeon, on our trip tomorrow and he'll continue doing his laboratory work in secret only as long as he wants to. This is Sasha's choice to make, not yours, not your government's. Your job is to tell us what wonderful San Francisco sight Sasha is about to see."

Katya took Sasha's hand in hers and was gratified by his look of appreciation for her support. Sasha was absolutely right. He should have made such a decisive change years ago.

Peter sighed. "I can see a compromise, but S-Branch will have to authorize it. We can get you reinstated at the University of Sydney, but your inventions, including the prostheses and brain implants, are going to have to remain the intellectual property of Australogic Laboratories. You will be a neurosurgeon who, shall I say, 'installs' them. Sorry, I have no idea what the medical term would be. That's the best I can do."

There was no comment from Sasha, but Katya was sure he was far from satisfied. She didn't understand why he let this S-Branch control so much of his life. Since he was seventeen. But then again, maybe that explained it. He'd been convinced from an early age that they had his best interests at heart. Maybe he really was much more vulnerable than she'd thought. Maybe this vulnerability reached back to his childhood, to that sick, controlling SS officer, to life in a concentration camp... She didn't want to think how his history of physical abuse, of torment, he had called it, had affected his life choices. He was a concentration camp survivor. That would always be who he was.

Peter's first stop was Coit Tower. The driver and the additional guard accompanied them inside. The other car full of security remained parked outside. Peter had arranged a private visit at night, and they were able to admire the murals and the view from the top by themselves. The next hour was spent driving to several high points in the compact city, viewing the bay and the lights of the bridges and city from many angles.

When they arrived at the Consulate around one in the morning, Sasha worked with the Sydney lab for an hour using the Consulate's secure network while Katya filled up on painkillers and rested. Then they were shown to two adjoining rooms, each with a private bathroom. They both already knew they would be needing just one room, although nothing was said. Katya was amused to see Sasha, looking rather embarrassed, emerge from the bathroom in the fine silk-like bamboo fiber pajamas that Peter had handed him. His hair was still damp from a shower. She'd slipped into her modest nightgown.

Sasha didn't confess that he'd never worn pajamas since his youth in Sydney, that he always slept nude. Katya didn't confess she usually slept in her underpants and a ragged t-shirt. That night they again chastely tucked up against each other's bodies, Katya's hand gently massaging Sasha's chest under his pajama top, each thinking how they had not slept apart in the seven nights they had known each other.

Morning brought a light breakfast served in the room and more painkillers for Katya. Sasha had discovered all of his clothes neatly folded on a chair, freshly laundered. He'd managed to exercise at dawn in the room and shower before Katya awoke. She was surprised to find Sasha had made the bed while she took her turn in the shower. Peter showed them around the Consulate before hustling the two of them into his limo for a quick tour through the Palace of the Legion of Honor art museum and a walk starting above the old Sutro Baths along the Land's End trail for the splendid ocean views, the same guards following behind them.

At noon they stopped for the best dim sum Katya could remember. She had to remind herself not to order pork buns. She knew Sasha wouldn't see what was inside the bun, but she was determined to stay pescatarian; she was really going to miss eating pork buns. She noted that Peter didn't order any meat dishes either. He laughed that he was missing his favorite crispy duck. Sasha acted like he hadn't understood him. They headed on to Golden Gate Park, strolling through the Japanese Tea Garden, the de Young Museum, and its neighbor the Asian Arts Museum, and across to the California Academy of Science where Sasha could not get past the Steinhart Aquarium. He grew more and more animated as they explored.

"Scuba diving is another passion of mine," Sasha told her, as they wandered through the colorful displays of fish. "I have reinvented the science of scuba three times over the course of the years, and I regularly discover and report new species, publishing under another name, S. Alexander."

Of course you have, thought Katya. Why am I not surprised? She had to laugh to herself at his total lack of humility. In his mind, he was just stating a fact. His genius was going to take some getting used to. Katya envisioned herself learning to dive with him in Bora Bora if her arm healed quickly. Then Katya asked that they be taken shopping so Peter could buy Sasha some appropriate clothes and supplies for the trip, including a small duffel. She knew he had nothing but the clothes he was wearing and that original pair of old work boots he was so attached to; he seemed grateful for the opportunity to purchase what he needed. Katya bought a few items for herself, keeping careful track of her dwindling cash.

"Don't forget swim trunks and some sort of beach shoes, Sasha. The resort I chose has no stores, just laid-back French Polynesian style. We'll have our own villa on its own cove, completely private. Bora Bora as it was a hundred years ago, far from the big resorts and cruise ships."

"You must let us reimburse you for the resort," Peter said.

"You can pay me back only if I lose my new job as Sasha's bodyguard and anti-publicist. I hope I caught all the musicians who were trying to take photos and videos last night. Maybe with Sasha's new declaration of emancipation, once he comes out as Dr. Borodin and has a job at the University of Sydney, I won't have to worry so much about publicity."

"Oh no, Katya, we still won't want publicity of any kind," Peter warned. "Keep watching out for cell phone cameras, please. I'm sending guards along on this trip to assist you and Jake, although I can't think of a more isolated, safe location than Bora Bora!"

"Of course we'll be safe in Bora Bora," Sasha growled. "Jake and Katya will be security enough. You send any of these men following us and I'll create a scene at the airport. I'll claim they're terrorists."

"You wouldn't!" Peter blanched. "Katya, tell me he's joking!"

Katya looked closely at Sasha's poker face and caught his near smile as Peter spun away from them to get control of himself.

"You know Sasha doesn't have a sense of humor, Peter."

Peter turned back to Sasha, his face carefully composed.

"All right, Sasha. You win this time. I'll call and cancel their reservations."

Peter's quick acceptance didn't fool Sasha. He knew his victory would be small and short-lived, but it felt good in the moment. His developing sense of humor was proving to be useful.

Katya insisted on one more stop. They had time for just a quick stroll through the Museum of Modern Art. Sasha enjoyed some of the artwork, especially the Impressionist collection, but declared the most abstract pieces beyond his understanding or caring. They crossed the busy street to walk around Yerba Buena Gardens, Peter and the guards trailing at a respectful distance. Katya knew Sasha would appreciate the Martin Luther King, Jr. Memorial with its thundering waterfall.

She watched Sasha's face as they walked under the waterfall and read the quotes and viewed the photo displays, listening to the roar and feeling the cool spray. The moving tribute seemed to have triggered something in him. His hair was wet, but apparently not from the spray, and he seemed to be in a deeply reflective space. He remained standing before a photo, his face growing increasingly anguished. Katya put a hand on his shoulder and found it damp through his shirt. She looked at Peter, but he just held up a hand in a stop and wait gesture, then moved back and took a seat on a bench outside the falls. People were beginning to stare at Sasha as they walked around him. It was a very long time before he turned to her.

"It's a list in my head," he said quietly. "I can't stop it once it starts. Maybe I can explain it to you some day, but not now... I can't talk about it now."

Katya imagined this was something to do with his experiences at Bergen-Belsen and decided to let it be. There had to be so much he couldn't talk about.

They returned to the Consulate in time to prepare for departure to the airport. Sasha used most of the time to shower and work with the labs. Katya used his absence as an opportunity to talk with Peter alone.

"If you haven't done so already, could you please give Sasha a good amount of cash for the trip? My funds are barely going to last and besides, he may get tired of being a kept man."

"You are droll, aren't you? Thank you for bringing that up. I will be sure to do so."

"And while we're talking about money, I don't understand why Sasha has never participated in any profit sharing with Australogic Laboratories. Or been paid a salary, for that matter. Australogic – could S-Branch have thought of a more purposely forgettable name? I don't know how much a captain makes, but it can't be much. With a valuation of fifty-eight billion, his laboratories could actually pay him what he's worth. Maybe quite a bit of back pay as well."

"How do you know this? You can't know this!" Peter sputtered.

"Markus Cutter's people hacked into S-Branch's information records. It was all there for me to read in Sasha's file. There's little I don't know."

"Well. I guess we'll just have to kill you then," Peter said, but now he was smiling.

"Ha. Get in line behind Mason and the CIA. Be serious, Peter, because I sure am. Maybe Sasha would like to invest in some of his

160

own products that the laboratories couldn't sell because only poor people would profit."

"You *are* a bit of a leftist revolutionary, aren't you Katya?"

"No, just a Berkeley Socialist."

"It may interest you to know that your fellow Socialist friend Sasha insisted he didn't want anything more than his captain's salary. He thought S-Branch providing free prostheses for the poorest recipients, outfitting his boat with everything high-tech and paying his men was enough. We always gave him what he asked for."

"So you make billions from the laboratories and you outfit the boat he designed with the high-tech gadgets and weaponry he invents and tests for you, which you then sell on at great profit, sharing none with him."

"You make a very good point, Katya," Peter sighed. S-Branch didn't know what they were in for with this woman in the picture. A whole new ball game, the Americans would say. Sasha was a different man. Peter decided he liked her. A lot. "I promise to bring it up immediately with S-Branch."

"Sasha wants to make some changes in his life and having a meaningful income will make a big difference."

"You've already made a big difference, Katya. I've never seen Sasha look so... satisfied."

"Wipe that ridiculous grin off your face, Peter. We slept next to each other, but that's all. Your Sasha is still very much who he was, and will remain so." Katya worried that her words were all too true. Sasha seemed reluctant to do more than gently stroke her face or hands. He remained cool, but so appreciative of her touch.

The two moved on to discuss the trip to the airport. Katya told Peter that she had just a whisper of concern that Sasha would not get on the airplane and she wanted to arrive early. Peter took a call, smiled broadly, and said he had one more big surprise for them. He gathered the staff in the main reception hall and sent for Sasha. A S-Branch agent had just arrived from the airport with three items, hand-carried from Sydney: a beat-up duffel, a rectangular violin case, and a laptop computer. Sasha ran across the room to take the violin case from the man's hands.

"We almost missed you!" Peter said. "One more delayed flight and we would have been chasing you on to Tahiti! Sasha, you and your violin are finally reunited. I wanted you to be able to take it with

161

you, and of course your laptop to work with the labs, but I can see you only have eyes for the one. I doubt that I will have to twist your arm to get you to play for us. But I do warn you we have to depart for the airport in less than an hour and you have some repacking to do!"

Sasha needed no coaxing. He eagerly opened the case and stroked the dusky red-brown wood of his Artemisia. His violin was a "she," never an "it" to him. The violin looked old and scuffed, but then only Sasha knew that her sad outward appearance had helped her hide her secret identity as one of the finest and rarest violins in the world. He tenderly picked her up, tuned her strings, adjusted the tension on the bow, rubbed the horsehair with rosin, and began to play. Bach's first violin sonata for solo violin resounded through the Consulate in all its precision and perfection.

Chapter 26

Katya was the first to see Jake at the airport. She'd half hoped Mason would have changed his mind about sending him, maybe be discouraged by the amount of his own money he was going to have to spend. But there Jake stood, small suitcase in hand, looking like another tourist on vacation. Sasha looked surprisingly calm, but Katya took no chances and waited for moments when they could avoid crowds and lines, and they got through security without trouble. Peter had provided him with a diplomatic pass and medical certification of his haphephobia, which helped. Sasha and his carry-ons were waived through, avoiding even the metal detector. Katya wasn't surprised that Sasha had abandoned his newly purchased duffel for his old beat-up one. Their first flight would take them only to Los Angeles, but even this short flight had a first class section.

First class preboarding was a breeze. Katya offered to take the window seat, but Sasha insisted, and looked silently and intently at the view over the summer seared-brown California landscape below them for most of the flight. Finally, he turned to her, a new and eager look on his face.

"Eccentric smart people who are as stubborn as I am miss out on a lot in life. I absolutely love it up here. I'm going to work on getting my pilot's license at the first opportunity."

Katya wished she could kiss him. She had never loved him more. All she could do was take his hand in hers and smile.

The seats in the first class section on the flight to Tahiti were amazingly comfortable and reclined almost flat. Katya had never traveled first class. They settled in for the long haul after a late light dinner. The painkillers were no longer making much of a dent in her discomfort, but she didn't complain. She saw Jake try to peek at them through the curtain separating the first class section from the main cabin. Calling over the flight attendant, she asked that he be warned away. They would have to deal with him soon enough. For now, there was plenty of time to talk and then sleep undisturbed.

As on the flight to Los Angeles, Sasha removed his violin case from the overhead compartment as soon as he was allowed.

"I'm never leaving Artemisia behind again," he told Katya, as he settled the case on his lap.

"Tell me what your day is like on the *Retribution*. Do you call her a boat or a ship?" Katya asked, snuggling against Sasha's shoulder. He became as animated as he'd been at the aquarium as he spoke.

"I've never told you her name. You remember everything from Cutter's file, don't you? We call her the *Trib*. Most people would say ship but we call her a boat, a two-masted sailboat, but with both masts removable, just over thirty meters, 99.7 feet, in length. She has hydrogen-powered motors of my own invention and a special design that make her the fastest boat in the South China Sea. Everything about her is my design. I'll give you a quiet, non-clinic day – no two days are exactly alike for us. We start with exercises and training right at dawn. There are always two men on watch duty in the pilothouse, so those two are excused.

"Chen does most of the food preparation, alternating with Hiro, so one of them will set out breakfast. Both are terrific chefs, you'll love their cooking. Chen and Hiro are also fine doctors! Then there's always work to do cleaning, preparing, putting away. Several of the men will find places to practice their instruments – I might do some mentoring. Lunch and dinner are communal too. Then there's music – solos and duets up to octets, but especially quartets, for whoever's in the mood late into the evening. Wait until you hear my quartet!

"Add to that days when we're in a good location for scuba explorations, snorkeling, or fishing. We accomplish a good deal of scientific oceanic research, checking water temperatures, acidity, and pollution levels, for example. We pull a small trash catcher behind the *Trib* and empty it regularly to determine what needs dealing with. You wouldn't believe the kinds of plastic we find, how microplastics are working their way into every sea. What do people think happens when a plastic item disintegrates! I look for methods to stop the polluting and invent ways to sift out what's already there, and design alternatives to the use of plastic. I spend several hours on the computer daily with all my labs.

"Our clinic runs have us all rushing. Every man of us is a doctor or has extensive medical training. We have a hospital with a state-of-the-art operating theatre, and the main cabin and all the sleeping cabins get turned into clinic spaces. Villagers come from all over when we enter a harbor, all the sails unfurled as a signal, or tie up at a river dock. We might see fifty to ninety, or even hundreds of patients each stop, do everything from baby well checks and inoculations to treating burns and broken bones, and perform not a few major operations. We speed to help out at disease outbreaks and disasters. On those stops we're more like an emergency room."

"But you're a brain surgeon, a neurosurgeon!"

"I do everything at the clinics, from triaging because I speak so many languages, to general medicine and surgery, but you would be surprised by the number of brain and spine tumors, spinal injuries and brain traumas, like subdural hematomas, and birth defects, that our sophisticated equipment picks up. I deal with cerebral aneurysms, blocked arteries, peripheral nerve issues, strokes, sciatica, low-back pain, pinched nerves, epilepsy, and more."

"Do you implant those miraculous computers in people's brains and attach your prosthetic devices on the *Trib* as well?"

"So Markus Cutter knew about those... No, there is much brain mapping and preparation to do before one of those operations, training and physical therapy afterwards. Those operations are done in Sydney or at major hospitals. You've learned that I haven't worked for the Prosthetics Department in Sydney in decades, but I perform the surgeries in five countries in Southeast Asia. I meet potential recipients on board, though, measure and order the prostheses. I quietly pay for the hospitalizations and staff, but Australogic donates the prostheses. I'm proud of the work I do."

Katya enjoyed hearing him speak with such enthusiasm. It was clear to her he loved his life on the *Trib*, his home for around three decades, Katya calculated. She could see how one could be jealous of a boat. She looked forward to meeting the crew. Ten men, seven doctors and three physician assistants, who, like her, had left their former lives behind to follow Sasha, to be a part of his grand mission. It surprised her Sasha didn't talk about his other work, his dangerous missions against human traffickers and criminals.

"How long have Maxim, Dima, Hiro, and Sonthi been with you? They seem to be your oldest mates," Katya asked.

"You know my crew well, too, from Cutter's files! Maxim, Dima, and Hiro are also my primary quartet partners, and with Sonthi, my finest mates. Maxim is German, a general surgeon and my First Mate, or First Officer, as we call him."

Katya stifled the urge to smile every time Sasha said "mite" for mate. She loved his Australian accent. It was going to take some concentration to say "Mahx eem," with the accent on the second syllable, because she was used to the American way, knew several Maxims in Berkeley. This was the German pronunciation. And the Russian. "Sun tee," "Hee rro," and "Dee ma" were easy for her.

"Maxim's been with me since 1984, and Hiro, from Japan, my Chief Communications Officer, joined later that same year. I met Maxim at a Doctors Without Borders event in Indonesia. I had been invited by a former crew member who was then high up in the organization and was always on the lookout for recruits for me. It was love at first sound with Maxim. He was providing a bit of entertainment playing his violin."

"I must admit I was surprised to learn that your First Officer was a German."

"He was born in 1951. I judge a man by what he does. But he speaks English, British English, without a trace of a German accent. Maxim's family found themselves on the East German side of Berlin after the war. His parents tried to be good Communists, but Maxim wanted out. As soon as he finished his general surgery residency, he traveled to Vietnam to work in a hospital, and from there he defected and joined Doctors Without Borders."

"How did you find Hiro?"

"Hiro found me. He was traveling in Thailand, escaping a bad marriage and an orthopedic practice he hated. He heard about me and the *Trib*, came looking for us in the harbor. Only went back to Japan long enough to divorce and pick up his cello. Hiro is my partner when I work on board with patients needing prostheses, and his cello is the heart and soul of my quartet.

"Dima, my Russian construction genius, and Sonthi, a Thai, an infectious and tropical disease specialist, joined the next year. Dima is a superbly trained violist; he was also on the run, escaping some very dangerous choices in the Soviet Union, on the wrong side of what passed for the law there – an anti-government activist. He was lucky the Soviets only broke his nose. Dima was working odd construction jobs and busking with his viola in Manila when I discovered him. He didn't hesitate a moment at my invitation, got his medical training on board. You'll love his Russian accent. He can't seem to lose his accent at all. Sonthi and I met during a typhoid epidemic in his country, on

166

one of the smaller islands. The *Trib* had arrived to help out, and Sonthi left with us, taking nothing but his violin. We bonded over our mutual interest in Buddhism, and music, of course. He's been my spiritual advisor and psychologist, my psychiatrist really, ever since."

"But no one else has stayed with the *Trib* long term?"

"It's not easy to live your life on a boat. I try to find land jobs for anyone ready to move on. With what little money I have, I help fund four refugee and rehabilitation centers, and quite a few of my former crew members work for them. The rest of my crew is fairly young, in their 20s and 30s, and have been with me three to eight years. Their English is excellent. Only my newest crewman, Aashir, a Malaysian, still has a strong accent."

"How much shore leave do they get? We're talking about a lot of men without women here."

Embarrassment colored Sasha's face. How could he tell her the thought had never entered his mind? To him, his crew were soldiers in a war against crime, poverty, and disease.

"What they do on shore leave is their business. They can have it whenever they request it. And our boat is in dry dock in Sydney one month a year, every July, for retrofitting and maintenance. Everyone scatters. I used that opportunity to take one of my freighters to New York, my fateful trip, though I thought no one would find out. Since I have no other home, I often stay with Dima, who has a flat in Sydney, or sleep on a cot at the labs and work almost twenty-four seven that month. And throw the residents of my adoptive parents' old house out long enough to play the piano every day."

"You have another home now, any time you need it, Sasha."

"I look forward to returning."

They talked on for hours, until sleep started to overtake them. Katya leaned in close and spoke into his ear.

"This will make eight nights we've spent together. I've never slept with a man before. I've kept a One Pill unused in my purse for the last ten years. I never knew it was your creation."

Sasha contemplated her meaning. How was it that he had loved only two women in his life and had met both of them as virgins. What he felt for Katya could only be love, he thought, even if he couldn't tell her.

Chapter 27

When Katya awoke, the sky was bright and Sasha was again peering out the window. She bent over him to look and saw the startling green of those long-anticipated jagged volcanic mountains below them. They'd arrived at Papeete. Sasha took advantage of the long wait for the connecting flight to work out in a far corner of the waiting area, ignoring the stares. This time he was free to leap and kick, moving in a much more forceful, but equally graceful, manner. His blond hair, still untrimmed, flew around his face.

Katya stretched too, glad for the chance to move after the long flight, then sat back to watch Sasha, along with everyone else in the waiting room. She'd hoped to keep a low profile on this trip, and here was Sasha making a spectacle of himself, albeit a glorious one. Guarding someone as stubborn, headstrong, and oblivious as Sasha was going to be more of a challenge than she'd thought. At least one of them already felt comfortable, safe, here in Tahiti. She noted Jake watching both of them, his face inscrutable. She was relieved when a much smaller plane arrived to take them on to Bora Bora.

A car was waiting for them at the airport curb, the name of the resort, le Hédonisme, on a sign on the dashboard. The temperature was a perfect eighty-two degrees and not uncomfortably humid, the air fragrant with unseen blossoms. Jake appeared beside them and, nodding a greeting, got into the front seat. The drive to the resort was spectacular, the volcanic mountains and water as beautiful as Katya had imagined. The dirt driveway in to the resort was long and winding, affording views at every turn. They passed a row of twelve identical small villas, packed close together, facing a strip of rocky shore. Katya was glad theirs was a single unit isolated on the other side of the resort, well worth the extraordinary price she'd paid for their privacy.

Upon arrival, their driver, Manahau, introduced them to their hosts, a handsome French couple in their mid-forties, Luc and Sylvie Roussel, who took them on a quick tour of the resort. Both were casually dressed and darkly tanned by the sun. Luc's black hair contrasted with his wife's fair, which she wore loosely swept up on top of her head, adorned with a hibiscus. The office was in their home, a lovely structure in French Polynesian style with a huge airy front porch that looked to be a gathering place for the guests, offering a stunning view of a long white sand beach and turquoise water. The grounds were lush with plantings, blooming trees, bushes, and flowers, native and non-native tropical varieties. Orchids clung to every palm tree. A large Polynesian-style wooden structure with a high ceiling accommodated the dining room, bar, dance floor, massage studios, and private meeting rooms. Jake wandered off to explore on his own as the rest returned to the office.

Katya and Sasha learned that Sylvie was also known as Dr. Roussel and ran a small clinic for the local population in a room attached to their home/office. She and Sasha talked medicine while Katya checked them in with Luc. Katya made it clear that she was Sasha's assistant, not his partner or spouse and double-checked that there would be two beds. She wanted to be sure Sasha could choose where, and how, to sleep. Luc informed them cell phone usage was not permitted outside the villas. Fine with us, Katya thought. No one would be sharing photos of them or trying to record Sasha's violin playing. Jake came in from the porch to register as they were leaving, but they only nodded to each other in passing.

Sylvie walked them to their villa. Katya was thrilled that the reality was even better than the advertisements. The villa was in the same Polynesian style as the main hall and completely private, a ten-minute walk from the house on its own small volcanic rocky cove, allowing both a view of the volcano behind them and a small but private ocean beach to the right. The large room had grass walls, ceiling fans, French-style furnishings including two queen-sized beds, and a luxurious bathroom with a two-person jacuzzi tub and double shower. Phone and television were noticeably absent. Snorkel gear and paddleboards were arranged along one wall. A large open-air lanai contained two hammocks, a table and chairs, and two thickly padded lounge chairs.

As soon as Sylvie left, they hurried to change into their swimsuits, eager to get into the turquoise water. As Sasha stripped off his dark blue shirt, now limp and sweaty with travel, the humidity, and his airport workout, Katya was struck by the beauty of his bare torso. His shoulders were broad, his waist narrow, his sculpted arm muscles bulged. His skin was a deep tan, but laced with a strange pattern of fine, thin scars, his abdomen a six-pack that would make a gymnast jealous. A ballet dancer, she had thought, but no, she had never seen a ballet dancer who looked this good.

She looked more closely at the scars she had only felt, never seen. They were raised lines that seemed to have been deliberately carved with a knife, some cut and recut multiple times, covering the skin on his chest from a few inches below his neck to the bottom of his pectorals. She knew from massaging his back that the same pattern of scars continued across its entire surface. Her first thought was that the raised lines had somewhat the appearance of African tribal scars. Sasha's were alternating horizontal and vertical parallel cuts of six lines each, the lines around six inches long. Such scars might have been the result of deliberate, systematic torture, she realized with horror. Then Katya caught sight of the faded line of numbers tattooed down his left forearm and she lost her breath for a second time. She walked over to him and held his arm gently.

"They did this to you in Bergen-Belsen? You were just a child!"

"It was done to me only two months before liberation," Sasha intoned quietly, speaking hesitantly. "I have never talked about it, not to anyone... That SS officer... Krüger... the camp overseer, my tormenter, the sadistic monster... Krüger quickly figured out my ability to memorize anything, my talent for music...

"The other SS officers got sick of his bragging about how much he could make me learn and hated my non-prisoner status. Four of them caught me alone, held me down, and used indelible ink on a very dull needle to tattoo these numbers on me, like the ones on the prisoners transferred from Auschwitz. I still see the officers' faces laughing at me, I remember the pain of their grip, of the needle. Krüger was furious when he discovered what they'd done, dragged me over to them. But when they told him the numbers were meaningless, he started laughing too, all five of them roaring with laughter. Then he beat me senseless."

Katya gasped, visualizing the scene. "And your scars?" she managed to ask.

"I won't talk about the scars," Sasha sighed, stopping abruptly and taking a deep breath. What he wouldn't say was that he couldn't talk about them. Another repressed memory. Then he continued in the same calm voice.

"But don't ever think of me as a concentration camp survivor. That's as false as the numbers on my arm. I was abused and beaten, yes, but nothing like the abuse and horror the inmates behind the barbed wire faced every day." Sasha couldn't bring himself to speak of the other torments he had suffered, the reason for his touch phobia. "I had better shelter, relative safety from disease, from the raging typhus, the lice, though I seemed immune to both plagues. Life in the camp was brutal. Prisoners were beaten, hanged, shot at random. Near the end, inmates died by the thousands, tens of thousands, their bodies stacked in piles. The stench of death, of burning bodies, of human waste, was everywhere, inescapable.. Everyone was starving, so many were sick. The sickest survivors upon liberation were barely living skeletons, and then only about half survived the displacement camp, too far gone to live. I am not worthy to be considered one of their heroic and honored number."

Katya was appalled, but also amazed that Sasha could tell his story with no apparent emotion in his voice. How many unspeakable acts had he survived and witnessed in that concentration camp? Once again, she thought about how much his experiences there would have shaped who he became, defined who he was. Katya thought about her own grandparents' families who had all perished in Auschwitz. Katya shuddered to think of their tattooed arms, their horrible fate. Here was a man who had lived through that horror. Sasha was most definitely a concentration camp survivor in her mind, but she could understand his denial, his survivor's remorse. Then she noted that he had begun to sweat, his hair was damp, that his breathing was becoming rapid, similar to his reaction at the MLK memorial in San Francisco. Katya stroked his face, then put her hand on the back of his neck and began massaging.

Taking a number of deep breaths, Sasha successfully calmed himself, something he could never do before, not without playing his violin. It had to be Katya's touch. He shook his head to make it clear the subject was closed. Katya held his arm and kissed it.

Sasha remembered with a jolt that Le had done the exact same thing. There was so much more to tell about the camp, about Krüger. Maybe someday he would be able to share all of the horrors, tell her what had been done to him, share the secret fears that he still held.

But now was not the time. Katya had seen his scars, his tattooed arm. That was enough. He decided not to slip on his long-sleeved

172

swim shirt. The two of them had this beach to themselves. There was no one else in the water.

"Let the past be the past," he said, changing moods. "I want to be here now, with you. Look where we are."

Sasha took her hands off of him and started unwrapping the bandages that covered her entire upper arm. He replaced them with four small bandages over the bullet wounds, then placed two of the large waterproof coverings carefully over them, one on each side of her arm.

"Just let this arm hang in the water, don't try to swim with it. We'll float close to shore today. I'll be right beside you if you need help. The water looks quite calm, you should do fine. We're really in a vast lagoon here. Use my sunscreen after me. Put it on everywhere. I picked some up from Peter when I first visited the Consulate, and there was also a jar in my duffel. I'll do your back if you do mine. You'll be the first person since... since... in a long time to be able to do so."

"This sunscreen is your development, too, isn't it?" Katya asked, to distract him.

"That it is," Sasha answered simply. "Still in development. This formula isn't on the market yet."

Katya felt the presence of Sasha's first wife in the room. Which was more alarming, she pondered, Le's ghost or the specter of Sasha's unfathomable genius?

They grabbed the snorkel gear, dipped into the cove, and swam out to the lagoon. They found the cove to be teaming with young fish and discovered a spectacular barrier reef with dozens of varieties of larger colorful fish less than a hundred feet from the beach. It was only 10:30 in the morning on their first day in paradise, but Katya's mind kept returning to Sasha's description of the scene from the camp and his physiological response. There was so much hinted at, but unsaid, so much she didn't know.

As careful as Katya tried to be in the water, she was still exhausted when they returned to the villa to separately shower and change. Her arm ached terribly but she didn't want to complain. She just asked to lie down in the hammock and rest while enjoying the view. Sasha took out his violin and played for an hour, performing all three of Bach's solo partitas. Katya was again transported, as in love with the music as she was with the man who could create such heavenly sounds. The tone on his violin, his Artemisia, was extraordinary: warm, deep, rich, and resonant, and yet such power. She found Sasha's virtuosity unparalleled. When he finished, he carefully wiped down his violin with a soft cloth, loosened the tension on the bow, and returned violin and bow to their climate-controlled case, his own invention. Sasha then opened his laptop and tried to set up communications with the labs. He discovered there was no Wi-Fi in the room, so he would have to ask the Roussels for a private place in their home when they went to the main hall for lunch.

The food in the dining room was exceptional, but Sasha was eager to head over to the office, so they ate quickly. The Roussels were not happy to comply, as theirs was a technology-free resort, at least for their guests, but they gave him a time late in the afternoon of the next day. Sasha took Katya to explore the rest of the property. He surprised her by introducing himself to the kitchen workers, groundskeepers, and maids, chatting and asking about their lives in French. He even wandered into the partially underground laundry, following a curved ramp from a shack down to the closed door that protected the guests from the roar of the machines. Katya asked him about his friendliness with the staff.

"There are lots of reasons," Sasha replied. "These are the kind of working people I like, that I serve as a doctor on my boat. This is their country, their island, their home. These are also the people who know everything that goes on here. If they think of themselves as my friends, it's like having a dozen extra eyes and ears."

Katya informed Sasha that she had a long hike planned for them. She kept quiet about their destination, but made sure they were dressed in long slacks and solid shoes despite the warmth of the day, surprising Sasha with his work boots she'd put in her own luggage when he couldn't find room in his duffel. They wound their way up a verdant hill behind the Roussel's house, stopping often to take in the gorgeous views of ocean, white sand beaches, lush green volcanic cliffs, and motus, the tiny palm-tree covered islands that surround Bora Bora. The well-worn path ended at a small cluster of buildings consisting of another French Polynesian house alongside two barns in a similar style, several corrals, and a brilliant green pasture.

A horse let out a loud whinny in greeting, and Sasha counted four others in the corrals, all beautiful creatures with some definite Arabian ancestry: two bays, a chestnut, a paint, and a huge, muscular gray. As Sasha delightedly stroked their necks and noses, a short, black-bearded man of around forty-five came out of a barn towards them. He introduced himself as Alain Desmarais. Through the travel agency and the Roussels, Katya had arranged a ride on the beach to surprise Sasha, thinking of his stories of experiences with horses at the Romani circus. While Sasha was enjoying the horses, she had a long quiet talk with Alain. He looked skeptical but nodded. Sasha helped Alain saddle and bridle three of the horses, including the gray gelding, a beast by the name of Claude that Alain said was half Percheron and half Arab. Katya watched Alain tie a coiled-up lunge line to Claude's saddle and lead the horse over to Sasha. Alain had saddled a bay half-Arab for Katya and he would be riding the chestnut.

Katya had ridden a few horses in her life, but never in a more breathtaking setting. They took a different trail offering fabulous views down to a long, deserted, white sand beach. She'd always dreamed of riding through the waves along a shoreline and was enjoying herself immensely, especially when they began to canter. They stopped to rest in the middle of a broad, flat stretch of sand.

"You are sure?" Alain inquired, looking even more dubious.

"Let's ask him," she replied. "Sasha, how would you like to ride bareback, see what you can still remember from the Romani circus?" She thought he might refuse. If this wasn't just a romantic story, it had been forty-three years. But then Sasha didn't seem capable of forgetting anything.

"I would love to!" he called out. "Claude has a perfect broad back and just the right smooth canter."

He gracefully dismounted, removed the saddle and bridle and took off his boots and socks. Alain hooked the lunge line to the halter and swung the end of the line to get the horse moving in a circle at a slow canter. Sasha watched the horse move. He seemed to be counting, a look of utter concentration on his face. With a quick run, he placed both hands on the horse's back and vaulted on. After a short distance, he stood up, steadying himself as the horse circled on its lunge line. Sasha made a few low forward jumps, adjusting his landings so he would descend in exactly the same spot on the horse's back. Then to Katya's and Alain's amazement, Sasha did a complete somersault, quickly correcting his balance.

After that, there was no stopping him. He somersaulted forward two more times, then backwards, and again forwards, bounced down onto the horse's back and up to his feet several times, jumped, twisted,

175

and landed on his seat facing backwards. Finally, he jumped to his feet again and gracefully did one more backwards somersault with a twist to leave him on his feet facing forward again. After this phenomenal display, he leapt off the horse, managing one more somersault in the air before rolling on the sand to break his momentum, and stood on the far side of the circle. Alain, grinning, brought the horse to a halt and walked over to shake his hand, but Sasha stepped back, did a deep bow and walked to join Katya.

"Remind me to never, ever doubt your stories again, Sasha," she said, grinning as well.

"I cannot begin to tell you how much I enjoyed that," he said breathlessly. "I felt like a fifteen-year-old again. Let me saddle up and we'll ride back."

"So, Sasha, tell Alain and me how you started doing gymnastics on horseback in a Romani circus when you were fifteen. I bet you have a story for us that will take us all the way back to the corrals."

They had all remounted and the horses moved out easily, eager to head home.

"You have a way of getting me to talk, don't you Katya? I'll tell it in French so Alain can understand it better."

"Oui, merci!" Alain shouted out, laughing.

"It started with a beautiful black stallion sold to us to slaughter for food for our two lions. The owner couldn't bear to shoot it himself. The beast was terribly underweight, his eyes wild. He was tied to the back of a wagon bearing a dead pony. Zeus, the stallion was called. The stallion had apparently gone mad a few months before, rearing and bucking, and had seriously injured three people who had tried to ride him. The local vet was useless. The owner then hired an abusive trainer who made things much worse. Now the horse bit and kicked as well, lashing out at everyone who neared. We purchased the horse and pony, and since I had been stuck with the job of butcher, the horse was given over to me to kill."

"And that wasn't going to happen, was it?" asked Alain.

"No, it wasn't. We got Zeus into a small round corral by himself. He was the wildest horse I'd ever seen, rearing and trying to bite us over the fence. I told everyone I'd butcher the dead pony first, keep the horsemeat fresh until needed. We were well settled and had no plans to travel on for quite a while. When I was done with the pony I sat alone eating an apple, watching the stallion race around the corral.

I could see that the stallion was in extreme pain. Zeus saw me eating the apple, pricked up his ears, and ran over to me. He was hungry. I left the rest of my apple on a post and backed away. After a while Zeus stopped pawing and shaking his head and came over to eat the apple. I did the same thing day after day, standing closer each time."

"Are we getting to the gymnastics?" Katya teased.

"Please! You asked me for a story and this is the way I tell it. I gave him an apple each day, a stress-free environment, kindness, the right feed, including Romani healing herbs with acid inhibitors because I was certain he was suffering from severe ulcers, asserted control with nothing but a twirled rope. That was my method. Zeus was eating an apple out of my hand at the end of two weeks. I only worked with him when there were no witnesses. Of course, I had to raid the neighboring farms for the occasional sheep or calf, though, but as long as the lions were fed, the Roma didn't care where the meat came from.

"Zeus still acted plenty wild and scary around other people and I encouraged that. You could say I trained him to act aggressive with other people. But now he was ulcer-free and back to his well-trained self. Soon I was riding him bareback, then standing on his back. Then I tried some of the gymnastics I'd seen the other riders do in our show. When I was ready, I gathered the clan to watch me try to ride him for the first time, or so I told them. Most were sure I'd be maimed or killed and didn't want to miss the action. So I walk out in the corral, Zeus snorting and rearing, hold out an apple, and he trots over like a child's pony. I hop on bareback, move him into a canter, and do all the somersaults and trick riding you just saw. I was proclaimed a miracle worker and a true "Gypsy," a real Roma, and put into the show. Zeus and I became the main attraction."

"And someone else had to butcher animals for the lions."

"Oh yes, Alain. I was done butchering."

Sasha then told Alain about his long black wig and moustache, and about the tent pole routine and aiding the local vets and doctors. Alain was still laughing as they finished unsaddling and brushing down the horses.

"You were one crazy, lucky boy. You are welcome to come and ride for free next time!"

As they walked back to the resort, Katya had an additional question.

177

"So were the Roma left with a worthless wild horse when you returned to Australia?"

"Mais non, I trained the horse to work with Mikaela, the object of my affection in the show, although she never touched me. She became the Romani woman who tames a wild stallion with a single apple."

"You really are a romantic at heart, Sasha. You just got separated from that part of yourself. Your stories prove it is still there deep inside."

Chapter 28

Jake was sitting on the front porch when Katya and Sasha returned to the resort office. He stood up immediately and came over to them. He looked apologetic, desperate, and more than a little worn out.

"Please, I'm sorry for the way Mason treated you, Katya. I'm sorry I was not in a position to interfere. But if I'm going to help guard Sasha, we need to stay connected. You've been gone for hours."

"I understand the position you were in, but it's still no excuse," Katya replied curtly. "If you'd asked the Roussels, they would have told you where we were. But I am willing to start over."

"Thank you! We have much to discuss," Jake continued. "I will say, I'm happy to see you looking so well."

"You do know the morphine craving was just an act," Katya reminded him. "And the pre-torture pain."

"I figured that out after you punched me."

"I bet you did. Did you find some decent accommodations here? I can't imagine Mason put you up in a villa."

"Sadly, yours was the last available villa for several days. I'm sharing a room with the driver-slash-jack-of-all-trades. I'm lucky they're not making me carry suitcases and serve in the dining room."

"But here you are in shorts and flip flops in Bora Bora."

"I'm not really complaining. But let me tell you what's going on this afternoon and this evening. They're holding a welcome celebration in your honor. No extra charge, I checked. Part of your pre-paid package in that expensive villa of yours. There are flower crowns and leis waiting for you there, all included. I'll walk you over to the main building at four-thirty. There's a welcome ceremony in Tahitian, and beachside dance entertainment and dinner afterwards. I understand every local islander around comes to these things for the free drinks. You don't speak Tahitian, do you Sasha?"

"Not a language I've had reason to come across," Sasha answered.

"But I bet he'll be fluent by the time we leave here," Katya added, only half in jest.

"Well don't get started yet. You just have time to get cleaned up and dressed. I'll be over in a half an hour to get you. Please, no backing out of this! Our hosts would be devastated! The Roussels have gone to great lengths to prepare."

"What do you think, Sasha? Are you ready for some Polynesian culture?" Katya asked.

"I'm not ready for rowdy drunken Polynesians, but I think I can handle the rest of it. Jake, we're not going to inform you every time we move, so use your spy skills. Keep an eye on us from a distance. Do your job."

Jake nodded and headed into the office. Katya didn't want to follow him and decided to thank the Roussels at the celebration that evening for the introduction to Alain. She found herself looking forward to the event, although getting ready would be a rush. She wondered why no mention of the celebration had been made, either online or by the Roussels. Katya had no concern about Sasha. He was proving himself more competent in social situations than she would have imagined. And they would be on the beach at sunset. It would be a perfect ending to a perfect day.

Jake arrived promptly, dressed in a rather loud multi-color Hawaiian shirt, white slacks, and sandals. Katya tried to imagine him hurriedly shopping for something "appropriate." She'd been impressed by Sasha's taste in making purchases in San Francisco and by the quality of the bamboo-fiber shirts, shorts, and slacks that emerged wrinkle-free from his duffel along with a pair of comfortable-looking eco-friendly sandals. She thought about his new heavy leather flight jacket and her warm peacock blue silk jacket, along with her burner cell phone; they'd left all three items behind at the Australian Consulate. She didn't see any reason she would need a cell phone again. Sasha claimed never to have used a cell phone. He'd never had a need for one.

Katya and Sasha took turns in the shower and dressed separately in the bathroom as well. Sasha emerged in a newly purchased long-sleeved, light blue collarless shirt, sharply creased tan khakis, and his recovered sandals, then stepped out onto the lanai to wait with Jake. Katya dressed in a blue and white patterned Tahitian-style dress she'd purchased in Berkeley that bared her shoulders. She had to use her teeth to help wrap a blue and white silk scarf around her bandages, then chose several flowers from vases in the room to tuck into it. Both men seemed genuinely pleased with how she looked when she stepped outside. She couldn't have been happier.

"I'm not wearing a flower crown; that's asking too much of me," Sasha said firmly.

"You might get swept away in the moment," Katya laughed. She had to agree with him, it was too much. "Maybe just the lei, then."

"Hurry up, you two," Jake ordered. "No one can eat or drink until you arrive."

"What happened to laid-back Polynesia?" Katya asked.

They entered the dining hall to applause. There was no meal in sight, but lots of appetizers, and the drinks began to flow. At the sound of a conch shell, six young Tahitian women came forward, all incredibly lovely, Katya thought, with their long straight black hair and red bare-shoulder dresses. Katya was shown into a small room on one side of the hall and Sasha to one on the other. Inside was nothing but a massage table elegantly covered in colorful cloth.

Three of the women followed Katya into the chamber and motioned for her to lie down. Two began gently touching her face and shoulders, and the third tickled her all over with a long, soft feather. *Sasha!* she suddenly thought in concern. Screams from the other side of the hall confirmed her fear. She jumped off the table and opened the door. The other three women came bolting out of Sasha's chamber. Katya ignored the startled looks of the crowd as she ran to find Sasha. To her great relief, he was looking bemused, not angry.

"That wasn't the response they were expecting, was it," Sasha stated, with a rueful sigh.

"No, I bet it wasn't. Did they touch you?"

"Things would have been a lot worse if they had. I saw what they were up to in time and pushed them out rather violently, I'm sorry to say."

"Are you all right?"

"Just a little embarrassed to rejoin the celebration."

"Don't be. They shouldn't have assumed. I'll make this right. Hold my hand as we exit."

"I have no doubt you can talk our way out of this one."

Sasha held Katya's hand tightly as they left the chamber. All eyes were on them.

"No one touches my man but me! He has taken a vow for the length of this trip, and a very big wager, I will add, so the next person who tempts him will have to answer to me!"

The room erupted in cheers and laughter, and the drinking resumed. Katya and Sasha found their appetite and began nibbling at the appetizers. Katya looked around at the crowd. There were twenty-four wealthy-looking resort guests, not including themselves and Jake, most of them Caucasian, but also several Japanese and Chinese pairs as well, the Roussels, Alain with a woman she assumed was his Tahitian wife, and around thirty other Tahitian men and women. She smiled at the six young women who had been in her and Sasha's chambers, and hoped they weren't losing out on expected tips.

At the sound of a conch shell, the crowd gravitated away from the appetizers to the front of the hall, where a small raised platform was decorated with Tahitian fabrics and a multitude of flowers. A bowl made out of a conch shell stood on a tall stool. Three drummers and a conch blower, handsome bare-chested young men in white loincloths with red flower headdresses, assembled around a Tahitian elder dressed in a floor length short-sleeve red robe, a feather cape, and a tall feather headdress, and holding a few large green leaves. Two of the young women approached, also dressed in white with colorful headdresses, each carrying a flower headdress and a lei. A third woman joined them, holding a small sheet of cloth made out of bark.

The Roussels gestured for Katya and Sasha to step forward. The elder began speaking in Tahitian, cut a leaf in two, then reached out and tried to take Sasha's hand. When he resisted, Katya held his hand out steady and mimed for the elder to not touch him. The elder nodded and carefully tied the leaf around Sasha's wrist, allowing only the leaf to touch him. Katya's wrist received the same treatment, and the elder mimed putting both their wrists together in front of them.

After a lengthy pronouncement in Tahitian, the elder poured a small amount of water over both their wrists from the conch shell bowl. Still speaking only Tahitian, the elder bade one of the young women to come forward. She handed the lei to Sasha and motioned for him to place it around Katya's neck, then the second woman brought Katya a lei for Sasha. The scene was repeated with the flower headdresses. Katya held the headdress to one side to give Sasha the opportunity to pass, but he reluctantly nodded consent. The elder looked right at Sasha and spoke a word in Tahitian, gesturing for him to repeat it, and did the same using a different word with Katya. Katya found herself growing increasingly nervous. This was no welcome ceremony. Then the elder held out his hand for the bark cloth. Sasha

182

saw what was written on the cloth before Katya did. But she didn't need to see it, she knew. Sasha's face altered instantly from apparent bored acceptance of the ritual to absolute fury. He turned on Katya, grabbed her by the wrist of her good arm and pulled down hard, forcing her to her knees.

"What is this! I trusted you!" he fairly shouted in her face.

"Sasha, I didn't know! I figured it out just as you did!"

Katya's heart was pounding. She was losing him, perhaps for good. This had to be Jake's doing. She turned to find him in the shocked crowd. He was smirking.

"All you know how to do is lie," Sasha retorted, throwing off the headdress and lei, tearing off the leaf bracelet. He pushed Katya's wrist away and stormed out of the hall.

Chapter 29

Two of the surprised drummers helped Katya to her feet. She continued to stare at Jake and pushing past the young men, walked rapidly towards him. Jake backed away grinning malevolently, then turned and disappeared into the crowd. Sylvie and Luc came rushing up to her, inadvertently blocking her path.

"Katya, Katya, we're so sorry," Sylvie cried out. "We don't understand what just happened!"

"Tell me what Jake told you," Katya was able to stammer, still looking for him. "Tell me in French. There are too many people listening."

The assembled guests and Tahitians were excitedly talking among themselves, but several guests were crowded in close. Katya felt like she was going to be sick. She was conflicted about what she should be doing at this moment – chasing down Jake or running after Sasha.

"Jake made all the arrangements. He said he was making them as a surprise for you from Sasha, that he wanted to marry you," said Luc.

"Dr. Borodin wanted to marry me. That's not even remotely possible. You saw for yourself his violent reaction. Jake told us this was a welcome celebration, that's all. What did Jake tell you his relationship with us was?"

"Doesn't he work with you? He said he was a personal assistant to Sasha, to Dr. Borodin, and had to be here. We struggled to find a bed for him."

"I am Dr. Borodin's only personal assistant, and his primary bodyguard. I told you I was not his partner, that we needed two beds. Jake is an outside agency bodyguard we didn't request and Sasha didn't want. I'm sorry I allowed it. I think Jake's agency ordered him to drive a permanent wedge between me and Dr. Borodin. Merde, he may have achieved his goal."

"Mon Dieu! We didn't know!" Sylvie looked shaken.

"When did Jake start making these arrangements? You couldn't have made all these preparations in the half-day we've been here."

"We received a call from him two days ago from the States. Jake was very specific about what he wanted us to do. Even that was last minute for us, but he offered a good premium… and Jake has been working with us here since you all arrived."

"Wait, are you saying the caller – Jake – paid for this entire fake wedding?" Katya asked, incredulous.

"Well, no," Luc said rather sheepishly, "he said to put it all on your room bill. The ceremony, the drinks and appetizers, the beach-side entertainment this evening, the feast for the entire resort afterward…"

"My bill?" Katya felt even sicker. "I've prepaid everything. I have no more money. I spent everything I have on your extravagant villa and the airfare. You just took a caller's word? How much money are you talking?"

"Close to four thousand U.S. dollars," Luc said, sounding like he too was going to be sick, his wife Sylvie blanching as well.

"We have all been played for fools. I know who will make good on the payment, so you two will be all right. Go ahead with the entertainment and feast while I sort this out," Katya said, knowing now she would be asking for Peter Hammond's financial assistance after all.

"Oh, thank you, thank you," they said at once, grasping her hand in gratitude. "What can we do for you, though?" asked Sylvie. "Do you know where Dr. Borodin is?"

"He cannot be far, at least his person. It's his spirit I worry about. And our relationship."

"You do know that he loves you, don't you?" Sylvie asked softly. "I have seen the way he looks at you."

"Sorry, but that's impossible. You don't know the man."

"But you are in love with him, no?"

"That… that is neither here nor there. And now I have lost his trust… and I will lose my job."

"We will explain to him. And the wedding is not a legitimate marriage – it is just an enjoyable celebration. There is no legal binding."

"I don't think that will matter to him. But thank you."

"Give him a little time," Sylvie told her. "Men are rash but then they are sorry. Come, have some more appetizers, then look for him."

"I couldn't possibly eat," Katya said, turning away to hide the tears forming in her eyes.

186

She wandered over to the bar side of the hall and stood along a wall, watching the men and women laughing and drinking. She was sure everything she had worked for was gone. She couldn't imagine Sasha trusting her, ever touching her again. The three Tahitian women who had attempted to give her a massage approached, the sight of their sweet solicitous faces making her heart ache even worse. They placed their soft hands on her, one even leaned her head on her shoulder. One of them spoke for them all.

"Katya, we feel your pain," she said in French. "We saw you were speaking French with Luc and Sylvie. My name is Taiana, and these are my friends Erita and Vaea."

"Thank you for coming over," Katya said in French. "I do feel in the need of friends right now."

Katya looked over at the bar and couldn't believe Jake had reappeared and was casually ordering a drink. She tensed and started towards him, but the women held her back.

"Wait, Katya, who is that? You don't need more heartbreak," said Erita.

"That's the man who set me up, there, with the Hawaiian shirt. He says his name is Jake McGill; I don't know what his real name is. I'm going to kill him."

"Now you are talking like a Tahitian man," Vaea admonished. "That is not how we women handle things. Tell us what he did."

Katya explained about Jake arranging the expensive wedding celebration and charging it to her, that he had lied to her and Sasha, that he wanted to drive them apart.

"So that is what happened. But you must have done something to him first. This sounds personal," whispered Erita.

"I must admit he and his friends were being very menacing to me so I beat him and tied him up. I even shot him up with morphine, stripped him, and left him in a hospital gown. I guess he could be wanting a little revenge for that."

The women's laughter caused many heads to turn, but Jake continued to nurse his drink. The three women put their heads together and started talking in Tahitian, looking around the hall as they did. They finally arrived at an agreement and came back to Katya, smiling mischievously. Erita and Vaea nodded to Taiana to talk.

"See that pretty young girl in virginal white sitting at a table with two others? With the yellow lei? And see the really big tough tattooed young man leaning against the end wall, watching her? That is Atea, she is desperate for a white husband, that one is, and that is her brother Tehei, who is charged with keeping her a virgin and away from the white tourists. So let us turn Atea on to Jake and see what happens."

"I really like how you ladies think," said Katya. "I can't thank you enough."

She left the women to work their revenge plot on her behalf and walked past the tables full of appetizers on her way to the door. She couldn't keep herself from looking for Sasha any longer.

Chapter 30

Katya walked slowly down the long path to the villa, trying to imagine what she could say to Sasha. Where else would he be but there? He thought her a liar. He had called her a liar. And she had lied plenty. Her elaborate fake identities – why had she felt the need to do that, she wondered, except to manipulate his feelings? Everything at the St. Francis and at her home in Berkeley had been an attempt to manipulate him, cold calculation. She did love him, even Sylvie could see it. What would Sasha think but that she was trying to trick him into greater intimacy?

The villa was empty. All the clothes Sasha had been wearing were dropped on the floor. The Sasha she knew would have neatly folded even a rag. She took off her headdress and lei, left them on a table, and continued her search. He was not in the cove so she started walking down the small strip of their private beach. There he was, sitting motionless on the sand, facing the quiet lagoon, legs tucked in a meditation pose, hands in his lap. He was wearing his swim trunks, but she could see they were dry. She approached quietly and sat down a couple of meters away, gazing out at the waves. Neither spoke a word for the next several minutes, then Katya found the nerve to address him.

"I'm sorry, Sasha, it's my fault. Jake was getting his revenge on me and he hurt you too. Mason wants to drive us apart."

"I know."

"You know?"

"I only needed a moment alone to figure it out."

"And what else have you figured out?"

Sasha didn't answer, didn't change his pose. Didn't look at her.

"Sasha, tell me what you want me to do," Katya pleaded with a sigh.

"I want you to sit next to me. I want you to forgive me."

"Forgive you? Forgive you for what?"

"I behaved abominably. I behaved like an ordinary loutish man. I purposefully and angrily hurt you. I think myself so much better than that, yet I sank down to the lowest level in a heartbeat. I didn't think at all, I reacted, in a totally illogical way. Violently."

"I understand why, Sasha."

"No, I don't think you do. There is no understanding. There is no logic to it."

"I will forgive you if you forgive yourself for being human, for having feelings."

"I have far too many feelings right now."

"How do you feel about me?"

Sasha turned to look at her for the first time. He crossed his arms and seemed to hug himself. The silence lasted so long Katya became more and more certain he had no feelings at all for her. She looked back at the sea and resigned herself.

"Katya... you are everything to me," Sasha said at last. "You once told me you did not want to live without me. I don't think I could live without you now, without your touch. I don't know if I can love you the way you deserve to be loved. The way that I feel you love me. It took me until now to see that you do love me. But if you can accept me as I am, I am yours."

Tears streamed down Katya's face. She wordlessly stood up and walked the two meters and the many miles separating them and sat down close to Sasha. He unfolded his arms and reached out to her. They held on to each other and together watched the endless pattern of the low waves, listened to the small boom as they hit the sand, the swoosh as they retreated. No, she did want more from him, she thought. She was fooling herself to think otherwise. She felt a profound sadness that he had not moved to kiss her, that he might never do more than chastely touch and be touched.

The quiet was broken by the sound of conch shells, drums, and loud voices from the main beach. The music and dancing were about to begin, with or without the guests of honor.

"Katya, we should go. But let's go separately and meet there. Let's keep Jake thinking he's succeeded in ruining our relationship until we can figure out what to do with him. He might try something far worse next time."

"I already have some new local friends working on that. He might just find himself in enough personal danger to keep him away from us."

"What have you been up to, Katya?"

190

She told him about Jake charging the four-thousand-dollar cost of the celebration to her, and about Atea and her big brother Tehei.

"Save me from the vengeance of Woman," Sasha commented, but with his near smile.

They returned to the villa and Sasha pulled his clothes on over his swim trunks. Katya snuck into the bathroom to put her bikini on under her dress, not caring that the straps showed. When she returned, she asked Sasha to help her put water shields over her bandages. She kept quiet about the pain. Lean into it, her Buddhist teachers would tell her. He untied the blue and white scarf from around her arm, the flowers falling to the floor, then rewrapped and tied it for her afterwards. Katya put the lei back around her neck. They walked quickly up the path, Sasha a few paces ahead, as the sound of the drumming grew louder.

Sasha joined the ongoing celebration on the ocean side while Katya wandered over to the office and main hall to look for Taiana, Vaea, Erita and any sign of Jake. Couples were still arriving, holding hands. Sasha felt many were staring at him in judgment. Two tall wicker chairs were set up facing westward, overlooking the ocean and a section of the beach marked off for dancing. A few dozen white folding chairs were arranged around them in a semi-circle. The early winter sunset was just starting to brighten up the evening sky as powerful bare-chested young men raced to light the tiki torches to the blowing of conch shells. The volume of the drumming increased dramatically. Assembling outside the main hall were dancers dressed in red outfits and adorned with red flowers glowing in the evening light.

Katya saw her three new friends. Erita nodded in the direction of the front of the hall, beyond the dancers. Atea's white dress was visible in the darkness of the entryway, and there, whispering in her ear with a hand on her hip, was Jake. Erita then nodded toward the sinking sun. Moving through the assembling crowd of guests and natives on the beach was a tall bulky figure, frantically searching. Tehei. Atea and Jake sank back into the darkness. Katya kept watching, and soon two figures emerged out a side door and disappeared into the lushness of the palm trees and gardens.

Katya breathed a sigh of relief and asked the Tahitian women to escort her to the beach. They arrived just ahead of the dancers, with Katya taking a seat on one of the wicker chairs as the conches were

191

blown. Sasha saw her from the far side of the dance area and made his way to the second chair. There was pointing and murmuring from the other guests as they noticed the "wedding" couple was back together.

"Jake is well occupied. Let's enjoy the rest of this evening, shall we?" Katya said with a satisfied grin. "I've been looking forward to my first sunset in Bora Bora. It's already spectacular."

The drums and sticks sounded out a pounding rhythm as the dancers swept onto the beach, the rich red of their clothing, flowers, and feathers flashing in the torchlight. There were six young men, muscular, handsome, bare chested, most with shoulder or leg tattoos and all wearing red, buttock-baring g-string loincloths, and six young women, all with long black hair and nearly bare themselves in short grass skirts topped with red flowers riding impossibly low on their hips, breasts undulating inside miniscule bikini tops. Their hips moved almost faster than the eye could follow. All of them were resplendent in leis and towering red headdresses. They danced in two lines, men in back, the women in front, arms gracefully swaying. A raw sexual power pulsed from the women's gyrating hips, the movement hypnotic.

Katya had seen a number of Hawaiian dances on vacation with her father, but nothing prepared her for the pure sensuality and pagan energy of this performance. She looked around at the crowd and everyone seemed to be swooning, mesmerized. Sasha was staring, wide-eyed. The Roussels didn't have to cater to a family friendly crowd like the big resorts did. All of their guests were couples who had sought out this resort for its unapologetic carnality. The frenzied dancing and the driving, pulsating rhythm of the drums added to the sensuality of the moment. The sunset was a glorious backdrop that heightened the drama enfolding in front of them.

The dancers swirled into close pairs, the women moving in small circles in front of the men, the men's hips moving almost as fast as the women's. The men were dancing on the balls of their feet, their knees moving rapidly in a scissor-like motion. Never interrupting their dance, the male dancers bent backwards with the women moving forward to gyrate over their groins. Then the dancers would reverse, and the men would thrust themselves over the women, this pattern repeating itself again and again, ever faster. Katya had never experienced a dance so close to pornographic and yet so beautiful. Suddenly a pair of dancers whirled forward to where Katya and Sasha were seated, an unbearably handsome man with sculpted muscles dancing in front of Katya, a gorgeous woman before Sasha, her swiveling hips so close the flowers swished against his knees. The dancers turned around completely twice, their hands touching each other, before moving off, to be replaced by each of the other pairs in turn. The glow of the torches reflected off their now glistening bodies, the dancers' eyes half closed in apparent ecstasy.

Katya felt herself totally aroused. Her hand flew out to find Sasha's reaching for hers as well. She could feel him trembling... or was it her own trembling she felt. Holding hands, they somehow managed to sit through the rest of the performance, until the drums and pounding sticks came to an abrupt stop. The moment the dancers left the beach, Sasha jumped out of his chair, pulling Katya with him, and still holding her hand, ran with her all the way to their private beach. Katya was sure she heard a cheer from the dance audience louder than the applause as the two of them raced away. They threw off their outer clothing and dove into the pristine warm lagoon, embracing each other underwater and coming up for air locked in their first kiss. Katya didn't want the kiss to end. She had waited so long for it. When they were finally able to break apart, they held hands again and pushed their way through the shallow waves to shore, racing up the beach to the villa.

Inside the door, Sasha turned on the lights and they stood a few feet apart, suits, hair, and bodies streaming ocean water onto the floor. Katya pulled her suit off first, fearlessly standing wet and naked in front of him. Sasha pulled off his trunks and they stood drinking in each other's bodies with their eyes. Katya caught her breath. Sasha was more spectacular unclothed than she could have imagined. She could see past the scars now, just take in his intense look of desire, his stunning build, the sheer naked maleness of him. Sasha walked slowly towards her and ran his hands along her shoulders, neck, belly, hips, breasts, touching her, caressing her. Katya was so aroused she could not stand quietly any longer. She reached to touch his face, then her fingers slowly slid down his chest all the way to the tops of his thighs. Sasha arched and stepped back.

"Wait, we must go more slowly. I want to touch you more," he whispered, seeking to gain control over his body. He leaned back in and held her face while he kissed her on the lips long and hard. Her hands moved down his back to his buttocks and she pulled him tight

193

against her. They moved slowly in a circle, clenched in that second kiss, then he picked her up and carried her to one of the beds. Laying her down softly, he sat beside her, touching her everywhere, his hands searching out her most sensuous areas, her body arching in response. He was amazed how every single part of Katya's body responded to his touch, even her ear, palm, throat, knees. Sasha's hand trailed down her belly to her pubic bone and found what she told him was her trigger, rolling it under his fingers as she cried out in pleasure.

Knowing this was her first time, he went slowly, thrilled by her wild arousal, her loud cries. Katya moved her body to the rhythm of his hand, moaning, and came to a seemingly endless orgasm. Sasha leaned down to kiss her mouth again and her hands reached to touch and stroke him, then she guided him into her as he moved to straddle her. At first she felt a confusing pressure so strong she gasped and feared she would have to ask him to stop, but the sensation melted away to one of intense pleasure as they began to move in unison. Before they both could come, Katya rolled him over and moved on top of him, luxuriating in the totally new sensation of having a man inside her, her fingers sliding over his muscular chest. She climaxed just as Sasha came with a loud cry. Katya leaned forward, keeping him inside her, and kissed his mouth again. She lay on top of him for a long time, feeling him pulse inside her, and thrilling to the aftershocks of orgasm. Sasha's hands stroked her buttocks, the sensuous line of her hips. They were both deliriously happy and completely satisfied. At least for the next half-hour.

The second time, they were able to go even slower, kissing, exploring each other's bodies more with their hands and tongues, then they moved to face each other on their sides. He entered her again and they both came with a long rush of orgasm that led them to a simultaneous climax. As they lay spent in each other's arms, they finally felt the wetness of the bed. Their hair was still quite damp, the pillows and sheets gritty with sand and soaked with ocean water.

Laughing at the mess, Katya pulled Sasha with her to the second bed and they slipped under the clean dry sheets. Katya draped herself over him as he lay on his back, touching his face and chest, his hands caressing her. They quietly spoke the words of love and affection Katya had so longed to hear, so longed to say. She had never imagined sex could be this good, this fulfilling, that Sasha could be so passionate, so attentive a lover. Katya still felt the sensation of his tongue in her mouth, her ear, on her breasts, taste the salt on his skin. She wanted more of him, but it could wait until morning. They had all the time in the world.

Chapter 31

Sasha awoke at his usual hour, just at dawn. He attempted to rouse Katya, but she only smiled and hugged her pillow tighter.

"Let me sleep a few more hours. Then you can come back to bed with me," she murmured.

"Don't move. I want to watch you sleep."

"I *can't* move. Please come back when the sun is actually up," she sighed. "Then I want you to make love with me again, but not yet."

Sasha touched her hair and ran his hand down the small of her back, but when she did not respond, he kissed a shoulder blade, showered and dressed. She loved him, he marveled, and he was himself in love again after so many years. He had made love for the first time in decades. He had thought he would never know such happiness again in his life.

What had allowed him to open up his heart? Had it been the sensual Tahitian dance? Dance had meant so much to him since childhood. Back in Europe, he'd danced all the wild Romani dances, never touching or being touched of course, astounding the clan with his athletic leaps, with the Russian and Chinese dances he'd learned for *The Nutcracker* in ballet class... danced alone in his room at Mandelbrot House, the music turned up loud, hiding from Harrison, then from his minders... Had purchased a sound system for his small boat, an even better one for his first house, so that he could dance with Le... His desire to dance had died with her...

Striding outside to the beach, he stretched and worked out for his usual ninety minutes. He stepped back into the villa to check on Katya but she hadn't moved, was sleeping. Sasha thought for the first time about the nearly undetectable tracker on his back, that someone at S-Branch had been listening in on their lovemaking, and tried, unsuccessfully, not to care. He had escaped the leash, well, at least extended it, but he had not escaped the collar.

He quietly stepped back outside and sat on a lava rock by the cove splashing water on his face and reflecting on the night with the kind of detail only he was capable of. Katya had been magnificent, so unexpectedly uninhibited, so passionate. He thought about how insatiable she'd been. How she'd totally opened to him. Sasha could still taste the salt from licking her ear, feel her fingers moving down his chest to his thighs, hear her excited breathing, her loud moans and sighs. And now his brain was back at full function. A dozen new ideas and plans began to work themselves out simultaneously as he watched the young fish dart in the water. It took him a moment to notice he was not alone. Jake had appeared, looking disheveled and self-satisfied, but cautious. He sat down on a lava rock a few meters away.

"It looks like your night was as good as mine," Sasha said to him calmly.

"That it was," Jake answered, eyeing him warily. "I'm trying to figure out how much danger I'm in, but it sounds like you two survived my little prank."

"Is that what you're calling it? By rights I should punch you in the jaw or drown you right here in the cove, but you've caught me feeling magnanimous this morning. I do want to know if this was all your idea or if Mason had a hand in it."

"Not going to answer that one. But I come offering a truce. I need to stay out of sight for a while. I knew you'd be up and thought we could climb together to the top of the volcano above us. There are supposed to be some amazing petroglyphs in a cave there, not to mention a stunning view. Should take us less than two hours round trip."

"I suppose I shouldn't ask who you're hiding from."

"Let's just say my amazing night has some potentially dire consequences."

Sasha thought it best that Jake didn't know Katya's part in his evening adventures and their consequences. They didn't need another round of revenge "pranks." He mulled over the idea of a hike. The petroglyphs were intriguing, and the climb would do him good. He shouldn't play his violin at this early hour and there was no Wi-Fi for work. Katya was still asleep. He didn't think he could stay away from her if he didn't leave.

"I'll go. But I'm working on something in my head so no talking," he said, gesturing to Jake to lead the way.

ॐ

A few minutes later, Katya stirred to the sound of a light tapping on the villa door.

"Room service, breakfast," an accented voice called out.

198

God no, she thought. Was this another of Jake's pranks? She just wanted to luxuriate in bed, just wanted more sleep, but she grabbed her unused nightgown off the table between the beds, ducked under the sheets, and slipped it on. The door opened, and she heard the squeak of a cart as it crossed the still wet floor. She thought of just keeping the sheet pulled over her head, but now she was wide awake. She sat up, holding the sheet up to her chin, and found herself looking down the barrel of a dart gun, two small dark men behind it. Not again, she thought, as she threw herself off the far side of the bed across the side table, crashing the lamp to the floor. If she couldn't escape, at least she would leave Sasha a clear message that she'd been taken by force. The dart caught her in her lower back and she lost consciousness almost immediately. The two men wrapped the sheet around her body and stuffed her into a large tub hidden under the white cloth pleats of a housekeeping laundry cart. They rolled it quickly back the way they'd come.

Katya awoke sitting in a wooden chair, the nearly deafening sound of washing machines and dryers filling her ears. She tried to move her hands but felt them handcuffed behind her, the strain making her injured arm throb. Her feet were bound to the chair with clothesline. There was a piece of tape over her mouth. A small dark man with a gun sat to the right of her, and before her stood an even more terrifying sight: a corpulent man with the unmistakable look of a Cutter family member, placing an array of scalpels and other sharp cutting instruments on a black cloth on top of a tall stool between the two of them. Katya took a deep breath and worked out in her head the next steps she must take to survive.

"You're back with us," the unknown Cutter said, as he roughly pulled the tape off her mouth, leaving one end attached to her face. "My name is William Cutter. My headquarters are in Indonesia, so it took me no time at all to join you here in your little paradise. Our time together will be short and anything but enjoyable for you, so I will cut to the chase, pardon the pun. I hold you personally responsible for the death of my brother Markus and the loss of his compound. As this is a full-service resort, I intend to give you the complete facial treatment, that is I intend to remove all the skin from your face as painfully as possible. I've already given you an injection of one of my favorite drug cocktails. We just need to give it a few more minutes to work. It will stop the bleeding and keep you conscious. It also tends to paralyze

199

your feet and numb your hands, but you won't be needing them anymore, will you, my dear."

"Don't you want to know who paid me to protect Sasha? That seemed to be the question on your late brother's mind," Katya said, as coolly as she could.

"I suppose you will answer that and all my other questions in due time, my dear."

"And don't you want to know Mason's role in setting up your brother? He's the one who pulled the trigger. Why do you think Mason planned the assault on your brother's compound when he did? Why do you think he wanted to be sure your brother didn't survive? I can tell you these things much more clearly before I'm in too much pain to speak."

"Ah, clever girl. Yes, I most certainly would like to know. But don't make me wait too long to get started. I'm most eager to see your new look. And I'm sure Sasha will be thrilled with it as well."

Sasha and Jake had only walked for a short distance up the volcano when Sasha felt a sharp pain in his chest. He stopped. Katya. Something was wrong, this hike was wrong, Jake being here with him was wrong. He spun on his heels to look Jake in the face. Jake looked startled, then frightened, and most certainly guilty.

"There are no petroglyphs, are there?" Sasha said, with ice in his voice.

Sasha grabbed Jake by the throat, lifted him off his feet, and held him over the side of the steep trail, a sixty-foot sheer drop to the tropical vegetation far below.

"Tell me what you know when I put you down or I will drop you the second time."

Jake gave the smallest of nods, terror in his eyes, and Sasha swung him back onto the trail. Jake held his throat, gasping, and it took another moment for him to regain his voice.

"I received a text..." he rasped, "from Mason... I was to get you out of the way so Katya could be interrogated again... People coming in... but..."

"But what!" Sasha shouted at him.

"Having doubts... it just isn't right, to interrogate her again. And Mason never texts, always calls..."

Sasha started running down the mountain trail before he finished and after a moment's hesitation, Jake ran after him. In fifteen minutes, Sasha was racing through the villa, taking in the broken lamp and the empty bed, and racing on to the center of the resort. How could he have left her alone... this was all his fault, he thought, uselessly.

"Do you have a gun with you?" he called over his shoulder to Jake.

"No, so sorry, I couldn't. I'll check the office to see if any cars have come in or out," he panted breathlessly.

"I'll start talking with the staff." Sasha wished he knew where to start looking. In this amount of time she could be in a trunk on the way to a private plane or boat. Or in another van.

Katya spun her stories about Mason with as much detail as she could imagine. She needed some sort of distraction to carry out her next step and had yet to come up with any possibilities. Time was running out. She sensed Cutter's fingers were itching to start carving up her face. Suddenly she knew Sasha was not far off, he was already looking for her. It was completely illogical, as Sasha would say, but she knew what to do next.

"You do know, Mr. William Cutter, that all I have to do is call out Sasha's name and he will hear me. He will come for me."

"No one can hear you outside this room," Cutter laughed.

"Sasha!" she screamed.

Cutter, despite his certainty, panicked at the sound and slapped her hard across the face. He replaced the tape over her mouth and walked over to the small ground level window for a long look outside. He turned back to her with a sneer.

"Time is up, no Saint Sasha on the horizon."

A voice in his head, her voice, called to him to check the laundry area. Sasha spied two of the maids sitting under a palm tree, carts piled high with dirty sheets and towels parked next to them. They readily confessed they'd been paid the equivalent of twenty dollars each by a strange young Indonesian-looking man to let him have the laundry room for two hours. They'd thought he wanted a place to be alone with a girl. Sasha told them to run and get the Roussels and all able-bodied staff to hurry to the laundry, but to wait outside. He signaled to Jake, who was just leaving the office.

201

"Black car came in an hour ago, still there," Jake said, as he ran towards him. "Two Indonesians and a big white man. Said they were meeting one of the guests. I have Manahau guarding the resort entrance to make sure no one comes in or out – he and I put up a barrier before I went into the office. There are already two couples who aren't guests loudly arguing to get in!"

"I've found her. Laundry."

They entered the small grass shack that served as a social area for the maids and the hidden entry to the underground laundry. Sasha opened the door and quietly slipped down the curved ramp. He made a lightning-fast peek around the last bend. A guard stood at the heavy, closed door, gun in hand, with his ear to the door, listening. Sasha retreated back to the shack. Reaching in his pocket, he took out the matches and switchblade he and Katya had taken from the van; it seemed like a lifetime ago. Katya had given them to him and he'd transferred them from pocket to new pocket ever since. His diplomatic pass had ensured that he hadn't even been asked to go through a metal detector at either of the airports. Sasha pulled some dried grass from the side of the shack.

"Grab that coconut on the ground," he demanded to Jake.

Sasha took the coconut and slammed it against a palm tree twice, creating a crack. He used the knife to open it wide enough to stuff in some of the dried grass, then lit it with a match, blowing on it until it caught. Signaling Jake to follow him, he quietly walked down the ramp and heaved the smoking coconut around the bend.

୶

Katya tensed, waiting for the right moment. Sasha had heard her, whether he knew it or not. He would come in time. Cutter was glaring at her, reaching for a scalpel. The guard leaned forward, eager to see the first cut. But instead of reaching for her face, Cutter sliced one of the bandages on her arm in two, revealing the bullet hole underneath. He poked and prodded at it a moment, then took a deep, vicious slice right through the center. The pain was excruciating but Katya held back a reaction. She didn't want to give him the satisfaction. A single small drop of bright red blood formed at the bottom of the cut.

"Ah, the drug is working. I'm ready for your face!" William Cutter said with excitement.

A sudden pounding on the door and loud shouting distracted both men.

202

"A bomb! Open the door, let me in! Now!"

The sound of an automatic gun firing and the thump of a body against the door followed. Katya was in motion at the first sound. She had freed her hands from the cuffs five minutes before – her right hand flashed out and stabbed one of the scalpels deep into the wrist of the gunman's hand, then knocked his gun to the floor. Cutter reared back more in annoyance than fear. She grabbed and threw one scalpel and knife after another at Cutter as he staggered backwards. Katya yanked the tape off her mouth and was reaching down with the last knife to cut the bindings on her feet when Sasha and Jake, using combined shoulder thrusts, burst through the door. They regained their balance and looked in astonishment at the carnage in the room. Katya made a last successful swipe with the knife and smiled up at them.

"I'm sorry. We'd thought you might be in need of assistance, but I see we were wrong," Jake said, shaking his head.

Jake leveled the liberated gun taken from the now unconscious hall guard at the man gripping his arm in pain, a scalpel sticking out of his wrist. Sasha checked the big man's vital signs. He was alive, but maybe not for long. Sasha didn't want Katya to see the potentially fatal location of one of the thrown scalpels and blocked her line of sight. He turned back to her. She stood up and tried to take a step towards him but fell forward instead. Sasha caught her in his arms and held her tightly, then kissed her passionately, but gently, on her bruised mouth.

Chapter 32

A small crowd had gathered outside the laundry. When the maids told their fellow staff members that it was Sasha who needed help, they all came running. The sound of gunfire put everyone on edge. The faint thump of the dryers suddenly stopped, and the silence made them even more nervous. Luc and Sylvie waited anxiously at the closed door in the shack and were relieved to hear Sasha's voice calling up.

"Everything is under control. We need two stretchers and Dr. Roussel."

Luc sent some staff for the stretchers and he and Sylvie held hands as they opened the door and started down the ramp. Sylvie was shocked by the scene in front of her – an unconscious man tied hand and foot with clothesline at the bottom of the ramp, a smoking coconut, the open, broken door, a second man sitting on the floor also with his hands and feet tied and a scalpel sticking out of one wrist, an obese white man full of knives and scalpels, Jake with a gun, and Katya, her face bruised, cradled in Sasha's arms.

"She can't walk," Sasha declared to Sylvie, his voice urgent and full of concern. "I'm carrying her to your clinic. I don't think the big man is going to make it. Do what you can here, then meet me there."

"Go through the house!" Sylvie called out. "The entrances are wider. Clinic is first door to your left."

He rushed up the ramp with Katya in his arms, through the agitated crowd and on towards the house, passing men arriving with stretchers. Katya was surprisingly quiet when Sasha set her down in a chair in the clinic. He was sure she was in pain, but he didn't yet know the source. He got some ice from the Roussel's kitchen, wrapped it in a cloth, and applied it to Katya's face, then started a quick examination. Sasha noted that one of the bandages on her arm had been sliced in two. He pulled off the pieces and was furious when he saw the nicks and the long, deep slice in the bullet hole, and even more furious with himself when he saw that the wound had taken a turn for the worse. This could not wait until his boat arrived. He laid Katya carefully on the one examination table, got her to take the strongest painkiller he could find, then searched the small clinic for more supplies. The clinic was woefully ill-equipped: antiseptics and bandages, an unlocked cabinet of basic medicines and syringes, a sterile surgical kit appropriate for removing large splinters and fishhooks and sewing up small lacerations, a box of examination gloves, and not much else. No X-ray machine, not even a basic laboratory, no lights over the exam table.

But his search netted him what he needed, including a local anesthetic, saline solution, a face mask, a sterile scalpel and forceps, tissue retractors, and a suture tray. Sasha scrubbed up, undraped the sterile equipment, put on gloves and mask, prepped her skin, and injected a local anesthetic. He needed just a moment to inspect the wound, finding and removing what he had suspected, a bone chip. Katya should start improving now that it was out. He would X-ray her arm when the *Trib* arrived to be sure there was nothing more, would start her on a different antibiotic immediately. Why had she been so stoic: he'd told her to tell him if the pain worsened. Katya must have been hurting for quite a while. Sasha cleaned and closed the wound, redressed it, then covered her with a blanket. In a very quiet voice, she asked if once again she could have some clothes.

Sasha didn't tell Katya that Cutter was dying. He still needed an antidote to whatever drugs Cutter had given her and would contact the Sydney lab as soon as possible to see if they might identify them from their effects. The drugs in Katya's system were similar to the ones he'd been given in New York but seemed worse. In addition to lack of bleeding from her wound, he could detect no sensation at all in her feet, no reaction to a pinprick. Likely, Katya had been given a mix of drugs, another Cutter special.

Sylvie and Luc arrived along with the two men on stretchers, both covered with sheets. Sylvie shook her head when Sasha looked at the big man's stretcher.

"The young man will wake up with a headache, but there's nothing to do for him. I could use some help with the hand injury though," she said, then whispered, "It's deep... You were right. The big man didn't make it."

They looked over at Katya, but she appeared to have passed out. Jake and a beefy gardener led in the second young Indonesian, a short, surly thug who looked ready to bolt. Sasha had them sit him in a chair and tie up his legs again.

"So who are these creeps?" Jake asked Sasha.

Sasha tended to the injury while talking. "Mr. William Cutter, brother to Markus, from his size and the look of him, and associates. William is based in Indonesia. We've had quite a few run-ins with his human trafficking and slavery organization. Since he was after Katya and not me, I'm assuming this had to do with her role in taking down his brother."

"Human traffickers! Slavers! Such horrid men," Sylvie said, looking aghast at the angry young man tied to the chair. "I thought you were a neurosurgeon on vacation..."

Sasha ignored Sylvie, but regretted speaking to Jake in front of her and Luc. Too late now.

"Jake, contact your people and get all three of these men picked up and out of here immediately," Sasha commanded. "Then find out how and when they got here. Maybe you can persuade this one to tell you."

The man spat on the floor for an answer. Maybe I should just render him unconscious too, Sasha thought. Jake stared at Sasha in confusion, having no idea who Sasha expected him to call upon. Sasha pointed to his ear, signaling Jake that his government was listening. Jake nodded, catching on, then looked back with what Sasha took unhappily to be sympathy. Jake didn't know the half of it, and Sasha didn't want his sympathy. Sasha knew he was going to have to deactivate the listening portion of his tracking device, whether S-Branch liked it or not. Katya must never know he'd still been wearing his tracker last night.

"I'm on it," Jake said loudly as he pulled out his phone and left the clinic.

"Is there someplace we can use as a holding pen, someplace secure?" Sasha asked Luc.

"We have a small room we use occasionally for belligerent drunks, but it's not very secure. There would need to be a guard," said Luc, looking ashen.

"Let's take the two survivors there after I remove the scalpel from this one. We'll need to keep them securely tied. We can hide the body there, too."

"I'll stay with them," volunteered the gardener, Tamatoa.

"Sylvie, are you all right?" asked Sasha. "I know this is not what your usual clinic practice looks like."

"I'll be fine. It's just such a shock. Let me put Katya in my guest room and I'll go to your villa and get her some clothes and personal items."

"Thank you, Sylvie, Luc. We're sorry this happened. These men will be gone soon and you can get back to your lives. I'll bring Katya in later."

"We are honored to have someone with your medical skills staying with us," Sylvie said. "I'm afraid I can do very little doctoring with what I have here."

"Make me a wish list of everything you would like to have, no matter how extravagant. I will make sure you get what you need. You must have an X-ray machine, for certain. I have a fully staffed hospital boat arriving in five days from Sydney. My crew will live on the boat, so you won't need to worry about accommodations for them. Normally, I live there too. I will contact them and they will bring all the supplies and equipment you ask for. This will be my thank you for what we've put you through."

"Dr. Borodin, you are a godsend! I am truly overwhelmed." There were tears in Sylvie's eyes. "Your crew will be most welcome here."

Katya began to stir. Sasha stroked her face.

"Luc, Tamatoa, I'm finished here," Sasha said. Tamatoa was beaming that Sasha remembered his name. "Please take this man away. Sylvie, there is one thing you can do for Katya and me. We haven't eaten much since lunch yesterday and I bet Katya is as starved as I am. Could we have some food brought over to the guest room? Fish or vegetarian, no meat? I'll carry Katya over there now. And could I make one call and use your Wi-Fi while we wait?"

Sylvie nodded, gave him directions, and left the room.

"No calls, no Wi-Fi. You're going to deliver me to the shower," Katya demanded, speaking for only the second time since Sasha had probed her wound. She relented when he told her whom he was contacting and why. Sasha picked up the phone and pretended to punch in Peter's number, letting his tracker carry the message. These charades were really getting embarrassing, Sasha thought. He explained what had happened, pled with Peter not to send in a plane full of guards, just to supply him with a credit card number. He repeated Katya's request for funds to cover Jake's fake wedding prank. Sasha couldn't let her know that Peter had already heard about it through his tracker. He hoped Peter would understand his coded

208

message about the voice deactivation – Sasha promising to check in twice a day through his secure computer. As soon as he'd hung up the phone, Sasha carried Katya into the guest room's bathroom, sitting her on the floor of the shower to wash her. She was entirely helpless. He would have to dress her when Sylvie arrived and carry her to a chair. Safe, peaceful Bora Bora, he thought. He was morbidly amused to find himself thinking ironically quite often since he met Katya.

Sylvie brought breakfast along with clothes and items from the villa. After giving them a few minutes of privacy, she sat in the guest room with them while Katya and Sasha ate at a small table. Sasha placed Katya on the bed after she had eaten. Sylvie was as curious as the natives about this strange couple.

"Dr. Borodin, I'm so sorry. I bet she'll be back on her feet tomorrow. She seems remarkably tough. I'm happy you and Katya have reconciled. I could see that you loved each other, even if you two couldn't see it yourselves." Sylvie waited a beat, then asked her first question. "You said you lived aboard your hospital boat, Dr. Borodin. Will Katya be living on board with you?"

"Please call me Sasha. I'm sorry I stormed out of the ceremony yesterday. I was taken by surprise, but now I'm glad it happened. We've never discussed where we'll live. This is all too new. Katya lives in California and I'm at sea in Southeast Asia most of the year."

"And I was surprised that Katya said she paid for this trip herself, that she'd used all the money she had."

"That is a long and complicated story. I'm not... I'm not a hospital-based surgeon on holiday, like I implied when we arrived... I don't take a surgeon's salary. I have very little money of my own. I'm more of a simple soldier, bringing free medical care to the people who need it most. And yes, my boat deals occasionally with unsavory criminal elements who prey on our clientele. The sponsors of my hospital boat pay my expenses, which are few, pay my crew, and will be buying your medical equipment. Katya has helped me to see that I need to make a change. I've been avoiding any kind of public life far too long."

"If you don't mind my asking, how did you end up living on a boat? What made you give up public life?"

Sasha thought for a moment how to answer, how much to reveal. He decided to be partially truthful, but not reveal too much. He and Katya seemed to be making a habit of it.

209

"Grief. I lost my wife tragically a long time ago. I had been a neurosurgeon at the University of Sydney, but ran away from the world, unable to bear the loss. Katya has been instrumental in bringing me back to life, and now back to love. I've been estranged from the modern world, and I'm so eccentric, I must admit, that my sponsors hired Jake and Katya to watch over me when I chose to leave the security of my boat to travel here."

Katya stirred again and sat up further in the bed with Sasha's help. She could hardly believe what she was hearing, Sasha talking so candidly, if not completely truthfully, with Sylvie. His trust in her was an encouraging step towards normalcy.

"We're taking this one day at a time, Sylvie," Katya added. "We're also assuming I'll be on my feet again soon. But I'm not staying inside, nice as this room is. Sasha can just carry me to the beach after breakfast."

"I understand there's quite a crowd of admirers out there. I'm afraid your privacy is a thing of the past," Sylvie warned her.

"Maybe we can make a deal with them," Sasha said. "Let them know that when my hospital boat arrives, there will be a free clinic for everyone. And I just talked with my friend Peter Hammond in San Francisco. He'll pay for last night's banquet and celebration, and he would like to pay for a second feast with everyone invited when Katya is ready to walk out of here. Katya and I never got to enjoy the first feast. The only cost will be a guarantee of our privacy for the rest of our visit." Sasha had no doubt Peter would not argue.

Sasha looked to Katya to see if she was in agreement.

"Brilliant," she said. "Maybe a promise of some music would help, too. I noticed you have a small piano as I was being carried through your house, Sylvie. I take it you're the pianist?" Katya hoped that Sasha would begin to play for an audience now that he'd opened so many other doors.

"I am, but the piano is completely out of tune," Sylvie answered with a sigh. "Tropical weather is not kind to pianos."

"Let me tune it for you," Sasha said. "I would like to be able to play it myself, and Katya would too, when she has two arms and at least one leg. Perhaps you could accompany me, Sylvie. You may have heard me playing the violin."

"Everyone within a mile has been enjoying your playing, Sasha. You're quite good. More than quite good! If we find some easy enough pieces for me, I would be honored."

"And I have one more idea for keeping your locals busy. Your clinic is far too small for all the medical equipment my boat will be bringing. I've already designed in my head a two-room expansion. Your building materials are simple here. We could get started tomorrow. And perhaps one of your employees would like to train with me to be your part-time medical assistant."

"This is all too much. Again, I am overwhelmed!" Sylvie effused.

Word of the assault in the laundry spread quickly and soon all the Tahitians in the area knew that Katya had taken down two attackers single-handed, that Sasha and Jake had taken down a third, and that there was a coconut "bomb" involved. Great care was taken to ensure the resort guests knew nothing of it. There were rumors that Katya had killed both attackers with her bare hands or with a single scalpel, that she was permanently paralyzed, that the attackers had cut her hamstrings, that they had carved up her face, that the attackers were mobsters from the U.S. looking for ransom money. The rest of the day Sasha had to fend off a steady stream of Tahitian well-wishers and the curious. He left the sorting of fact from fiction to Jake, who seemed to relish the attention.

Together they'd come up with a plausible story that kept close to the truth: the attackers were in a human trafficking and kidnapping gang, and Katya had killed the leader's brother accidently in her role as bodyguard to a previous client. Tahitians understood revenge for a family member, and everyone, guests included, loved the story that the doctor guest had fallen in love with his new assistant/bodyguard and married her right here at their resort, after a rather juicy hiccup at the ceremony. And they loved that Katya was a woman warrior who had bested her abductors. They were all thrilled to help build the clinic expansion and eagerly awaited the hospital boat. It was a long, expensive trip to Papeete for care. The two Indonesians and the corpse were whisked away on a private jet that night; life at le Hédonisme returned to normal. Sasha found time alone to temporarily remove his tracker and deactivate the voice transmitter. It was his invention after all. For once his privacy was going to come first.

Sasha carried Katya back into the guest room late that night and put her to bed. She still couldn't wiggle a toe, but her hands were only tingly, no longer numb. They were encouraged that Sasha's lab suggested nothing more than a combination of over-the-counter medicines from Sylvie's clinic cabinet, Sasha's painkillers, and patience. They'd managed to have lunch, and then dinner with a fine second sunset, on the beach. Even though the natives were respectful, a few of the resort guests peppered them with questions. The bothersome guests were shooed away by a sweet looking Australian couple Katya hadn't noticed before, an attractive young blond woman and her strapping husband. Another couple seemed to be following them. Katya didn't understand the displeased look Sasha gave them. That evening, Katya was happy to be placed on a living room sofa listening to Sylvie and Sasha run through some music together.

"Not how I pictured our first full day in Bora Bora," Katya said, snuggling close in the guest room bed.

"How can anyone picture what almost happened to you?"

"I had it under control. I never pictured failure."

"That is one of the many things I love about you. And my crew will love about you. The *Trib* will be arriving in just a few days. The Roussels are no longer limiting my Wi-Fi usage so I've been having long talks with everyone. I think they'd be here tomorrow if they could. They are excited to meet you."

"They're not the only ones who are excited. Being French, I don't think the Roussels will mind if we make love loudly in their guest room tonight. I'm not wasting this night with you just because I can't move my feet and one arm. We are on our honeymoon, after all."

"I swear I'm going to make you scream in ecstasy, Katya," Sasha said, smiling inwardly at the multiple ironies. "When they hear you, the Roussels will start having sex at the same time. You just lie still, not that you have much choice, and let me make love to you. Just feel free to touch any of my body parts that come anywhere near your one good hand."

He could deal with the Roussels hearing them. Katya was right; they would probably even enjoy it. But this time they would be the only ones listening. He lay on top of her and started to kiss her, making good on his promise.

Chapter 33

"When were you going to tell me that William Cutter is dead? That I've killed another man?" Katya said Sasha, after her visitors left.

The young Tahitian women had arrived early that morning and fussed over her for an hour. They'd happily shared all the news and rumors floating around the resort and helped her to shower and get dressed. Now she lay on top of the bed again, propped up with pillows.

"I would have told you today. I thought you had enough to deal with yesterday."

"I didn't throw that hard. I don't think I meant to kill."

"A scalpel went through an eye, Katya."

"Oh God... I didn't know... And just how many Cutter brothers are there? Is this revenge cycle going to be repeated again and again?"

"Sorry to tell you there are, were, four brothers, all deep in crime, all evil specimens. I feel that we're safe for now, but we'll need to be more vigilant."

"Two more Cutters out there. What does Fate have in store for us next?"

"Fate will have nothing to do with it. We'll make our own destinies."

"Well, I plan to make my own destiny right now by getting out of this bed and walking to the bathroom."

"You're not serious."

"Watch me."

Katya had been wiggling her feet under the covers for the last half-hour and hoped that she wouldn't fall on her face if she was wrong. She swung herself to a sitting position on the side of the bed but did not refuse Sasha's offer of a helping hand. She stood up and took one step forward with great difficulty. She rested to the count of ten and tried a second step. It took a long time, but she made it to the bathroom. She could not have done it by herself.

"Progress," Katya said happily. "Please tell Sylvie and Luc to start preparing the beachside feast for tonight. I'm going to work on this all day until I can walk there under my own steam. Let's keep the news among us four if we can."

Sasha was encouraged but stayed with her in the bathroom. He made her promise not to try walking anywhere without him by her side, then helped her to a chair and sat down next to her.

"How is your arm today?" he asked.

"Much better. I knew it shouldn't have hurt so badly. Thank you for finding that bone fragment before things got even worse. Maybe I should thank the late William Cutter for slicing me open. How soon do you think I will gain full use?"

"In a normal person, I would give it three more weeks. You, on the other hand, I'd say a few more days. You can start doing careful exercises with it. No pushups, please."

"Irony. Part of humor. Part of being human. You, too, are making progress."

"What are you talking about? I was being serious. You seem quite capable of trying to do pushups."

"I should have known. Maybe I could notch poles or plait thatch at the clinic construction site today. I can't sit here feeling useless. How is it going out there? Even with the door from the house closed off, it certainly is noisy."

"There must be over thirty men, women, and a few of the older children hard at work. Even some of the guests are pitching in. You know, I *will* carry you out there. It will cheer you up to see the progress and everyone will be happy to see you."

Sasha noticed Katya's face suddenly darken and he guessed what she was thinking. He remembered the photographs in her Guatemala album of Katya helping the villagers build a school and clinic.

"Katya, we will not let the past repeat itself. I know you can't forget what happened to the villagers you loved any more than I can forget the horrors and loss I've experienced in my life. I am incapable of forgetting anything. The memories crowd my mind and often make my life a living hell. But I am as close as I've been in over thirty years to being able to see through them to the light on the other side, the light you bring to me."

Katya was so moved by his words she couldn't speak, just nod her head. She was still in awe of his expressions of love for her, of the depth of her love for him. She ran her fingers through his hair and was surprised by how damp it was and could see that he was starting to get his inward look again. He sat silently for a long time, sweating through his shirt. Katya was sure that the mere mention of his hellish

214

memories had sent him away from her. She took both his hands in hers while she waited, hopeful that he might be ready to confide in her this time. His hands were icy and tense. When he finally looked down, she knew he had returned.

"Sasha, I need you to tell me where you go at times like this. Please don't lock me out. I know you don't want to talk about it, but I want to understand you. You know there is nothing you can't tell me. Let me share your burden."

"I'm sorry, I can't stop once it starts," Sasha said, looking as anguished as he had at the Martin Luther King, Jr. Memorial in San Francisco. "And you're right, it is time for you to hear this. There is a list I can't forget. Name, city, birthdate, date of death."

"What names and dates, Sasha?" Katya asked, breathless. "Whose deaths?"

"Those who died at Bergen-Belsen whose names I was given." Sasha's voice was again calm, detached, but his face held a look of horror, like he was staring into a pit of the dead. He pulled his hands away and seemed to withdraw into himself. "It started about four months before the camp was liberated. Thousands of new prisoners had begun arriving, exhausted, sick from forced death marches from the East – then tens of thousands arrived from all over. The horrible conditions in the camp got much worse... there was another typhus outbreak. Everyone was afraid they were going to die of starvation, or typhus, or dysentery. Or be murdered. There seemed to be no hope left anywhere.

"One of my newest teachers, my Polish teacher, had just lost her sister to typhus. Word had spread from the other teachers that I remembered everything I was taught, and from her experience teaching me, she thought that it was true. She asked me to remember her sister if I survived. She gave me her name, the city she came from, her birthdate, and the date of her death. I didn't know if I could do this for her, but I promised. I was just a child who was never sure I would survive my next beating by my Nazi tormenter.

"Her sister became the first name on my list. So many people were dying; no one wanted any one of them to be forgotten. Soon she was whispering other names, cities, and dates. Inmates in her compound asked her to pass on more names and dates, then word spread to the other compounds. Prisoners would find ways to whisper to me as I walked by. I would find names and dates scratched with charred wood on scraps of cloth that fluttered through the barbed wires. My violin and music teacher, Herr Silber, and my other surviving teachers brought me more. I stole pieces of paper and pencils from the SS barracks and my teachers smuggled them out. Small scraps were returned to me with more names and dates. All of the inmates who taught me perished. All their names are on my list. And still more names came...

"I memorized all the information in the order I learned it, and I repeated the list to myself every day. Anne Frank's name is on my list, her sister Margot's, too. Both died of typhus before liberation. The world has never forgotten them, but there are hundreds whose lives and deaths might have been. I became the memory of the camp, a living archive for the names of the dead. As the day of the announced turnover of the camp to the British approached, I saw the camp officials destroying records, and I knew my memory would be the only record left of many inmates' names and deaths. I could not fail them. I learned later there were so many deaths since the camp opened – over 50,000... The names of some twenty thousand people who perished were lost when the records were burned. As long as my list was, it was only a small fraction of the deaths those last months. I had memorized a mere two hundred and eighty-four.

"After my tormenter Krüger killed himself, I moved into one of the women's compounds and stayed with a Dutch group during those last days. With starvation and typhus continuing to take their toll, I added more names to my list as I waited for liberation. I tried to recite my list to the British liberators, and when they didn't understand me, I later asked for the head of the Jewish Refugee program at the Bergen Displacement Camp. The woman in charge understood immediately and called for a volunteer to copy down every name, check every spelling with me. I thought I had discharged my duty, that I was done forever with the list, but it comes back to haunt me again and again..."

Sasha stopped suddenly. Such an unimaginable burden of responsibility for a child, Katya thought, as she steeled herself against her own strong emotions. Sasha needed her to focus on what would come next. He didn't need her pity. He needed her help.

"I have only fifteen names on the list in my head, Sasha, my relatives from Vienna all murdered in Auschwitz. The dates of their deaths were carefully recorded by the Nazis. My father and I visited

Auschwitz together on a trip to Poland and paid our respects. They have not been forgotten either."

"David told me. I have no words."

"We stood and said the Mourner's Kaddish together aloud, my father and I. Then behind me, I heard other voices joining in. Before we finished, half the visitors around us were reciting the Kaddish with us. Nearly everyone was in tears. When we were finished, strangers started shaking our hands, each other's hands, starting conversations, sharing stories of why they were there, who they had lost."

Katya glanced over at Sasha. He still appeared stricken, lost himself, but he looked back at her.

"Do you know the Mourner's Kaddish, Sasha?" Katya asked, keeping her eyes fixed on his.

"Of course I know it. The Mandelbrots raised me Jewish in Sydney. I can't forget anything I've learned. But I don't believe in a God who would let this happen. There is no God."

"God didn't do this. Man did. Do you imagine God as a Superhero, able to smite your enemies, destroy Evil? That you could stop a tsunami... a bullet... with prayer? A belief in God, in a higher power, gives you hope, courage, inner strength. I'm not just talking about praying to the God of the Torah. I have also become a doubter, but I've learned to think of God in a different way. I pray to the God inside me, inside you. Think about what you've learned from Buddhism. Prayer changes who you are, not the world around you... Listen Sasha, would you recite the Mourner's Kaddish with me, now, aloud? You need to make peace within yourself. You need to let this be finished. We'll imagine we have a minyan: the dead will be here with us."

Katya took his cold hand in her warm one, giving him a squeeze of encouragement. Turning to face him squarely in her chair, she moved to place her forehead against his. He bent down to her, his eyes closed. She waited a full minute, then started reciting the Mourner's Kaddish softly at first, then louder. She could see Sasha's lips moving, then heard him speak the ancient Aramaic prayer with her, the printed form floating before her eyes, as it must have been for Sasha, the alphabet the same as Hebrew, the transliteration following...

Yit'gadal v'yit'kadash sh'mei raba b'al'ma di-v'ra khir'utei...

217

Katya kept her body still through to the end of the long prayer, her head firmly against Sasha's, afraid to move too soon. When he straightened, she noticed his hair was drying, his face no longer looked stricken. Katya could sense the tension leave his body. His hand relaxed and his thumb began caressing her hand. Maybe, just maybe, she thought, this had been the release he needed. Maybe he was ready, maybe he could finally put the List to rest. Sasha gave her his near smile, and she was certain that he held the same hope. Clearing his throat, he let go of her hand and touched her face.

"Thank you. That meant more to me than I can say. I'm sorry for the loss of your family in California, too. You're not alone anymore."

She reached out her arms to him and he picked her up as if she weighed nothing at all. They shared a long kiss before he carried her through the house, out the front door and around to the construction site. People stopped work to smile and greet her and Sasha, then returned to their jobs with renewed effort. He found a place for her to sit.

Katya was not at all surprised that Sasha was offering greetings and giving directions in Tahitian and knew everyone by name. The framing was already up, and workers were starting in on the raised floor joists and steps. Sasha showed her where the covered porch waiting area would be. There would be an in-patient unit on the left with two beds and an isolette for newborns, and a new space for outpatients in the middle. The original clinic room that had opened into the house would contain a small but high-tech one-bed operating room, along with an ultrasound and an X-ray machine and other medical equipment.

The basic construction would be completed in just four days using the basic building materials on hand, plus lots of bamboo, screw pine, known here as pandanus, and naiu, plaited coconut palm leaves for the roof, over hidden sheets of tin. Sasha was taking no chances with water leaks from the current daily twenty- to thirty-minute rains of Bora Bora's drier winter, June to August, or from the torrential downpours of its summer, December to February. The seasons were the same as Australia's, although here the average temperature year-round was in the 80s. Just the way he liked it. He showed Katya how the rainwater recovery system would work and told her that his crew was also bringing his own version of solar panels that would meet the

218

electrical needs of not only the new clinic but of the entire resort as well.

"Sylvie asked around if anyone wanted to train as her assistant and she received fifteen responses," Sasha told her. "Maybe we'll train them all in basic medicine and see who wants to continue. Then we can see who does the job well."

"That's a great idea. But you'll have sixteen trainees. I know next to nothing about medicine and need a crash course, but I promise I'm a fast learner."

If she were going to manipulate her way into joining Sasha's crew, she would have to develop some medical skills quickly. Sasha took her hand in appreciation of her interest.

"We'll start this morning, just you and me, then we'll meet with the others after lunch. First let's find you something you can do here with one arm and just your fingers."

The day went by swiftly. Sasha proved to be a hard taskmaster but seemed to have infinite patience, and was an excellent teacher of basic medicine and first aid. By late afternoon, Katya's mind was reeling from all the information she'd learned, and the list of interested potential clinic assistants had been whittled down to seven, including Tamatoa and Taiana. Katya had Sasha carry her to the guest room once every hour so she could practice walking. After the Tahitians left, Sasha began tuning the baby grand piano, Luc helping scrounge appropriate tools. Luc, Sylvie, and Katya watched, fascinated. Katya was amazed by his new manic energy.

"How... how did you learn how to do this?" Sylvie asked.

"Our piano tuner came twice a year. I was always underfoot, finally convinced him to teach me. I could tune the piano myself by the time I was nine."

Katya smiled at their hosts' dropped jaws, caught Sasha's look. He was being indiscreet and knew it, didn't care. Even with a superb tuning and voicing, Katya knew the old piano would be just passable. It would have to do. The tuning took a long time, Luc and Sylvie checking in often to watch. Sasha then went to work, practicing technique, remembering pieces he had learned so long ago. No sheet music needed, the notes forever in his head. He would read through the sonatas Sylvie chose to play with him. One reading and he wouldn't need sheet music for them either. Katya was as transfixed as she had been first hearing his violin playing. Even on this second-rate piano, Sasha's artistry was unmistakable. Rhythm, subtlety and strength in a range of dynamics, an exceptional expressive and poetic depth – Katya wished she could play half as well.

Two hours passed, his audience of three unable to leave the presence of such mastery. Debussy. Then Bach. Scarlatti. Rameau. Chopin. Beethoven, followed by Brahms: some of his last works for piano. Contemplative pieces, quiet, Romantic, with just flashes of drama. Luc and Sylvie were finally torn away by the call of business. Sasha stopped abruptly upon their departure, like he'd been waiting for them to leave, not wanting to hear their words of praise. Katya understood. She leaned over him and kissed the back of his neck and stayed quiet.

"Sylvie has told everyone our piano and violin performance will be right before the beachside feast," Sasha said. "She's a little nervous, she says, but then she has no idea I've never played before a seated audience."

"Are you telling me you're nervous?" Katya asked.

"I don't ever get nervous about anything. I may just ignore the audience altogether."

"Just play as if I'm the only one listening, Sasha. You can't ignore me."

"I will consider the audience in my choice of music, though. But I won't play Haydn or Mozart. Or anything baroque except Bach, Scarlatti, and Rameau. My taste runs much more to music this audience would find difficult to listen to. Bartók. Prokofiev's sonatas. Shostakovich. Messiaen."

"Then save those pieces for me, Sasha. But you're missing out on some wonderful music. Tell me more about your piano in Sydney."

"A fine old Steinway, much like yours in Berkeley, but a full-size concert grand. It was rebuilt just five years ago and sounds sublime. I gave the Mandelbrot's house, and their money, to the University of Sydney when I shipped off to Vietnam. The University keeps the house for visiting professors, with all of the furnishings intact, although I imagine they've updated some of them. Sadly, Harrison's extensive Oceanic and Southeast Asian art collection went to various museums. That I miss. Nothing but dull framed Australian travel posters on the walls now. I don't leave the living room."

Katya thought for a moment. "You told me you play cello, too. Don't tell me you play cello as brilliantly as you do violin and piano."

"Then I won't."

The newly tuned baby grand piano was rolled onto the front porch and turned sideways. Chairs were set up in the living room for the resort guests and all the doors were opened wide. More chairs were set up on the lawn, but there was standing room only by the time the performance started. Katya was already sitting on a stuffed chair in front of the piano before the other guests arrived. Jake sat near her, and she flashed him an all-is-forgiven smile.

Sylvie and Sasha played through some Bach and Fauré sonatas. Katya thought Sylvie a modest and timid pianist and wished she could have been at the keyboard herself, but it didn't matter. The audience was listening to the magnificent sound of Sasha's violin. Everyone present had heard Sasha's violin from a distance but nothing prepared them for the excitement of watching him perform. Facing the piano, he didn't have to acknowledge the listeners on either side of him, nor was his back to any of them. For most of the locals, this was their first experience with live classical music. Neophytes and jaded world travelers alike were mesmerized by the intensity and passion he brought to his playing, his music engulfing their senses. No one moved, no one took their eyes off of him for a second.

Then Sylvie left the stage to Sasha, and the evening quickly grew even livelier. Sasha launched into wild Romani music that made everyone sit up, then worked through some of the most beautiful music for solo violin in the repertoire, beginning with the complete Chaconne from the Bach second Partita he'd played backstage at Davies Hall, followed by the Romanza Andaluze by Sarasate, and ending with an exquisite interpretation of the brooding Recitation and sprightly Scherzo by Kreisler.

Cheers and applause erupted from the audience. Sylvie and Sasha took another bow, then Sasha carefully put away his violin as the applause continued. He turned to Katya and held out his hand. She stood up and slowly walked to him and held his hand tightly as they descended the stairs to renewed wild cheering. They were thronged by ecstatically happy Tahitians congratulating both of them. Katya was sure someone would try to take Sasha's hand or pat him on his back, but the Tahitians already knew him well enough to give him space. The guests followed the Tahitians' example and kept a respectful distance.

Banquet tables soon groaned with fresh fish, Tahitian specialties like poisson cru, raw fish marinated in coconut milk, and chevrettes, freshwater native shrimp, po'e, sweet pudding made with taro root, breadfruit, called uru here, crab legs, mussels, papayas, pineapples, mangoes, coconuts, and much more. Bare-chested young men lit torches along the beach. Sasha found a table for Katya and went to fill two plates. They sat back to eat while watching their third spectacular sunset.

Sasha began to relax for the first time since Katya was attacked. The past days had been difficult emotionally, a roller coaster for a man unaccustomed to dealing with emotions. He was trying hard to accommodate all the challenges to the Zen Buddhist peace he aimed for, but it was an impossible task. Everything about this place and the situation was new and different. Sasha had never experienced such a laid-back lifestyle as Bora Bora offered, busy as he was trying to keep himself with numerous projects, in sharp contrast with his decades of well-ordered shipboard life. He had been living in unaccustomed luxury ever since the St. Francis in San Francisco. He had just played music publicly for the first time in his life before a seated audience and was even accepting applause, albeit reluctantly. The memory of the applause and standing ovation after his speech at the Global Human Rights Conference washed over him.

Recognition. Acknowledgement. He had made a few steps out of the shadows. He had to admit it felt good.

And Katya. Maybe he would not have been able to make love with her if they hadn't experienced the unexpected wedding ceremony. Despite how he'd ended it, and its unofficial nature, the ceremony made him feel in his heart that they were husband and wife. His love for this young woman was almost more than he could bear, the thought of losing her too terrible to consider. He felt he'd suffered more trauma from the attack on Katya than she appeared to. Her calm, unfazed demeanor was admirable but inexplicable. His desire to touch her and be touched, for sex with her, after so many years of celibacy was emotionally overwhelming as well. Sasha knew he was fortunate his mind could pursue a dozen thoughts at once, because one of the most irresistible every moment of the day was of having sex with her.

Sasha felt himself very much in a free fall. The sensation he felt most was hope, though he couldn't seem to find the right words to describe it. Hope that his recitation of the List had ended forever. A hope for lasting happiness, perhaps. Was that even possible again, he wondered. Hope for happiness that would not be snatched away in a day, like it had almost been, or after an all too short year and a half like with Le.

Chapter 34

Katya and Sasha snuck away from the feast while the celebration was in full swing. Katya insisted she wanted them to sleep in their own villa. Taiana and Vaea went back to the guest room to gather up their possessions and Sasha's violin case. Erita couldn't bear to leave Katya's side and kept kissing her and crying as she helped support her. Katya was finally able to disengage herself when they reached the cove in front of their villa. The young women handed over to Sasha all the items they were carrying, kissed Katya one more time, and slipped back to the feast.

Once inside their villa, Sasha saw that Katya was looking pale and depressed. He got her to sit on the sofa and brought her a glass of water with her antibiotic pill and another Australogic painkiller, then sat close beside her.

"Time to slow down," he said to her with concern. "You look terrible. I'm sorry I didn't notice sooner."

"That's not all of it. Yes, I'm exhausted, but I also feel sick about having taken another life, as awful as that life was. I can't get the image of Cutter with the scalpel in his eye out of my mind. How do you manage to cope every day with the images in your head?"

"I can't smile and I can't laugh. I've never shed a tear. No one but you can touch me. Most people would say I'm not coping well at all. There are good memories sometimes, but the images that prevail are those of the horror of the camp. There is only music when I play. Music is my one escape. I guess playing music is how I cope. But talking about these things with you has also been a tremendous help to me."

"As listening to you has been for me. If you feel like talking now, we may both feel better."

"I... I would like to try. I want to tell you about Le."

Sasha settled Katya down to where her head was resting on his shoulder. He stroked her hair and neck as her hand snaked under his shirt to caress his abdomen and chest. He collected himself to tell the still painful story.

"I remained with my medical unit, fulfilling my duties as an army captain and surgeon, although I lived with Le on my boat. Somehow I kept my work at the laboratories secret from her, made sure she never saw the guards sent to watch over me. I continued the free clinic, with Le helping me when she wasn't in class at the university."

"She didn't know about your history, your protected genius status?"

"No... not really. Or very little of it... She cried when she saw my scars and tattoo for the first time... but accepted that I wouldn't talk about them."

"You should never keep such secrets from those you love... but go on."

Sasha nodded absently, too caught up in his memories to reply.

"When Le and I bought a house together – a small place on a riverbank with room for the child to come – we were so happy. Le had reached her eighth month and we were preparing the house for the baby's arrival. My happiness since I'd met her spilled over into my work and we had friends from my unit, fellow doctors and nurses, and from her university. I'd never had friends... Several were musicians and we played music together – the first time for me since... since Herr Silber, my music teacher at the camp..."

Sasha closed his eyes, and Katya could feel him reliving his loss. Of this Herr Silber. Of Le. Of his unborn child.

"My pain was doubled because I lost her twice. The first time, I had just been dropped off at home by friends after surgery rounds and she didn't come rushing to the door to greet me as usual. I found a note on the kitchen table, but I knew at first glance it was a forgery. The note said she was leaving me and going home to her family in the North to have the baby. I ran to the bedroom and discovered a dead pregnant woman on the bed. I knew she was not Le in an instant. I grabbed my two violin cases and ran out the back door towards the river – somehow I knew she'd been taken by force, that she was still on that river.

"But before I could run down the slope to my boat, I was thrown to the ground by a tremendous explosion. Our house had been obliterated, and had I tarried a moment longer over the note or the strange corpse, I would have been killed. As it was, I was injured, but not seriously. My friends had turned their car around and were staring in shock at the burning ruins when I staggered to the street. The police thought I'd lost my mind when I tried to convince them that the burnt skeleton of a woman with an unborn child found in the ruins was not my wife. My friends and my unit, even S-Branch, were also convinced my wife and child were dead, and they weren't much better at supporting me. I was certain that her father, General An, had kidnapped her and tried to kill me.

"For over six weeks, I was a total wreck. I would not work for my unit or in the laboratories S-Branch had built for me in Saigon. I exploited every connection I'd ever made in the country trying to find her. Finally, a contact got a message from her to me. She had escaped her father and was on her way home, with a place, date and time when she would cross the border on the Mekong River from Cambodia into the South, where I would meet her. Not a word about the child.

"I took my boat and was there, breathless with excitement, waiting, when I saw her making her way through the trees. I stood up from the tall grass where I'd been hiding so she could see me, when to my horror, shots rang out from somewhere halfway between us, and Le crumbled to the ground. I ran forward and found two American snipers lying in the grass. In my fury, I knocked both men unconscious, nearly killing them, then raced on to Le. She was still alive, but I knew at once the shots were fatal. She told me… she told me she loved me and that she never would have left me, and that the child had been born early, a boy, and that… and that was all, she was gone. I picked her up and carried her to my boat on the river to bring her home to Saigon. There must have been a hundred people at her funeral, and although everyone now knew that I had not lost my mind before, I was truly out of my mind this time with grief and depression, obsessed with finding my son. But that door was closed to me, then and since. I have been searching for thirty-three years. I am still searching."

Sasha looked down, then gathered himself to continue.

"S-Branch did what they could to get information from the Americans and to keep them from prosecuting me for beating their men. The Americans admitted they'd received a tip that a dangerous female spy would be crossing at that moment from Cambodia and had sent the snipers to kill her. I never did learn who betrayed her or why. When my unit and S-Branch insisted I return to work after a month, I took my boat and fled. I dyed my hair black and disappeared. I exchanged boats several times, made it as far as Malaysia, Indonesia, and the Philippines.

"It was during this year of constant movement that I ran into the horrendous aftermath of a pirate attack. I rescued the one survivor, a young woman, a teenager, who had been raped and left for dead in the midst of her murdered family on their boat. I was again obsessed, this time with finding the killers and punishing them. When I located three of them, I used my boat and the girl as bait to get them aboard, then captured them and tied them to chairs. I set up a poison administration system in each man's arm, activated by a simple push of a button. I asked the girl if she wanted to push the button to kill them as she watched... The men were begging for their lives... As traumatized as she had been, she could not push the button. But I could. And I did."

Sasha stopped for another long moment. This had been the lowest moral point in his life, and he was still appalled at what he had become: a killer of killers.

"The girl wanted nothing more to do with me after that. She thought me insane, and she was probably right," he continued. "I took her to her older sister's home and traveled on, my grief and anger dissipating month by month, although my deep depression continued. It finally dawned on me to practice medicine instead of hate, so I started my traveling clinic, living off donations and payments of food.

"S-Branch tracked me through my medical work and caught up with me in Indonesia. They held out the promise of more freedom from surveillance. I demanded a much larger boat with the most modern medical equipment and a big crew if I were to return to work for them. I would design the boat myself and do my work for the labs remotely for eleven months out of the year. They readily acquiesced. Little did they know I would take up pirate and human trafficker chasing before two years had passed. I couldn't stand by while terror reigned on the rivers, bays, and coasts we traveled. No one else seemed capable of doing much about it."

"So it was your choice not to return to the world, to live on your boat."

"I couldn't face a world without Le in it. Until you, I never thought of returning to my career as a publicly acknowledged surgeon, or of ever loving another person as I had loved Le."

"Your son is still out there waiting for you to find him, Sasha."

"I still think of him as a small child. He's several years older than you now."

Katya moved over to kiss him, straddling his lap. He responded with an even deeper kiss as her fingertips caressed the back of his neck. Sasha reflected that the incredible sex of the last two nights mirrored his lovemaking with Le during their all too brief marriage. He was touching Katya in ways that had put Le into ecstasy, ways Le had taught him to pleasure her, using the outrageous, ribald banter that amused her, so opposite his normal speech. And yet it felt right, it was as it should be. For the third night in a row, he carried Katya to bed and let himself be lost in the wild pleasures of uninhibited sex.

Chapter 35

The next several days flew by with a predictable pattern and flow. Sasha woke at dawn and exercised for precisely an hour and a half while Katya slept in. He talked Jake into sparring with him twice, but Jake left the second time so bruised and beaten he swore that Sasha was still taking vengeance on him. Exercises ended, Sasha swam to the main beach and back to cool off, then returned to the villa to wake and make love with Katya before they snorkeled and showered together. She couldn't stop him from making the bed each morning – he told her it was automatic, that he'd been making beds since he was a small child. Katya didn't ask why. There was story there she was sure she didn't want to hear.

Sasha hadn't been able to resist sitting down at the keyboard after the concert and spent part of each afternoon methodically playing more selections by Debussy, Bach, Scarlatti, Schumann, Beethoven, and Chopin, his music vying with the sound of rain on the tin roof. A small crowd gathered on the front porch to listen after lunch, although the audience thinned considerably when he started playing through the last three Prokofiev piano sonatas. Katya loved them and jokingly told Sylvie the detractors were all philistines. He won his audience back when he began playing Schubert: an astounding "Wanderer" Fantasy, Franz Schubert's most technically demanding composition for the piano, then all eight of his impromptus.

Sylvie confided she was enthralled by Sasha's playing and was plotting another concert for him. Katya knew Sylvie had convinced him when she heard him practicing some particularly challenging pieces well after the resort guests had retired to their villas.

Each day, Sasha worked with the Sydney labs via his computer, advising on current projects and beginning new ones, and supervised the construction project. While Sasha was gone, Katya did vocal exercises and sang in the villa, then plunged herself into various modified workouts to regain her strength. Later, she would join Sasha at the Roussel's house to practice technique and melodies on the piano with her right hand, carefully trying out her left, and to chat with Sylvie. Sasha taught Katya and the dwindling number of candidates for clinic assistant for two sessions of an hour each and played his violin. Somehow he found time just to laze with Katya on the beach or walk the property with her, barefoot or in sandals, dressed in shorts and a light-weight long-sleeved shirt.

Katya's arm was healing quickly. She agitated for a scuba lesson, but Sasha insisted she wait until the *Trib* arrived so she could learn on his newest line of high-tech equipment, arguing that the resort's scuba gear was old and out-of-date. She settled for a second snorkel with Jake while Sasha worked. Jake spent several hours a day on the construction project, working closely with Tihei.

Jake was a hero to Tihei after the laundry room rescue. Atea and Jake were becoming quite an item, much to Katya's amusement. Jake told her he felt under no obligation to return to the U.S. and Mason's employ, that he'd been hired muscle, an ex-intelligence agent, as Sasha had surmised. Sasha and Katya wondered if Jake would ever be able to leave Bora Bora.

Nights were spent in vigorous sexual explorations, apparently by everyone in the resort, Katya mused, not just her and Sasha. No one but Sasha was stirring in the early morning. Katya didn't know how he did it. She knew she would have to become an early riser if she were to join his crew, but sleeping late was such a joy.

On the seventh day, news that Sasha's sailboat was approaching the small harbor unexpectedly early brought nearly everyone to the dock after lunch. The staff hurried to their homes to gather their children and the guests rushed down as well, marveling at the sight of the boat. Luc, Sylvie, and Sasha stood at the end of the dock to welcome the crew. Sasha was beside himself that Katya wasn't there. She and Jake missed the sighting, having just embarked on a particularly long and difficult snorkeling adventure at a distant beach, believing they still had several hours. Sasha knew Maxim must have put the *Trib* into "overdrive."

Fresh from dry dock and refitting, newly painted a gleaming white with well-scrubbed teak decks and all her white sails up on her two tall masts, the *Trib* made as beautiful an impression as Sasha could have wished for. Knowing the crew had motored the entire way, he was pleased they'd unfurled the sails for show as they approached the island. Sasha was surprised, however, to see his crew uncharacteristically dressed in colorful tropical shirts with white shorts, but he appreciated the huge smiles on their faces as they caught

232

sight of him. The crowd cheered as sails were furled and the crew motored into the dock. The crew had to shake dozens of hands before reaching the one hand they most wanted to grab but were sure they would never be able to.

Sasha stood by awkwardly as backs were slapped, and leis and kisses bestowed on his mates. He introduced the crew by name to a number of people who stood close by, starting with Luc and Sylvie Roussel. The best greeting he could manage was to put both hands on each crew member's shoulders. He held Sonthi the longest, seeking some sign that he'd been forgiven for surreptitiously placing his tracker on his back and sending him off to his Buddhist silent retreat in Thailand without him. Sonthi shook his head, smiling, then touched his forehead to Sasha's.

"You are with us again, Sasha, that is what counts," Sonthi said in his soft Thai accent, pulling back to look at him. "But we definitely need a long talk."

"I owe you that, my friend," Sasha replied.

Sasha had to explain multiple times that they would meet Katya in just a while, that their arrival had caught her on a distant part of the island. He had so wanted to have her at his side at this moment. The crew disappeared below deck a few at a time and returned carrying gifts for the resort staff and their families – prized gourmet goods in recyclable pouches and fresh kiwis they'd picked up in New Zealand on the way, with an especially big box for Luc and Sylvie to share with the guests. Strong arms were then enlisted to help haul up the medical equipment to be taken straight to the newly finished clinic.

The crew also handed over a two-year supply of biodegradable soaps and detergents that Sasha had ordered. Sasha's first glance into the underground laundry had shown him that le Hédonisme needed to make a green change. The crew had also brought the supplies he needed to reclaim the resort's drain and sewage output for watering, and the promised solar panels, enough to supply the entire resort with free electricity. Maxim told Sasha the main cabin had been filled with material, Sasha's sleeping cabin as well.

The crowd cheered again and there were many volunteers. When all the items were safely stored or in place, Sasha asked the crowd on the dock for some time alone with his crew, and all but four guests dispersed. Two Australian couples remained, smiling broadly. Sasha turned to his crew to introduce them.

"All right, mates. This trip is going to be a real vacation for you all. There will be no watch duty for any of you while we are here. S-Branch has sent us four agents to guard the boat twenty-four seven. SB had no trouble getting volunteers, as you can imagine. I know these agents and they know our boat. They helped install and test the new equipment while she was in Sydney this last month. They've been quietly patrolling the resort and keeping guard these last several days. They arrived the morning we did, but there were no villas open for them. Who could have imagined an attack coming so soon? They hurried here as fast as they could, but Jake had already closed access and our good gatekeeper wouldn't let them in! Mark and Sherry, Doug and Laura. Not their real names, but that's what they'll be going by, since they're now lodged in two of the villas here at le Hédonisme. They know all of you by name and sight. And the infamous Jake will be on guard as well. But still, we should all stay alert. The aftermath of the attack on Katya could well lead to yet another attempt at retaliation."

The two groups greeted each other warmly with vigorous handshakes. The crew was in even higher spirits as they retreated back to the boat. Doug and Laura followed them but headed up to the pilothouse. Quiet returned to the harbor.

There was a moment's silence as Sasha and the crew assembled in the large, now empty main cabin. Then on cue, all ten crew members mimed holding up glasses and shouted, "to the groom!" Sasha pressed his palms to his forehead and pretended to beg mercy. Maxim had been named spokesman for all.

"My dear Sasha, never in a million years did we expect to hear that you'd eluded S-Branch and hopped one of Australogic's freighters to come alone to New York. Or that you'd given a public speech. Or that you'd met the perfect woman and she was taking you to Bora Bora and paying for it all. Or that you had actually gotten on an airplane to get there. And then, to hear that you'd fallen in love and gotten married in a Tahitian wedding ceremony. I think we are all just too jealous for words that she can do all that honeymoon stuff, and we can't even shake your hand! We're all exceedingly happy for you, Sasha. You deserve happiness. We're all behind you, as always."

"Hear, hear!" resounded from most of the crew, laughing at Sasha's look of embarrassment. Only one man, Aashir, hung back, looking distraught.

Maxim continued. "We were shocked but less than surprised, however, that you almost got yourself killed multiple times in the process! Here's to this mysterious Katya for rescuing you!"

Whistles and wild applause followed.

"Maxim, friends, thank you, truly, something I never say enough to you," Sasha responded, recovering his composure. "I want to take issue with the way those statements about 'never in a million years' sound… but I can't. I do love Katya and although the wedding ceremony was just a meddlesome prank, I feel married to her. Was it a simple question of Fate that I decided to hop that freighter to New York? That this perfect woman, yes, she is that, as you will see when you meet her, decided to hop a plane to New York from California and was there to save me again and again? That she could touch me? That I could fall in love again at my age? That she could fall in love with me, at *my* age?

"Yes, I *am* happy, not a word you've probably ever heard me use about myself. And I'm happy that you are all here to experience this beautiful island with us and get to know her. I wish she'd been with me when you made landfall, but now I have this opportunity to talk with you first. Let's have a real toast, find a glass and fill it with whatever you want. This toast will be from me to you, my colleagues, my friends, my musical mates. How I've missed you!"

Sasha and a few of the men retreated to the galley to pour drinks of various sorts, water as usual for Sasha. The men were laughing and joking, thrilled to be back together with their captain. Chen, Hau, and Keung remained in the main cabin, looking out at the gorgeous volcanic island. Hau pointed out two people walking along the dock, holding snorkeling gear and carrying small duffel bags. Chen thought the woman must be one of the natives, with her mixed-race face, sun-browned skin and wet, dark hair. She was wearing a bikini that showed off an attractive and exceedingly athletic body.

The three men were discussing how good-looking she was and what a waste that she was with that nothing white dude when she stopped to comb her hair and slip a Tahitian-style dress out of her duffel, pulling it over her bikini. She carefully removed the water shields and then the bandages from her upper arm, revealing two unmistakable bullet wounds. The men stared. This was Katya. They called the others to come quickly and they were all gaping out the windows when Sasha returned with a tray holding four glasses. The

235

man she was with applied fresh bandages and then tied a colorful scarf around the dressings. He then turned towards the resort buildings carrying both sets of snorkels and she started walking right towards them.

Sasha observed his rapt crew. This meeting was not going the way he had wished.

"Eyes front!" he shouted out.

It was his crew's turn to look embarrassed as they spun to face him.

"Aye, Captain!" they shouted in unison.

"I see you've discovered Katya has arrived. I would appreciate your treating her as if she were a new crewmate and not as just a woman. Do you think you can do that for me, *boys*?" he asked, emphasizing the last word.

"Aye, Captain!" they shouted together, sensing that they were forgiven for gaping at her, and completely surprised by Sasha's ability to show good humor. Sasha put the tray down, and the men holding glasses did the same. There would be time for toasts later. The crew noted how Sasha bounded up the stairs through the companionway to the deck to greet Katya. It was no wonder he was in love. They were all a little bit in love with her themselves, or at least envious.

The crew lined up for a formal greeting, trying to be casual and not stare. Katya, returning on Sasha's arm, found herself looking at ten of the most handsome men she had ever seen, Sasha included. Most shared a similar body build – well-proportioned, muscular, broad-shouldered – which could not just be the result of their training routine. Clearly Sasha had a deep appreciation of male beauty, Katya mused. These men would be a pleasure to look at. She was especially looking forward to seeing them with their shirts off.

"Sasha has told me so much about each of you," Katya began. "He couldn't ask for a finer group of mates. I look forward to getting to know you all."

It was time to make a strong first impression. She had been quizzing Sasha for days about his crew, memorizing names, nationalities, personalities, and job skills, matching names with the small, indistinct photos she remembered from Markus Cutter's files, and even looking up some Malay expressions to get her past the level of restaurant greetings she knew. She'd found it amusing that all of the doctors used their title informally with their first names. Katya also appreciated that the crew had not lined up by rank, that relations seemed looser and much more egalitarian than she'd supposed. She would meet each man's gaze steadfastly in turn, giving him her full attention.

Katya held out her hand to the first man standing in the row, Kiko, a licensed physician assistant from the Philippines. He was twenty-seven, the second youngest, short and dark, with long eyelashes and a sweet face. His name, "kee ko," was as charming as he was. She remembered he'd been with Sasha for five years already. Kiko ran a hand over his unruly black hair before awkwardly taking Katya's outstretched one. She greeted him in Tagalog and continued speaking the language.

"Kiko. I understand your viola playing will soon rival Dima's. Sasha feels you are as skilled as any doctor. He's told me often how much he appreciates your expertise in so many areas."

Kiko nodded deeply, flushing a little when Katya gave his hand an extra squeeze before letting go. She moved on to Sonthi and spoke in Thai. Sonthi was tall for a Thai, golden-skinned with dark brown hair, a youthful forty-seven, and handsome in an almost feminine way. He had the serene countenance of a Buddhist monk, which he had been several times in his younger days. Sasha had called him his spiritual advisor and Katya could see why. She was curious to discover what Sasha meant by calling him his psychiatrist as well. She offered Sonthi a wai, the traditional hands-together Thai greeting, which he returned, then she held out her hand.

"Dr. Sonthi. I look forward to discussing Buddhism with you. Sasha has appreciated your advice and help these last fourteen years, more than I'm sure he's told you. I hear you are also a fine violinist. I understand no one knows tropical diseases like you do. You and Sasha have already found better treatments for so many, even a couple of cures. I bet you two will put an end to all of them in my lifetime."

Katya gave Sonthi's hand a lingering squeeze as well and turned to Hau, Vietnamese, thirty-six years old, a general practitioner and another violinist. Hau had a sly, mischievous look, no doubt the crew's prankster. He wore his black hair long; his face could have been that of a Vietnamese film star. Katya decided to throw away her prepared greeting and ad lib. She gave him her hand as if she were meeting royalty and spoke in Vietnamese.

237

"Dr. Hau, I can't believe you've survived eight years with Sasha's total lack of humor. You will be happy to learn he is starting to develop one, but he still has a long way to go." Hau laughed, revealing perfect teeth. They all seemed to have perfect white teeth, Katya noted. Like Sasha.

"I think we all got to see a bit of his new sense of humor just a bit ago," Hau said, in English, and the rest of the crew chuckled.

Tuan, standing next to him, made a melodious, high-pitched giggle. Hau leaned down and kissed Katya's hand. She turned her head to Tuan while slowly removing her hand from Hau's. Tuan was five years younger than Hau and had only been with the crew four years. His dark hair was neatly trimmed, and he displayed several coral and shell necklaces in the V of his open shirt. This one, Katya thought, is most assuredly gay, if still in the closet. She took up his hand and spoke again in Vietnamese.

"Dr. Tuan. You're also a fine cellist, I hear. I understand you will be returning to the outside world next January to complete your medical training, a neurosurgery residency. I hope you decide to return to the *Trib*. Sasha tells me you are already one of the finest doctors he knows."

She removed her hand quickly from his to prevent a second hand-kissing, but kept her eyes fixed on his a bit longer to make up for it. He nodded to her, smiling, and she turned to Maxim. The oldest member of the crew at forty-eight, Maxim was a rugged-featured German with greying light brown hair and light brown eyes to match. Katya knew him to be the only other surgeon. She had noted how he'd been watching her. Wary, skeptical. Protective of Sasha. His handshake was painfully firm. Ah, she thought, this one has dominance issues. She lowered her eyes and chin in a subtly submissive gesture, then looked back into his eyes before she addressed him in German.

"First Officer Maxim. It is an honor to meet you. Sasha tells me what a superb surgeon you are, that he has counted on you for over fifteen years. No one is a closer or better friend to him than you. I look forward to hearing you play violin in the quartet."

"We meet at last. The pleasure is mine, Katya. Welcome on board," he replied in his British English, giving her hand another crushing squeeze.

Katya worried she shouldn't have spoken to him in German. Sasha hadn't said anything, but maybe German was forbidden due to his past... She relaxed when she noted how unconcerned both Sasha and Maxim appeared.

Dima was next in line, a forty-three-year-old Russian who towered a head or two above the rest of the crew. His hair was a few shades darker blond than Sasha's, his eyes a dazzling green, his features as perfectly regular as Maxim's, but with a slightly broken nose that gave him an intriguing character. She remembered Sasha telling her how Soviet goons had roughed him up, how he'd had to flee Moscow before he was arrested for anti-government activity. Katya was relieved that he took her hand gently, and she spoke to him in Russian.

"Dima. Our quartet violist. I see the members of the quartet keep together even in line! I hear you are the construction genius who can transform the *Retribution* into as many guises as you please, and that you are the boat's chief storyteller. I'm sure you have fourteen years of stories to regale me with."

Dima smiled, and gave a rather formal bow. Hiro, the quartet's cellist was next, a forty-six-year-old orthopedist with a peaceful aspect and a lion's mane of black hair without a trace of gray. Katya addressed him in Japanese, first giving him a respectful bow, then a handshake.

"Dr. Hiro. Chief Communications Officer. Sasha tells me you have been an indispensable font of calm and wisdom these last fifteen years. I look forward to hearing you in the quartet. Sasha speaks so highly of your cello playing."

"Welcome to the *Trib*, Katya," he replied in Japanese.

Hiro returned Katya's bow as he released her hand. Three more, Katya thought, just three more. She didn't dare look at Sasha. She moved on to Chen, an internist and infectious disease specialist, thirty-five, another striking figure, taller than anyone but Dima, with a neat chin beard and soul patch, the only facial hair in the group. He stood straight as an arrow and had a studious, serious mien. Katya continued in Mandarin Chinese.

"Dr. Chen. I hear you are also a fine violinist. Sasha may not have told you, but Mandarin was my first language, even before English. It would be an honor for me to be able to speak with you in the language I learned at my grandmother's knee."

"You speak flawlessly, Katya. It would be my pleasure."

Katya turned to Keung, standing next to him, and reached out her hand. She liked his masculine name, "kung," meaning "universe." Keung was also Chinese, but from Hong Kong. His black hair was wavier and shoulder length, his eyes blacker, and he held himself in a more relaxed and laid-back posture than Chen. She'd learned from Sasha that Keung had been a thief, a low-level gang member, unlike Chen, who was already an idealistic doctor when he first stepped aboard the *Trib* to visit. Now thirty, Keung had been with the crew for six years already, a year less than Chen, working as another physician assistant. He'd been trained by Sasha, like Dima. Like Aashir, Keung had no background in music or medicine before he joined the crew. Katya found him the most physically attractive of all. She addressed him in Cantonese.

"Keung. I understand your cello playing is coming along well under Hiro's and Sasha's tutelage. Hong Kong is the only place in the East I have traveled to with my sifu. He was born and raised there. I understand from Sasha that you were a great street fighter, as was my sifu. I would love for you to show me your moves some time."

"If Sasha deems it appropriate," he replied in English, looking suddenly nervous.

Katya took the hand of the last man in line, Aashir, from Malaysia. He was the youngest at twenty-six, with just three years on the crew, but already making great strides on the viola, Sasha had told her. The smallest man, Aashir had dark, smooth skin, floppy black-brown hair with blond tips, liquid brown eyes, and long eyelashes – an exquisite young man. She noted how he glanced over at Sasha with an unmistakable look of longing, of love, as she approached. Even taking her hand would seem like a betrayal for one so lost in unrequited love. She would have to work this one carefully. Was everyone blind to Aashir's passion? Or did they all just choose not to see? She carefully repeated the words in Malay she'd memorized. She felt exceedingly fortunate that they seemed so appropriate now that she'd met him.

"And Aashir, I must apologize that Malay is new to me. I want you to know that Sasha holds you very dear to his heart and that will not change." She held on to his reluctant hand a moment longer.

Katya looked up and down the line of men. A lot of challenges lay ahead. They were certainly welcoming of her as a visitor to their boat, but they would not easily accept her as a member of the crew. She'd been naïve to once think Sasha had needed her as a non-sexual partner

240

and protector. She was now sure Sasha had been wrapped in a cocoon of devotion and protection for decades, even long before this current crew. Here were ten men who she could see loved him selflessly, but they could not touch him. Sasha needed her for a love he could return, for her touch, for a deeper one-on-one relationship. The men must all be curious but also worried about what changes lay in store. It was time to address the entire crew in English.

"I know that I am a complete stranger to you. I'm the woman who stole your Sasha's heart. But I'm not stealing Sasha away from you. I'm the one who brought him back, alive and well." The crew erupted in cheers. Right direction, she thought. "I don't know what is going to happen next between us. Right now, we're enjoying a well-deserved vacation in paradise, which is what you all will be doing if I ever stop talking," she continued to laughter. "So please, let us take the time to get to know each other and we can all decide together how to proceed. Sasha considers you family and I would like to think of you as family, too."

There were more cheers. Katya could feel a lessoning of tension in the cabin. Some of the men came up to clap her on the back or shake her hand again in gratitude, and a few even hugged her.

"Let's try that toast again," Dima called out over the noise, in a strong Russian accent, "this time to Katya, for bringing Sasha back to us!"

"First my toast to all of you," countered Sasha. "Dima, get one more glass for Katya, non-alcoholic."

Everyone found a glass and waited for Sasha to begin. He looked around the cabin at the men he had lived and fought alongside, practiced medicine and played music with, and at Katya. Hopefully he could find a way not to have to choose between them.

"To my crew. There was never a moment in all my adventures and misadventures these past weeks that I wasn't certain I would be back among you. Now that I'm able to speak of love again, I want to say how much I love each and every one of you. Thank you, mates, for putting up with me all these years. You are the best men on the entire planet. Now drink up before I get even more uncharacteristically sentimental. But save a sip for the second toast."

Katya raised her glass to the crew. The men laughed at Sasha's unaccustomed emotionality, raised their glasses and drank, then the cabin quieted. Sasha raised his glass again.

"To Katya, who never faltered in securing my survival, even at the risk of her own life, over and over again. I, we, owe her everything. My love for her, mates, like my love for you, knows no bounds. Because of you, Katya, I am not the same man I was before. I know I am a better man, a man more at peace with himself, certainly a more humorous one. I thank you for my life, for love, for happiness."

"To Katya!" the crew called out in unison, raising their glasses and drinking to her.

"And now, I want you all to get off this boat and start exploring the island. Luc and Sylvie have invited us to join them for a lavish Tahitian dinner buffet in the main hall starting at 1900 hours. Enjoy the sunset! You are welcome to use our villa during your stay, but with nude swimming at the villa's beach only, not the main beach. Please wear togs there! I'll show you where our villa is later. I'm giving you all five minutes to clear the decks!" Sasha commanded.

The men laughed and joked with each other, happy to follow Sasha's orders. Within minutes they were all standing on the dock holding day sacks, deciding among themselves what to do first. Chen looked back at the boat and did a double take, tapping Keung on the shoulder, then they all turned to see. The big boat was rocking gently back and forth on the calm water.

"You don't think they're..." Kiko began. "We just left!"

"Oh God, yes I do. But what could they be doing that would move the whole boat!" ventured Chen.

"I'm trying to picture Sasha..." snickered Hau.

"I really don't want to even try to picture what they're doing," Aashir sighed, and they all hurried off the dock towards the resort.

Chapter 36

Breathless and spent, Katya lay next to Sasha on the teak floor of the main cabin, her fingers intertwined in his. They were both drenched in sweat. The day was a warm and humid eighty-five degrees and all the portholes and windows were still closed. Sasha had made love to her in gymnastic moves she hadn't thought possible, literally bouncing off the boat's inside walls. He didn't look the least bit winded, despite the sweat.

This was the first time they'd recklessly thrown themselves into midday sex and both of them hoped it wouldn't be the last. They were doubtful there would ever be another time possible on the *Retribution*. Sasha stood first, naked and glistening, and pulled Katya up to stand beside him. They pressed their wet bodies together tightly, allowing themselves another long kiss as their hands slid over each other.

Katya looked out the cabin windows. Sasha had convinced her the glass was one-way, but it was strange to feel so open to view. She would have a lot harder time gaining the trust and confidence of the crew if they knew she and Sasha were having raucous sex on their boat, in their home, right in the main cabin. She looked around her, noting built-in padded benches along two of the walls, a low table, and a swivel commander's chair oddly placed facing the closed port side cabinetry. Most of the space was open. For music, she imagined.

"Now that you're well acquainted with the main cabin, I believe I'm going to have to start my tour of the boat with the showers. Don't expect any touches of luxury and you won't be disappointed," Sasha said into her ear, before he licked it. "You taste like the sea, just like our first night together."

They grabbed their scattered clothes and he led her down a few steps towards the stern of the boat, but she slowed.

"I thought your cabin was forward in the bow," she said, confused.

"That it is, but both the aft crew's cabins have double showers. There's hardly room for me in my forward shower. We'd be all elbows in each other's faces."

"And isn't the main cabin on a boat called the saloon? Or is it salon?"

"Not on my boat!"

"Main cabin it is then! I want to use the right vocabulary. I have to ask what 'togs' are, though."

"Swim attire. Or swimmers, in Sydney. And just so you know, 'pants' are underpants in British English."

"I'll remember that! I call them slacks, but I think I've heard you call them trousers."

"Slacks it is then," Sasha said, kissing her.

Katya looked around the crew's quarters as they passed through. There was an identical cabin on either side of the narrow hall, each containing four cleverly built-in narrow berths across from each other in pairs, and teak storage cabinets in a beautiful finish. Nautical ropes held in a large collection of books by each berth. Each cabin ended in a door to a spacious head with two sinks. They dropped their clothes on a berth in the port-side cabin and Sasha pulled her into the head, turning on both side-by-side showers.

"All the water comes from the ocean under us, goes through my purification and desalination filters and is ready to drink, or in our case, get clean with," Sasha said, not without a touch of pride. "The solar heating system takes the edge off the cold, but I've felt no need for hot water where we travel. Hope you don't mind."

"It feels wonderful. I'll soap and shampoo you, if you'll do the same for me."

Once they were dressed, Sasha continued the tour. He opened the thick metal door to the hospital that took up the rest of the stern. Katya thought the door seemed more like an airlock on a jet plane's emergency exit, but much larger. Sasha reminded her not to touch anything unless he asked her too, as freshly washed as she was, even as he pulled on medical gloves.

"Not quite a Class One Clean Room, but I'm working on some new devices, more advanced than the HEPA filters now in place, that will keep the hospital and our cabins even more free of pathogens. I have something better in mind than this sticky mat to clean shoes, too. I recently added laminar air flow and the hospital is hit with ultraviolet germicidal irradiation when it's empty. The starboard-side bathroom has a space where we scrub and gown up; there's lots of water-proof storage for our PPE and surgical drapes and a secure sliding door from the bathroom into the hospital that opens on voice command. Remember I told you why the cabins are so undecorated –

because we use them as our doctor's offices, waiting and recovery rooms. Everything personal is stored in the cabinetry. Berths and bookshelves get zip-covered; we scrub and sterilize the whole boat after each clinic. Well, my crew does. I take up my violin to unwind."

High-tech medical equipment filled all the space between long oval portholes on the sides and even hung from the ceiling. Only one hospital bed was set up, but there was room for several. Shallow cabinetry surrounded the door and deep built-in cabinets on the stern wall contained more equipment, supplies, medicines, and additional folded-up hospital beds.

"The beds also serve as examination tables and for some non-invasive procedures," Sasha informed her. "The hybrid surgical table with its segmented, radiolucent, floating tabletop handles the brunt of our work. I know the operating theatre is small, but it's fully integrated and flexible. There's never more than three of us in here at a time. The clear partitions separating it from the rest of the hospital allow us to communicate better while keeping the field sterile. Air flow and filtration are critical; air is exchanged twenty-five times per hour. The temperature and humidity are carefully controlled as well."

Katya could only nod in wonder. Sasha strode over to the deep storage wall. A wide pullout drawer held a dozen examples of Sasha's unique prostheses. Some looked like they belonged on robots – the hidden framework, Sasha told her, while others were covered in life-like skin in a variety of hues. Sasha held up arms and legs, hands and feet. Katya marveled at the detail: freckles, tiny hairs, and veins. Sasha explained how the electronic skin he'd developed could sense touch, temperature, and textures; the prostheses also contained a heating system that made them feel warm. Sasha turned one on and held it out for Katya to touch.

The tray of example bionic eyes fascinated her the most, each eye a different color, the elaborate inner workings on display. These were older models, but Katya didn't think they could look more futuristic. Sasha explained that all his prosthetic devices were individually constructed, completely custom for each patient. Katya took another look at one of the hands.

"You've recreated Luke's prosthetic hand, just like in *Star Wars*!" Katya exclaimed.

"Star wars? I don't know what you're talking about."

"Of course you don't. Never mind, but congratulations anyhow! I think you're much more than forty years ahead of the rest of the scientific world! I hope I get to meet one of the recipients of your futuristic hands one day."

A small vault-like case with a clear lid contained several of the tiny pill-sized computers and neural implants that connected the prostheses to a human brain, all of his invention as well. He closed the drawer and moved on. There was not enough time to explain it all now, he said, although Katya thought he looked like he wanted to. He pointed out some of their many pieces of medical equipment. Sasha's own version of an ultra-low-radiation CT scanner pulled out from the same deep storage wall, its platform folded up until needed. He then showed her the compact but complete diagnostic lab with not one but two microscopes, an ultrasound, a defibrillator, a low-radiation digital X-ray machine, an electrosurgical unit, EKG/ECG machines, cardiac and other patient monitors, a phoropter for eye exams, dental equipment, and something he called an A.I.-driven anesthesia machine, his own invention. Katya couldn't take it all in. She looked up.

"I've never seen a hospital with a skylight," Katya commented.

"You'll see skylights in each cabin. They also serve as escape hatches. Or a quick way to the deck from the crew's cabins. One-way bullet-proof glass here as well, but they can be made dark, like the rest of the windows."

They walked back up the steps, through the main cabin, and down to the galley and dining area. Three long padded benches formed a U-shaped booth around a table. A single chair for Sasha was pushed under the open end. The tiny galley would be crowded with even two crewmen but was long and well fitted out. Katya noted a washer and dryer under the counter. Mostly for their hospital scrubs and linens, Sasha told her. Their personal laundry was usually handed over in labeled bags to trusted cleaners once a month in ports. Sasha informed her that behind the door next to his cabin were ladder-like steps that went down to the engine room, Dima's workshop, and holding cells. They continued on to the three forward officer's cabins.

The small cabins, each with a miniscule private head, were all about the same size, although Hiro's and Maxim's were longer and narrower. Sasha's cabin was across from the galley and shared an inside wall with Hiro's. A tight passage between Maxim's and Hiro's cabins led to storage in the tip of the bow. Katya peeked in and noted extra mattresses and shelves of clothing amid the assorted material; she thought she spied a variety of wigs, but didn't comment. All three officer's cabins had similar narrow berths and cabinetry in the same teak. Katya couldn't imagine where she would fit into the sleeping arrangements. Sasha's berth wasn't much wider than he was. His entire cabin wasn't much bigger than a queen-sized mattress. Maybe a king, if you included the cabinetry.

"Where do you keep all your musical instruments?" Katya asked, as they returned to the main cabin.

"Ah, take a look," Sasha said, as he opened cabinet doors on the starboard side of the stairs on the stern end wall.

There was a surprisingly large space inside, where three cello cases, three viola cases, and four violin cases rested in a climate-controlled setting. Sasha's violin stayed with him, stored in her own climate-controlled rectangular case. Sasha showed Katya carefully wrapped ribbons of pure white Siberian horsehair for their bows, hundreds of packages of extra strings, and what he told her was best the rosin available. Other cabinets held music stands and drawers of sheet music.

"Each music case holds three bows, but we have two dozen extra bows as well, including several carbon fiber ones for the hottest, most humid days. I rehair each of my bows every three or four months, and rehair the men's bows when they need it. They're happy to let me change their strings, too. I've got replacement bridges, pegs, and such, but any needed major repairs get done in Sydney at a luthier's once a year."

"Then what's in the cabinetry on the port side?" Katya asked.

Sasha pressed a button and a series of panels slid open to reveal a computer whose keypad glided forward. A dozen monitors plus a large screen and a vast array of additional technology popped forward as well.

"My primary communication system with the laboratory and my secondary command center," he said, as he flicked on the large screen. "This is my captain's chair, the only piece of movable furniture in the room, as you can see, except for that low table. We have three sturdy bamboo folding tables and lots of folding chairs in storage for the men to use and for our patients when this is a waiting room. We've room for Mendelssohn's or Shostakovich's octets!"

The image on the large screen was a live view of the docks from the pilothouse. Sasha rotated a dial to show a 360-degree view around the boat. He toggled another button and there was the resort as seen from above, a satellite view. As he rotated the dial, the image zoomed out to reveal the entire island, then, reversing, zoomed in on their villa. The image was clear enough to reveal her beach shoes on the steps of the lanai. Sasha pressed another button and all the equipment disappeared behind the cabinet doors.

"That's impressive!" Katya then looked across the main cabin to a handsome set of steep wooden steps leading up to a closed door. "And those steps?"

"To the inside entrance of the pilothouse. We're heading there."

Sasha led her up the companionway stairs to a vast expanse of teak decking, pointing out the comfortable outdoor seating area and the two masts, the shorter foremast and the slightly taller mainmast he called the aft mast.

"Ah, so she's a schooner, not a ketch," Katya remarked.

"You do know your sailboats!" Sasha exclaimed. "I like thinking of you and your father sailing in San Francisco Bay."

Looking up to the large, fully-enclosed pilothouse, Katya saw two people she recognized. No one-way glass here, she noted. She followed Sasha up the outside stairs where he introduced her to Doug and the blond-haired Laura, explaining their role as part of a security team, including another Australian couple. Laura gave her an admiring smile.

Guards from S-Branch, Katya thought. For the past two days, they'd been staying here at the resort, fellow guests. Had they arrived in Bora Bora the same day she and Sasha had, or not until the next day? He hadn't called for their help during William Cutter's attack and had seemed upset to see them on the beach keeping back the well-wishers and curious, so he must not have known about their presence beforehand. They must have been staying at another resort until villas opened up at le Hédonisme. Why hadn't Sasha told her about them? Did Jake know? She knew who the other couple must be, the ones she'd seen following them. She would have to talk to Sasha about not keeping such important security information from her. Katya tried to imagine that more guards were a good thing, in light of the attack on her, and continued exploring the pilothouse. She'd never imagined so much technical equipment on a boat. Sasha grew excited pointing out the pilothouse features.

"There's a lot more here than steering and engine controls, as you can see. Weather instruments, depth sounders, sonar, radar, communications, including satellite, plus defense and weaponry control and spyware, all of my own invention, and so much more. That's why there are two crewmen on duty here every hour of the day, spelling each other. Our two Australian couples have taken over watch duty so the crew can enjoy their freedom. There will be no unforeseen attacks on this boat or this island, I assure you."

Sasha said he'd show her the engines and the solar panels on the pilothouse roof another day, and how the boat lift worked for the dinghy and two Zodiacs attached to the stern, along with a diving platform with lockers for scuba gear and snorkeling equipment. He promised a tremendous surprise when they could take her out on the open ocean away from prying eyes, then led her back down the outside stairs to the main deck.

"We'll unfurl the sails for a while when we take her out, too. You missed how beautiful the *Trib* looked when she arrived."

"I'm so sorry I wasn't there. She really is a magnificent boat. I see your touches everywhere. She's brilliant, practical, unfussy, logical, and beautifully masculine. I can't wait to sail on her... But speaking of beautifully masculine, I want to talk with you about your crew."

"Let's sit outside here. I hope you aren't referring to the resort wear clothes they showed up in. I don't know what they were thinking. That's not how we normally dress on board."

"Well, the clothes didn't help. Your crew members are the most gorgeous men I have ever seen. As Dostoyevsky had Prince Myshkin say in *The Idiot*, 'The world will be saved by beauty.' I can tell you love looking at these men."

There was a stunned silence as Sasha took in her meaning. He'd worked alongside these men for three to fifteen years and their "beauty," and his physical attraction to them, had never entered into his consciousness. But what was she trying to say about his unconscious mind?

"I ... I don't see them that way. Not at all. I chose them, one by one, over the years because they were right for the job. And I was proved right every time."

"I'm just saying you have a special appreciation of beauty. Maybe there's a reason for this, maybe it's just part of who you are. You pay no attention to beautiful women passing by, and yet you chose women to love who were good looking, if I can include myself in that category. I've seen a picture of Le. She was indeed beautiful, Sasha. I for one appreciate your judgment, because looking at your crew is going to give me great pleasure. But it's going to make it more difficult for me to become one of your crew if that's what we decide."

Katya chose not to share her observation that Sasha had stared at the muscular, bare chested male dancers at the frenetic, sensual Tahitian dance that first night, had hardly seemed to note the women. Or how he watched the handsome torch lighters. What had happened in his past to make him untouchable by men, to make him incapable of acting on his desires... or recognizing that he had them.

"You do love these men, Sasha, in your comradely way. But that doesn't mean they don't love you in their own various and personal ways. Maybe I'm not saying this right. You seem to have a system that works for everyone here on the boat in such close quarters, day in and day out. Throw me in the mix, touching you, kissing you, having sex even as quietly as possible in your narrow berth, and all hell is liable to break loose. I'm going to have to win their hearts and have them rooting for me to be accepted."

"You've given me a lot to think about. But I can tell you have something more in mind."

"You're not going to like it, but I think it will work."

Katya shared her plans, and she was right, he didn't like it, any part of it. Sasha reluctantly agreed to most of her ideas, but said he'd have to think about the last one. He couldn't risk losing her.

They sat in the shadow of the pilothouse in silence, Sasha stroking her hand. Katya could tell he'd gone to a dark place and hoped she would be able to talk him through it. Sweat was beginning to bead on his brow. Her hands moved to caress his face, neck, and shoulders.

"Sasha, where are you now? What are you seeing?" She could feel him trembling.

"Bergen-Belsen. My tormenter, SS Obersturmführer Krüger, the camp overseer, was an extraordinarily handsome man. I'm seeing him now through adult eyes, not the eyes of a frightened child."

250

Katya was mortified, afraid she'd gone too far. "Sasha, don't do this to yourself! His looks have nothing to do with your perception of beauty."

"Maybe they do. I've told you very little about my years there – almost two – so Krüger told me. I believe I wasn't yet four when I arrived in that cattle car."

"You don't have to do this…"

"Shhh… don't speak. I might not be able to continue. Somehow your touch is keeping me from sinking into a memory attack. I can't believe I can talk about this…"

With great difficulty and many pauses, Sasha told her about his life in Bergen-Belsen. He took slow deep breaths frequently, and his hair and shirt were quite damp by the time he finished. He tried to leave nothing out, but there was so much to say.

"Krüger couldn't find enough ways to torment me. When he found me reading German, discovered how quickly I could learn, he found sick amusement in forcing me to parrot back anything I was taught. I absorbed information like a sponge, had total recall. Since part of the camp was designed to hold high-value prisoners the Germans might be able to exchange, there were numerous professors and teachers interred there – he'd pick them out and have them sent to me daily. He wanted history, math, chemistry, and physics teachers especially, speakers of every language in the camp, ones who knew English, too. He enjoyed watching them squirm, fed on their fear. There were almost no books, hardly any paper. Where were they to even start? There I stood before them trembling, so impossibly young, so fearful for them. He would hold a gun to the prisoner's head. *Teach him all you know,* he'd laugh. The first woman, ordered to teach me Hungarian, had been too frightened to speak. Krüger pulled the trigger."

Sasha paused so long Katya thought he was going to stop. She took his hands in hers as he breathed slowly and deeply. When he continued, his voice took on a strange monotone, as if he was trying to distance emotion from words. Katya remained silent, too horrified to speak. Sasha pulled his hands away. She sat quietly beside him. His voice remained calm while his face grew tortured, strained.

"There were so many – neutrals from Spain, Portugal and Turkey, along with Dutch, Polish, and Hungarian Jews in the Exchange camps... French and Belgian prisoners of war until their compound became a women's camp, too many women being brought in... Russian and Italian P.O.W. s. There were prisoners the Nazis called Zigeuner, Gypsies – Roma and Sinti, and all kinds of political prisoners... Later, Jewish prisoners from every part of Europe arrived from other camps if they were too sick to work. Not that anyone was treated medically. They were sent there to starve. Or to be... subjected to... horrible medical experiments... Although the SS guards were sadistically cruel, Bergen-Belsen wasn't called a concentration camp at first, was never an extermination camp like Auschwitz... I can't talk about how the camp was divided up, how it was run... not now, not yet...

"Hungarian, Dutch, Polish, Romanian, Albanian, Czech, Russian, Spanish, Portuguese, Italian, Turkish, Romany, French, English, I was forced to start learning them all. I didn't know if I was supernaturally gifted, or if I was just willing myself to learn to save their lives. Or worse, but I can't talk about that, maybe ever...

"Krüger forbade me to learn Hebrew or Yiddish, but I heard so much around the camp, I picked up a lot of both. My German advanced into fluency. The few books belonging to officers in the camp were all in German or English, and Krüger borrowed them for me. He commandeered books in Dutch and Russian. I learned to speak, read, and write those four languages fluently.

"Then there was music... The piano was missing half its keys, but I learned. The cello was a small beat-up student model, but I learned. Then Herr Silber was brought in, with his two battered violins, a full-size and a quarter-size. He was forced to entertain the officers frequently. I'd heard him play. I knew what a treasure he had – the tone of his violin was magnificent. We became close, Herr Silber and I, although I learned nothing about who he was, only the city he'd come from, when he was born. He took over my piano lessons, became my cello teacher, too, and soon I was playing well. My arms and my fingers were long, the quarter-size violin was a stretch, but I could reach when I began. I was around four and a half.

"Krüger had no idea of the value of the violins under his nose, only saw their nicked wood, their dull finish. He just wanted to hear them played, along with his favorite instrument, the cello. Herr Silber was the only adult who wasn't afraid of me... of what failure with me would cost them. All my teachers were fated to die, one by one, of typhus or dysentery, Herr Silber last. I will never forget any of their

252

names or faces. Herr Silber left his battered valise containing the two violins with me before he died. I had no idea then that they were both made by Antonio Stradivari."

Sasha took a moment to take several deep breaths. Katya could see he was growing more agitated. He shook his head when she tried to reach out to him. His gaze settled on the open water of the lagoon and remained there as he continued.

"I was especially adept with chemistry. Krüger thought that was amusing, music and chemistry. He'd had no name for me at first, called me 'slave' or 'you.' He started calling me Alexander Borodin. With your knowledge of music you must know who he was, the Russian 19th century Romantic composer, doctor, researcher, and chemistry professor. It was a joke to him... He called me Sasha, a diminutive of Alexander. His little Russian. His Russian doll. I've been Sasha ever since.

"Outside of lessons, it was just Krüger and me, meaning him finding an excuse to beat me, or I was left alone in his room. The other SS seemed to avoid him when they could, never interfered in my beatings. As camp overseer, he had unlimited power. I did once befriend a child on the other side of the barbed wire, a boy about my age. It was my first winter there... I would sneak him food, we spoke a few words of Czech together. Krüger caught me, surprised me by bringing the boy into the room we shared in the SS barracks. We had an hour of play, stuffing ourselves with food Krüger brought us. I avoided coming near his bed or the pile of rags next to it where I slept. At the end of the hour... Krüger led the boy back towards the Czech compound. I ran off after them. I had forgotten to ask the boy's name. I saw the boy... lying on the ground, the snow turning red around him, Krüger standing over him, the Luger in his hand trailing wisps of smoke into the cold air."

Sasha paused for a long time again. Katya could see him willing himself to go on. She smothered her horror, struggled to keep herself from reacting, speaking out.

"Two days before the date set for liberation, Krüger's madness played itself out. I heard the officers panicking; the camp was to be handed over to the British... the typhus epidemic had overwhelmed the camp. Although he could have fled, left the camp a free man, Krüger stayed for the transition, then chose to put a gun in his mouth. He wanted me to play a simple cello line Herr Silber had written for me, as he… as he died. I sat in the adjoining room, the door open between us, where we could see each other. I would not put the bow on the strings. I wanted him to die without the grace of music. I watched him die."

Sasha continued, his voice choking again and again. He would tell her everything he remembered, although he knew he might have some of it wrong – Krüger lied to him often – everything but the overwhelming sense of nameless guilt that haunted him. He knew pieces were missing, that there must be many repressed memories, not just concerning his scars, his refusal to eat meat. He spoke in detail of all of his teachers, what he knew of their deaths. The tens of thousands of deaths, fifty-thousand over the span of the camp's existence as a typhus epidemic raged, the piles of bodies – two, even three meters high – the stench of burning bodies, the hangings, the vicious dogs, the gunshots. The recurring, terrifying images, smells and sounds he could only shut out with music. The starvation and dysentery and typhus and lice... the mountain of dead prisoners' shoes. How Krüger would pull him by his elbow off his pile of rags and into his bed at night and sexually abuse him.

"Oh God, Sasha." Katya turned pale but forced herself to stay calm and listen.

"I've not willingly allowed any one to touch me since, not until Le, now you. I've never told anyone but you."

"What this man did to you…" Katya had to stop. The thought was too terrible.

"He controlled me completely, tried to break me. I didn't tell you yet," Sasha hesitated, took several long deep breaths. "I didn't tell you about the leash and collar Krüger made me wear, pulling me around the camp, often forcing me to crawl on my hands and knees. After a month, I finally bit his hand hard enough to draw blood, and I kept on biting, jumping at him, scratching wildly, pretending to *be* an animal. The guards and other officers were laughing at him, but no one moved to pull me off. Krüger savagely beat me, but he never put me on a leash again."

Katya had to work hard to keep her emotions in check. She wanted to cry but held back. "How did you survive? How did you not turn into a monster?"

"I have no memories before the camp. There was another language, another culture, lost. I was already speaking some German when I was brought to the camp. The other officers taunted me that I was not an ethnic German, that despite my blond hair, I was just another subhuman. But from birth to three or three and a half, someone had cared for me, taught me love – a parent, caregiver. I remained that same empathetic, loved child throughout the horror. I've been able to remember almost everything since, but never the face of a mother or father, never a face from before," Sasha sighed, a great sadness in his voice. "I know there are other memories I've repressed..."

"Didn't they try to turn you into one of them in the camp?"

"Krüger did. I would take no part in his cruelty. When I was about four and a half, Krüger had a miniature Nazi uniform made for me, boots, hat, whip and all. Made a big show of presenting these things to me in front of his fellow SS officers, commanded me to put them on. Instead I threw it all into a bonfire in the yard... into a hellfire of burning bodies. Krüger beat me nearly to death. If it wasn't for my music, he would have killed me. Piano, cello, violin, Krüger loved listening, kept me alive to play."

"So you also owe your life to your music," Katya said, softly placing her hand on his. This time he did not pull away.

"Music is everything to me. My whole life I've been made to feel I was a freak of nature – my unnatural musculature, genius IQ, an extraordinary memory. You'll tell me it's not logical, but this is what I've feared for fifty-four years – that I was the product of some advanced Nazi experiment."

"Sasha, you know in your heart as well as your head that's not possible! If it was, there'd be more of you, and there's only one. If I still believed in God I would say you are as God made you. However you came to be, you have used your gifts for the good of mankind."

"I have also made weapons of war and intrigue. I have killed. I have... a deep well of violence inside me I have to work to control. Hunting down human traffickers and other criminals releases some of that urge..."

"And yet, you've done much good. Your other inventions, your prostheses, your medical work. What would it take to convince you that you are not some experiment?"

"Seeing my abilities passed on to the next generation. Finding my son and discovering that he is as brilliant as I am."

255

"Then we're going to find your son if that's what it takes. I know you've been searching a long time, but we won't ever give up."

Katya was disturbed and frightened that nothing he told her explained the terrible deliberate scarring across his chest and entire back. There was still more he could not talk about, had repressed along with the memories of his earliest youth, even more unimaginable traumas than she'd just heard. Katya enfolded him in her arms and held him tight for a long time, then she turned his face towards hers and kissed him. Sasha returned her kiss. He looked relieved, unburdened.

"You cannot begin to imagine how much it means to me that I can tell you all of this. I shared nothing with my adoptive family, nothing with the trauma therapists they took me to, and nothing with Le or my crew, even Sonthi. But I will not speak of any of this again. Maybe someday I will ask you to share my story with my crew. They deserve to know. But not until I'm ready."

And now S-Branch knew some of his story, he thought back, from before he disconnected the audio portion of his tracking device. He was relieved they hadn't heard more.

"You have my word, Sasha. Please know you can always confide in me."

"But now, here we all are on Bora Bora," Sasha said, his face brightening, his mood suddenly switching gears. "You have your master plan ready to put into action, I have my role to play, and we all have sweet hours of island pleasure awaiting us. This opportunity may never come again."

Chapter 37

Seven o'clock found the crew assembled outside the main dining area. Their few hours of freedom and exploration made them hungry for more, and hungry for the Tahitian feast they could see being laid out on the banquet tables. Katya had arranged with Sylvie that no meat dishes would be served. Sasha arrived alone and spent some time talking with his mates before they entered the hall together. Katya arrived a few minutes later and struck up a conversation in French with Sylvie, who nodded and smiled with excitement.

Sylvie hurried back to her office and Katya fixed herself a plate. She chose a chair between Hau and Keung, across from Chen, and tried to join in their conversation. The men studied her intently and turned away when she looked back at them. Sasha was already seated at the opposite end of the table conversing with Maxim, Dima, Hiro, and Kiko. He didn't look at her. The others found places as they arrived with brimming plates of food. She needed to get herself on a normal footing with the crew. Sitting here, away from Sasha, was a start. She was just one of them. Sylvie returned and hit the announcement gong before the first dinner guest had left the hall.

"Good evening guests, and another warm welcome to the crew of the *Trib*. The crew will be hard at work early in the morning getting our new medical equipment up and running and installing the solar panels. Luc and I have been so excited setting up the three clinic rooms. We feel like children at Christmas opening boxes. We really can't thank the men of the *Trib* enough.

"The crew wants you all to know there will be a free clinic on the boat starting at ten o'clock tomorrow. Please come by with any medical issues, large or small, vaccination needs, or just for a well check. My clinic will be open the day after at ten, and several crew members will be on hand to help demonstrate the new equipment. Our special entertainment this evening will be another concert by our own Dr. Sasha Borodin, this time on the piano. He will be playing Chopin's Grand Ballade Number One, a Schubert Impromptu, and Ravel's *Gaspard de la nuit*, starting at seven."

A cheer erupted from the crew. Not one of them had ever heard Sasha play the piano. They knew Sasha had given the Mandelbrot family home with all its furnishings, including the grand piano, to the University, that he arranged time to play whenever he was visiting the laboratories, but they'd never been invited to hear. As far as they knew, no one except those listening to his tracker had heard his playing in decades, not since he left for Vietnam in 1965.

Sylvie, Luc and their staff set up chairs and moved the piano as before. The staff brought their families this time, making a loud and boisterous crowd on the lawn. There was absolute silence however as soon as Sasha sat down without preamble at the piano. A full minute passed before he placed his fingers on the keyboard and began to play. The crew was as enraptured as the rest of the crowd.

"I think Aashir just had an orgasm," Hau said a little too loudly, as the Chopin rose to a central crescendo. Aashir flushed and sank into his seat.

So Hau knows about Aashir's infatuation, Katya thought. Maybe they all do and just accept it. Maybe I'm wrong and they're all in love with Sasha, she mused. Sasha knew the Schubert Impromptu was her favorite. He told her he had chosen it for her. The wildly virtuosic and haunting *Gaspard* left the listeners breathless and there were immediate calls for an encore when Sasha finished. He obliged them with a precise and exquisitely articulated selection by Bach, then abruptly stood, and without bowing, left to join his crew amidst the loud applause, taking in the congratulations without reaction. Performing on the piano before a seated audience had left him emotionally drained. All he really wanted to do was be with Katya. He kept his distance, but it wasn't easy.

"Let's find a quiet spot on the beach to talk," he called out, as he strode towards the ocean, walking quickly away from the cheering crowd.

The crew and Katya hurried to follow. She left them there an hour later and headed back to the villa. She would wait for him to come to her, make love with her. Hopefully he would not leave her too exhausted. She was determined to be up at dawn with him to join the group workout on their beach.

Sasha arrived around 11 p.m. and found her half-asleep in a chair over a medical text. He bent and kissed the back of her neck, sliding his hands down over her breasts.

258

"Stop, I'm pretending to read," she murmured, turning to smile up at him.

"The crew asked about you when they noticed you'd left," he said in her ear.

"Absence makes the heart grow fonder," she replied, closing her book.

"Absence makes me grow harder. I can't stand being apart from you,"

Katya laughed. "We're together now. And I'm ready for some easy, gentle sex. No more acrobatics for me today."

"A woman who knows what she wants."

"A woman who knows what she needs. I need to be able to keep up with your crew exercising at dawn tomorrow, and I need to be able to walk."

"I'm so sorry, did I hurt you? Was I too rough?" Sasha asked, genuinely concerned.

"Not so that I need the night off," she said reaching her arms over her head. "Carry me to bed?"

Sasha didn't need to be asked twice. He swung her onto the closer bed and removed her clothes slowly while kicking off his own. They kissed long and passionately as he touched her, stopping and starting to make her writhe in anticipation. She rolled over on top of him and moved her body against his until they were both too aroused to continue, then she let him enter her. They both came in a flash, but she stayed straddled over him until he was relaxed. She dropped down beside him, and they lay caressing each other.

"Sasha, tell me two things I don't know about you. Nothing serious," Katya pleaded, in a playful mood.

"I don't know what you mean. Everything is serious with me," Sasha said, sensing this was supposed to be a lighthearted moment. "You go first, tell me two things I don't know about you and then I'll have a clue what to say."

"Fair enough. First, I don't like cats. Can't stand them. When I think of the millions of songbirds they kill every year, the diseases they spread. Always ready to dig into you with their claws."

"That's a pretty harsh assessment. I guess I see cats as necessary ratters on the wharfs. So, no kittens for you. What else?"

"I'm not really a vegetarian, or a pescatarian as you call it. I don't eat meat now because you don't. Sometimes I hallucinate the smell of

259

bacon cooking and think about convincing the chefs here to make me some. I don't like to eat beef, but I miss chicken, duck and lamb chops. And pork buns."

"You can have meat anytime you want to, Katya," Sasha said, amused that she'd chosen to give up something she enjoyed to keep him company in his eccentricity, that she'd implied she was already a pescatarian. "I've watched Maxim and Dima put away a big steak each, and Hiro an entire chicken when we were on leave together." Sasha knew this wasn't true as soon as he said it. That was fourteen years ago. He now remembered watching them eat for a few minutes, then gagging, excusing himself, not knowing why he was sweating, in a panic, and that he didn't return to the table. None of his crew had ever eaten meat in his presence again. He chose not to share this recalled memory with Katya.

"Well, thank you, but I'll keep my diet meatless. Your turn."

"I too have a secret food craving. Chocolate covered marzipan."

"No! I've never seen you tempted by anything sweet here. You always choose a piece of fruit for dessert. How did you ever get a taste for marzipan?"

"When I was in Europe, my Romani mates shoplifted quite the assortment of chocolates from a fine emporium and I discovered a taste for it. There's a store in Sydney I buy a piece from every year or two, but I think about the taste more often than that."

"And?"

"And I've never driven a car, never learned how," Sasha continued. "I wasn't interested when I was young and then I never needed to, nor would I have been allowed to. I know I could if I had to, though."

"You won't miss driving in California. You've seen the traffic between San Francisco and Berkeley. I can imagine all big Asian cities have traffic as bad as I experienced in Hong Kong. I'll be your chauffeur when we don't have Peter's car and driver."

Sasha leaned over and kissed her, then put his arm around her and pulled her close. They were conversing like a normal couple, well, almost normal, getting to know each other. He was enjoying being an ordinary man if only for this moment in time, the man he had imagined himself to be when they were in the van together.

"Tell me about your childhood in Australia," Katya requested, caressing his chest, her fingers tracing the lines of his scars.

260

"Are you sure? You know I'm not brimming with happy memories to share." Nothing ordinary in his childhood, Sasha thought.

"I want to know," Katya insisted.

"I'll skip quickly over the horrors of getting there, the boxcar... Bergen-Belsen... Then the Bergen Displacement Camp afterwards. Standing alone, watching Bergen-Belsen be burned to the ground to try and contain the typhus and lice epidemics. Witnessing thousands more deaths of privation and typhus, finding the Bettelmanns, an older couple who had passage to Australia, where a relative lived, who would take me along, pretending I was their grandson. The Bettelmanns didn't make it, died of a fever during an epidemic on the ship.

"There I was in Sydney in quarantine, alone, yelling at the officials trying to take my battered valise with Herr Silber's two violins hidden inside away from me. They backed down, but they were impressed with my English skills and the amount of knowledge I threw at them, desperate not to be sent back to Germany. Somehow I came to the attention of Harrison Mandelbrot, a physics professor at the university, who ended up adopting me. He and his wife Maddy knew I'd come from Bergen-Belsen, so they used Celle, Germany for my place of birth, chose January 1, 1940 for a birthdate for my papers. I refused to use their name, kept using the only name I knew, Alexander 'Sasha' Borodin. I have no idea why, except maybe stubbornness."

"What was Harrison Mandelbrot like?"

"Hard-driving, tyrannical, at least that's how I saw him. Pushed me unmercifully to learn, then eventually took credit for all my inventions. My adoptive mother Maddy was another story. Sweet, accepting. Their wealth came from her side of the family. I had no idea physics professors couldn't afford anything like the huge home on an enormous view lot I moved into. They showed me the bedroom they'd fixed for me. I actually asked where I was going to sleep. I'd never imagined a bed like that, covered in blue pillows and teddy bears."

"Maddy was in a wheelchair in the picture I saw."

"Maddy was well into the downslide of MS, multiple sclerosis, couldn't play the piano anymore. You'll hear her piano someday when I get you to Sydney. I was surprised to see a piano with all its keys. But I didn't touch it for a while. Didn't open the valise. The memories of the camp would be too much... I was entranced by their extensive record collection, though. I listened to almost every one of them, then they borrowed others for me. Discovered books, too. Read everything on their shelves, especially science and history. The library was like heaven to me. They borrowed books from the university in the other languages I knew how to read – Russian, German, and Dutch.

"I stayed quite solitary, to their dismay. The Mandelbrots tried to get me to open up, be social. I was solemn, unsmiling, humorless, only spoke when spoken to. The first months, I wouldn't look people in the eye. I didn't tell the Mandelbrots I was beaten if I looked a guard or officer in the eye, was used to hearing 'Eyes on the ground, worm.' Harrison forced me to make eye contact. I told them nothing about my life at Bergen-Belsen, wouldn't even speak to the therapists. One therapist suggested 'play dates.' The first time Harrison brought a boy my age to the house, I ran and hid under my bed. How could I tell him about the Czech boy in the camp? Never did have a friend in Sydney growing up."

"How did you get back to music?"

"They took me to a piano recital a month after I was adopted. When we came home, I sat down at the piano and recreated the entire program, not perfectly of course, but amazing enough, even to me. In the middle of the night I got out the violin and started playing a Bach Sarabande I'd heard on a record. That opened the floodgates. When I told them I also played cello, they procured me a decent small cello, and music teachers for all three instruments. They continued to take me to music events, concerts." *As long as Mozart or Haydn weren't on the program,* he thought to himself.

"How did they know to investigate your violins? I wouldn't think that would occur to them."

"The violin teacher they hired looked both instruments over after hearing their tone. I screamed and fought when they took them away to have them analyzed. They were made in 1723 by Antonio Stradivari. There was record of them being made for a father and son who both died before the violins could be delivered, then all records ceased. No provenance, no story, other than a rumor Stradivari knew the father and son, destroyed the violins out of grief. No explanation for how the violins got into the hands of Herr Silber, or even who Herr Silber was. The violins were in good shape except for their deceptive outward appearance, were restored and restrung. The process took months. Harrison procured me another quarter-size violin to play while waiting. You can imagine my relief when they were returned to me. I... don't know why, but I've never told anyone on my crew that my Artemisia is a Stradivarius, just that she came with me from the camp. I let no one else touch her."

"Did you name your beloved violin after the artist Artemisia Gentileschi?" Katya found his possessiveness over his violin just a little ominous.

"Yes, I did. I'm surprised you know about her."

"And where is Artemisia's little companion now?"

"I didn't want my quarter-size violin sitting unused – the violin I'd learned on meant so much to me. I entrusted her to the dean of the Sydney Conservatorium of Music and to every dean since then. She is played by the most talented young student until he or she moves on to a larger instrument. But my quarter-size violin stays in the Conservatorium."

Sasha didn't add that it was innocent young Artemisia's rape and her torture at the trial to test the truth of her accusation that had caught his attention. Not to mention her violent, controlling father and her splendid if nearly forgotten masterpieces of Italian Baroque art. That her father had taken credit for some of her work.

"I like that. You never performed for an audience when you were young?"

"I refused to play outside the house, never for visitors. Harrison worked up several opportunities with good orchestras, but I always said no. He tried to surprise me by hiring a hall and an orchestra when I was eleven, thought I would be thrilled to perform the Mendelssohn Violin Concerto I'd been playing at home with a recording. Even with just a half-dozen listeners in the audience, I walked away. He was furious."

"You might yet get that chance to perform with an orchestra."

Sasha didn't respond. He held onto that hope, the offer made in San Francisco. He gave her his near smile and continued.

"I preferred to be with Maddy. I read what I could find on MS. invented devices to help her with her disability. Harrison patented and sold my devices as his own... Maddy called me her hundred-year-old midget. I was so outrageously literal, I corrected her every time. She found it amusing. It drove Harrison crazy. He kept waiting for me to be grateful, to smile, to let him hug me. He still tried. I must have had a panic attack all the way to blackout once a week. Then the Bergen-

Belsen memories would come, usually in the middle of the night, and I would scream when they tried to get me to stop playing the violin. Or I would just sit and look inward for long periods, drenched in sweat, reciting the List in my head. I wasn't an easy child to live with."

What an understatement, Katya thought, her heart breaking. So little had changed for him in all this time. He'd had a respite with Le, and now with her. If Sasha had indeed found peace with the List, could his other issues be dealt with eventually as well? She kept quiet and encouraged him to continue.

"Harrison thought maybe I could succeed in sports with my hypertrophic musculature. I could lift three-kilo weights straight out to my sides at six – the 'Iron Cross.' I refused all group sports like soccer, but I excelled at martial arts. I was excited to discover I could block kicks and punches without triggering a touch phobia attack. Harrison enrolled me in gymnastics as well, but I wouldn't compete. Other children made fun of me, tormented me because I looked, and acted, so strange. Harrison hired a driver to take me to classes. Later, a tutor would take me, and to the beach to swim.

"I looked forward to the classes as an escape from the daily drudgery of learning. I also got the entire day off on my birthdays, free to choose one or two distractions. My favorite was sailing. Harrison was a sailor, taught me to sail in Sydney Harbour. I never felt so free as out on the water. Sailing was the one thing we did together that wasn't a battle... As I grew older, I exercised hard to make my body look like I'd sculpted it in training. I swam, always wearing a long-sleeved swim shirt, and took ballet classes, though my partner had to be careful not to touch me. I could still support and lift – I was so strong. The ballet students tolerated me."

"How on Earth did you get into ballet?"

Sasha gave her his near smile again. "I couldn't sit still listening to music on their records. I ran, leaped, and twirled around the vast living room. Maddy loved to watch me – she'd enjoyed dancing when she still had her mobility. The next December she had Harrison take us to a performance of the Nutcracker by the Sydney Ballet at the Opera House. I was hooked. It took Maddy a year of uncharacteristic begging and persuasion, but she finally convinced Harrison to let me start ballet at eight. Harrison hadn't wanted me to take any more time away from my lessons, from his rigorous instruction..."

"That's where you got your wonderful shoulders. I always thought you looked like a dancer. You move with such grace."

Sasha looked embarrassed. "I'm going to ignore that. Maybe I've talked long enough."

"No, don't stop. You haven't told me about your laboratory, your work with Harrison Mandelbrot." Katya began massaging the back of his neck and he reluctantly continued.

"I don't want to say much. I was desperate, foolish, egotistical. When I was ten, I wanted to save Maddy, cure her MS. Got Harrison to buy me mice for pets, did hopeless experiments. I set up a lab in the carriage house. Had a hundred other scattered ideas, started building physics projects, scrounged my material. Harrison discovered my lab, and when he was done laughing, turned it into a genuine lab and put me to work on some real projects, bought me whatever I needed, worked with me. After a couple of years, I was creating devices he could market and sell, but he claimed they were his own. He made a lot of money, became well-known. I started to grow resentful."

"You said you were never sent to school before college?"

"I caught a break for my first year in Sydney. No schooling, just a barrage of tests to see what I knew, what I might be capable of. I practiced my languages, had all those records, books, and my music lessons to keep me occupied. Then Harrison home-tutored me himself, hired trusted tutors when my abilities outstripped even his knowledge. The tutors were sworn to secrecy; none of them knew about the others. At Mandelbrot House and in my own laboratory, they taught me an entire secondary school curriculum, then on to college-level work, and I continued to study languages, added new ones, perfected the ones I'd started learning in the camp. Harrison pushed me mercilessly, wanted to find out how far I could go, how much I could learn. I swear, Katya, there were times I felt like I was back with Krüger. Harrison knew he could no longer keep my genius a total secret. But my lab work, my inventions, would belong to him and him alone.

"Harrison wielded his considerable influence to convince the University to let me enroll at twelve, settling on chemistry for my major. With my physique, and an early growth spurt, I looked much older. I lived at home, of course; a tutor drove me. I sat in the back of my classes, when I would bother to show up at all, continued to learn on my own, avoided the other students, aced my tests, and tried not to draw too much attention to myself. I found it all a terrible bore but graduated at fifteen. I preferred tinkering in my lab and helping Harrison with his life's work: trying to create a commercial car motor based on Nikola Tesla's radiant energy research, a truly fuelless engine. All of his advancements came from my ideas... Plus I still had gymnastics, martial arts, and ballet, languages to learn, my music... Meanwhile Harrison became famous, and even richer, from marketing my inventions as his own. Relations between us grew more adversarial.

"Then that summer Maddy died and I lost it, ran away. Or should I say stowed away. When I returned from my year in Europe, all I wanted was to be a doctor. I was devastated that the University of Sydney medical school wouldn't accept me so young. Harrison tried to make it clear to me no medical school anywhere was ever going to accept me with my eccentricities, as he called them, no matter what age I was. Maybe he just wanted to be sure I wasn't distracted from creating inventions he could sell. Maybe he really did think I couldn't handle medical school. I boycotted my own lab.

"In response, Harrison somehow managed to get me enrolled in both Bioengineering and Biochemistry graduate programs, thought that would placate me. I became fascinated with the science of prosthetics, studied robotics and computer science too, and on my own as well. I made sure I'd completed all possible pre-med classes, worked harder at fitting in. I wouldn't give up my dream of medical school. But I was tired of playing Harrison's games, of playing down my genius, and worked individually with the professors, moving ahead faster than he wanted me to. Harrison gave in and helped me make a name for myself as a gifted albeit eccentric student, as I began to improve and design medical devices for the University hospital.

"So when I finally did start medical school, I already had a reputation with the University and its teaching hospital. Given my personality traits, I'm sure the dean was hopeful I'd go into research, would disappear into a lab somewhere. Or maybe become a pathologist and hang out in the morgue. But I matured a great deal my first year. I impressed the school with my double load of classes, my surprising competence with patients, and eventually, my skills with a scalpel."

"And with your undeniable brilliance."

266

"And yes, with my undeniable brilliance, as you put it. I found that if I made physical contact first with patients, putting a hand on a shoulder or a head, I had time to ask politely not to be touched. Not that most patients would even think of touching their surgeon, even a lowly resident... The entire staff watched out for me. Touch panic attacks and blackouts were rare. I kept my violin with me, managed to escape into a soundproof private place S-Branch created for me in the hospital if I felt a memory attack or List recitation coming on. I may have had no friends, been unpopular, as Peter told you, but I was respected. As the years passed and I finished my residencies, I took on the persona of a holier-than-thou surgeon. I was certain that I was better than anyone else. I'm ashamed to admit my attitude worked for me in that environment."

"But wait," Katya asked, confused, "I think I missed something. How did you get into medical school? If I remember correctly, that was only a year after you returned from Europe, right?"

"Harrison, died, had a heart attack. Everything changed. The government discovered me and my precocious talents and stepped into his role. They promised me anything I wanted."

"And you wanted to go to medical school. How did you get found out?"

"I bragged about my lab to a visitor after the funeral. I told him the hydrogen fuel cell was mine, that all the work Harrison claimed as his own was really mine, told him about my medical equipment innovations, showed him around the lab. He came back a week later with two other men. They listened to me go on again, then offered me a job working for the government. But it would have to be secret. To protect me, they said, like Harrison had protected me from celebrity, from notoriety. Appealed to my patriotism, frightened me with visions of real-world adversities if I were to become famous, the impossibility of a normal life given my eccentricities, flattered me. They called me a genius...

"I was ripe for their exploitation. I was angry over Harrison claiming my hydrogen fuel cell, even angrier that he'd sold the process to an American oil company, thinking that they'd market it immediately. It never saw the light of day again. Still, I blamed myself for Harrison's death, thought his guilt over the success of my fuel cell, my anger over its burial, had contributed to his heart attack. I was not yet eighteen, a selfish, resentful, but also frightened teenager, alone and unprotected. Looking back, I think Harrison may have loved me in his own way, wanted to keep me safe, protect me from fame at too early an age. I'll never know for sure.

"The government officials offered me my own state-of-the-art laboratories. I demanded early admission to medical school and a role in creating a new Prosthetics Department for the University of Sydney. They didn't hesitate, thought my being a doctor would be a great cover. I found myself enrolled for the fall semester. But now I had a handler, and a minder who was also my driver, who escorted me everywhere I went, stayed nearby at the medical school and hospital while I took classes or worked, even moved into Mandelbrot House with me. A series of minders, all of whom I hated. Then guards, in addition. Such as it was, my youth was over."

"You never did have a childhood. This was your Fate, Sasha. This is what made you the man you are, the man I fell in love with."

And this is what is going to make learning to live with him a daily challenge, she thought. She had been able to forget his genius status, enjoy the sensuality of the island, the passion of their lovemaking. She was about to be introduced to the reality of his life: S-Branch constantly looking over their shoulders, declaring what they could and could not do, dealing with his bouts of manic, wild restless energy, his depressions, his resentful commitment to Australogic. His past was going to continue to rear its ugly head at any moment. She would experience life as the only woman aboard his boat with his crew, be subject to his iron rules as Captain, that is, if she could manipulate her way forward. She loved this man madly. She would make it work. They shared a long kiss, then he scooted back a little so he could look at her, holding her hands.

"Katya, there's something I want to tell you, now that it's my crew members' turn to have you manipulate their emotions. You didn't have to go through all that mystery about who you were, trying to get me to want you, to get me to fall in love with you. All those stories, your complicated maneuverings, were completely unnecessary."

"You saw through my intentions? And you weren't angry?" Katya asked, surprised, particularly that he used the same word "manipulate" that she'd just used in her head.

"No, I was never upset. On the contrary, I was moved by how hard you were trying to win me. I wanted you even when we were holding our noses in the darkness of the van, when I couldn't remember what

268

you looked like. I loved your humor, the self-confidence you projected, even though I knew you were frightened. Our, dare I say, mystical connection. Then everything I learned about your life made me want you more. I was pretending to be just an ordinary person while you were pretending to be someone you imagined as extraordinary. You should have had faith that your ordinary life, as you called it, could seem wonderful and extraordinary to me. You and I were more alike than you thought. I fell more in love with you... I knew I loved you when we escaped from the van, when I really saw you for the first time."

"But you gave me no clue you were interested in me that way. You were so formal, always the gentleman, cold even at times."

"I felt I was too old, too humorless to be romancing you, that it wouldn't be fair to you... or that you'd reject me. You must admit it took you longer to fall in love with me."

"Sasha, we've only known each other two weeks! But I wanted to be with you before I fell in love, before I knew how extraordinary you are. I thought you needed me."

"I do need you." Sasha kissed her. "I'll always need you."

Chapter 38

Sasha swung out of bed wide awake at dawn as usual. Katya stumbled out of bed after him and took a quick, cool shower before dressing in workout clothes. Honeymoon's over, she thought. Now she had to figure out how to share Sasha with ten men. Or more precisely, how to get them to want her as part of their crew. Reasonably awake, she followed Sasha's fast stride out the door and over to their private beach. She was half hoping the crew would be out swimming in the nude, but they were busy stretching or still arriving. Like Sasha, they were dressed in soft, loose clothing in various neutral shades, looking even more attractive. She grew even more curious about this bamboo-fiber fabric. Morning greetings were friendly and informal. The men took their time finding places to stand on the beach. Katya found an open spot and joined them, facing Sasha. Other than only being able to punch with one arm, Katya felt she was not embarrassing herself and was able to keep up. When Sasha called for pushups, she got down in the sand as well.

"Katya, I told you no pushups until that arm heals. What do you think you're doing?" Sasha yelled at her, sounding angry. The men stopped at the unexpected tone and watched to see what would happen. Katya squirmed in the sand a bit to get positioned and proceeded to do twenty-five one-arm pushups with her uninjured arm, then sat up on her knees looking at Sasha. Most of the crew burst out in cheers and laughter. Sasha continued to look angry but dropped down to start two-arm pushups, and the men joined him.

When the time came to choose sparring partners, Tuan stepped towards her, volunteering. He folded his left arm over his waist and bowed to her. They would spar equally handicapped. Sasha opened his mouth to object, but instead just nodded once. With her injury, Katya knew she should not get knocked to the ground, so she went after Tuan with everything she had, and took him down again and again while staying on her feet. By the fifth takedown, the rest of the crew had stopped their own sparring to watch. When Dima, Sasha's partner, stopped too, Sasha put his hands on his hips and stood looking annoyed. Katya and Tuan battled on until she took him down hard for a seventh time and sat on him, twisting his arm behind him. Tuan slapped the sand furiously in surrender. She helped him up and bowed. Tuan bowed as well, then shook her hand. The crew started to cheer again, except for Aashir, who glared at her. They were silenced immediately by Sasha.

"What just happened here? I gave no one permission to stop. This is practice, not a tournament, Katya. Follow instructions or leave."

Katya bowed low, took a step back, and moved into rest position. The crew was stunned. Sasha never spoke to them like this, and Katya was sparring no differently than they were, just with more ferocity. The exercise continued for another half-hour, ending with Tai Chi, the more combative Chen style, with spiraling jumps and quick thrusts, after which the men started wandering back towards the boat and showers. They could see and hear Sasha still standing with arms crossed, berating Katya.

When Katya and Sasha got back to the villa, he grabbed her and kissed her. They stripped off each other's clothes and stepped into the double shower together.

"Please, Katya, don't ever make me do that again," he said, as he lathered her with soap. "My men trust me. I felt like an ogre out there."

"They'll forgive you. Did you see how the men reacted when they thought you were being unfair? I'll have them eating out of my hand in no time."

"You cunning little vixen. Just don't try manipulating them, or me, that way ever again," he said, with a twinkle in his eye and his near smile.

"I wouldn't dare," she replied, as she lathered his rising member. They were back in bed making love in minutes.

After yet another shower, Katya walked over to the new clinic building alone to help Sylvie finish setting up. Dima, Keung, Chen, and Tuan would be arriving any minute. Sylvie had been unable to decide between the powerful Tamatoa and the empathetic Taiana to be her clinic assistant as she needed both traits. Sasha had told her to go ahead and hire both, since it was a part-time position, and they would be continuing their other jobs at the resort. Sasha's sponsors would pay their salaries, he assured her. Both were there and excited to get started. Erita and Vaea, along with many of the other Tahitian women at the resort, were hanging around hoping to get a closer look at the handsome crew and to try to interest them in a massage, or something else.

Sylvie was excited to tell Katya she'd found a good guitar for her to borrow and wanted to show her the outfits she'd put together. Sylvie would announce at dinner tonight that she had two special guests for the evening's entertainment: gypsy jazz guitarist Django Reinhardt and singer Edith Piaf. Katya begged to try the guitar now in case her arm would not allow her to play, while she could still back out. She tuned and was warming up when the crew members arrived. She started playing a Bach transcription that she knew well, and they stood around her listening, joined by the Tahitian staff. Katya was pleased with her playing and the guitar's tone, and with the positive reaction of her listeners. She put the guitar back in its case and joined the workgroup.

Sasha walked over to the *Trib* to prepare for the morning clinic, but since the crew had everything so well organized, he asked them all to join him in the main hall for breakfast. He tried hard to be especially easy going and even struggled to be humorous to help make up for the scene at the beach. He could detect no difference in their attitude towards him. *Katya was right*, he thought, *they will forgive me anything*.

The clinic workgroup joined them in the dining hall, and Sasha kept up the pretense of coolness towards Katya. She was right again; he could see the crew fawning over her, at least everyone but Aashir. She had been quite impressive with her one-arm push-ups and her sparring skills, he had to admit. It was the first time he had witnessed either. He listened to her regale his crew with how she came to perfect her one-armed skills. The prospect of having to teach for six months with a broken arm had convinced her she could not afford to be weak. Katya trained with her sifu on one-armed strategies and worked with the other arm once she had healed. She'd kept up the practice ever since. She told them of the fight clubs in Hong Kong and had them in awe of her, especially Maxim, the skeptical First Officer.

Sasha told them the story he'd heard from her sifu about her last fight club experience and how she'd used her wits to win with that broken arm, then about breaking both of Gunner's arms in the California fight. He hoped the crew had gained a deeper respect for her and would feel just a little self-concern about who was going to have to spar with her one-armed tomorrow. Sasha nodded at her. He

273

was looking forward to the evening's entertainment. Katya hadn't told him exactly what she'd be doing but he knew she would be performing on the porch stage. He thought about her singing in a club in Berkeley, her "alter ego" hippie clothes in the footlocker that David had shown him. Katya was certainly full of surprises.

The morning went by quickly. Dozens of natives and guests stopped by the clinic on the boat. Most were just curious and wanted a tour. The crew did well checks on everyone from babies to adults, gave advice, took care of vaccinations and pre-natal visits, picked up a couple of infections they could treat, made a few key diagnoses, and performed a hernia repair. The guests had no health issues past sunburns and the native population was fairly healthy.

By noon the men were looking forward to having the rest of the day free. Sasha told them he would stay, and they could all go hiking or snorkeling or else just lay on the beach, as they wished. He found he was enjoying the simple banter, especially with the last group of natives to visit, a staff family with two boys, a seven-year-old, Hitiura and a five-year-old, Iki. Sasha listened to Iki's heart and lungs with his stethoscope, then Hitiura's, and tried to engage them with his steadily improving Tahitian. He noted that Hitiura's speech sounded a little slurred, and asked him several questions in French, then English – if he had been having any headaches, any problems walking or with his balance, if he'd thrown up recently. He replied yes to all the questions, and added that his vision was a little blurry, that he was having trouble reading his book. Sasha could hear the same slight slurring of words in his replies in English.

"Have you taken any falls lately?" Sasha asked, growing concerned.

Hitiura shook his head no, but his little brother spoke up and said Hitiura had climbed a palm tree to get a coconut a week before and had fallen to the ground.

"Did you hit your head, Hitiura?" Sasha asked, keeping his voice casual.

Hitiura looked up at his shocked and disapproving parents, a kitchen employee named Manua and his wife, Tarita, a server, but managed to nod yes. Sasha asked him to show where on his head he had hurt himself. Sasha put his hand on the boy's shoulder and turned to the parents.

"We have a wonderful machine here that can look inside Hitiura's head and tell us if everything is all right. It doesn't hurt a bit. Can I show you how it works?"

The parents eagerly agreed, and Sasha set Hitiura up in the CT scanner, making the trip into the donut seem like a game. The brain image showed on a computer screen the whole family could see. Sasha, damping his concern, explained that there was a subdural hematoma, a collection of blood on the brain's surface, that needed to be drained immediately. The boy's life was in danger, but the outcome with surgery and medicine for this kind of condition was excellent. He would need to drill a small hole in the skull to relieve the pressure by draining off the blood. Manua and Tarita were unsophisticated people, but they trusted Sasha, and although frightened, they would do whatever needed to be done. He asked them to sit in the main cabin and talk with their sons while he got ready.

What Sasha needed was an assistant and he'd sent the entire crew away. He excused himself to the family, then casually walked up the steps to the pilothouse, nodding to the two S-Branch guards. He didn't want to have to raise the alarm to bring his whole crew back and was relieved to see Katya walking towards the dock, with Aashir at a distance behind her. Slipping down the outside stairs, he hurried across the deck.

"Katya, Aashir. I need you both STAT," he called down, and returned through the companionway to gown up and scrub.

Aashir, in a despairingly jealous mood, had been following Katya as she headed to the boat. His jealousy was forgotten in an instant as he ran past her to heed Sasha's call. Katya started running, too, and they arrived breathless at the main cabin, startling the waiting family. Katya squeaked out a greeting as she and Aashir slowed to walk down the steps into the hospital area at the stern. Sasha explained the situation and told them both to scrub quickly.

"This will be a good learning experience for you, Katya," Sasha informed her. "This is a chronic subdural hematoma, not acute. I won't need to do a craniotomy. I'll only need one burr hole. Aashir will assist me, and you will assist both of us as needed. I think it would be best if you talked with the parents one last time before bringing Hitiura in. They know and trust you, too."

Sasha set up the operating room with the sterile tools they would need laid out on a Mayo stand. Aashir helped Katya get properly

275

scrubbed, gowned, and gloved, then shaved and prepped the back of Hitiura's head. They stood on either side of Sasha as he placed an IV in the boy's arm and gave him a local anesthetic. He would be sedated but conscious for the procedure. Katya told Hitiura how brave he was being. The procedure would be painless, she assured him.

Sasha was quick and precise, using his scalpel to expose the skull and then drilling a small burr hole. The blood and fluids were under pressure and drained quickly while Aashir expertly suctioned and irrigated. Katya found the procedure fascinating, and did exactly as she was asked, handing Sasha items from his surgical tray, and then carefully replacing them. She couldn't help noticing that Aashir was staring at her for long moments, nothing visible of his face except those liquid brown eyes and long lashes. In less than thirty minutes the opening was closed and Aashir nodded that all Hitiura's vitals were good. Sasha informed Katya that this tine no tube had to be left in to continue draining fluids, and asked her to go see the family once she'd removed all of her protective clothing.

"Tell them the procedure went perfectly. We'll keep him quiet here for a few hours, and then transfer him to Sylvie's new hospital clinic for a few days for monitoring. He must restrict his physical activity for a while and they must let us know if he has headaches or memory problems, but he should make a full recovery. Tell them I'll come out to get them as soon as we move Hitiura to a bed."

Katya followed his instructions and soon the grateful family was gathered around Hitiura's bed, wringing Aashir's and Katya's hands, bowing deeply to Sasha, and listening to his care instructions. Iki laughed at his brother's partially shaved head but Hitiura said he couldn't wait to show it off. Aashir found a moment to talk to Katya privately. He looked chagrined.

"Katya, I am sorry I doubted you," he said. His accent was strong but she was impressed with his language skills, and with the noticeable Australian accent to his English. He'd been avoiding talking with her. "It's hard to believe you have never done anything like this before. You handled yourself very well. You seem to handle yourself well in everything. Sasha is extremely fortunate to have found you."

"We found each other. Aashir, I know you love him too and you know he loves you in a different way. Let me help you find what you're looking for."

Aashir surprised her with a long, tight, heartfelt hug. Progress, Katya thought, progress.

Chapter 39

News of the "miraculous" surgery traveled like wildfire around the resort and neighboring areas, bringing in more Tahitians seeking medical care. Katya was concerned that Sasha was attracting far too much attention, but there was not much she could do about it. Aashir's new friendship and advocacy did much to endear her to the rest of the crew. He had stayed with Hitiura on the *Trib* and helped him make the transfer to the clinic. Sylvie was enjoying having her first ever in-patient and a livelier clinic. When several crew members brought Aashir a plate of food, since he'd missed lunch, he couldn't stop talking about Katya. Katya decided not to overplay her hand. It was time for her and Sasha to disappear for a while, time to tour the rest of the boat, especially the diving platform and the scuba gear.

Sasha wanted to stay close to the *Trib* while Katya was learning how to scuba. The reefs off the resort, while quite shallow, were teeming with life. The waters around Bora Bora were lagoon-like, protected from large ocean waves by the motos encircling the entire island. After less than a half-hour's instruction on land, they stepped off the platform and submerged into the crystal-clear water. Sasha's third-generation equipment made diving easy and natural. He warned her to breathe slowly, that excited new divers used up their oxygen at a faster rate. Katya found she didn't need to use her arms at all, just barely move her fins, and she was propelled easily through the water.

On her first dive, she thrilled to a multitude of new sights, including mantas and stingrays, sea turtles, moray eels, several passing black-tip and lemon sharks, and many new varieties of fish she hadn't seen snorkeling. The colorful cliffs of coral took on new beauty and impressive dimensions as she swam around and over them. The water at this depth was a perfect temperature, cooler than nearer the surface. There was only the bubbly rush of their breathing and the rasping of parrotfish beaks against the coral. Sasha promised her they would take a Zodiac out to deeper water the next time. He had already scouted out several great dive sites that would guarantee them humpback whale sightings.

Back at the *Trib*, Sasha showed her a drawing pad filled with dozens of pages of exquisitely drawn sea creatures, some enlarged from microscopic images. She remembered that he'd been the first to discover some of them, that he had shared his findings with the scientific world as S. Alexander. The drawings were as beautiful as they were scientifically detailed, his artistic skill another aspect of Sasha's life she'd known nothing about. Crew members were coming and going so they had to behave themselves and they headed back to their own villa for afternoon sex and showers. Afterwards, Katya took a nap in the hammock while a twenty-minute downpour drenched the island. The sound of rain on the roof and nearby palms was deeply soothing. She could get used to island life.

When Katya awoke, Sasha was gone, so she headed over to the Roussel's to rehearse. Her arm felt stronger and her guitar playing sounded even better. She didn't see Sasha until he and the crew joined her in the hall at dinner.

When Sylvie made her announcement about the evening's performance, there was much conversation about what was in store. Enough guests knew of Django's and Edith's music to spread the word of who they were, but they had no idea who the performers would be. Sasha kept quiet but was curious to see what Katya would do. She excused herself and slipped out of the hall.

The porch stage contained two chairs, the piano, and nothing more. When the audience was seated, an unrecognizable Katya appeared, holding a guitar and wearing a thirties-style men's suit with a polka dot tie, boots, a fedora pulled low over her face, hair slicked and pulled back, and a pencil moustache drawn on her upper lip. Sylvie followed her with a second guitar. They bowed to polite applause and sat down. Sylvie accompanied on rhythm guitar while Katya played her interpretation of Django Reinhardt's gypsy jazz music, although she played with four fingers; Django had played amazing music with just the two unburned fingers of his left hand. The crowd quickly got into the swing of the music.

Katya allowed herself several show-off moments and a couple of solos before striking the final chords. She and Sylvie took a bow and she swept off her hat and let down her hair, to roars of laughter, cheers and lengthy applause. They left the porch and made their way through the chairs to Sylvie's bedroom to change for the second act. Luc removed one of the chairs from the stage, and Katya returned minus

280

the mustache, in bright red lipstick, wearing a black dress and curly dark red wig, carrying her guitar. When the crowd quieted, she stood and accompanied herself to a half dozen Edith Piaf songs, including her most well-known "Non, Je Ne Regrette Rien" and "La Vie en Rose," belting out the songs in a near perfect imitation of Piaf's voice and bold style.

When the wild applause started to slow, she put down her guitar and started singing "To Dream the Impossible Dream" from *Man Of La Mancha* in French, still in Piaf's voice and style, wandering down the stairs and through the audience, sliding her hand across the shoulders of each crew member in turn. She sang the last lines in English, but still as Edith Piaf, as she reached Sasha, then bent over to kiss him full on the mouth. He stood and took her into his arms, returning her passionate kiss before spinning her into a graceful dip.

The crowd, and especially the crew, were shouting their acclaim, laughing and cheering. Katya was relieved the song had gone over well. It had started out as just a joke between her and Broadway-loving Sylvie. Sylvie had shared her small record collection and had been delighted to learn Katya had performed in musicals since she was eight, had sung the role of Dulcinea in a college production. Katya hoped David hadn't shared that information with Sasha. She chose to sing the knight's song in French because she knew no one on the crew but Sasha spoke the language. She worried that Sasha would be embarrassed, or worse, offended, but his reaction showed an increasing sense of playfulness that Katya found thrilling. Perhaps he hadn't caught the reference to Don Quixote or the line "covered with scars," wouldn't think of Aglaya's teasing of the idealistic and saintly Prince Myshkin with her at first mocking, then serious recitation of Pushkin's "The Poor Knight" in Dostoevsky's *The Idiot,* a book Sasha knew well. He'd already angrily refuted any comparison between him and the "positively good man" Myshkin represented.

Katya gently pushed Sasha down in his seat and returned to the stage to take a bow. She turned away from the audience, quickly wiped off the lipstick, and turned back as she pulled off her wig and bowed again to increased applause. Sylvie sat at the piano and Katya took a more formal, upright pose, hands clasped loosely in front of her and began singing Schumann's unsentimental lied, to the words of Heinrich Heine, "Du bist wie eine Blume" in a lovely mezzo voice, slowing the lied's tempo to enhance its languor, emphasizing the melancholic mood. Lifting her hands, she reached out to Sasha as she sang the words "so hold und schön und rein." Katya's natural voice was a surprise, and the applause longer still. The vocal exercises she'd managed to fit into her days had paid off; her voice was small but well-trained, and she'd put her heart into her singing. Amid calls of *encore!* Katya picked up her guitar and sat down, this time launching into a guitar solo, the beautiful "Memories of the Alhambra" by Granados. By the time she finished, she'd won every heart among the crew. Maxim and Dima were in tears, and Sasha had fallen in love with her all over again.

Music took center stage for the rest of the time on the island. Mornings might be spent snorkeling or scuba diving, but the afternoon rains, short as they were, sent Katya and crewmates inside the Roussel's house to begin playing in various groupings. Her success playing the guitar with her healing arm encouraged her to try the piano, and after much practice, she began accompanying Sasha, then the cellists, violists, and other violinists wanted their turns for duets, trios, quartets, and quintets. Sylvie printed out any music they asked for. There was no audience to impress, although guests and employees would stop by to listen. When Sasha retreated to the *Trib* to work at the command center with his labs, Katya and the crew played through music with joyous abandon, unconcerned with mistakes and restarts. She enthralled Tuan and Aashir with her piano playing in the Beethoven Trio Number 2 in G Major, Hau and Kiko in the Mendelssohn Trio for piano, violin, and viola in C Minor. Katya knew she had the complete support of Chen and Keung after they laughingly faked through Dvorák's heartbreakingly beautiful "Dumky Trio."

Maxim, Dima, and Hiro would do anything for her after they finished playing the Brahms' Piano Quintet in a much more serious run-through with Sasha back playing first violin. Kiko threatened to exhaust her making her play piano/viola pieces until she convinced Sasha to take over as accompanist.

Once she had Sasha at the keyboard, it was easy to convince him to play piano quintets and other chamber works, with Sonthi or Maxim on first violin. Katya marveled that the crew members could be such fine musicians. Sasha had told her most were musicians when they arrived, but that he had a test for musical ability that never failed him when he was recruiting. If a new crew member was not already a musician, he learned quickly under Sasha's tutelage.

Sasha needed no cajoling to let her hear him play the cello. Taking up Hiro's cello, he played Bach's first solo cello suite in its entirety. Katya hadn't thought he could astound her yet again. Virtuosic was the only word that would suffice. The Brahms quintet put Sasha in mind of his first cello sonata, the E Minor, and with much more practice and rehearsing, Katya joined him for a run-through that attracted half the resort and the entire crew to listen in.

When Katya could escape from her accompanist role, she played gypsy jazz or classical music on the guitar anywhere she felt moved to. Sasha continued to play solo violin, and to play solo pieces on the piano as well, settling in to work through more of Bach from *The Well-Tempered Klavier*. Sylvie convinced Sasha to perform two more concerts, one with Katya accompanying him in more challenging piano and violin pieces: Ravel's Sonata Number Two, Prokofiev's second, and the Debussy Violin Sonata in G Minor, along with a string concert featuring Sasha and his crew. Sasha chose to start with the intensely romantic Borodin second string quartet, causing some amusing confusion with his name, then the Schubert two cello quintet, and the rousing Mendelssohn Octet. The Mendelssohn had long been one of Katya's favorites, but she had never heard anything as moving or as beautiful as their performance of the Schubert, the acclaimed pinnacle of chamber music.

To hone their musical skills, crew members practiced wherever they could find a place to be by themselves – on the beach, by the cove, on a trail, in the villa, on the deck of the *Trib*. Keung told Katya that Dima's workshop in the hold had been a sought after place to practice on board, but that they were all pleased to escape its crowded confines. Guests and staff alike seemed as happy to listen to their practicing as to their performances. Katya continued to do her vocal exercises whenever Sasha was busy elsewhere, and found time to read Sylvie's medical texts and to start running again, climbing over volcanic outcroppings to go from beach to beach.

The villa became the daytime hangout for the crew. All of them, Sasha included, spent much of the day shirtless, although Sasha wore his long-sleeved shirts at the main resort. Much to Katya's delight, the crew began to feel comfortable enough with her to return to their predilection for nude swimming off their private beach. Someone

283

would begin, then they would all strip and race each other, Sasha always the fastest swimmer by a wide margin. She noted that Aashir and Sasha were the only two circumcised men, but that's about all they shared in common physically. Although exceptionally fit, Aashir was small, dark and delicate, standing a mere five feet, a full ten inches shorter than Sasha.

Aashir and Tuan had quickly become a couple, thanks to Katya's machinations. She was amused by the change that came over Aashir, how happy he seemed, although she still caught him giving longing glances at Sasha. Sasha spent no less than two hours a day on the *Trib* working with the laboratories, giving Katya a chance to hang out with the men and get to know them better. On one of these occasions, she invited Aashir, Tuan, Hau, and Kiko to spend some time with her on the villa's lanai. The two new lovers caressed and kissed each other, ignoring the friendly teasing of their mates. Hau and Kiko had their own interesting sexual proclivities: Katya had seen them flirting as a pair with the native women, and disappearing with one onto the *Trib*, both men holding hands with her... when they knew Sasha was not on board.

"What does Sasha think of your relationship?" Katya innocently asked Tuan and Aashir.

An uncomfortable silence fell over the group.

"Sasha doesn't know," Tuan finally answered. "He is not to know. We can only be amorous here out of his sight."

"Surely he's not homophobic!" Katya exclaimed, shocked.

"No! I mean, he just can't see men sexually involved with each other..."

"He freaks out, panics," Hau explained. "Starts to sweat heavily, gasps for breath, worse than when he's haunted by his past. At least then he can grab his violin. Playing music snaps him out of it."

Kiko nodded. "We've all witnessed this. When we're on shore leave in a bigger city, or even on the docks, there are often young men soliciting sex, or pairs of men who are loving partners. We've learned to steer his attention away."

"Have you asked him why he reacts this way?"

"He said he won't talk about it, ever. Try asking Sonthi."

Sasha's revelation about his childhood sexual abuse was private information, not to be shared with his men. Somehow Katya was certain there was more to his aversion to viewing homosexual

284

relations, perhaps something that had happened to him as a young adult. It was clear to her Sasha loved men, even as he seemed unaware of his feelings.

Katya sought out Sonthi, but Sasha had confessed nothing to him, refused to talk about Bergen-Belsen or anything at all in his past. He too suspected that Sasha had suffered further abuse beyond his childhood. She and Sonthi talked about Buddhism, psychology, and his own past instead. She discovered that his father had been a well-known psychiatrist in Bangkok.

"My father pushed me to be a psychiatrist, but I never went into practice after getting my degree," he told her. "I finally rebelled and went right on for a residency in internal medicine, then a fellowship in infectious diseases. I have made tropical diseases a specialty as well since I have been on the *Trib*."

Now she knew Sasha had been serious when he'd called him his psychiatrist. "Do you consider Sasha your patient?" she asked, not sure if her questions had been appropriate.

"I am sorry to say Sasha chose to stop having sessions with me a year ago, Katya," Sonthi confided to her. "I still help him deal with crises and we practice meditation together on board, when I can get him to sit still, but his connection to Buddhism is tenuous at best. There is not much I can do for him but help him cope when he won't open up about his past. All we know is that his memory attacks, as we call them, are a return to the horrors of Bergen-Belsen. He has not had one that I know of since we've arrived, and that must be because of you, Katya. I am pleased with his current state of mindfulness. Whatever you are doing with him, keep it up."

Sonthi stopped to give Katya an appreciative touch on her hand. Katya couldn't keep from laughing, despite the seriousness of the discussion. Sonthi didn't seem to understand what was funny, but he looked hesitant to continue.

"I don't want to embarrass you, but I could never picture Sasha being physically intimate with anyone, even though I knew about his Vietnamese wife; to us on the crew, he was an asexual being. He was also humorless, driven, much more rigid, and sometimes deeply unhappy. Don't misunderstand me – he loves living on the *Trib*, loves us, in his own way... making music, practicing medicine with us... away from Australogic and S-Branch's control. Sasha is such a different person since he met you. But I have no doubt there will be difficult times ahead. Sasha is prone to depression, and although you may not have witnessed them, you seem to know about those memory and touch phobia attacks, his long silent spells. You have experienced his highs, his manic behavior. I do what I can for him. I am here for you too, if you need help."

"That means a lot to me, Sonthi."

"None of us are going to tell you Sasha is an easy man to live with."

"I'll take all the help you can give me," Katya replied, smiling. "Do you think he's ready to be back in the world?"

"I don't know. I am surprised he has begun performing, but le Hédonisme is not the world. The concerts are private and he feels as safe and protected here as on the *Trib*. Some of us are always with him on shore leaves and when visiting hospitals, and in Sydney, he is escorted by armed guards and has a private car and driver. But the fact that Sasha used subterfuge to escape alone to New York to give a talk at a conference, even anonymously, speaks volumes about his mindset. Something had changed in him, even before he knew you. He seemed to need something more. We'll see what happens when he is back on the *Trib* full time."

Katya mulled over the news that the crew didn't know about Sasha's plan to start part-time work as a teaching neurosurgeon with the Prosthetics Department at the University of Sydney, or his thwarted desire for recognition for creating the prostheses and neural implants he worked with, or his cautious, and uncertain, wish for public acknowledgement of his genius. She would have to get used to armed guards and drivers, like in San Francisco... but how would the crew of the *Trib* take his absences? They were all there because of him.

By the crew's fifth morning, everyone was desperate to fit as much as possible into each day. No one knew how long they were going to be able to stay. No one wanted to leave. Most of the crew joined Sasha and Katya on their next scuba expedition into deeper water. Katya was thrilled at the great number of whales and sharks they sighted and looked forward to exploring more dive sites. Keung and Chen set up a second dive after music for just the three of them later that afternoon while Sasha worked with his laboratories.

Katya was beginning to feel at home on the *Trib*. She and Sasha could move onto the boat if the Roussels needed the villa back, although she was relieved to learn their hosts were in no hurry to see them go. She and Sylvie had grown close. Katya's paid reservation had ended, but she and Sasha were invited to stay on as guests. Bookings for the expensive unit were few and far between. Sasha paid for their and the crew's meals with the money Peter had given him. If the money ran out, he could charge on Peter's credit card. Sasha told her that he had never possessed a credit card of his own.

Sleeping together in Sasha's cabin would be problematical with that extremely narrow berth. Exploring the small room, Katya had to laugh when she discovered the huge container of sunscreen and the long brush he must have used to coat his back. He'd brought along both jars from San Francisco and they were almost empty. She used it daily too, finding it to be the finest face and body cream she'd ever tried. Sasha seemed to look younger every time he used his product. *What else was in that sunscreen*, she mused. She was also amazed by the cabinet full of sheets – at least thirty sets. She'd learned the crew stopped to have their laundry cleaned once a month. *Why so many? Did he change his sheets every morning?*

Katya was disappointed, though, that Sasha put off discussing their future. Was she or was she not coming with them when the *Trib* departed? She had no doubt of his love and his desire for her, but she thought she could see him struggling with the idea of such a profound change in his life; he had to be concerned about the disruption in his daily shipboard routine, about sharing that tiny cabin with her. Katya refused to even imagine the *Trib* sailing off without her, Sasha only an occasional lover.

The arrival of the crew had already brought about a change in Sasha's personality, his restlessness and distractibility growing increasingly stronger. The honeymoon was definitely over. Even though his ardor for her continued unabated, Sasha seemed to be reverting to what she imagined were the decades-long habits of a ship's captain, of a man used to being in charge, and he grew even more obsessive. Katya also sensed an intense sadness in him that occasionally rendered him incapable of movement – not quite the depression Sonthi spoke of, but she could see how it could develop. Her method of coping was to get even closer to the crew.

287

Katya found them all remarkable men, fearless and powerful and yet tender-hearted and emotional at the same time, and only slightly less idealistic than Sasha. They laughed as easily as they cried. Music or a beautiful sunset could move them to tears, even serious Chen, serene Sonthi, and the dependable first officer, Maxim.

She chatted often with Hiro in Japanese or English about Japan and Shintoism. She discovered that Hiro had achieved his excellent English with four years at Harvard before returning to Japan for medical school, a fact Sasha had for some reason omitted sharing with her. Hiro was nearly as calm as Sonthi and also full of good advice.

Like Dima, Kiko, and Hau, Hiro had seriously contemplated a career in music. Bowing to his parents' wishes, Hiro became a doctor instead, although music remained his passion. Dima, the son of a woodworker, had just auditioned for a seat in the viola section of the Tchaikovsky Symphony Orchestra in Moscow when he had to flee the country to avoid arrest for his dissident activities. Kiko had attended a music conservancy in Manila for a year on a scholarship, before the money ran out and he went for a physician assistant degree. It amused Katya to no end how Kiko sighed whenever Sasha played, how he followed Sasha like a faithful puppy. Katya learned that Hau had successfully modeled in his youth, and had unsuccessfully auditioned, several times, for the Saigon Philharmonic, falling back on medicine as a second career choice.

Chen's and Tuan's parents gave them no choice of careers – they would be doctors, but both had been well-taught musically growing up. Tuan and Aashir described life in their native countries, how difficult it was to be gay in their cultures. For Tuan, playing a straight man was mandatory for advancement. Katya never would have guessed Aashir, like Keung, had no background in music. Maxim had been concertmaster in a youth orchestra in East Berlin, but always knew he wanted to be a surgeon. For Sonthi, music and medicine remained equally important in his life. No one in his family was musical, and he admitted that his commitment to violin playing was another way to separate himself from his domineering father.

Maxim and Dima relished recounting many of the *Trib*'s more memorable missions. Katya found Dima to be a big, lovable Russian bear who adored her and she returned his affection. She and Maxim grew particularly close; she saw him as the older brother she'd never had, and sought his council as often as she did Sonthi's or Hiro's. She asked Maxim and Dima a question that had been bothering her.

"Since you're busy telling Sasha stories, can you explain to me why he doesn't like Mozart and Haydn?"

"He says they're 'boring and predictable!' Those are the words he uses!" Maxim laughed. "He's never allowed us to play any of their music, even on our own."

"I can't think he really believes that."

Dima shrugged. "Sasha is stubborn when he get idea, Katya," he said in his strong Russian accent. "He doesn't like changing mind. Doesn't care for Vivaldi, Handel, or Telemann, either. We just go along. Plenty of other great music to play!"

"I love their chamber work! That's unfortunate. Maybe I can change his mind."

Now both men laughed. Maxim put his arm around her. "Save your breath for other issues, Katya. There will be plenty!"

Katya particularly enjoyed the company of Chen and Keung, learning about life in Beijing and sharing her experiences of Hong Kong. Chen took little convincing to teach Katya how to make more of the various nautical knots used on the boat; she'd only known two. They often conversed in Mandarin, sitting cross-legged in the sun on the *Trib*'s open teak deck. Keung, Chen's constant shadow, liked to participate, cajoling Katya into translating into Cantonese when he had difficulty following what they were saying. Keung had learned Mandarin in school, what little he'd attended, but his fluency was limited, and he struggled with the different sounds. Both of them teased her that she had to be half Chinese, not quarter. When she told them that her Chinese family name was Zhang, they started calling her "Katya Zhang," and it caught on with the rest of the crew.

When Katya discovered Keung was in charge of trimming hair, she conspired with him to get Sasha to sit still long enough to allow his overlong hair to be cut. Watching Keung struggle, Katya realized how difficult it was to cut hair without touching the person's head. She would have to learn how to cut Sasha's hair herself. She offered to trim Keung's hair afterwards. With her free hand, she played with his long black locks after releasing them from his top knot, running her fingers through his hair, giving him a scalp massage.

She caught the look on Sasha's face as he watched. Here was a side of him she hadn't experienced before. He was smoldering. Saint Sasha had another chink in the armor of his saintliness besides a hidden well of violence under that calm, logical exterior. Katya decided not to let it pass unnoticed.

"Sasha, I never took you for the jealous type!" she teased. "You look positively green."

Sasha flushed through his dark tan, and Keung almost jumped away from her, making her laugh. Katya held him down with one hand on his shoulder.

"Stay still, Keung, I'm holding sharp scissors here! Sasha, you must know by now that I'll never love anyone but you. Your crew is my family now. You're going to have to get used to the idea that I like touching people. Why don't you come over here and massage my lower back while I finish this haircut?"

Sasha did as she suggested, throwing in a long kiss on the back of her neck for good measure. Katya could still sense his continued discomfort.

"I apologize to both of you," Sasha said, putting some muscle into his massage. "Katya, you must be the most sensual person alive. I wouldn't have you be any other way."

Katya filed the moment away in her memory. Was Sasha concerned because Keung was near her age, instead of thirty years older? Because Sasha was often rigid and hyper-focused, while Keung was relaxed and laid-back, with no devasting history weighing him down? Did he really imagine she couldn't handle his complicated and difficult personality? Katya wondered how Sasha would react if he ever thought he had reason to be truly jealous.

Sasha hadn't made time to get back to riding and Katya knew he missed it. She decided to surprise the crew with Sasha's Romani horse acrobatics before their time on the island was over. Arranging with Alain for a morning ride, she brought along Luc and Sylvie, and told the crew to meet them on the beach. The crew had all heard Sasha's reminiscences of his Romani days, and Katya delighted in seeing their faces, and Luc's and Sylvie's amazement, when Sasha demonstrated his skills. Sasha was emboldened to try more daring stunts. Katya let Maxim ride back with Sasha and returned to the resort with the crew. Dima entertained her the whole way with more stories of the crew's exploits over the years, including a few tales about Sasha, some of which were heroic, and some amusing and not so heroic, Hau keeping up a comic commentary. Katya had the distinct feeling that Dima would never dare tell such stories in Sasha's presence. Despite the humor, she never doubted the men's love for Sasha for a moment. Some of them, like Kiko and Aashir, seemed to worship him. No, they all worshiped him, as did she. She had no doubt they were willing to give their lives for him. As was she.

Early on the morning of the crew's sixth day, after their morning workout and breakfast, Sasha decided it was time to take the *Trib* out on the high seas to show Katya what she could do. With a crew of four, plus Doug and Laura watching the defenses, the boat motored slowly out of the harbor and away from the island. Keung and Aashir unfurled the sails. Katya found the *Trib* a glorious sight as she tacked in the trade winds, the island breathtakingly beautiful from this distance. After a half-hour of silent sailing, the sails were furled, and Sasha brought Katya to the port gunwale, telling her to watch over the side. They were motoring again at twenty-five knots, and the island was now lost to view.

Katya's eyes widened as a long wing-like structure separated itself from the lower side of the boat. She felt the *Trib* rise above the water as the speed increased. Sasha explained there was an identical wing on the starboard side, that the *Trib* was lifted entirely out of the water. The boat was now a hydrofoil, with twin jet-like engines propelling it forward, making it seem to fly over the water. No matter how rough the sea, the *Trib* would move ahead smoothly. He explained how he'd adapted his hydrogen fuel cell discovery to run the engines, that all he needed was water to make the hydrogen fuel, with water and heat the only by-products, for the first pollution-free motor. His unique invention used electricity created by his solar panels on the roof of the pilothouse to separate the hydrogen constantly with a ninety-five percent round-trip efficiency, renewing the hydrogen reserves in safe fuel cell packs. Nanotechnology kept the devices cool. He'd told her why he couldn't share his hydrogen fuel cell motor with the world, but that he and S-Branch had no problem using it for their own purposes.

"With the sails unfurled, the *Trib* can do sixty-five knots. With the engines at top speed, and sails furled, we can do two-ten," he shouted proudly into the wind. "That's 407 kilometers per hour, 253 miles per hour."

"If you ever get your hands on some money, you should try to buy back the process from the oil company. The world needs your motor," Katya shouted back.

"I've tried to get S-Branch to do so many times. They see my motor as their own secret weapon. They take advantage of its speed with my boat and our freighters. I don't think the oil company will sell the process anyway. Too much competition for their own polluting products. Someone else will come up with it eventually. I don't need the credit – as if I could take credit for anything."

"You're too humble, Sasha," Katya protested.

"Humility has nothing to do with it. I've never been humble. This is what I signed up for at seventeen. I'm resentful every day. Resentful but resigned."

Katya was surprised by the unexpected depth of anger behind his statement. She could well imagine this would become a major issue one day soon. She knew he was still terribly disappointed that S-Branch would not let him claim credit for his prosthetic devices and brain implants. When this island vacation was over, S-Branch had promised to renew his connection with the University of Sydney Prosthetics Department, but he would still be pretending the prostheses were not his own, but products of unknown geniuses at Australogic. He would be the "installer," as Peter had so crudely stated. Katya couldn't think of a solution that would keep Sasha out of the public eye.

The *Trib* lurched forward, forcing her to grab the railing. The speed was beyond anything Katya could have imagined, the wind whipping her hair painfully against her cheeks and into her eyes. She staggered back down the companionway to the security of the main cabin as the speed continued to increase, appreciative of the absolute smoothness of the ride. The *Trib* returned to a leisurely fifteen knots for the trip home, hydrofoil wings again unnoticeably tucked back against the undersides of the hull. She could understand their use for speed when dealing with criminals, but she preferred a pleasure sail any day.

Fate eventually intervened, and their island pleasures came to an end on the crew's eighth day. Word came from Sasha's personal contacts in the Philippines that the fifteen-year-old daughter of an important Cabinet secretary who was a close friend of the President's had been kidnapped. A human trafficking ring had threatened to sell her into a bleak and untraceable future if unpalatable political and financial demands were not met. The Philippine government had been given just four days to comply.

When Sasha learned that the young woman was being held with dozens of other female trafficking victims, he decided on his own to get involved. He had to rescue them. He knew he would never get permission from S-Branch, so he didn't ask for it. Gathering the crew and Katya in the main cabin, they discussed what to do. The crew was unanimous – they would create a plan together and leave for the Philippines as soon as possible. Katya asked Sasha for a private moment while the crew talked among themselves. They retreated to Sasha's cabin and she reminded him of her earlier request.

"Let me be a part of this. And you step back after the plan is made. If I'm going to be a member of this crew, you cannot be over-protective of me. And the crew cannot risk you putting yourself in harm's way again so soon after getting you back."

"I'm the captain. I can't step back, as you put it," Sasha retorted. "This is what I do. I will not put my crew's lives in danger unless I'm willing to risk my own."

"Then you're going to have to face the fact that I am willing to risk mine as well. And I won't let you risk getting yourself killed trying to protect me." Katya hesitated before continuing. This was it, no more dancing around the big question. "I *am* coming with you, aren't I? That decision has to be yours as captain. You know what I want to do. You know that I love you."

Sasha stared at her in disbelief. "How could you imagine for a moment that you weren't! You *are* a member of this crew. You are an integral, an essential part of me now! Oh, Katya, have I been that opaque?"

"Then I can throw away my return airline ticket? I've already changed the return date for a week from now."

"Let's have a miniature bonfire!" he said, kissing her. "I guess I'm not much better at reading and understanding other's emotions than I was before. I had no idea you had any doubt."

"You didn't want to talk about it."

"Because I thought there was nothing to discuss!"

293

"Now that's settled, what about the first question? Am I going to be participating in this mission?"

"Let me think about it," Sasha replied, not wanting to think about it at all. "Wait until I see what information we can gather and what we're up against. We still have just the barest facts. I will have a lot more intelligence coming in a few hours. We'll start taking leave of our friends here on the island while we wait."

Katya's relief was enormous. "I feel so at home here, Sasha. It's never seemed like just a vacation," Katya sighed, snuggling into his arms.

"Could you have imagined any of this when you handed me that roll of paper tickets in San Francisco?"

"That you could love me? That we would be having wild sex multiple times a day? That I could be so accepted by your crew? I could go on and on, Sasha. The answer is no, these past two weeks have been wonderful beyond all imagining, maybe subtracting William Cutter's little visit."

Chapter 40

Katya took it upon herself to let Luc and Sylvie know they would be departing that day. Sasha decided to use the excuse of a medical crisis in New Guinea, an epidemic that needed their immediate attention. He climbed up to the pilothouse to inform their S-Branch helpers that the Philippine situation was urgent and, permission or no, they would be leaving. When he returned, he sent the crew off to enjoy their last hours at le Hédonisme and left to join Katya. Dima insisted on staying behind on the boat.

Luc and Sylvie were both in the office when Katya arrived. Sylvie's smile faded when she heard the news, and Luc momentarily took her hand. Sylvie quickly got control of her emotions and started making frantic plans.

"We'll need to do a farewell lunch. We'll have a Tahitian dance. I know several dancers who will gladly donate their time and talents, plus a few drummers. Luc, tell the staff to put together some large baskets of fruits and vegetables for the boat. Do you need fresh water? Oh yes, you make your own fresh water. Drinks, what about other drinks, and fish? And I'll need to let all the staff know so they can say goodbye. Hitiura just went home, I know his family will come…"

Katya took both Sylvie's hands in hers and held them firmly.

"Whatever you come up with will be most appreciated. We would all stay here forever if we could, but duty calls us back. I don't think the crew and Sasha have ever had what you would call a vacation together where they could do as they pleased. I can't imagine you two could have made them any happier than you have. Thank you for your warmth, your hospitality, your friendship. You know this trip has changed my life, and Sasha's as well. Your resort, our time here, has made us a couple, a couple madly in love."

"Nothing could have made me happier, not even Sasha's incredible gift of my new clinic. Please find a way to come back and be our personal guests."

"We will certainly try, Sylvie."

"I think Erita and Vaea are visiting with Taiana in the clinic. I left her changing the dressing on a chef's burned hand. The way those girls chatter, I'm sure they'll still be there, if you want to have some time with them," Sylvie said, a deep sadness creeping back into her voice. She had found a friend in Katya and already missed her.

"Thank you. I'll bring Sasha over in a little while and we'll talk more," Katya said, as she gave Sylvie's hands an extra squeeze before releasing them. She hugged Luc and he returned to work.

"I wish you luck with Sasha," Sylvie said under her breath as they walked to the door.

Katya was taken aback. "Meaning?"

"I think I know who Sasha is now, what he is. I've been putting it together. I couldn't help listening in a few times when he was in the living room on his computer talking with his laboratories before the *Trib* arrived. He needs you, the crew around him. He's no more ready to be out in the world than the world is ready to understand his remarkable genius. There is no one like him."

Katya smiled. "That, Sylvie, is the truth." She gave Sylvie a long hug, then walked on to the clinic.

Katya could see how devastated the young Tahitians were that the *Trib* would be leaving. Vaea had set her sights on Dima and a few free massages had gotten her what she wanted. Maxim and Hiro had their private cabins; she'd seen them several times in the close company of two of the beautiful women dancers. Erita and Keung had successfully managed to couple a few times but finding a place to be alone had been an ongoing challenge. On the *Trib*, lanyards on the door handles of the two crew's cabins had become quite popular. Katya let them use her villa once, without Sasha's knowledge. Taiana flirted outrageously with Tuan and didn't understand why he failed to respond. Katya had sent her after Chen. She had no doubt all the crew had managed to find plenty of recreation during their stay, even Sonthi. But the women told Katya they would miss her the most.

Katya asked if they'd seen Jake. He'd made himself scarce since the arrival of the *Trib* and had moved in with Atea and her brother Tehei. Katya had been right – Jake would not be returning to work with Mason and was doing what all visitors wished they could do, planning to stay on. Katya made sure to tell her friends to get Jake, Atea, and Tehei to come to the farewell celebration.

Sasha caught up with Katya as she was leaving the clinic. They savored a long kiss, not knowing when they could be so openly affectionate again. They would have to be more circumspect on the boat. Sasha's tiny cabin and all too narrow berth would be their only refuge. The trip to the Philippines, all 9,492 kilometers, would take less than two days using the hydrofoil wings, traveling full speed day and night, slowing only if another ship crossed their path. Days on the boat would be full of planning and preparation, This would not be an easy rescue and all of their lives might well be put in danger. Love, and perhaps music, too, would be put on hold, island hedonism left far behind.

Katya thought of Aashir and Tuan, how they would manage their new relationship in the tight confines of the boat. She was happy she'd successfully steered the two towards each other, had even given them the privacy of her villa when she knew Sasha and the rest of the crew would be elsewhere. Tuan's departure date for a neurosurgical residency in Vietnam was already set. Now Katya was sure Sasha was going to be looking for two replacement crew members instead of one. Aashir had been assiduously studying Vietnamese, even practicing with Katya, and his affair with Tuan was no secret to anyone on the crew but Sasha. None of them had any idea how Sasha would react if he discovered the two were lovers when life resumed on the boat. To the crew, Sasha seemed clueless that love between men could exist. They all feared a panic attack if he caught Tuan and Aashir being physical with each other.

Sasha made dispassionate farewells to Luc and Sylvie, making sure Sylvie didn't have any questions about her new clinic equipment. Katya could tell his mind was already on the task that lay before them in the Philippines. He seemed aloof and distracted with everyone but her. For his sake, she wished they could just sail away and not have to prolong their departure. She could see he was in no mood for the emotional storm that would come with the lunch and farewell celebration. Katya had hoped for a last hike or snorkel but getting Sasha through the next several hours was going to be a full-time job. She needed to be with him, wherever he was in his head.

"How can I help, Sasha?" she asked. "There must be so much you need to do to get the boat ready." Sasha was too focused on the departure to respond to her shoulder massage.

"Sylvie is helping with food supplies – her staff will bring them on board," Sasha replied. "I need to go over every inch of the engine room, make sure everything is functioning perfectly. I've got to check the bilges and pumps, inspect fluids, check that the dinghy and

Zodiacs are properly stored, that the solar panels are putting in amps, check the weather, tides, and currents, and check the local charts for the water we'll be navigating."

"Stop! You have a crew of ten," Katya interrupted. "Maybe we should head back to the boat and pick up whomever we see along the way. Dima is already there, he'll help you."

"But it's their last day. I already gave them these few hours free."

"Life just isn't fair when you're a sailor. Let's hope they won't see us coming and hide."

Sasha turned to her and gave her his near smile. Taking her hands, he gave her a quick kiss.

"Thank you. I needed that. I need you. Come with me and we'll go bother Dima."

They walked hand in hand back towards the boat. Katya breathed in the flower-scented air and took in the spectacular views of the emerald volcano, turquoise water, and white sand beaches she'd grown so accustomed to. There would be nothing to see the next couple of days but open ocean. Sasha would be steering a route that would avoid coming anywhere near the other islands along the way, with fabulous names like the Cook's, Tuvalu, the Solomons, Palau. Maybe the men *were* in hiding, she mused, because they saw no one but resort guests and staff on their way.

Once on board, Katya followed Sasha as he made his rounds, checking lines, instruments, fluids, his hydrogen fuel cells, water system, and everything else he had mentioned. They saw no sign of Dima. When they returned to the main cabin, they found him standing in the galley with a drink in his hand, a big smile on his face.

"Dima, we were looking for you. I could have used your help," Sasha said, sounding vexed.

"Oh, I've been helping all right. Follow me, you two," he replied, walking towards Sasha's cabin. At first sight, the cabin looked just as it always did to Katya, but there was a slight scent of freshly sawn wood and oil, and she saw the porthole was open for ventilation. Sasha walked over to the berth. The storage unit under it was noticeably shorter, and the mattress level considerably   higher.

"Allow me to demonstrate," Dima said mysteriously, motioning for Sasha to stand aside. He reached under the mattress, folded down the top-dressing board of the storage unit, and slid out a solid wooden frame that self-assembled its two stacked sections to triple the size of the bed. Supporting legs automatically dropped down to the floor. Dima then unfolded the mattress, already dressed in sheets and blanket, to entirely cover the supporting platform and pulled a second pillow out of a cabinet. Katya recognized the bedding as belonging to the resort. Luc and Sylvie must have been in on this, must have given Dima sets of queen-sized sheets and a larger blanket, the extra pillow. She would have to thank them, too. Katya guessed that Dima had stitched two of the extra mattresses from the storage room together at their top edge with Sasha's original. There was just enough room in the cabin to walk around it. It was pure genius.

"Dima, I think I love you!" Katya said, eliciting an even broader smile on Dima's face. Dima removed the pillows, refolded the mattresses in thirds, and slid the wooden frame back, where it neatly stacked itself. He raised the dressing board that matched the storage cabinet wood to cover the edge. Then he casually tossed the pillows back onto the perfectly made berth. Katya stepped into the newly opened space and gave Dima a hug, reaching up to give him a big kiss on the cheek. Sasha looked like he didn't know whether to be grateful or embarrassed. He finally came over and took his turn giving Dima an awkward one-sided half-hug.

"Dima, I cannot thank you enough," Sasha sighed. "I had no idea how we were going to share that berth. I thought I might have to move into the main cabin to sleep."

"Dima has your back," the big Russian said simply, but he looked pleased his work was so appreciated.

Chapter 41

The time of the farewell celebration had arrived and the hall was packed with the resort guests, even the newest arrivals, a couple from the U.S., and all the staff members and their families. The kitchen staff stood by the doorway of the kitchen. Alain and his wife Rava chatted with Luc and Sylvie. Jake appeared with Atea and Tihei. He'd told Katya he liked the name Jake, was keeping the name that matched his passport, was happy to ditch his old identity.

Assembling on the lawn were six female dancers and three drummers. Katya held on tight to Sasha's hand. She could feel this was all too much for him in his present state of mind. She had insisted that the lunch itself be just for the crew and their hosts, the Roussels, but had allowed Alain and Rava to join them, and it had been a lovely, quiet affair. The members of the crew were wandering among the crowd, shaking hands, saying good byes. Hitiura and his family came up to Sasha and they talked for quite a while, the rest of the crowd standing back. As they turned to leave, Hitiura rushed back to try and give Sasha a hug. Katya stepped between them and expertly caught the hug herself, squeezing Hitiura affectionately.

"I promise to give Sasha your hug, Hitiura," she crooned. "You stay well and stay out of coconut trees!"

At that moment, the new American guest, a brash Texan, pushed through the crowd and swung a big, hairy arm across Sasha's shoulders in greeting, squeezing hard. Sasha dropped to one knee, grabbed the big man's arm and twisted himself free, then pushed the man backwards with such fury that he crashed through the crowd and against a table. Sasha's face contorted in pain. He clutched his chest and began shivering intensely, breathing heavily, and sank down to the floor on his knees. Sylvie ran to him, but Katya shouted out to her.

"Don't touch him, Sylvie! Please, everybody stand back. Sylvie, go see to your guest."

Sasha's crew rushed to the scene and they formed a circle, facing outward, around him and Katya. Sonthi dropped down into a crouch next to Sasha but stayed quiet, watching what Katya would do.

"I'm so sorry, Sasha, I didn't see him coming," she whispered to him, but his eyes were tightly closed. He was unresponsive, still shivering, sweat beginning to pour off his face, his breathing ragged.

"Not your fault, Katya, we were all off our guard," said Maxim, turning to look at his stricken leader. "I'm just thankful it wasn't the boy who caused it. You were quick."

"What do you do?" asked Katya, beginning to panic herself, as she knelt beside Sasha.

"There's nothing we can do but keep him safe," Sonthi replied. "He will be unconscious in a few moments and he'll be easier to move. Usually an episode like this is over in thirty minutes, but you can touch him, we cannot. You might be able to get him through this faster."

"Sasha," she called out, working hard to keep her voice calm, massaging the back of his neck, his shoulders, caressing his face. "Sasha, it's me, Katya. He's gone, you're just with me now. I'm here."

He soon began to breathe more normally and the intensity of the shivering lessoned, but his eyes remained closed.

"Sasha, can you hear me?" Katya asked him quietly, feeling relieved when he nodded. "Let me know when you're ready to stand up. We'll walk over to Sylvie's clinic and we'll come back later if you want to."

Katya could hear the big American bellowing across the room, complaining he'd been assaulted. She heard Sylvie tell him his gesture constituted an assault on Sasha's person, and if he and his wife didn't leave the hall immediately, she would have them thrown out. The anger of the crowd convinced the man to back down and he retreated, confused but unhurt. After about five more minutes, Sasha stood up with Katya's help, and with eyes and head downcast, dripping with sweat, walked with her supporting him out the hall door, past the stunned dancers and over to the clinic. Sylvie, Maxim, and Sonthi followed close behind. The celebration room was silent.

Katya got Sasha to sit down in a chair and fixed a cold cloth to wipe his hands, face, and neck. His hands were clammy when she held them in hers. Maxim brought a glass of water and he drank it down, then put his head in his hands, elbows on his knees, breathing in long, slow breaths. When Sonthi pulled up a chair and sat next to him, Sasha reached over and placed one hand on his shoulder without looking up. Maxim, Katya, and Sylvie moved to the next room and spoke quietly.

"Haphephobia. I should have known the way he so neatly avoided being touched. The natives sure seemed to understand. How often does this happen?" Sylvie asked.

"I've never witnessed it, just helped prevent it," Katya replied, still shaken. "Maxim?"

"It's rare that someone gets past his guard, or our guard," he answered. "I'm just astounded that Katya was able to keep him from passing out. It takes a lot to put him into this state, not just a light touch. That just makes him cringe. Sparring doesn't faze him though, blocking doesn't trigger it."

Katya knew he couldn't mention fighting in front of Sylvie, but she might have witnessed him working out with the crew in the mornings. Sasha wouldn't have lasted very long in his often violent world if physical contact during combat could devastate him.

"How is it that you can touch him?" Sylvie asked in wonder.

"I don't know," Katya answered honestly. "Only two people have been able to touch him. His first wife, and me."

"Do you want me to give him a sedative, or maybe an anti-depressant?" Sylvie asked.

"God no, he never takes anything," Maxim insisted. "No drugs, unless he has a serious injury. He'll be himself in a few hours."

"I hope so," Sylvie said. "I can only imagine what he's lived through. I couldn't help noticing his birthplace and year. I thought at first he must be using someone else's passport, he looks so much younger. I saw that he was born in 1940 in Germany and didn't believe it until I saw the numbers tattooed on his arm when he was swimming past our beach without his usual swim shirt. And the scars..."

"I think you can understand where his phobia comes from, Sylvie," Katya said quietly. She didn't want to say more than was necessary.

"I'm so sorry. What a horror for a child, for anyone," Sylvie responded, holding back her emotions with difficulty.

"Maxim, do you know anything about his life in the camp?" Katya asked. Maybe S-Branch had shared whatever they knew with his First Officer and closest friend.

"Sasha made it clear to me, to all the crew, even Sonthi, that he wouldn't talk about it under any circumstances," Maxim answered. "We'd all seen the numbers on his arm, his scars, witnessed his long spells of silent sweating, his sudden grabs for his violin at all hours,

303

his full-blown panic attacks like this one. We could only imagine what terrors he endured there. We knew he was in Australia already before he was six. We never knew how long he'd suffered in Bergen-Belsen before then, but we'd hoped it wasn't long."

"Nearly two years, Maxim. It was far worse than you or anyone could imagine. Sasha told me I'm the only one he has ever confided in and even then, I'm sure much has been left out. It's not my place to tell his story without his permission. I hope someday he chooses to share it with all of you. I know he wants to. What he doesn't want is pity, ever."

Katya knew how emotional Sasha's crew could get, even tough Maxim. His loyalty and devotion to Sasha were unquestionable. Maxim looked as stricken as Sylvie. Sonthi remained a quiet, calming presence next to Sasha. Katya could see Sonthi's lips moving in Buddhist prayer. Sasha had not moved his hand from his shoulder. She walked over to them and picked up Sasha's other hand. It was no longer clammy and his shivering had stopped.

"Sasha, are you ready to talk? Tell me what you want to do," she asked.

"How long have I been gone?" he asked, his throat still dry.

"You were out of it for just a few minutes. Less than fifteen minutes have past. You stayed conscious the whole time," she said, stroking his wet, blond hair. "Welcome back."

"Think there's anybody left in the hall?"

"I imagine there might be," Katya said with a smile. "Shall we find out?"

Sonthi stood and nodded gratefully to Katya, then bowed low in a Thai traditional wai, his hands pressed together.

"My dear Katya Zhang. I would not have believed it if I had not seen it with my own eyes," he said in his quiet voice. "Sasha has never been able to stay conscious before. Thank you from all of us. You are going to be a most welcome and most useful addition to our crew."

Katya could only return the wai, feeling too emotional to speak. She helped Sasha stand. His eyes remained unfocused, his shoulders hunched. He may have been able to stay conscious, but he seemed to be falling into a depressed state of mind.

The hall was full of quiet chatter when Katya walked back in holding tight to Sasha, with Maxim, Sonthi, and Sylvie following. Katya could tell Sasha was making a heroic effort to hold his head high. His wet hair dripped onto his shoulders, his shirt was soaked through. Everyone turned to look, then the crowd slowly started applauding the man they had come to love. Sasha nodded his head slightly in acknowledgment but did not speak. Katya thought he looked a little embarrassed, but mostly like his mind was still far away. Maxim signaled to Aashir, who hurried over with another glass of water.

"Maybe now would be a good time to start the dancing," Katya whispered to Sylvie.

She nodded and walked out to talk with the entertainers. Soon the sound of drumming filled the air and the crowd began to head outside. Sasha placed his hand on the shoulder of each of his crew members as they filed past, and each placed his hand over his own heart in return. Jake waited until they had passed, then paid his respects as well. Sasha gave him a slight bow in response, and Katya wished him and Atea every happiness.

Luc pulled down two chairs in front of the hall, and as on their first night, Katya and Sasha sat together and watched the incredibly fast and hypnotic movement of the dancers' hips. The dancing was sensuous and beautifully choreographed, but much less erotic than before. The six women were dressed in white with multi-colored feather headdresses and flower leis, the shirtless drummers similarly adorned. Katya could feel Sasha's weariness and his growing depression as she held his hand. Her mind wandered to all that had to be accomplished before their departure and then to the planning session that awaited them. Sasha looked in no shape to be accomplishing anything. It was time to pack up their few belongings from the villa and take them to the boat. As extraordinary as her time in Bora Bora had been, Katya was ready to move on.

Maxim stood next to her and seemed to sense her distraction. He leaned over and spoke in her ear, but she didn't think Sasha would have heard him if he had shouted.

"He'll snap out of it. He gets into a deep depression first, then turns manic. Wait until he starts the planning session. He'll be bouncing around like an agitated molecule."

"Thank you for that, Maxim. He does have me worried."

"And thank you, Katya, from all of us, for this time here on this island. We understand this was your idea. This dance is the perfect ending," he said warmly, placing his hand on her shoulder.

She reached up with her free hand and held his, knowing he was representing the feelings of all the crew. She remained holding both his and Sasha's hands until the dancing and drums stopped for the last time.

Chapter 42

The crew and Katya gathered in the main cabin two hours later, ready to hear the intel Sasha was about to impart, as a late afternoon rain pounded the boat. It would be over as usual in less than thirty minutes, but the darkness and rain added a dismal note of foreboding. Sasha had showered and changed at the villa while Katya packed and took one last look at the commodious, luxurious accommodations they would be leaving behind. They made it to the boat just before the rain started. Sasha had covered a table set up in the middle of the room with charts and papers and the command center was open. The men had pulled out chairs. The monitors were filled with live feed from a dozen sites. Maxim was right. The importance of the task at hand revived Sasha completely, and he bounced from table to monitors and back again. There was a spark in his eye and excitement in his voice when he began the session.

"Ready. We've gotten excellent intel from a number of reliable sources. We will be the ones going in, but we'll have good backup from S-Branch and the Philippine government. Our young woman, her name is Sandra, here's her photo on the screen, has been moved from location to location, but she has now been taken to the holding area where we know the rest of the women are being kept prior to transport and sale. We know that women are still being purchased or kidnapped for this major transport as I speak and taken to the site. Let me show you where that location is and you will see the bad news."

Sasha pointed a device at the main screen and the live satellite image of an immense metal clad ship appeared, a half-dozen smaller boats arriving and departing in exceedingly choppy waters.

"And I'm sorry that's not the worst news. The person behind this operation, with his headquarters on that ship, is Jack Cutter."

Of course it is, thought Katya. Fate and the Cutters were not finished with her yet. There was some discussion among the men, then Maxim spoke up.

"What is the estimate of his manpower?"

"Intel shows Cutter has close to forty of his soldiers on the ship, plus an estimated twenty additional personnel. We can assume advanced weaponry, perhaps torpedoes."

"And where is the ship sitting right now?" Chen asked. "It looks in deep water not far from shore, with all the dinghy traffic."

"On the west coast opposite Manila, off a private villa owned by Cutter. No villages or other inhabitants nearby. Not much of a harbor, so it's a rough ride for those dinghies."

"Would we be able to reach this ship with one of your disablers?" Hiro inquired.

"Definitely. We could disarm the weaponry, but that still leaves him with Sandra and approximately thirty to fifty other hostages, plus all the armed men."

"You need someone on the inside," Katya said.

Everyone turned to look at her. The idea seemed too impossible at this late a date to take seriously. No one had expected her to participate in the planning.

"Listen, let me continue," Katya pleaded, noting their dismissal. "Sasha, you said Cutter's men are still taking in women. We sell one of our own female agents, wired for tracking and sound, hidden devices all over her, to the buyers. She will be right where you want her, in the midst of the captive women. First night, she lets herself out, creates a way to allow a small group of commandos on board and they start quietly taking out the soldiers on patrol. Prisoners and commandos are ferried off the boat before Cutter even knows. Then you can hit him with the disablers. I don't know exactly what those are, but I like the sound of them, and bomb the heck out of the ship if you need to. A whole fleet could move in once the ship's been disabled."

"We could use darts on the patrols, stun canisters for the soldiers," Sonthi added.

"And a communications distorter for the beginning of the raid," Hiro said, nodding. "They wouldn't be able to detect the small boat bringing the commandos or the women's escape with their security cameras. This could work."

"You're asking much of one female agent," Sasha said, shaking his head. "There's a lot that could go wrong. Does the Philippine government even have such an agent who would be willing and ready, who would have the skills? How would we look for one without risking a leak?"

"You send me," Katya said, looking straight at Sasha. "I speak Tagalog, I know the culture. There's not a lock I can't open if I have the right tools."

There was a stunned silence, and then the men looked nervously at each other and at Sasha.

"Absolutely not," Sasha replied sternly. "What are you thinking! You could be beaten or raped, or killed. You've no experience in these kinds of operations."

"What do you call our escape from the van, from our pursuers, my help with your raid on Markus Cutter's compound? My escape from William Cutter?"

"I said no."

"I accomplished all that with no training, no assistance, no high-tech devices hidden in a watchband. Now I've got two days to train with the best and everything in your arsenal."

"No, Katya," Sasha repeated. "You don't look the least bit like a Filipina. And you're already on Jack Cutter's kill list. He'll know what you look like."

"Not when Hau gets done disguising me. Kiko will be disguised too. He's the one who's going to sell me."

"Katya, I said no," Sasha declared again, still calm, but his eyes were flashing anger.

"Open it up to discussion," Katya responded.

The crew listened with growing concern. This was sounding like open rebellion. Or the middle of a domestic squabble. Maxim tried to diffuse the situation.

"Let's see what other ideas we can put on the table."

No one spoke. The men looked at each other. There were no better ideas.

"Sasha, what about you?" Maxim asked, keeping his voice neutral.

"Her idea is a good one but she's not going to be the one going in," Sasha answered, his voice cold.

"And why not?"

"You know why. Don't make me say it."

Maxim stared him down. "Just say it, Sasha."

"I'm not going to risk losing her," Sasha said quietly, after a long pause.

309

"But you risk your life, you ask us to risk our lives, and we do it willingly. Katya is not just your partner. She's a member of the crew now. She volunteered. It's her plan. I for one have trust in her abilities and her judgment."

Sasha sat silently for a moment longer, trying to contain his anger and concern, weighing his needs against the needs of the crew, of the mission. Maxim was right. Katya was right. And yet even the possibility of losing her tore at his heart.

"Hiro, what do you think?" he asked at last.

"I don't see a better option. Katya's plan is an excellent one. If she feels she can do this, we should at least explore the option."

"Kiko, Hau? Are you in with this?" Sasha asked.

"Aye, Captain," they both answered.

"Dima? Aashir?"

"Aye, Captain," they replied together.

"Chen, Keung, Tuan?"

"Aye, Captain."

"And you, Sonthi? Do you think Katya can do this? What is your psychological assessment." Sasha glared at Sonthi, daring him.

"Yes, I do. Let go of your own fears, Sasha."

Sasha looked defeated. "Then it's unanimous. We'll explore the option Katya's laid out for us," he said without enthusiasm. "We'll need to decide who goes with me to take out the patrols. Dima, we need a disguise for the boat that hasn't been seen before. No one can think we arrived so quickly in the *Trib*. Jack Cutter must still believe we're in Bora Bora. We'll use silent motors for a flotilla of large Zodiacs to take the prisoners off the ship and we'll need a driver for each one."

The logistics planning continued for another hour, then Maxim asked Katya and the rest of the crew to leave, saying he needed to talk with Sasha alone. He decided the deck would be the best place and the two stepped up through the companionway into the steamy sunshine.

"I'm taking lead on this mission, Sasha," Maxim said firmly. "You shouldn't have talked aloud about not wanting to risk Katya. Your feelings for her could put us all at greater risk. These are your rules. You are not going on that ship."

"You knew how I felt, you wanted me to say it. I'm not sitting this out." Sasha pounded one fist in his other palm to punctuate his words. His eyes flashed with fury, but Maxim did not back down.

"You'll do comms instead of Hiro with Aashir. Listen to yourself. You're nearly out of control just talking about it."

Sasha glared at him, then his shoulders collapsed. He stood with a hand on the main mast, looking out at the open sea, his back to the Bora Bora skyline, the post-rain trade winds ruffling his blond hair. He felt miserable.

"Maxim, I don't know what to do. I've never experienced such inner conflict before a mission. I'm not myself... I can't be who I was before. I could not survive losing her."

Maxim's voice softened. "Give it time, my friend. Everything has changed for you... Katya has changed everything. I know you're thinking about returning to the University of Sydney, taking up where you left off."

"Who told you that?" Sasha asked, caught off guard.

"Word gets around. No, it wasn't Katya. I've been talking online with Peter Hammond."

"It wouldn't be full-time if I did. I'd still work and live on the boat. I thought I could travel now that I can use air – demonstrate my prostheses, new surgery techniques, be a public figure. Then I completely lose it in the hall when some stranger just puts an arm around me. Eleven people watching out for me and I'm still vulnerable. How can I return to the world outside this boat?"

"I wish I had some answers for you, Sasha. Don't think you have to make any decisions right away. We have a long trip ahead, you've never slept on the boat with Katya, we've got Jack Cutter to deal with. Just know I'm here if you need me. Dima and Hiro, too, and Sonthi. We've all lived with you more than fourteen years. We're always here for you. But it's time to sail, Sasha. Send up Dima and Keung for watch duty and I'll relieve our Aussie mates in the pilothouse to enjoy the rest of their stay on land with the other two. Go be with Katya."

Sasha put his hand on Maxim's shoulder and nodded his head. No one had known him longer than Maxim and there was no one he trusted more. He was indeed his friend, not just his First Officer. Maxim nodded back and sounded the departure whistle. Sasha saw the crew scrambling to prepare, and went down to locate Dima and Keung.

Katya was waiting for him in their cabin when he finished his part of the preparations. No one had thought to give her a departure job, so she'd decided to just get out of the way when the whistle blew. She

311

hadn't expected Sasha to be so devastated by her plan, but she understood his reluctance.

"I had some visitors while you were with Maxim. You just missed them," she said, watching his face for some clue as to what had been discussed with Maxim. "Luc and Sylvie brought me the guitar I'd been playing. Seems the crew pitched in and bought it from the owner. I told them you'd made a complete recovery and they were most pleased. They said bon voyage, of course."

Sasha tried hard to not look as miserable as he felt. He nodded and sat down on the narrow berth next to her. He knew these deep mood swings always occurred after a panic attack, but that didn't make it any easier to cope. He was upset with himself for succumbing to an innocent touch in such a public way, angry at losing his leadership position by being too honest, depressed about his uncertain future, concerned about Katya's fateful decision to be taken inside Cutter's ship as a prisoner, a human trafficking victim.

"Talk to me, Sasha," Katya whispered.

"Not now… please."

"Then come with me topside and we'll watch the last of Bora Bora."

She took his hand and pulled him up, and they walked back to the main mast Sasha had just left. She took his arm and together they watched the island that had changed their lives recede until there was nothing to see but a small bank of clouds as the boat slowly motored away, then returned to the main cabin as the *Trib* lifted on her hydrofoil wings, accelerated, and flew across the sea.

Chapter 43

Work began in earnest preparing Katya for the mission when Maxim returned from the pilothouse. Hiro and Sonthi laid out a multitude of miniscule lock-picking devices for them to choose from, then they moved on to several high-tech items Katya could not have dreamed existed.

"Are all these yours, Sasha? Very impressive."

Sasha became more animated discussing his inventions and demonstrating how she could use them. By dinner time, he felt much more like himself. Chen put together a meal that rivaled anything the chefs at the resort had created, using the fresh fish, island fruits and vegetables sent over by Sylvie and Luc. Sasha found his appetite had returned, which usually meant his dreaded deep mood swings were over and he could put the panic attack episode behind him.

During dinner, he noted Katya watching him eat. She confessed she'd thought he'd eat more enthusiastically and less methodically back in the familiar confines of the *Trib*. This is just how I eat, he'd told her. She had a lot to learn about his eccentric nature, he thought. *Hopefully, living with me on the Trib won't scare her off.* He sent Tuan up to the pilothouse with plates of food and drinks for the duty watch.

After dinner, Hau signaled to Kiko and Katya to follow him, and Sasha saw them disappear into the storage area at the bow of the boat. He knew Hau would be showing them disguise ideas and he didn't want to think about it. He also didn't like the mischievous look on Katya's face when she returned.

Another hour was spent in planning and preparation for the mission, then there remained a short time for music before the crew retired to their cabins. Katya took out the guitar and played a few quiet Spanish pieces, followed by some masterpieces as a thank you to the crew for their gift: Tárrega's "Capricho árabe;" the "Grand Solo," by Sor, his Opus 14; and the jaunty "Choro Number One" by the Brazilian Villa-Lobos. When she finished, Sasha gave her his near smile as the men cheered. Katya didn't play violin, viola, or cello, but she was going to be a valuable addition to their musical world. He was already imagining her joining his quartet for a few guitar quintets he knew of... and then there was her singing... Sasha took Hiro's cello from the cabinet, and exercising his newly found sense of humor, started to play a mournful dirge. To a laughing chorus of boos and thrown objects, he switched to an upbeat movement of Bach, the Bourrée from the third suite. Sasha found himself reveling in their amusement. Maybe he wasn't entirely hopeless, he thought.

Hiro had one more gift for Katya and Sasha before they headed to their cabin. He waited until the others had all departed the main cabin before he made the presentation. It was a small square box, some sort of electronic device.

"I call it the sound eater," Hiro told them, trying to look serious. "Sasha's not the only one who's creative on this boat. It makes a kind of white noise that masks other noises around it for about five meters. Others can't hear you and you can't hear them. I invented it when I had a snorer in the next berth. Dima tells me he's tripled the size of your berth, so now you can enjoy your time together without worrying about Maxim and me hearing you. If your sounds reach the other end of the boat, I can't help you."

Katya laughed and bowed as she accepted the box. Sasha felt a deep embarrassed flush rising up his face, but he managed a bow, and stood watching Hiro enter his adjoining cabin.

"Well, Sasha, I know this has been a difficult day for you," Katya said, smiling. "But Dima and Hiro are giving us no excuses. We don't want to disappoint them, do we? Waste all their hard work and thoughtfulness?"

Sasha answered by picking her up and squeezing carefully through the door to his cabin. He closed the door with his foot and they kissed until he was too aroused to continue. He set her down and together they pulled out the expanding berth, turned on the noise eater, and they proceeded to test the limits of both. When Katya was happily exhausted and nearly asleep, he dressed and slipped out to the main cabin for a few hours of work with the labs.

෨

Katya awoke in the middle of the night, surprised to find Sasha's side of the berth empty. After a moment's confusion, she threw on shorts and a shirt and went looking for him. She had a good idea where he'd be. She heard his voice first, coming from the main cabin, quietly asking questions, a female voice answering. The secondary command center was wide open, every monitor active, including the big screen.

He was connected to his laboratories, completely focused. Katya knew it had to be around midnight in Sydney. She stood back and watched him for a while, never having seen him at work. A South Asian woman, Pakistani or Indian, white-haired and somewhere around her late seventies, was going over results of product testing in the pharmaceutical or chemistry lab. Sasha's hand touched a knob and the woman's image jumped from a monitor to the large screen, then the camera focused on her work on the table in front of her, then back to her face. The woman looked up and smiled.

"Hello, Katya. Nice to meet you. I'm Priya Anand."

Sasha spun around in his captain's chair. Katya walked closer and put her hands on his shoulders, turning him back around. She was amused by how startled he looked and kept her hands where they were, gently massaging.

"I'm sorry to interrupt. Nice to meet you, too, Priya. Now I know about Sasha's other woman!"

"Ha! Finally, someone with a sense of humor! As old as Sasha is, I'm old enough to be his mother. I've been with him since day one, except for the Vietnam era. I refused to move. But I'm not his only woman. There are thirty-two more of us, and thirty men. And we're just the ones he has contact with. There's a couple hundred more supporting staff who don't know he exists! Not to mention around ten thousand other Australogic employees. Outside the Research and Development labs, only the CEO knows Sasha, and Sasha can't stand him!"

"How do you prevent leaks? How has Sasha never been outed?"

"Outed! I like that word. Makes him sound like a spy! And there's another kind of 'outed' but I'm not going there. And dear Sasha never is either! My guess is you know your Sasha better than he knows himself... But in answer to your question, we all had to sign quite the draconian nondisclosure agreement with our Aussie government. The charge would be no less than treason, very nasty penalties. We're a loyal bunch! Sorry if I'm staring, but I heard you could touch him, and I'm still blown away to see your hands on his shoulders. I'm so happy for him. You can tell I love Sasha like a son, and I already feel like I've gained a daughter. I look forward to meeting you in person when the *Trib* is in Sydney again, although I'll have to wait a year. You've changed the course of history with what you've done for Sasha! He's alive, thanks to you, and full of great new ideas!"

Katya laughed. She loved Priya's humor, her nonstop chatter. She couldn't see Sasha's face, but she imagined that he was embarrassed, and impatiently waiting to get back to the business at hand. He hadn't said a word since she arrived.

"You don't work around the clock there, do you?" she asked Priya, marveling at the dedication of Sasha's staff.

"Just ten of us at a time take a night shift, two for each lab, even me, as head of the Chemistry Lab. Your Sasha contacts us any time he can, or anytime he feels like it. If you just arrived, you missed the others filling him in and taking their orders. There's a camera on one dozen projects as you can see. I should have him back with you in about twenty more minutes."

"Please continue. Don't mind me."

Priya and Sasha went back to their discussion and Katya studied the monitors. Most of the views made no sense to her, but she recognized robotic parts for a hand on one screen, for a prosthetic eye on another, a disassembled dart gun on a third, and what looked like a screen of computer coding on a fourth. Priya was still going over lab results. She waved at her and headed back to bed. Sasha was so engrossed he didn't notice her leave. The last words she heard made her smile.

"Sasha, she's…"

"Don't, Priya!"

Priya's friendly cackle followed her down the hall. Katya was pleased. Seemed like Sasha had a mother figure watching out for him all these years after all, she mused.

ॐ

Sasha looked carefully at his crew at dawn, trying to determine if his night's sexual activities with Katya had been overheard. Maybe Hiro was playing a joke on him with his box. The item looked like a commercial white-noise generator, incapable of blocking the loud sounds Katya made during sex. He didn't tell Katya. Hopefully only his fellow officers would be able to hear her. But Maxim, Hiro, and the rest of the crew went about their morning routines and no jokes were fired his direction. Exercise topsides was impossible at 210 knots per hour, so they divided into two groups to work out for shorter sessions in the main cabin, with Sasha leading the first group, and Maxim the second. Katya was grateful for the extra sleep and watched the end of Sasha's session before joining Maxim's. The day was filled

316

with preparations for the mission, especially training for Katya, and the evening with the quartet playing Shostakovich's Eighth, a rather foreboding choice, Katya thought. At least they didn't play Schubert's "Death and the Maiden." That night Sasha felt comfortable enough with their arrangements to be bolder and wilder with their sexual explorations, though he found himself imagining Hiro pounding on the wall separating their cabins at any moment.

Land was sighted at the beginning of the third day. They had arrived at the southwestern edge of the Philippines just north of Caraga. The *Retribution* was slowed, hydrofoil wings retracted, and they anchored far offshore to let Dima and the crew work their disguise magic before continuing. The *Trib* was too small to be of use in this mission but it was crucial she not be recognized. Jack Cutter could not know they were there. Dima had been busy in his engine room workshop prefabricating panels that would fit over windows and portholes, changing their shape and the shape of the pilothouse. The *Trib* was painted a bright red halfway to the water line. One mast was taken down and the Turkish flag raised, the newly appointed boat moved closer to shore. Kiko, wearing a wig with a ponytail to his waist, ran the dinghy into Caraga and picked up three trusted Philippine sailors who would take care of the boat during the mission.

Sasha relaxed a little once the boat was motoring north to their next rendezvous, a quiet port, where they would leave the *Trib* and be whisked to a Philippine patrol boat. He let Maxim have the helm and sat down in the main cabin with a glass of water, checking charts. A sudden commotion sounded topsides and an unknown Filipina burst down the companionway, Hau and Kiko in pursuit. She stopped in front of Sasha and stood swaying uncertainly. He motioned for Hau and Kiko to back away. They remained at the top of the steps, ready to intercede.

The woman appeared to be in her mid-forties, dirty, dressed in ragged clothes, her black hair touched with grey and chopped terribly at many lengths, as if she'd gone at it wildly with a pair of scissors. Her look was friendly but daft, like she was simple-minded, and her black eyes stared at Sasha with curiosity and entreaty. She started nodding her head and speaking in Tagalog in highly nasal half-sentences. Sasha could see sharp buck teeth and the pocked skin of her face. She asked if she could work for him – she cleaned, cooked,

317

never made trouble. Nodding her head all the while, she took a step closer and he could smell a terrible pungent odor of fish coming off of her. Bounding down the steps, Kiko squeezed around her and apologized.

"Captain, she stowed away on the dinghy, under the tarps," he said breathlessly. "We've been trying to catch her."

"It's all right," Sasha said, holding up his hand. "What is your name?" he asked her soothingly in Tagalog.

"It's … it's … K-K-Ka … tya," the woman stuttered.

Sasha stood up. As much as he stared at the apparition before him, he could see no trace of Katya, the disguise was so complete, the mannerisms so convincing, the voice so different.

"Not bad, eh Captain?" asked Hau, coming the rest of the way down the stairs.

Sasha walked around her, still in disbelief. Katya remained in character, nodding her head and swaying. Then she stood up straight and the simple look vanished.

"We may have gone a little overboard with the fish paste in my underwear, but I think that and the sharp teeth should discourage any playing with the merchandise," she stated boldly in her own voice.

"Katya, you're a wonder," Sasha said. "Hau, amazing job. But why would Jack Cutter's men buy someone who looks like this?"

"We've learned they're desperate to get their numbers up," Hau said, proud of his craftsmanship. "Cutter wants as many women as possible so Sandra will be hard to trace when they start selling them if the government won't negotiate. Plus, I hear there are jealous wives in Arab countries who want a slave maid they can completely control that their husbands won't lust after, so this one fills the bill."

"And I'm really cheap," Katya chimed in. "My nephew Kiko is also desperate – to get rid of me. Kidnapping is harder work, and the less they have to pay for me, the more money they get to keep."

"They also take them just as they find them. I learned clean-up for sale presentation will happen at the other end of the trip," Kiko added.

"If you're trying to make me feel better about you taking on this risk, you've only partially succeeded," Sasha sighed.

What was he going to do if she didn't come back? How would he survive? Did Katya really know what would happen at the end of this voyage to these women, her among them, if Cutter prevailed? For most, there would be beatings and forced drug addiction, multiple

318

daily rapes to break their spirits, a short and miserable life of prostitution. Sandra would be sold to the highest bidder, then eventually discarded, either killed or sold on as a prostitute. For the others, a life of servitude awaited, either in a private home or a factory, with no pay, no passport, no escape, no hope. Tens of millions of people were enslaved world-wide – girls sold into marriages, children and women trafficked into prostitution, and along with men, forced into slave labor. Sasha's anger at the relentlessness and ruthlessness of human trafficking and modern day slavery knew no bounds.

"I'm going to finish my disguise," Kiko told Sasha. "We're taking off in the dinghy in less than a half hour. Cutter's men have been spotted and we need to be roadside and ready. Wish us luck, Captain."

"I'm going to be on a government boat doing comms with Aashir," Sasha said, looking right at Katya. "Maxim will be your captain for this mission. I wish you more than luck. I wish you success and safe return," he said sadly, holding out his hand to the grubby hand Katya offered in return.

Chapter 44

Katya's purchase and transportation to the ship went just as expected, although Katya was laughingly disappointed that the traffickers bargained Kiko down from the tiny sum he was asking for her. She was not bound, as she went willingly with the traffickers' promise of good employment overseas, and she didn't pretend to resist until the dank holding cell was right before her.

To her relief, all the women were being held in one giant barred room. Getting them all out together would be so much easier. Some of the women were crying, some praying, some looked too stunned by their turn of fate to do anything but stare out the bars. She counted forty-six prisoners including herself and those lying down on cots. She wandered through the women casually, looking for Sandra. Katya knew there would be security cameras, so she stayed in character. She found Sandra lying on one of the cots, her fingers twisted around her rosary beads, her eyes red. She didn't look injured or molested, Katya was overjoyed to see. She whispered her intel in a way that only her listening device would pick up and moved on to check the locks on the doors. They looked like they would be no problem, once the security cameras were frozen. She would wait until the right time to inform the women what they must do to earn their freedom.

Maxim had chosen 3 a.m. for the communication disrupter to be activated. It would hopefully take quite a while for the guards to realize their views were unchanging and they would not know their weapon systems were off line. Katya would convince the women to pretend to sleep and not move for the half-hour before, so that the guards would be used to the stillness. Maxim had chosen five crew members to join him on the commando style raid, Hiro, Tuan, Sonthi, Chen and Hau. They were each carrying minicam watches with a close-up satellite view of the ship to help locate the patrols, courtesy of S-Branch. Dima, Kiko, Keung, and two Philippine sailors would be following with the five Zodiacs to pick up the women when signaled. Two Philippine patrol corvettes, of the three in the entire navy, would be waiting ten miles out and would move in when Cutter's ship communications systems were disrupted. Sasha and Aashir were running comms on one of them. Only the ship captains knew the purpose of the night mission. The sailors were informed it was an exercise to prevent leaks to Jack Cutter's group.

At precisely three, Sasha informed Katya the disruptor was successfully activated. She roused the women and had them get into groups of up to ten while she unlocked and slipped out the door. She took out the first guard with a neck choke, and now had a weapon to stick in her belt. Leaving him bound and gagged, she moved on. She dealt with the next guard in the same manner but found her way topsides blocked by a steel door. She used a silent lock exploder and ran on up to the ship's rail. When she could see the way was momentarily clear, Katya signaled Maxim with a light from her wig and the men threw up a rope ladder for her to attach to the rail. The men clambered up the side of the ship from their darkened, silent Zodiac. Within minutes, all topside guards appeared to be darted and down. The men went searching for the soldiers' sleeping quarters, planning to seal the doors, while Katya returned to the cell to bring up the women. The flotilla of Zodiacs had tied up along Maxim's and Katya helped each woman down to the waiting hand of the driver. Each Zodiac departed as soon as it had ten passengers; the last would take the remaining number.

All appeared to be going as planned until there was a sudden outbreak of gunfire from the other side of the ship. A guard must have gotten past Maxim's men and to the soldiers. Katya could see a swarm of them emerging from a door high above her. She chose the most capable looking of the remaining women to help the others and ran to where she last saw the crew. Pulling off her wig as she ran, she chose two of Sasha's stun explosives and a laser blinder to stick in her pockets. Chen and Tuan were hunkered down with five advancing soldiers firing in front of them. Katya threw one of the stun explosives and watched the soldiers collapse.

Then she saw Maxim on the other side of the ship take a bullet in his side and go down. Katya watched in alarm as he was collected by two soldiers and dragged towards the giant round pilothouse at the top of the ship. One of Cutter's soldiers grabbed her from behind as her attention was diverted. She spun to throw off her attacker. Blasting him in the eyes with the laser, she kicked him hard in the groin, then cracked the back of his head with the butt of her gun. It took Chen and Tuan ten minutes to fight their way with more stun explosives to

322

where Sonthi, Hiro, and Hau were holding back another group of soldiers. Katya made her way behind the soldiers and threw her second stun explosive. Sasha's voice sounded in her ear that all the women were safely off the ship, time to retreat.

"Maxim wounded, taken to pilothouse," she called out, not just to Sasha but to the crew in front of her.

They nodded as one and moved carefully up the multiple sets of stairs. Holstering their dart guns, Katya and the men pulled out hand guns. This mission had gone deadly. There would be no retreating without Maxim. Sonthi placed a powerful explosive on the pilothouse door and spun aside as a barrage of bullets rained through the empty space where the door had been. Hiro hit the ground and blasted into the opening with his handgun, then rolled back. A loud shout to stop broke the ensuing silence. There was movement inside, and Maxim, barely conscious, came into view, a soldier holding him up from behind with a gun to his head, with a second soldier to his right also pointing a gun at him. Katya quickly noted the second man's hand was shaking.

"Come in and join us or your Maxim is dead," said an unseen voice from the far end of the room.

Katya nodded to the crew to let her go first and she stepped into the room, Hiro following, guns held at arm's length ahead of them in a two-handed grip. Hiro signaled for the others to stay where they were. A tall and obese Caucasian man stood behind a desk. This had to be Jack Cutter. Four more soldiers flanked him, two on either side, guns drawn.

"What an absolute surprise. First Maxim, and now can that really be Katya under that hideous makeup? I remember seeing you among our women in the holding cell. I never would have guessed it was you. Hiro, what a pleasure to see you. The rest of your crew must be on this ship somewhere. I thought you were still lounging around Bora Bora after doing in my brother William. We'll take both of you and Maxim with us. William wasn't able to cut you to ribbons, Katya, but I'm looking forward to finishing the job properly. You can watch me work on Hiro and Maxim first."

"Sasha has other plans for you, Jack," Katya said, her gun never wavering. "No one is surrendering here."

"Don't tell me Saint Sasha is out there, too! Did you get him on another airplane? Or maybe he's aboard one of those ships moving in on us. The pleasure it gives me to think of him watching his crew go up in a ball of fire before he goes up as well. You may have ruined my little party here, but I have plenty of other ships."

He had said enough for Katya to know what he was planning. She had to act fast or they were all dead.

"Two left two right!" she shouted as she fired her gun first at the soldier holding Maxim then at the gun hand on the soldier to his side.

The four crew members outside the door rushed forward firing and each took out a soldier before he could react. The soldier holding Maxim dropped with a bullet between his eyes and Maxim slumped down on top of him. The second soldier was injured but very much alive.

Jack Cutter stomped on the floor and started to sink below the desk. Katya ran forward to grab at him. Hiro's bullet whizzed past her, striking Cutter in the head.

"Help me! Don't let him drop!" she shouted, as she grabbed Cutter's arm and held on.

Jack Cutter's tremendous weight was pulling her down a circular trap door that had opened on the floor. Hiro lowered his gun and ran to help her.

"Pull back, all boats!" Katya yelled desperately to Sasha at comms. "This ship is going to explode any second! All small boats out of the water!"

Chen came running to help hold Cutter's dead weight. This Cutter was so fat, he barely fit in the circular hole.

"I'm sure it will close after him if he goes down," Katya exclaimed. "He has an escape plan, a way to get off this boat before it blows up. Help me get him up to where just his feet are in the hole."

Chen and Hiro pulled. Sonthi, Hau and Tuan rushed to help.

"Hau, quick, down the hole, get ready to catch the next man! Chen, grab the injured soldier and slide him down," Katya ordered. "Now you, Chen – when you're down you and Hau get ready to catch Maxim. Then you three follow when Chen says he's ready. Hiro, you go last and signal me. Hurry!"

Sonthi, Tuan, and Hiro ran to pull Maxim over and slid him down gently when Chen shouted up, then they jumped down the hole one after the other. Katya heard the rumble of the first explosion before she heard from Hiro and rushed to push the dead Jack Cutter back down into the hole, squeezing in front of him, pulling the last of his bulk in by her weight hanging on his legs. As she had surmised, the hole closed above them, triggered by something on Cutter as she rode his legs down through the ship, a terrifying dark slide that ended with strong arms grabbing her away from him as he crashed onto the floor. She looked around at the inside of a submarine that looked built for at least twelve. Her comms were silent, nothing was getting into or out of the sub. Sasha would not know they were alive. One after another, her crewmates took off their comms, the silence as frightening as their new circumstances. Katya would not give up hope. She kept hers on.

"I hope to God one of you can figure out how to close us up and get us out of here," she said, as more explosions rocked the ship above them. Sonthi found a hatch above her head and she helped him secure it shut. "Where's the soldier?"

The injured soldier was sitting up against the side wall of the sub. He had no more wish to die than they did. He pointed out the controls and talked them into a rough but successful maneuver away from the ship and a full speed throttle forward. They hadn't been underway two minutes before a tremendous shock wave sent them pitching, but the sub stayed in one piece and they continued on. Katya went over to the soldier and shook his uninjured hand.

"My name is Katya. We owe you," she said in Tagalog. "I will see you stay a free man."

"Angel," he answered, pronouncing it the Filipino "ang hel." "Why did you save me?" he asked in English.

"Angel, how appropriate. Even if I didn't suspect you were the submarine captain from your uniform, I would have saved you. I could tell you weren't a killer. I was hoping against hope you'd still be conscious when the rest of us landed," Katya answered.

The others looked more closely and saw a small image of a sub on his jacket and shook their heads in admiration for her observation. Angel pointed out the medical kit, and since everyone except Katya was a doctor there was no shortage of good care on board for Angel and Maxim. Hiro and Sonthi tended to the injured Maxim, and Hau turned his attention to Angel's wound, the others assisting as needed.

৯০

Sasha and Aashir watched with growing despair as explosion after explosion racked the big ship, ending in a fireball of epic proportions. But for Katya's timely warning, both of the Philippine patrol corvettes would have been too close and would have been destroyed, Sasha,

Aashir, the rest of his crew, and all the just rescued women as well. There was no doubt all who had been aboard Jack Cutter's ship were dead. They both searched the roiling waters in vain for a Zodiac.

The ship's captain came down to stand with them. He was sympathetic, but said it was time to take their rescued women home. The mission had been successful beyond their wildest hopes as far as he was concerned. Sandra and forty-four other women saved, political and financial crisis averted, a major crime lord and his operation crushed. Sasha's worst fears had been realized. His Katya was gone, and he had lost his oldest friends and mates, Maxim, Hiro and Sonthi along with Hau, Tuan, and Chen. More than half his crew. He didn't know the depths of Aashir's grief for his beloved Tuan. They'd heard their last words in the pilothouse, but whatever Katya had tried to do, it had failed. They had died somewhere in the bowels of the ship. The sound from each comm had stopped when his crew went down that mysterious hole. The connection that he had with her was silent. It was like a door had been closed between them.

The thought of losing Katya, of being without love again, almost caused his knees to buckle. Alone. He'd been thankfully, finally, alone when his Nazi tormenter was dead and he could escape the SS barracks. But there were no good alone times since. Alone in the women's compound, surrounded by walking skeletons, typhus raging, prisoners dying all around him. Alone in the Bergen Displacement Camp, watching Bergen-Belsen burn to the ground. Alone when the older couple who were taking him to Australia died on the ship. Alone when he arrived on the Sydney dock, his grip tight on the battered valise nearly as big as he was, containing Herr Silber's incomparable violins nestled like Russian dolls inside. Alone in quarantine until taken home by Harrison Mandelbrot. Alone and feeling lost in the big house with the grand piano with a full set of keys, his own bed, and the two strangers he would not let touch or hug him. A childhood alone with no friends. Desperate and alone with the death of his first wife, an entire year alone on a boat, on the run from his handlers, from life. And now, would his remaining four crewmen stay with him, or would he be alone again?

As the patrol corvette turned to head back, Sasha saw something rising in the water, a sea of bubbles followed by a long gray form. A submarine. Hope started to rise with it. The sub popped to the surface and the hatch opened. Aashir saw the hope, then the certainty on

Sasha's face. But then he saw with terror that a dozen sailors were aiming their rifles at the hatch.

"Stand down, stand down, friendlies!" he yelled into his comms with the Philippine command, and he heard the order come back to the men.

"Keep your heads down," Sasha spoke into his comm, not knowing if he was connected.

Clear as a bell he heard Katya's voice in his ear.

"Sasha, we're all here, every last one of us. Maxim too. And an angel."

Chapter 45

The crew decided it would be best to stay in the submarine and follow the patrol corvettes back to their port. Maxim was in no condition to move through the small hatch and up the side of a corvette in the pitching seas. Sasha told Katya a private ambulance would be waiting at the port. The crew spent the trip learning about the sub's operation and stepping over the gigantic sprawling body of Jack Cutter. The sub motored on the surface with the hatch open so Katya could speak with Sasha the entire way. She stuck her head up occasionally to enjoy the fresh air and cooling spray of water.

"Just you and me," Sasha said. "Aashir is off comms. That makes one more time you've saved my life," Sasha said, keeping his voice deadpan. "Not to mention sixty-two Philippine sailors and officers, forty-five just-rescued women, Aashir, Dima, Keung, and Kiko, and all the men on the sub with you. I hope you're proud of yourself."

"I love how you make that sound like a rebuke," Katya replied. "That's almost funny, but it needs some work. I count about sixty dead on Cutter's side, one rescued. One dead by my hand. I'm going to remind you of a story you once told me and ask that there be no medals or award ceremonies. Can't we just sneak away to someplace more peaceful, like Myanmar or Beirut?"

"The *Trib* is waiting for us. And Jack Cutter is responsible for the deaths of all but five of those men by taking Maxim prisoner and then blowing up his own ship."

"Just get us where we can see each other again. I'm having nasty flashbacks to the van. How is Aashir holding up?"

"He was as desperate as I was, thinking we'd lost you all. He might have gotten his wish and ended up with me if you were all dead."

"I sense you're joking. But you knew how he felt about you?"

"Not all these years, no. Not until you started me thinking about how good looking my entire crew is, and how they love me each in his own way. Got me noticing, remembering. After so many years. Looking back, three with Aashir mooning at me."

"I can't comment. I'm hardly where I can speak freely in a submarine with half your crew. He's obviously not standing next to you." Katya smiled. Sasha still had no idea Aashir and Tuan were lovers.

"Got me thinking about something else, too," Sasha continued. "Let's take the *Trib* and see the world together. Five months. Wrap around the Philippines to Vietnam, Malaysia, Indonesia, Thailand, India, out the Suez Canal to the Mediterranean and Europe, across the Pacific to the Caribbean and through the Panama Canal, Mexico, back to San Francisco. Or up to Hong Kong, Taiwan, China, Korea, Japan, over to Hawaii, San Francisco…"

"I'm sensing a pattern here."

"Because I want to be in San Francisco with you. With the *Trib*, the whole crew, Katya, when 1999 turns into 2000. At that moment, the moment I turn sixty, I want to marry you. Officially this time. On the *Trib*. I'll name Maxim Co-captain and he can officiate."

Katya was stunned into silence. She had not seen this coming.

"Katya? Are you there?"

"Sasha, are you proposing to me, over comms, me on a submarine, you on a patrol corvette?" Katya could feel the eyes of the listening crew suddenly boring into her.

"Yes I am. So, will you?"

"Sasha, this is because you've had a scare. How do you know you'll feel this way when we're all back together?"

"Because we've already been married. I messed it up badly, but I promise not to jilt you at the altar this time."

"Oh God, Sasha, where is this sense of humor coming from? You're teasing me, and it isn't fair. I can't see your face."

"I'm completely serious. I'll even say the words. I love you, Katya Zhang Kaplan. Will you marry me?"

Katya looked down from her position sitting just under the open hatch into the sub. Maxim was out with a strong sedative, but Hiro, Sonthi, Tuan, Hau, and Chen were all smiles and head nods. Even Angel was smiling.

"I seem to have permission from my family. The answer, Sasha, is yes."

The next five months flew by for the crew of the *Retribution*. The crew had been excited about the voyage, and Sasha's first itinerary idea had been chosen unanimously, with the second itinerary in reverse for their return. All were happily sworn to secrecy about the

330

planned wedding. After three days laying low on the disguised *Trib*, they motored out of sight of land and restored her to her former white color, her original two masts and her shape, sailing back into port as if she'd just arrived from Bora Bora. Maxim's recovery had been slow but complete, and he was back to limited work within a month with his new title of Co-captain, although in reality his job was the same. He had chafed at being a mere passenger, a patient.

The crew had decided to break the trip into four parts, and to intersperse the frantic pace of medical clinics with days of hiking, touring, and beach activities. The Australian government cooperated fully by contacting each country and making all the arrangements and permissions ahead of them for the clinics as far as the Suez Canal and Syria, and for the other clinic segments of their voyage after their European sojourn. All they had asked in return was for the *Trib* to hoist the Australian flag and for the world to consider the free clinics a gift of the Australian people. They made sure the medical world knew the expedition was being led by Dr. Sasha Borodin, neurosurgeon, of the University of Sydney.

Their world tour had begun right where they were in the Philippines, with Kiko as Katya's personal guide in Manila, Maxim grousing about being left behind in the care of one of the men on watch duty. The *Trib* continued her journey around a few of the 7,640 islands, making frequent clinic stops at some of the 2,000 inhabited ones. Between clinics, Sasha and the crew took Katya to the best beaches, snorkel and dive spots, lucking out with only mild storms and no typhoons in the heart of the Philippines' rainy season. Kiko's claim to Katya that the Philippines offered some of the best diving in the world proved not to be an exaggeration. Diving wasn't just recreation for Sasha. His concern for the increasing fragility of the ocean's health matched that for his patients. He, Katya, and the crew spent hours restoring coral reefs after storms, using methods Sasha had developed to reattach broken pieces, testing temperatures and salinity, and calculating changes.

Putting on the hydrofoils, they sped around the top of the Philippines to sail west, past Hainan Island, China's southernmost tip, then down the coast of Vietnam, taking time to tour Ha Long Bay, with its mysterious karst towers and intriguing caves. Tuan and Hau rivaled each other to show the best of their home country; Sasha considered Vietnam a home country as well. Sasha toured Katya around his refugee and rehabilitation center on the coast of Vietnam; they would visit three of his four centers on this trip, including the ones in Malaysia and Thailand. Katya was impressed how well run they were and by the pleasant working conditions at their bamboo fabric producing facilities, but Sasha bemoaned not having the funds to improve them further. The *Trib* sailed up the Mekong River from Ho Chi Minh City to Phnom Penh, Cambodia and round trip to Siem Reap, where they visited such fabled places as Angkor Wat and the root-covered ruins of Angkor Thom. Another 290 kilometers by river through Cambodia to the Bay of Thailand and the *Trib* was back in ocean waters.

After coastal clinics in Cambodia and Thailand, the *Trib* traveled up the Chao Phraya River to Bangkok. Sonthi served as their guide to a multitude of temples and three days and nights in the city. Then south to Malaysia, making clinic stops before and after they rounded the peninsula, Sasha choosing not to stop at wealthy Singapore, to everyone's disappointment. Aashir was Katya's host for three days in Kuala Lumpur. Katya loved the panoramic view from the Skybridge on the forty-first floor of the eighty-two story Petronas Twin Towers, the tallest buildings in the world, and snacking on the delectable Malaysian street food.

Most of the crew members didn't reappear until the next day during their two to three night city stops. Only a few stragglers joined Katya and Sasha for their dawn workouts. Sasha couldn't understand why Tuan and Aashir always returned late at night to the boat; Katya knew they were eager to enjoy having their crew's cabin to themselves.

Katya stayed on board with Sasha every evening and night. Sasha played solo works on his violin or Hiro's cello when the crew was away; chamber works filled most other evenings. Katya introduced Sasha and the crew to Boccherini's guitar quintets; his wonderfully modern-sounding and buoyant rococo "La Musica Notturna delle Strade di Madrid" of 1780 quickly became a favorite, especially the passa calle. Sasha had long ignored Boccherini as a composer, and started exploring his other eight surviving guitar quintets plus literally hundreds of other works from duos to octets. Boccherini was a virtuoso on the cello; Sasha enjoyed playing some of his numerous two-cello duets with Hiro, then a few for violin and cello. Sasha couldn't imagine life on the *Trib* without Hiro and his magnificent cello playing.

Sex with Katya occupied Sasha's nights, but he was just as eager upon awakening, and disappeared with her into their cabin the moment they returned to the *Trib* from their day's outings, or at the end of clinics – after first playing his violin while Katya and his crew cleaned and sterilized the hospital and cabins. Katya had no complaints; no one worked harder than Sasha seeing patients and performing surgeries during the clinics. Their love life was the amused envy of the crew, their sounds carrying throughout the main cabin.

On their evenings alone together, Katya helped Sasha test water samples and classify the plastic trash collected from their drag, or watched him create his intricate sea life drawings of new discoveries, read medical texts given to her by Sylvie, practiced her guitar or vocal exercises while Sasha worked online with his laboratories, listened to him perform solo works on violin or cello, or visited with the two men stuck with watch duty in the pilothouse. She'd enjoyed keeping Maxim company while he recovered, but as soon as he was able, he was back to visiting long-time lovers. Maxim appeared to have a woman friend in every major port. Katya never felt bored for a second, although she missed experiencing night life in the cities. She had to settle for enjoying the view from the deck of the *Trib* and listening to the crew's wild tales of their adventures the next day.

To Katya's surprise, music was the *Trib*'s only entertainment. The music was all live: no sound system, no recordings. There were no games, not even chess, no sports – no kicking around a soccer ball on the beaches, but many stops for swimming or snorkeling and diving. Sasha introduced Katya to his favorite denizen of the ocean, the octopus, sharing many accounts of the remarkable intelligence of this endlessly fascinating creature. Over the course of their travels, he found twenty-eight species, of the world's some 300, for her to observe in their natural habitats.

Swimming was the only part of her triathlete days Katya was able to continue; she missed biking and running. At first she managed a few runs on longer beaches, but Sasha demanded that she stay in sight of the pilothouse. Dima offered to explore cities with her by rental bicycle, but Sasha declared the busy streets too dangerous and forbade it. Katya chafed under his strict rules but couldn't convince him to be

333

less protective. Keung and Kiko finally volunteered to start running with her. For a couple of months, Katya was able to return to her five mile routine, until the realities of living on a boat caused her to abandon her efforts. She grew to rely on Sasha's ninety minute dawn workouts to keep her in great shape.

Missions against human traffickers and their ilk were declared too dangerous as well, especially since the Australian government was promoting this world tour to the medical community, and they'd barely survived the last mission against Jack Cutter. There would be no missions, but Sasha gathered information about illegal activity from his patients and passed it on to local authorities, for what it was worth. Katya marveled yet again at Sasha's ability to speak so many languages, to remember everything he read or heard. She noted him studying more languages online, preparing for the South Asian and African segments of their expedition. He insisted on communicating directly with all his patients.

The *Trib* had been holding clinics for decades along these coasts, and local populations turned out in great numbers. Katya was charmed by how the villagers would excitedly shout "Dr. Sasha! Dr. Sasha!" whenever the *Trib* pulled into an oft-visited port, Sasha standing at the prow. The free clinics would last all day, or until the last patient was seen. The crew dealt with every case that presented itself, including mental health and dentistry. Any patient needing further assistance would be taken along to the nearest medical center or hospital. Sometimes whole families crowded the main cabin or deck, a loved one in the hospital section of the boat.

Sasha contacted coastal hospitals along their route, asking for patients they thought would be good candidates for free prostheses. At each stop, Sasha would inspect the solar power equipment along with fresh water and sanitation systems, most of his own design, and make any needed modifications, or make plans for the construction of new systems. His frustration at not having money to make more substantial improvements was clear. So far Katya's private lecture to Peter Hammond had produced no results. Sasha's meager captain's salary remained his only income. Katya had a few dollars.

Katya loved the clinics, her skills increasing with each new experience. She helped as a non-medical member of the crew, sometimes assisting in care, but at first mostly organizing and welcoming patients, fetching and hauling for the doctors, and placating small children. Women thronged her, glad for a female face. It hadn't taken long for her to become expert in giving shots and inoculations. She soon had the previously chaotic clinics organized to a point that astonished the crew. Sasha made sure to express his gratitude.

Of all the clinical activities, Katya loved assisting Sasha as he met with potential prosthetic patients the most, observing his care and concern as he made his examinations and precise measurements, and demonstrated his, that is Australogic's, futuristic creations. Sasha had quickly arranged with the five hospitals he regularly worked with for a number of long-ago-ordered, individually constructed prostheses and neural components to be implanted at their facilities during the time of the *Trib*'s medical expedition. The Australian government facilitated their timely delivery. Maxim, Hiro, Kiko, and the local hospital staffs assisted at the operations. Most patients were required to travel to the University of Sydney for their life-changing operations, but Sasha had determined travel would be too expensive and disruptive for these impoverished clients.

A woman in Manila received Sasha's unique prosthetic eye; in Ho Chi Minh City, there were new limbs for two older patients who'd had their legs amputated below the knee due to ulcers caused by type 2 diabetes; four patients, their arms lost to land mines, obtained new arms and hands in Phnom Penh, Cambodia; two young men each received a new hand in Bangkok, their hands lost in work accidents; and in Kuala Lumpur, a teenage girl received a new leg and foot. Katya was not allowed to view the procedures, but she met the patients before and after.

The prostheses were nothing short of a miracle, she felt. Australogic was almost ready to go public with these newest models. Katya could only imagine the world-wide excitement these prostheses would generate. The arm and hand recipients would be able to quickly return to their lives, their new limbs nearly identical to their real ones, with a full range of motion and sensitivity. The patients who had received a new leg walked right after the surgery, but they would need much physical therapy to strengthen their bodies due to a leg's load-bearing nature. The eye recipient would take the longest to adjust. The woman had lost her sight as an adult, but Sasha explained it might still take some time for her brain to learn to recognize the images it was receiving.

335

Seeing the prostheses on living recipients was much different than viewing them in a drawer on the *Trib*. Katya thought how these utterly brilliant prostheses were just a small part of Sasha's creative output. Maxim, Hiro, Sonthi, Dima and the rest of his crew had devoted their lives to Sasha and his vision of a better world, protected him with their lives, without ever viewing his Australogic laboratories in Sydney, without seeing the entirety of his genius. She might never see the labs either. Sasha kept his two worlds as separate as he could, and his men respected that. The difficulties living with him, of subjecting their will – her will – to his, were mere trifles in the overview of the cosmos.

Katya couldn't help but view Sasha in a new light. Sasha wasn't quite the saintly, selfless, or humble man she'd first thought, but he was a superb doctor, an idealistic humanitarian, and a genius without equal. And vulnerable. He needed her. He needed the crew, his disciples. He was one man with almost no money and no clout, no power, tilting against the specters of poverty, pollution, woefully inadequate health care, injustice, Climate Change, and cruel human greed. A man without a voice, but for one speech at that fateful Global Human Rights conference. But if anyone could save the world from itself, it was Sasha. If the world didn't crush him first.

The *Trib* made three more clinic stops along the Sumatran coast of Indonesia, then followed Katya's wishes to visit the quarantine center for orangutans at Batu Mbelin and hike in Gunung Lenser National Park, where they spied wild orangutans and elephants and explored the deepest, lushest jungle environment any of them had ever experienced. Their route took them back up the Indian Ocean side of Malaysia and Thailand, the famous beaches around Phuket quiet and peaceful for their dawn workout. Once they reached the long coast of Myanmar, the crew was in new territory, but even that dangerous country seemed to be in a moment of peace and gave its permission for several clinic stops. For Katya, every country was a new and exciting adventure.

The clinics continued along the coasts of Bangladesh, India, and Pakistan, around the Arabian Peninsula – Oman, Yemen – and up the African coast – tiny Djibouti, Eritrea, Sudan, Egypt – and through the Suez Canal. Since Katya had been encouraged to choose their free time activities, a sail down the Nile to the pyramids was on their itinerary, and she had also insisted on a day-long stop in Israel, just then starting to pull its troops out of Lebanon, causing a flurry of diplomatic negotiations for them to be allowed to hold clinics in both Lebanon and Syria afterwards.

Katya had been more concerned with how the crew was holding up under the onslaught of patients at every stop along the way. Bangladesh and India had been especially overwhelming in her view, but the men seemed to thrive at the busiest times. The *Trib*'s hospital served as a hectic emergency room more than once. Every country past the Southeast Asian peninsula was new to the entire crew. They reveled in the sights, sounds, tastes, and fragrances, the new faces and new cultures.

Katya also found she could be useful to the crew by giving neck and shoulder massages throughout the frantic clinic days. Sasha had been the beneficiary of her touch since the first day in the van, and he still melted under her full body massages. Sharing her healing touch with the crew was new and brought everyone even closer together. Katya was relieved that Sasha displayed only moderate signs of jealousy, which she ignored.

Over the course of their expedition, the Bergen-Belsen list did not return to haunt Sasha, but difficult clinical cases provoked two memory attacks requiring his violin when Katya was not nearby, and her touch had gotten him through four accidental contact episodes without his losing consciousness. She saw how the continued attacks deeply disappointed him. He confided to her that he'd hoped finally speaking out about his history would end the torments. He experienced a half-day deep depression with each episode, followed by a manic-depressive cycle that would last for hours. Katya found it difficult to keep up with his moods. The crew took it all in stride.

The success of the massages gave Katya an idea. She would try something new to help Sasha past his touch phobia. She started with giving Sasha a back massage with oil, with Sonthi sitting next to her, letting Sasha hear his voice, then having Sonthi try to massage him the same way. Sasha cringed and shuddered, begging him to stop. Kiko tried next with the same results, but she would not give up. Katya became convinced that Sasha had experienced another psychologically scarring incident past his childhood, one that he still would not talk about, no matter how she tried. She knew there would come a time when he was ready, and maybe then he could start to heal. There was already a sign of hope. Sonthi told her Sasha started up psychiatric sessions with him again, after over a year of avoidance, although Sasha's refusal to speak of Bergen-Belsen or to submit to hypnosis continued to thwart any noticeable progress.

The crew had been able to relax and enjoy the second part of their voyage, a pure pleasure cruise starting with the breathtaking Turquoise Coast of Turkey, then exploring many of the scenic Grecian islands, up the Adriatic and the gorgeous coast of Croatia, over to glorious Venice, and down around the boot of Italy, with stops at every port that interested them on the European side of the Mediterranean to the Strait of Gibraltar. Serious clinic work picked up again as they rounded the north of Africa, starting in Morocco and ending in Senegal, and they did nothing but make music across the Atlantic Ocean to the Caribbean, flying full speed on their hydrofoil wings.

The last leg of their voyage had them hard at work doing clinics again, and enjoying the beaches and bays, from Saint Martin, the Virgin Islands, Puerto Rico, the Dominican Republic, Haiti, and Jamaica down the coast of Central America to Panama. The Australian government got them a priority schedule crossing and they were through the canal in less than nine hours, continuing their clinics up the Pacific side of Central America and Mexico. Katya had many misgivings about the stops in Guatemala, but the familiar, welcoming faces of the people overcame her guilt, and she felt like her work with the clinics was in some small way a penance. She hoped now she could feel like she had atoned for the village she had caused to be slaughtered. Maybe now she could find some peace.

Katya had certainly found a new love – life on board the *Trib*. Everything about living on the *Trib* was a joy, excepting the lack of a piano; she would gather up several more of her instruments when they arrived at their destination. She had lovemaking with Sasha, the comradeship of ten handsome men – her new family. A new and worthy purpose. The beauty of the sea and the life under its surface. She loved clear night skies full of stars. Sailing with the wind was as exciting as speeding on hydrofoils. She loved how the *Trib* weathered storms with ease, when not outracing them. She missed the rocking of the boat when working or touring on land. Katya hadn't slept on land since she'd left Bora Bora.

The end of December found the *Trib* along the California coast, moving against large numbers of humpback whales heading to Baja, pods of dolphins riding her bow. The crew grew more excited as they entered Californian waters, finally reaching San Francisco Bay on December 28. They sailed under the Golden Gate in the early morning light. The rising sun gilded the freshly green hills of Marin on their port side, San Francisco sparkled on their starboard. Chen, Keung, and Dima furled the sails and the *Trib* slowed to five knots. They found the berth that had been arranged for them at the Marina Yacht Harbor and tied up.

Katya was thrilled to be back in home territory, eager to cross the bay to her house and friends in the Berkeley Hills. The Australian Consul-General, their mate Peter Hammond, looking sleepy, was there to greet them at the dock, offering the crew a large van and private guide for city tours, a welcome dinner for them at the Consulate, guards for the *Trib*, and a car with a private driver and a guard for Katya and Sasha. Even Peter was not let in on the wedding plans. Five months before, he'd happily agreed to forego all the tempting high society New Year's/ End of the Millennium parties he would be invited to and had accepted their invitation to a musical New Year's/ Birthday celebration on the *Retribution*.

The crew had hours of work to do scrubbing and battening down the *Trib* after her long voyage before they could be free to explore San Francisco, but they insisted Sasha and Katya take off on their own. Katya was only disappointed Sasha would not invite the crew to join them, even for part of a day. She would have loved to share her Berkeley home with them, let her colleagues hear her and Sasha play on a fine piano, her Steinway, wanted to fill her house with their music. Katya packed a duffel for the two of them, and taking Sasha's violin and computer, they stepped into the car. Katya and Sasha found themselves truly alone together for the first time since July.

Chapter 46

Traffic on the Bay Bridge heading into San Francisco was bumper-to-bumper on this Tuesday morning, but delightfully light towards the East Bay. Katya had the driver drop them off in front of her house and said they would call when he was needed again. Sasha refused to let the guard stay with him. Carlos, Sonya, and David were expecting them. All three had accepted the invitation to the New Year's party that Friday. Yan volunteered to stay behind and celebrate with the new refugees from El Salvador, three young women escaping a life of poverty and forced prostitution. They were shy and had declined the opportunity to join them for the celebration on the boat.

Katya worried about how David would take her relationship with Sasha, but she needn't have been concerned. As they entered the house, David and Sonya greeted them at the door, holding hands. But the two left after lunch for a three-day visit with David's parents in San Jose, so Katya knew David was not taking any chances with his heart. The house hadn't changed a bit in the many months she had been away, but it no longer felt as much like home.

The three days passed quickly. The only time they left the house was to slip into San Francisco to get their marriage license, swearing Peter's driver and the guard to secrecy. There was gardening and music, hour-long massages for Sasha, lovemaking in her single bed, and a total lack of routine past their dawn exercises, Katya's vocal warmups, and Sasha's work with his labs on his laptop, with plenty of time to just be alone in the spacious house and yard. They enjoyed frequent conversations in Spanish with their sanctuary guests and helped them practice their English. Sasha even dared to pet Cesar.

Katya loved sparring alone with Sasha. To Katya, their sessions felt more like a beautiful choreographed dance. They took turns being the attacker, Katya managing to stay on her feet, but just barely, Sasha effortlessly parrying all the moves she threw at him. Sasha matched her one-arm pushups just as effortlessly, something he would never do in front of the crew.

Her Steinway got a workout from both of them, but her favorite musical activity remained duets with Sasha playing violin. He didn't comment on her harpsichord performances, but he insisted she play each of her other instruments for him. The Chinese pipa and the Japanese koto were his favorites. Carlos felt too intimidated to play classical music after listening to Sasha, but he played them some jazz pieces he'd been working on. Katya got Sasha to listen to her favorite folk singers and some Stéphane Grappelli recordings. She took out her Martin classical guitar, put Yan on rhythm guitar, and enjoyed fooling around with some Django Reinhardt Hot Club gypsy jazz arrangements, but Sasha refused to try imitating Grappelli's unique violin style. Instead he improvised some "Gypsy" Romani tunes to the accompaniment of their guitars, then said he'd had enough. Katya knew better than to push him. Life with Sasha would be a delicate balance, a dance, she mused. He would do what he wanted and compromise would most often come from her. She could only manipulate him so far with touch, and with sex. Sasha insisted on accompanying Katya as she sang lieder and French art songs. He told her he found her voice magical.

The morning of December 31, Sasha and Katya snuck quietly away to the waiting car Peter had provided for them. They'd done their last two-person workout in the near dark by the lights in her garden and planned to shower on the *Trib*. Katya looked back one last time, wondering if and when she would ever return. She would miss her piano the most, but she felt eager to get back to the boat and the crew, her new family. She carried her mandolin and her Chinese pipa for part of the evening's musical offerings, and the guard placed her koto, her favorite guitar, and their one duffel in the car. Sasha carefully loaded in his violin case and laptop. They would send the car back for Carlos, Sonya, and David at two. Peter Hammond and Professor Takahashi and his wife Umi were the only other expected guests, since her sifu had declined. Her farewell meeting with him had been painful for both of them.

The day dawned clear and not too cold, with a forecast of perfect light winds for sailing. Hiro and Chen would be setting out appetizers at three, then the crew would motor into the bay and unfurl the sails for the beginning of a cruise that would last from 4 p.m. until 2 the next morning. The *Retribution* would keep circling the bay, then head out under the Golden Gate Bridge for international waters shortly before midnight. Sasha was set on the idea of a timeless moment with no fixed location, the time between centuries and millennia, between

1999 and 2000, between the 31st of December and January first, in a place that belonged to no one country, just over twelve nautical miles from San Francisco, traveling on the hydrofoils for smooth sailing. The late afternoon and evening would be filled with music, with all the crew members getting a chance to participate. Katya was putting together an entertaining surprise for Sasha with the help of Hau, Aashir, and Tuan. None of them could imagine anything going wrong with their impeccable plans on this beautiful day.

But once again, Fate was an unwanted guest. Sasha and Katya arrived at the boat at 9 a.m. to find Peter Hammond standing grim faced on the dock, talking with Maxim and Hiro, along with four other members of the crew. Peter looked like he'd been roused from his bed long before he was ready.

"You're here," Peter said. "Didn't want this to go over the car's phone. We've had some urgent intelligence from S-Branch. Careful as you were, somehow Cyrus Cutter discovered you and your crew were behind his brother's demise in the Philippines. He's out for blood and he's the worst of the lot. Word's gotten to him that the *Retribution* is in San Francisco and Cyrus has been putting out feelers about how to get to you. Nothing specific, but we have all our resources listening and watching for trouble. I have confidence in the defenses of the *Trib*, but we're still stationing extra men around the harbor."

"I appreciate the guards you've given us on the boat for the crew's shore leave," Sasha replied, now grim as well, taking Katya's hand, "but that ends now. No one knows the ship's defenses better than my men. We're going back to our two-man watch, but we'll spell them often so everyone can have time to celebrate and enjoy the music." He looked searchingly at his crew, who nodded in solemn agreement. "If you would rather not be aboard, Peter, I understand."

"I wouldn't miss this day for the world, Sasha," Peter replied. "This is going to be a birthday celebration you will remember, and Cyrus Cutter's little snit isn't going to stop us."

Katya would have felt more confident if Peter had brayed his big laugh, but he remained serious. "Should we disguise the boat?" she asked.

"Far too late for that," Sasha said, regret and concern evident on his face. "We'll just have to be on full alert from now on. I'm so sorry, Katya,"

"So how does this change our schedule?"

"I'm not changing a thing. We sail at four, return at two, and hell take anyone who gets in our way."

"Now you're talking like Peter, or me, Sasha."

Sasha didn't comment. He was focused and in charge.

"I'm going to take some time to check our motors and defense systems with Maxim and Hiro. You go ahead on the boat," Sasha said, giving her a distracted kiss.

Sasha remained on the dock talking with Peter and the six crew members for a while longer before he disappeared down into the hold with his two officers. Sasha returned to his cabin an hour later, his clothes dirty and grease on his hands. He saw Katya was in the tiny shower, so he grabbed a towel and headed to one of the crew's heads. He assumed all hands were on deck or in the pilothouse and that he would have the head to himself. He paid no attention to the lanyard hung over the handle and opened the door.

The sight of Aashir and Tuan naked, kissing in full embrace, hands exploring each other, sent him reeling backwards. Sasha felt a flush of heat run up his body to his head and the sudden shivers of an impending panic attack. Gasping, he sat down quickly on one of the berths, fighting to regain self-control. Aashir and Tuan, in a panic themselves, quickly wrapped towels around their waists and ran to him.

"Sasha, Captain, breathe, please breathe," Tuan urged, then motioned for Aashir to get dressed while he knelt next to Sasha. "Go get Katya, just trousers will do, go!"

"Tuan, I can't..." Sasha tried to speak, but he was having great difficulty. "You can't..." he tried again, but stopped, breathing hard.

He forced himself to slow his breathing. Aashir returned at a run with Katya, also partially dressed, wet hair streaming. She sat next to Sasha and held his damp head in both her hands, touching her forehead to his. Sasha sighed deeply and took her hands away, holding them in his lap.

"Tuan, Aashir, you can't do this, you can't do this and be here," he managed to say.

Katya knew of Sasha's physiological reaction to male to male sexuality, but she decided to try a psychological approach, aiming to reach Sasha's logical brain, appeal to his empathy.

"And how is what they were doing different from what we do?" Katya asked. "They are a couple as we are. Everyone knows except

344

apparently, you. They've tried hard to be discreet, more than we have."

"I don't care that they can love each other, I get that now," Sasha said, sounding wounded. "I just can't witness it... I can't help how my body reacts."

"You're still implying that what they're doing together is wrong. Maybe it's time you leveled with them, with the entire crew, why you feel this way, tell them what happened to you," Katya said soothingly. "There is more you haven't told even me. You will find it easier to live with if you talk about it. You know that's true."

"It's a completely different issue," Sasha countered. "These are consenting adults. I was never... was never…"

Sasha stopped. Katya looked deep into his eyes while she massaged his scalp, speaking to him without words. Sasha's panic began to subside. When he looked calmer, she took his hand in hers. Sasha gave the smallest of head nods. Katya squeezed his hand in acknowledgement of his permission to continue.

"I know you're concerned about Cutter's threat. You're feeling vulnerable. When you feel vulnerable, you're reminded of the helplessness and pain you experienced in your past. We're going to talk about that past, Sasha, bring it out into the light. I'm going to tell Tuan and Aashir what you told me...

"You were a small child, not yet four when it started. You were sexually abused in the most despicable ways by a sadistic German SS officer in Bergen Belsen. You were made to do things you hated and had terrible things done to you. You were beaten, tattooed, your body is covered with scars. You witnessed horrific acts of violence committed against equally helpless prisoners. You had no choice, nowhere to run, no one to turn to for help. The fact that your abuser was a man makes it difficult for you to abide seeing men touch each other, to accept any kind of touch. You were traumatized, Sasha, and you're still traumatized."

Katya dared to go further. Perhaps this was the moment when probing deeper would reveal the second abuse she suspected. Tuan and Aashir looked stricken.

"What else happened to you, Sasha?" she asked, keeping her voice even and calm. "Where did it happen? I think someone knew you had a visceral and uncontrollable reaction to being touched…"

345

"Stop. Just stop," Sasha begged, his panic returning. Sweat poured down his face, his shirt grew damp.

Tuan hurriedly dressed, surreptitiously slipping the lanyard into his pocket, and sat next to Aashir on one of the other berths. Aashir had thrown on a shirt. They were horrified by what they were hearing but nodded to Katya to continue.

"Sasha, listen to my voice. Put yourself back to that time. You have people who love you right here. Talking will help you. We'll keep it among us three. We can better help you next time you feel like this. But you have to let it out."

Sasha's breathing was still ragged. After a long pause, he nodded again. Curling up on the berth, he placed his head in Katya's lap; her hands caressed him. Several more minutes passed before he began.

"I won't talk about Bergen-Belsen. But there was another... incident... just after I arrived in Vietnam," he said, his gasps calming as he began to control his breathing, "an eccentric, socially naïve, virginal, puritanical, not at all humble, and untouchable twenty-five-year-old surgeon. I'd put together my own mobile medical unit. The Yanks had a R&R center there in Vung Tao on the coast, right where I was stationed. A group of them had taken an instant dislike to me, but then the feeling was mutual. I saw how some of them were treating the Vietnamese as subhuman, condescending at best with the men, treating the women like they were all prostitutes, every local like a potential enemy, and the attitude was starting to rub off on some of our men. Our women were as angry as I was, though; the Americans tried to hit on my nurses, but they ignored them. I... could not ignore them. We had a joint canteen for meals and the two groups spent far too much time together.

"My commanding officer didn't take my complaints seriously, and I asked to be allowed to give a demonstration. I put on a black wig and dark sunglasses, dressed in an ARVN uniform as a common Vietnamese soldier, and took a meal with my medical crew and troops when the Americans were there. The C.O. would be watching out of sight. I had no more eaten a bite before three Americans came over and started bullying me. I lost my temper, threw off the wig and sunglasses, and did a martial arts number on them, sending two to the hospital, although there were no long-term injuries. Needless to say, I made an enemy of every American in the room that day. My C.O. put an extra watch on me, knowing my value to our government and to his unit as a surgeon, and separated our two groups' meal times.

"A few nights later I was knocked unconscious and abducted by a gang of these angry Yanks, seeking vengeance, and awoke to find myself naked, gagged, and tied backwards to a chair in a deserted room. How they'd avoided my watch, I don't know."

Sasha stopped his story, and it was a full five minutes before he continued. Katya kept touching his face and running her fingers through his damp blond hair until he was able to start again.

"They knew full well I couldn't stand to be touched," he said, more quietly. "There were six of them, egging each other on, tormenting me for what seemed like hours. I knew my watchers would be looking for me and held out hope they would come, but they didn't find me in time... The Yanks touched me all over, with hands, cocks, bare buttocks, laughing at my reactions, my utter distress, even at my scars, calling me a gook lover, a queer... said they didn't like how I looked at men. I shook my head violently – I honestly didn't know what they meant... They faked making out with each other, mocked me with empty beer bottles, saying they were going to shove one up inside me............ When I started to go into full blackout mode, they would toss a bucket of water on me and continue... They either got bored or panicked when they couldn't wake me from a blackout, because my watchers eventually found me alone in the room, unconscious, still tied in the chair, and somehow got me back to my sleeping quarters.

"The American authorities were inclined to call the whole thing a friendly hazing that got a little out of hand, and I didn't want to press charges and bring what happened to me out in the open. Breaking all six of their noses the next day brought me a little satisfaction, but no peace, and I got permission to move my unit to Saigon. I redoubled my efforts to keep from being touched because my reactions thereafter were... worse. And that is everything. I've got nothing more to say," he finished in a whisper.

"Sasha, dear, dear Sasha." Katya spoke softly. She had a terrible feeling Sasha hadn't told everything that had happened. "I'm so very sorry. You know we will never let anyone abuse you that way again. Try and put it behind you. Find some peace. Concentrate on the movements of my fingers. You can accept being touched by me now. You have my love and loyalty, and that of ten men around you."

347

Sasha remained silent and motionless, but his breathing was back to normal. Katya continued stroking him as she turned her attention to Tuan and Aashir.

"I think you both understand now that it's not your love for each other that disturbs him. Seeing your physical intimacy triggered his memories and his response. Think of him as experiencing PTSD, because he is... he has been for all these years. I'll teach him what a lanyard means if you two can do a better job keeping your affair private while you're on the boat. Tuan, I know you're leaving us to start your surgery residency at the university in Ho Chi Minh City next month. What are your plans, Aashir?"

"I'm going with Tuan," Aashir answered, gazing sadly over at Sasha. "We know it's not going to be easy. Tuan's never been openly gay, and I've never not been."

"I wish you the best. I'll miss you both terribly. How did you two connect with Sasha?"

"Sasha was working with some prosthetic patients at my hospital and doing his neural implants," Tuan answered first. "I knew I wanted to be a neurosurgeon after watching him. I also knew I wanted to be with him. We talked about music, and I invited him to my apartment... we played a violin/cello duet... I was in heaven at the sound of his violin. I'd never met anyone like Sasha... I was so captivated, I had a hard time finishing my internship before I moved aboard the *Trib*."

"And I was working on a dock in Malaysia," Aashir said. "It was love at first sight when the *Retribution* pulled in and I saw Sasha standing on the deck. I begged to be considered for the crew. I knew boats and martial arts, my English was decent, and I promised to learn whatever he needed me to know about medicine. I nearly lost my mind when he began speaking to me in perfect Malay. Then I promised to learn a musical instrument. I was impossibly persistent. I've never regretted a moment."

Sasha stirred on Katya's lap, stretching out his hands to his mates. Both young men slipped quickly to the floor and took the offered hands in theirs, Aashir kissing Sasha's hand over and over. Katya felt a long shudder pass through him as they touched, but that was all. She was almost in tears watching them. When he was ready, Sasha sat up, recovered his hands and ran his fingers through their hair affectionately, something he'd never dreamed of doing before. He then held Katya's face and gave her a kiss.

"All right, mates, we have a long and wonderful day ahead of us. Please go finish whatever it was you two were starting in the showers and let me have some time alone with my bride."

Neither man knew whether to laugh or be embarrassed. They hopped up and disappeared together back into the head, but not before Tuan reattached the lanyard to the door handle. Sasha looked longingly at Katya. She took his hand, leading him to their cabin. They almost tripped over Kiko, sitting on the floor outside the crew's door, his face covered with tears.

"Ah, now you know too, Kiko," Sasha said, as he reached down and touched his face. Kiko braved reaching up and taking Sasha's hand in both of his. Once again, Katya felt a shudder pass through Sasha's body, but he didn't pull his hand away.

"I still want to keep this among the five of us. Let me decide if and when I'll talk to the rest of the crew."

Kiko nodded and reluctantly let go. Sasha and Katya hurried on, barely able to control their passion. As soon as they closed the door, Katya pushed Sasha down onto the narrow berth and lay on top of him, locking her lips on his. They didn't take the time to pull out the bed or even turn on Hiro's suspect noise canceler. When she came up for air, Katya sat up and removed her shirt, then Sasha's.

"Let's try letting me do all the moving and touching this time, all right?" Katya said breathlessly. "Tell me immediately if anything I do is uncomfortable for you."

Sasha nodded, and she stayed sitting on top of him, touching, then kissing his face, neck, nipples, arms. Sasha groaned with pleasure and let himself relax into her lovemaking. She rolled him over onto his stomach and worked his shoulders and back the same way, rubbing her body across his, sliding down his shorts and undergarment and caressing his buttocks and legs to his feet, then back up. Katya removed the rest of her clothing and rolled him onto his back again as she continued to stroke him. When they were both completely aroused, she slipped him inside her and started to move up and down, staying in control as long as she could until they both climaxed, one after the other. She remained astride him until she felt him go soft, then stretched out full length on top of him.

"My God, that was good," she whispered. "I love having over five months of honeymoon before the wedding."

"Just when I think we've tried everything, you surprise me."

"May we never stop surprising each other."

"I just wish we had more time. You're going to still be young and full of sex and energy when I'm old and feeble."

"Ha. You'll have replaced all, and I mean all, of your body parts with flesh-like robotic ones and your brain will be as good as ever when you're 110. Or you'll die happily in the saddle and I'll take up with any one of your young and handsome crew."

"In the saddle?" Sasha queried, rolling them onto their sides facing each other, holding her close to keep them from falling off the berth. "What do saddles have to do with it?"

"Having sex, Mr. Knows Everything."

"All I know right now is that I was heading to take a shower a couple of ages ago because you were using our tiny one. I think we have to start all over."

"You first this time," Katya laughed. "I'm going to sit on the floor and watch you, then you can watch me. I'll get almost as wet from your shower just sitting there."

"You know we could get our own lanyard and use one of the double showers."

"Now you understand about the lanyard! We'll have to choose a different color. Next time. I want to stay naked and look at you."

Sasha turned on the water and stepped into the shower, and Katya took great pleasure in admiring his perfect, beautifully muscled, ageless body. Even his remarkable pattern of scars were beautiful in their own terrible way.

"We're going to have to get dressed eventually. Seems we've invited a few people over and it's too late to get out of it," she tried to shout over the water. "We might have a thing or two we're supposed to be doing right now."

"Can't hear you," came from the shower.

"Never mind," Katya said to herself, smiling.

Chapter 47

Three o'clock arrived and with it the first of the guests. The entire crew had decided to arm themselves with compact handguns, not dart pistols, in light of the threat, and they slipped on unaccustomed shoulder harnesses requiring them to wear loose, unstructured jackets. Keung was holding Sasha's jacket when Professor Takahashi and his wife arrived on the dock. Sasha ran out to greet them, with Keung chasing after him. Sasha didn't notice the professor staring at the gun until Keung started helping him into his jacket. They all decided not to speak of it.

"Professor Takahashi, we are honored you have chosen to join us tonight," Sasha said a little too brightly, followed by a respectful bow. "I apologize that I met you under such false circumstances. This is one of my crew, Keung, a physician assistant and trauma technician."

"A pleasure to meet you, Keung." Short bows were exchanged. "Please call me Fujio. May I introduce my wife, Umi. This is the mysterious Dr. Sasha Borodin, who has won our Katya's heart. I understand you will be performing this evening?"

"Please call me Sasha. Everyone living on this boat is a fine musician and you will hear us all perform, including Katya. Please come aboard. Two of our doctors are also excellent chefs and have set out appetizers and drinks to get us started. Dinner will be at eight."

"I like your Australian accent, Sasha," Fujio said, still looking uncomfortable about having seen the gun. "But you did make an extremely convincing Dane."

The main cabin had been transformed, thanks to Tuan, Aashir, and the two chefs. Narrow serving tables were set up against the closed cabinetry walls on both sides of the stairs, and were now covered with colorful Hmong and Malaysian embroidered cloths and an elaborate spread of food. The cabinets on the starboard side had already been emptied of instruments and music stands; they were stored in one of the crew's cabins, to be brought out as needed later. Only five folding chairs were set up in the middle, joining Sasha's captain's chair, now pushed to the side. Down the steps on the other side of the main cabin, the galley dining table was heaped with more food and a variety of alcoholic and nonalcoholic drinks, and held a huge bouquet of exotic flowers. Katya hoped no one would trip on the steps during the course of the celebration. Space would be tight, but the guests could also wander the decks and outside seating area. Everyone had been warned to bring coats. Maxim left his cabin door open and guests were informed to use "the facilities" there. Kiko and Sonthi had drawn the watch starting at four and would be in the pilothouse. Sonthi would take the first helm as well.

Peter was next to arrive, then David, Sonya, and Carlos. Katya appeared from the back of the boat to greet her guests and introduce them around. All the men were dressed in their best clothes: slacks and shirts in various shades of tan and off white, their jackets, designed by Aashir, in muted earth tones. Maxim and Hiro had even put on solid shoes instead of sandals. Sasha still wore his. Katya's clothing matched that of the men. She would change later.

Keung had been busy earlier in the day giving much-needed haircuts, and Sasha had sat still long enough for Katya to properly trim his. When Aashir next reappeared after his haircut, he'd restored his blond highlights; in fact, he was considerably blonder. Katya had smiled at him, amused, then surprised Sasha and Maxim by announcing that the boat needed to make a stop in Sausalito at six for a special guest entertainer. They looked at her curiously. Aashir had grinned back at her, seeming to be in on her plans.

The mooring lines were just being loosed when an additional figure came bounding down the dock and hopped aboard the boat. Dima made a grab for him and held his arm tight while Keung ran inside to get Sasha's and Peter's attention. Katya hurried out behind them. The man was Mason.

"Absolutely not," Katya said heatedly. "I will not have that man aboard tonight. You can toss him in the bay for all I care."

"Katya, please. I think it would be a gesture of peace between our governments and our organizations," Peter countered.

"You knew? You invited him? The man is untrustworthy and corrupt. He tortured me, Peter!"

"In my defense, just a little bit," Mason said with a smirk Katya wanted to smack off his face. "I'm here to make amends."

"Sasha, please back me up here. I want him off."

"Peter, tell me why you invited him," Sasha demanded, reaching to hold her hand.

"To tell the truth, I thought he might be rather an insurance policy," Peter answered. "If you think he's corrupt, maybe the bad guys will leave us alone tonight."

"You are so wrong," Katya hissed. "He's the one who pulled the trigger on Markus Cutter. He's got to be as much of a target as we are."

"They don't know that. He may still be useful to them," Peter countered.

"People, please! I'm right here. And I'm taking offense," Mason laughed.

"Katya, let him stay. He's holding up our departure. Let Dima search him thoroughly and he or Keung will shadow him," Sasha said, regretting it the moment the words came out of his mouth. He had once considered Mason almost a friend, a colleague in arms, but that was long ago.

"Peter, you're on my shit list," Katya growled. "Mason, come within three meters of me and your private parts will regret it. And Sasha, I'm going on record now as saying this is a bad idea. It's also unfair to Dima and Keung."

Katya spun around, stormed back down the companionway, and disappeared into the crew's quarters. Sasha watched her go. He was sure she was right. He didn't need to be upsetting her on this of all days. He introduced the new arrivals to his crewmembers, and was relieved when Katya reappeared in a better mood.

The *Retribution* finally left the dock at four fifteen and motored slowly out into the bay. The guests, with the exception of Mason, were invited to the spacious pilothouse to watch the sails unfurling and to meet Sonthi and Kiko. Maxim took great pride in explaining some, but not all of their technology. The light winds kept the boat moving at a comfortable speed for walking on the decks and the city skyline looked glorious as it began to light up.

The *Trib* circled around Alcatraz Island, Katya regaling Sasha and the crew with its infamous history as a prison, then once around Angel Island. Katya told of its thirty years as an equally infamous detention center for Chinese immigrants, and how she and her father had often sailed there for a picnic and hike. Lines of pelicans and dark-bodied cormorants flew past the boat as the sun set in fantastic shades of tangerine. As the colors faded to dove grays, the wind whipped up colder and guests and crew alike retreated to the main cabin. Dima was the first to play, standing to perform solo viola, starting with Kodály's transcription of Bach's Fantasia and Fugue in D Minor, while Katya offered the guests appetizers of sushi and dim sum and took them on a short tour of the boat, only viewing the hospital from its doorway. Katya and Dima exchanged smiles as she passed. He had never played more beautifully. He'd told her he would be playing just for her.

When the applause ended, Hiro reported with Hau to the pilothouse for watch and helm duty, and Dima took Keung' s place keeping an eye on Mason, making sure he caught his angry glare as he towered menacingly over him. Sasha provided the next entertainment, and his solo performance of Rachmaninov's soaring "Vocalise," without its usual piano accompaniment, and Prelude in G Minor ensured that no one noticed Katya's disappearance, or even looked out the windows as the boat made a quick stop at the Sausalito dock. Their guests settled themselves on the padded benches to listen. The Takahashis, David, and Sonya had been thrilled with Dima's playing, but gasped with amazement hearing Sasha perform for the first time. Sasha had just finished playing and the applause was ending when a loud, unfamiliar voice sounded from the top deck. A strange apparition came down the companionway, carrying a beat-up guitar case covered with stickers celebrating the 1960s.

The newcomer introduced herself as Sara Skyfeather. She was dressed in a calf-length, less than clean hippie dress and tall, dirty, worn-out boots. Her long, messy blondish hair tumbled from under a gigantic hat. Huge sunglasses perched on her nose, although it was already getting dark out, and a strange assortment of bead necklaces hung around her neck. Her partially hidden face was pale, her lips white, and those closest were appalled by her broken, dirty fingernails and an overall odor of mildew. She said she was an old Berkeley friend of Katya's and called for her to come out and see her, but Katya, refusing to leave the starboard crew's cabin, instead exchanged a series of loud, mock insults with the visitor. The crew and most of the guests were puzzled. David was laughing, which added to everyone's confusion. The crew looked to Sasha. His eyes were twinkling in his otherwise inscrutable poker face.

Sara announced her first two songs, "Help Me" and "Pave Paradise" by Joni Mitchell, which she sang in an uncanny approximation of Joni Mitchell's voice, accompanying herself on a

354

guitar as covered with stickers as its case. Only a small handful of those on board knew what they were hearing, and they were astounded; Sara's voice was virtually indistinguishable from the famous voice they knew. Sara then launched into a rendition of the Eagles' "Hotel California" in Joni's voice, ending with a long Spanish guitar solo. The crew and guests were thrilled and applauded wildly. By now, most of the crew had caught on. David leaned over to whisper to Sonya and Carlos, and their eyes widened.

Sara gave a short, meandering diatribe about love and peace, then announced her next song, "Who Knows Where the Wind Goes," which she sang in a completely different voice.

"I'm supposed to tell Sasha this is Judy Collins; I understand he missed out on the American folksinger part of his otherwise thorough education," she said when the song ended, to David's renewed laughter.

"My last song is for any of you Joan Baez fans out there, and I see maybe three. Can I see a show of hands if you know this song, 'Blowing in the Wind?' Ah, well I'm pleased. Looks like maybe seven of you. I'm not surprised the shorter blond one doesn't know it," and she sang in her best Joan Baez voice.

By the time she finished, only Peter, Mason, and the Takahashis had no idea who Sara was. Sara stayed in character and joined the crew and guests as they partook of appetizers and drinks. She purposely got into a political argument with Mason, playing the far left Berkeleyite to the hilt. Sasha separated them by requesting one more song before she departed. Sara obliged with singing "Both Sides Now" as Judy Collins, while thanking Joni Mitchell for being the songwriter. Sara bent over low as she collected her applause, and pulling off glasses, hat, and wig, stood up straight as Katya, to redoubled applause. Sasha embraced her, then motioned for Aashir and Tuan to head up for watch and helm duty. Katya blew Sasha a kiss before she returned to the crew's quarters to quickly change her clothes. Her audience was left discussing the scene and laughing. After downing several drinks, Mason sidled closer to Peter and Sasha, Dima close behind him. Shaking his head, Mason engaged Peter.

"I couldn't see Katya in there anywhere. We talked face to face for five minutes," he admitted to Peter. "And how could she get up on the deck? She came down the companionway!"

"She had me fooled as well," Peter marveled. "She's got quite the voice. How did she do those fingernails, and her voice coming from the crew's cabin?"

"We've known her since she was born," Fujio added. "Neither Umi or I had any clue. I actually saw her singing as Sara in a coffee shop once. No clue," he repeated.

"And what did you think, Sasha?" asked Peter, looking highly amused. "I bet this little entertainment was mostly for your benefit."

"I'd discovered the outfit in her house when I went through her things with David before I really knew her, but the depth of her talent amazes me. In answer to your questions, Peter, she exited through a skylight from one of the crew's cabins. She must have prepared a recording of her own voice. She had some help – I noticed Aashir disappeared for a while – and used press on nails. Hau has a whole collection of them. Katya is a chameleon with a beautiful voice. She sang as Edith Piaf for us in Tahiti. And you should have seen a disguise she pulled off in the Philippines. She did successfully trick me there."

"I think her whole relationship with you has been a big trick," Mason said, snarkily. "She wormed her way into your heart with deceit and manipulation."

Dima looked like he was going to punch him.

"You're way out of line, Mason," Peter warned.

"And you, Sasha," Mason continued, "you found a young girl with a daddy fixation. You've got what, thirty years on her? You're more than twice her age! Tell me Sasha, where do you keep the portrait on your boat, the one that gets older while you stay forever young?"

"It's not too late for me to drop you over the side of the boat, Mason," Sasha replied with fury. "The water's just as cold as you are. Katya was right. I never should have let you on board."

Sasha turned away from him just as Katya entered his line of sight. The Takahashis were looking uncomfortable. The main cabin was so crowded, no one could miss the angry exchange and the room grew quiet.

"Three meters, Mason," Katya said icily. "That puts you in the galley dining area or topsides. I think I'll make that three meters from anyone else here. This is Sasha's birthday celebration besides New Year's, and you stand there insulting your host, not to mention me.

Maybe you and I need a little heart to heart alone instead. I'll treat you real nice, just like I did Gunner."

Mason's smile froze. He began to look a little panicked when he saw she was serious.

"My apologies. I didn't think I'd had that much to drink," he murmured, backing away.

The tension in the cabin began to subside. Sasha and Katya exchanged a long look. Maybe this would be the worst that would happen this day and they could relax.

At that moment a massive underwater explosion rocked the *Trib*, sending the boat heaving back and forth. Everyone tried to find something solid to grab on to. Sasha ran to the banquet tables and ripped the tablecloths away from the cabinetry wall on the port side, sending food and dishes flying. He pressed the buttons that opened all the technology panels filling the wall, including the big screen, and there were now keyboards and displays popping out low over the tabletop where food had been set out a moment before.

"Status report!" he shouted into a speaker.

"I.C.T. from another boat, Captain. Neutralized," came Aashir's disembodied voice from the pilothouse.

"Onscreen," Sasha called out. "Launch and light it up."

The big screen came to life with an image of the near darkness outside, just the running lights of boats on the now very choppy water and the innocent twinkle of lights from a shoreline. Most of the crew ran to their positions outside the main cabin, Maxim racing up the steps to the pilothouse ahead of them all. Only Dima, Keung, and Chen stayed with Sasha. Suddenly the nighttime scene was as bright as day, with a powerful spotlight following a large speeding motorboat from above. A drone, Katya thought. How did she not know they had one? The drone's light blazed on several men standing on the deck of the fleeing boat, looking up at the drone or back at the *Trib*.

"Painting it," Sasha called out again, as he quickly typed and pressed buttons on his array.

A loud whiz filled everyone's ears, like fireworks or artillery being fired off, followed by more. One of the men on the fleeing speedboat was suddenly covered in red. The guests gasped in horror, until the man was hit with a second color, blue this time, and many colors began to rain down on the vessel – green and yellow as well as purple – dripping down the boat and on the men on its deck. Gasps turned to laughs.

Sasha couldn't let their guests know how close they had all come to instant death. Aashir's I.C.T. was his quick-thinking code for incoming torpedo. He had detected the torpedo in time and had intercepted it with one of their own defensive weapons. The underwater explosion was still causing enough wave action to violently rock the boat, but conditions were starting to settle down.

Sasha looked over at Mason and saw real terror in his eyes as well as confusion. Mason was involved and must have just realized he'd been betrayed, Sasha was certain. He spun away from the control array and grabbed Mason by the throat, lifting him off his feet, and held him against the doorframe.

"What did they tell you?" Sasha demanded, under his breath.

"They just wanted to observe! That's what they told me, I swear!" Mason squeaked.

"You will tell Dima everything or I'll send in Katya," Sasha said quietly, with disgust, lowering him to the floor. "Dima, take him down to the hold, and when you're done, leave him in a cell. Make sure he'll stay silent."

Katya distracted the five civilian guests away from the scene with Sasha and Mason. She made up a story about a nasty gossip rag, not a very convincing one, but it was the best she could come up with quickly. She was all too aware of how close they had all just come to utter annihilation.

"The *Retribution* and its work are more famous than you might think," she told them. "We try to keep a low profile. We warned this rag not to film or bother our boat, even took out a restraining order. Sasha just found out Mason was paid by the rag to tell them where we were. The harmless paint cannonade was the *Retribution*'s response. That explosion that rocked the boat was their doing. I don't know quite what they used, but I think it was a sonic wave generator. Quite illegal, though harmless, but it sure got our attention, which was what they wanted. Sasha has contacted the authorities on shore and now the boat can't hide. Anyone who got painted topside will be easy to identify and arrest."

That last part at least was true. But the authorities would be Peter's men, and they would have their own ways of finding out who these assailants were, how Cutter had reached them, and how they happened

358

to have a speedboat with torpedo capacity in San Francisco Bay. Sasha sent Chen and Keung up to the pilothouse and demanded to see Aashir and Tuan immediately. Peter, looking ashen, followed. All the other crew members except Maxim returned to the main cabin. The remaining guests seemed satisfied with Katya's preposterous story, but they didn't quite understand the crew's overwhelming joy and spirit of celebration. When the two crewmen arrived, Tuan grinned and pointed to Aashir.

"You have Aashir to thank. He saw it coming – he did everything exactly right," Tuan said proudly.

Sasha motioned for Aashir to come to him, then shocked everyone in the room by grabbing him and kissing him hard on the mouth, ending with a long full-body hug. Aashir, dumbfounded but deliriously happy, wrapped his arms around Sasha and hugged him back, holding him through the long shudder and out the other side to peace. The crew erupted in loud cheers, and as soon as Sasha freed him from his arms, the rest of the crew began hugging Aashir, too. Sonthi was the first, tears in his eyes. Dima came up from the hold and was so happy when he heard, he too gave Aashir a hug and a kiss on the mouth, to roars of laughter. He whispered to Sasha that he'd given Mason a knockout sock in the jaw for him and had then given him a long-lasting sedative. He would share what he had learned later; useful information had already been called in to S-Branch security. Katya waited her turn patiently. She too gave Aashir a big kiss and stood for a long time just holding him tightly. She did not die this day. Sasha, the crew, her friends, they all lived, because of Aashir.

Sasha knew the crew had to settle down before they aroused suspicion among their guests. He also knew he was in no mental state to perform, and Maxim would need another hour or two, but music was what they needed. He called Kiko over and asked if he could pull himself together and gather a quartet.

"Something lighter, more familiar, upbeat," Sasha requested.

"How about Dvořák, the 'American,' Kiko suggested. "I'll grab Hau, Sonthi, and Tuan."

"Just get started as soon as possible before we lose our guests."

Sasha hurriedly arranged chairs and Sonthi brought out music stands and sheet music. Katya started to pick up scattered food and dishes from the floor, and David, Sonya, and Carlos bent to help her.

"Katya, I need to speak to you alone. Soon," David whispered.

"Help me get all this put away in the galley, then we'll find a place," she answered.

When the job was finished, David kissed Sonya and asked her to take Carlos up on deck for a few minutes, nodding towards Katya. They'd all known each other as friends for long enough that she got the hint and left quickly with Carlos, after grabbing their coats. Katya took David's hand and they slipped across the hall into her cabin and closed the door. Katya could see the concern on his face.

"What the hell, Kat? Tell me what just happened here?" David demanded. "I almost fell for your cock and bull story until I saw the crew looking like they'd just been saved from a watery grave. And Professor Takahashi told me Sasha was wearing a gun. Is everybody armed? Are you? This is so much more than a hospital ship, Kat. What have you gotten yourself into?"

"Slow down, David," Katya chided, keeping her voice calm. "I can't tell you what just happened, because nothing happened. We're fine. There was a problem and Aashir fixed it. And yes, we're all armed. This is sort of an Australian army boat as well. You could say I'm also in law enforcement now. It's just part of what we have to do to deliver medicine where it's needed. You know very well there are evil people out there, people who would hurt our clients."

"Good God, don't lie to me. What kind of law enforcement? Have you shot anybody, killed anyone?" David saw Katya blanch and look away. He hadn't been serious, and now he saw that she was. He pictured her deadly aim at target practice. "God, Kat, what kind of danger are you in? Are *we* in?"

"I can honestly say you couldn't be safer than on this boat right now. I can't tell you what happened to me when I disappeared in New York, but it changed me. I found myself in the position of having to do whatever it took to save my life and the lives of others. I found I was good at it. And I found the love of my life."

"Sasha? I know you two are together, but he's so much older, thirty years I just heard!"

"Sasha and I have been lovers for more than five months now. We couldn't be more in love."

"He didn't even know who you were when he came to our house the first time."

"That's right. And he found out. And he fell in love with me."

"So, you're going to live on this boat the rest of your life, just you and Sasha and what, ten other men?"

"Something like that. Making music, protecting the vulnerable, treating the sick and injured, and touring the world. Sasha is a complicated, difficult man, more than you know, but I love him. It's not a bad life, David. It's been a pretty wonderful one so far."

"I'm beginning to see it your way, Kat, not that I entirely believe you. I think I really don't want to know what that explosion was about. But please, please be careful. You know I'm with Sonya now, but I'll always love you."

"And you will always be my friend, David, my best friend. Listen, I'm giving you the house and my car. The signed papers and deed are on my desk. I prepaid the property taxes. When I get some money again, I'll help support our sanctuary and amnesty program. I'm afraid I have less than twelve dollars to my name right now."

David still seemed confused by what had just happened on the boat. Katya wasn't surprised he failed to process that she was giving him her house free and clear. He didn't even know she owned it.

"So, crime doesn't pay, but neither does fighting crime," David replied, confirming her take.

"Ha. Let's get back, I hear music. Or Sonya and Sasha will think we jumped ship together."

Chapter 48

The music, as always, brought everything and everyone back together. Peter returned from the pilothouse much reassured and sat with the Takahashis, David held hands with Sonya, Carlos leaned forward, entranced. Sonthi played first violin, and his rich tone lent an air of authority and precision to the piece. Hau, although not nearly as accomplished a violinist, was more than adequate on second violin, Kiko's viola was as heavenly as ever, and Tuan's ecstatic mood showed in his brilliant cello playing. After the "American" quartet, Sasha encouraged them to continue, and they moved on to Mendelssohn's Opus 12.

Katya whispered to Sasha during the applause. "Our celebration with Aashir might have an unexpected confusing side effect for our guests. We're about to be married and you just embraced Aashir passionately and kissed him on the lips."

"Do you think ravishing you on the bench would do it?" Sasha replied, a twinkle of amusement back in his eyes.

Katya stopped his talk with a long kiss. She took a moment to reflect how much Sasha had changed since she had met him, tried to imagine him saying such a thing just five months ago. After the music finished, Sasha wrapped his arm tightly around her and held her close as they stood talking with their guests around the surviving appetizers on the other tables. Hiro returned to the galley to make some fresh dishes, then sat and chatted in Japanese with the Takahashis to distract them.

"You or me next?" Sasha asked Katya.

"Oh, you certainly look quite recovered. Give them a best-of-concertos medley like you did at Davies Hall. Throw in some Mendelssohn and Bloch, a bit of Bruch and Sibelius, maybe some Korngold. Then your Bach Chaconne, of course. I'll tune up my instruments. None of them stay tuned for longer than one selection, especially my mandolin! Let's see if you and I can keep going until dinner. But don't forget to relieve Chen and Keung soon. Chen's our dinner chef and Keung is his sous-chef tonight."

"I'll send Sonthi and Kiko up again. They'll furl the mainsail and put everything on automatic. Sonthi's going to have to man the helm and help watch defenses when Maxim returns to perform. I would prefer two pairs of eyes solely on the defenses." The watch would be changed after every set of musical selections. He would let Maxim give the orders. Sasha deeply regretted not retaining Peter's men.

Sasha's virtuosity proved a perfect distraction. His playing was magnificent, drawing more gasps from Fujio, Umi, David, and Sonya. Afterward, Katya played one piece each on her guitar, now devoid of stickers, mandolin, and pipa, and then on the koto, to Hiro's, Sasha's, Fujio's, and Umi's delight. When she was finished, Sasha went up to the pilothouse to personally drag an anxious Maxim away from the helm so Sasha's quartet could perform the Ravel before dinner. Katya had never heard them play more rapturously, especially during the second movement's pizzicato. She'd insisted on the Ravel, one of her favorite quartets, and Sasha was happy to oblige for this day.

At eight, Chen outdid himself with a Chinese banquet featuring fresh fish and shellfish in a dozen styles, aromatic rice, stir-fried vegetables, and delicate noodle dishes. Maxim and Hiro invited the guests on deck; when they returned, four covered tables and sixteen chairs had been set up and awaited them and the crew, the appetizers replaced by the buffet banquet. Two of the crew ate quickly and exchanged places with the men on watch duty. After dinner, the guests were invited to revisit the pilothouse, and the main cabin was again made ready for music. Aashir, Keung, and Chen performed less challenging trios by Beethoven, his number one, and Bach's first three-part invention, then by popular demand, Sasha's quartet returned for Prokofiev's First. There was a pause for dessert: fresh warm egg tarts, dou sha bao – red bean paste buns, mango pudding, and fried sesame balls. Sasha ate one tart then left for his cabin. Katya made use of his absence to talk privately with Fujio and Umi.

"I hope you two are enjoying yourselves. Sasha and I are so happy you could come," she opened, knowing there would be questions she needed to answer.

"The music has been wonderful, Katya," Umi declared. "And the food! But who *is* this Sasha? Fujio and I saw that he was wearing a gun, in a holster! What kind of doctor wears a gun on a pleasure cruise?"

"I'm armed, too. Would you like to see my gun? Everyone is wearing a weapon, including our Consul-General. This boat is property of the Australian armed forces and we are on duty day and night to protect her. Sasha is not just captain of this boat and Chief Medical Officer, but a captain in the Australian Army as well. Peter volunteered our cruise to the local coast guard for extra eyes on the bay, in case of a boating accident or trouble on a New Year's Eve in San Francisco."

Umi found she had nothing to say, so wisely just nodded her head. Fujio laughed, amused at how Katya could still silence his wife, and said he liked Sasha, but he couldn't possibly be thirty years older than Katya, as he'd overheard.

"I'm afraid I have to correct you again," Katya said, looking forward to their reaction. "Sasha has held the rank of captain for thirty-four years! He was not yet twenty-six when he joined the Australian Army as a surgeon. We'll be celebrating Sasha's 60th birthday after midnight. I had him pegged at forty-two tops when we met. Amazing, isn't he?"

Fujio and Umi were staggered. Fujio had recently celebrated his fifty-seventh birthday, but he looked more than two decades older than Sasha. Katya smiled and promised to talk more later. It was past eleven and time for her to get ready. Sasha had just reappeared. He'd shed his jacket and holster and changed into his light blue shirt. Boldly rolling up his sleeves as he walked, he decided he would no longer hide his tattooed forearm from public view. He sat next to Fujio and ignored his staring at his arm as he engaged Umi in Japanese. Katya nodded to Aashir and Tuan, and they disappeared with her into the crew's quarters.

As she left, she observed Maxim, Dima, Hiro, and Keung, who would be playing second cello, arranging chairs and stands for the music that would set the stage for her and Sasha's big moment. No more drama, no more attacks, please, she prayed. She felt the speed of the boat increase as the motors augmented the headsail. The rocking intensified as they hit the heavier waves of the open ocean, then the *Trib* lifted onto her hydrofoils and all was smooth. The *Trib* had already sailed under the Golden Gate Bridge and they were headed far out of the bay at around twenty knots, twelve nautical miles to go to reach international waters by midnight.

At the appointed time, the quintet commenced the slow, heartbreaking Adagio from the Schubert Quintet in C Major, the "two-cello." Sasha had at first wanted something livelier, but again Katya insisted, reminding him the music was plenty lively in the middle section, that there was no more beautiful music in the world for her. She told him how moved she'd been by their astounding performance of the same selection on Bora Bora with Sasha playing first violin, Tuan playing the second cello.

A few minutes before the end, Sasha stood up and walked to an open space in front of the quintet, facing the stairs and hallway to the crew's quarters. Katya came slowly up the steep, narrow stairs, followed by Aashir and Tuan, each carrying an elaborate flower lei over one arm. Katya was dressed as she'd been at the "wedding" in Bora Bora, in the blue and white bare-shouldered Tahitian-style dress, the same blue and white silk scarf tied around her now healed arm, the scarf decorated with exotic flowers as before, the same kind of flowers in her hair. She was barefoot but wore an anklet of flowers around one leg. Sasha gave her his near smile, surprised and delighted with her appearance. Aashir leaned into her and whispered that he'd always wanted to be a bridesmaid, nearly causing her to lose her composure in laughter.

She and Sasha stood facing each other, holding both hands, until the music came to its glorious conclusion. Their small audience guessed something momentous was about to happen and held their applause, watching the couple. The crew set down their instruments and took on new roles. Maxim stood before them as officiator, Hiro moved next to Sasha, and Dima behind him. Keung hurried up to the pilothouse to relieve Kiko and Sonthi, Hau adjusted the cameras. Sonthi quietly took his place next to Dima. Keung had reluctantly volunteered to do double duty at the helm and watch during the ceremony, but only after Hau promised he would video record the ceremony for him to view later, and that he himself would replace him in a half-hour. Keung would be able to hear everything from the pilothouse with the door open.

"Friends," began Maxim, "we are here to witness the union of Katya Zhang Kaplan and Sasha Borodin. It has been Sasha's wish to have this union take place at the precise moment of transition between hours, days, years, centuries, and millennia, between the last moments of his fifty-ninth year and the first of his sixtieth."

366

Maxim glanced over at Kiko, who was watching the time, then back to Sasha, and nodded. Sasha remained calm and serious as he began his speech. Both he and Katya had decided not to use any sort of traditional vow.

"Katya, I don't know if two people have ever met and fallen in love under stranger circumstances. Fate has brought us together and has threatened to tear us apart time and time again. But we have persevered, and I have fallen more deeply in love with you with each passing day. You have taught me to live again, to love again, to discover the romantic in me you knew was there. I know that I ask you to accept much – permanent roommates," and here there was laughter from the crew, "tight quarters, and not much money. A captain's salary will just have to stretch for both of us. You and Peter well know if I had more I would just give it all away. I love you, Katya Zhang Kaplan, and I do not want to be separated from you for even a moment as long as I live."

Tuan stepped forward and handed him the lei. Sasha put it carefully over Katya's head and kissed her. There were a few audible gasps from their guests as Sasha spoke, but Katya didn't take her eyes off of Sasha to see from whom. It was her turn now and she spoke clearly and calmly. She had not written a speech ahead of time. She would answer Sasha's.

"Sasha, my love for you has also grown stronger every day. You have given me everything – your heart, your trust, your confidences. You amaze me constantly with your brilliance and your selfless consideration of others. You are not giving me permanent roommates, you are giving me the brothers I never had. You are giving me a family closer than any real family has ever been. And we will have no need of money. We can live on love, as they say, as long as we live on this boat. I have already given all that I have away, even my house. Let no one say either of us married for money," she said to more laughter from the crew. "I love you, Sasha Borodin, and I cannot, will not, live without you."

Aashir stepped forward with the second lei, handing it to Katya, and Sasha stooped a little to let her place it over his head. They kissed again.

"Do you, Sasha Borodin, wish to marry this woman?" Maxim asked.

"I do."

367

"And do you, Katya Zhang Kaplan, wish to marry this man?"

"I absolutely do."

Maxim smiled. "Do you have the rings?" he asked, catching Kiko's nod.

Kiko turned on a recording of a bell chiming the twelve strokes of midnight. Katya grew concerned that the entire crew, Maxim included, looked like they were choking up. Please no drama, she prayed again. Hiro at least was able to respond quickly and handed a plain gold band to Sasha – mercury-free artisanal Fairtrade gold, Sasha had assured her.

"With this ring I thee wed," Sasha said calmly, as he placed the ring on her finger.

Hiro handed the second band to Katya, who slipped it quickly onto Sasha's finger.

"And with this ring I thee wed."

"As Co-captain of this boat, I pronounce you equal partners, husband and wife," Maxim said hurriedly as the recording rang out its twelfth chime. The recording changed to loud wedding bells.

Sasha and Katya melted into a lei crushing full body embrace and a long, lingering kiss. There was applause from their guests, none louder than Peter's, who had been taken completely by surprise, and loud cheers from the crew. Sasha reached behind him and handed Katya what seemed to be a loose scroll. She opened it up and saw it was the bark cloth marriage certificate from Bora Bora, the one that had caused him to run. He'd already signed it and he now handed her a pen. She nearly broke down herself as she signed it, loving him even more for the thought. Maxim signed it after her as officiator, having received an online Universal Life Church ordination to augment what he'd discovered was his insufficient legal status as a ship's captain. Maxim, along with Hiro and Sonthi as witnesses, signed the official legally binding marriage certificate, and handed it to Peter to file for them.

"Happy New Year!" the crew shouted.

Peter and the other guests had been so startled by the surprise wedding they'd forgotten the moment of the new year and new millennium had arrived. Chen handed around champagne glasses, with sparkling apple cider for Sasha and Katya. The crew crowded around the newlyweds offering congratulations, and taking the opportunity to hug and kiss Katya: Sasha didn't mind for once. The

Takahashis seemed to have overcome their reluctance and looked almost accepting of the idea of their Katya marrying this older man. Sonya and Carlos were thrilled, and David gave Katya an especially long hug, his eyes moist. Hau held Katya's face and kissed her right on the lips, then rushed up the inside pilothouse steps to keep his promise to relieve Keung. Peter was beside himself, happy for them but teasing about how they could have left him out of the loop.

"It's all right. I'll get my vengeance," he laughed. He asked loudly for everyone's attention. "This moment after midnight on this special New Year's Eve marks not just the end of one millennium and the beginning of the next, but also the date that has been chosen to celebrate the birth of one of the most remarkable men on our planet. I'm speaking of course of our very own Sasha Borodin."

The crew erupted in loud whistles and cheers, and Peter held up his hands to be allowed to continue.

"Since Sasha gave me notice of this party five months ago, I've had plenty of time to put together a presentation about his life, and to arrange quite a few well-wishers, both live and recorded. I see Sasha looking concerned already! Sasha, my dear friend, I promise everything I'm about to present can be safely viewed by our civilian guests and will not embarrass you. This is a celebration, not a roast! So, please get Sasha a seat where he can see the screen and gather around."

Sasha was looking more than just concerned. He was already looking embarrassed, almost horrified. Katya got him to sit down and rubbed his shoulders until he resigned himself that Peter was unstoppable. The screen lit up, showing a small group of people on a live feed, two men, a woman, and a girl around sixteen. One of the distinguished looking men gazed out at them, then, recognizing Sasha, began speaking in good but accented English.

"Sasha, this is Joseph Estrada, President of the Philippines. Here with me is my Cabinet Secretary, his wife, and you know their daughter Sandra. Your prime minister informed us in strictest confidence just this last week of your involvement in Sandra's rescue. We're many hours ahead of you here, but it's still January first. Since I hear you won't allow me to reward you in any other way, I want to at least wish you a happy birthday and personally offer you and your crew the gratitude of our nation for saving Sandra and the other forty-four women caught up in that terrible web of human trafficking, for

369

ending the threat. I know you did so at great peril to your own lives and we will forever be grateful.

"I was already well aware of your decades of medical clinics around our island nation that have touched and enriched the lives of many of our poorest citizens. We are also eternally grateful for the clean water, solar power, and sanitation systems you are continuing to install in our remotest regions. Thank you, Sasha, and my thanks to the entire crew of your hospital boat. My good friend and his family would also like to thank you personally."

"Happy Birthday and thank you from the bottoms of our hearts from my wife and me for safely bringing home our Sandra," added the Secretary. "She has been speaking nonstop about your crew's bravery, especially of the woman who allowed herself to be taken captive in order to facilitate her rescue. Is she there with you? Is that her next to you?"

"I can't believe I'm seeing you," Sandra shouted out, when Katya nodded. "You had on such a disguise! I never would have recognized you! Oh, thank you! I still can't believe you all came for me. I had given up hope, then you came to us in that awful place and got us all out and off that ship. And I can see the man who drove my Zodiac behind you. Thank you too!" she said to Dima, who nodded, tears forming in the big man's eyes. Katya decided to answer for herself and the men, who looked incapable of speech.

"Sandra, you have your life ahead of you now. Enjoy it. Give back to the world, make it a better place. That is the best way you can thank us."

"I will, I am giving back! My parents are helping me change the lives of all of the women who were saved with me, with money, jobs, housing, whatever they need. We meet together all the time! I've made a film for you. All of them wanted to thank you personally, although they didn't know who you were! Please, please come, all of you, come and see us next time you are in the Philippines! I want to hug all of you!"

A video followed, with many groups of women, family groups, or occasionally a single woman, smiling and looking into the camera and saying the words *thank you*, in English or Tagalog. Katya could tell that Sasha was moved, as loathe as he was to receive thanks of this kind. A second video began as soon as the first had faded out, views of the excited crowds at the clinic stops all along the many islands of the Philippines at the beginning of their world expedition: the crew with stethoscopes listening to heartbeats and examining patients in their cabin/doctor's offices, using the X-ray and other machines, Katya smiling and speaking Tagalog as she organized a clinic, Sasha and Maxim in minor surgery, peering over their face masks, Kiko and Sasha advising in Tagalog on a clean water system with a village group. Katya tried to figure out who had been taking the videos. Was one of their own crew involved in Peter's plot to memorialize Sasha's work?

Katya was certain when the video moved on to a few scenes from some of the rest of their stops on the expedition that had taken them most of the way around the world – people crowding the docks in country after country, Sasha triaging patients, in surgery, Katya carrying a small child in Eritrea and in Guatemala, giving inoculations, the crew rushing to assist at the site of a disaster, Sasha examining a newborn in Somalia, the proud mother standing by... The clinic videos were occasionally interrupted with scenes from one of their day-off adventures – walking through the root-covered ruins of Angkor Thom, Katya and Sasha holding orphaned baby orangutans, the crew riding camels in Egypt, visiting the restored remnants of the ancient Roman port at Caesarea in Israel, the *Retribution* sailing past an isle in Greece. This last had to be a close-up satellite image. They had surely been watched every moment of their trip. Katya was certain that Hau was the missing crew member in the video. He must have been the one filming, the sneak.

The video continued with moments from their stops in local hospitals: Sasha being shown candidates for artificial limbs or eyes, demonstrating his models, taking careful measurements, asking about their lives in their native languages, making dates for the completed robotically enhanced prostheses to be attached, the brain implants inserted. The video faded out and another began: before and after photos of a dozen men, women and children with missing arms, legs, hands, feet, eyes, then with their prosthetic devices in place, smiling, well-dressed, followed by a scene of children in shorts and t-shirts playing. One had to look closely to see that they all had prostheses: the tell-tale flesh-colored sleeve that covered the connection of prosthesis to flesh on an arm or leg. The children stopped their play and ran to the cameraman, waving, laughing. The camera panned over a group of children at a different location and country, a school. All

371

were reading, and they turned their eyes to the camera. All had one barely noticeable artificial eye. They all smiled and waved.

The video faded again and a new one focused on a group of older doctors in white coats in front of a University of Sydney sign, waving and smiling, and shouting out "Happy Birthday, Sasha." The oldest looking doctor spoke, saying how thrilled they all were with the news of Sasha's latest medical tour, how they had been made aware of his amazing clinic work over the decades in Southeast Asia, how they welcomed him back to a leading role in their prosthetics department. He went on to say they were astounded by the present generation of prostheses coming out of Australogic Laboratories and couldn't wait to work with Sasha again in person.

Another fade out, and the camera focused on the unmistakable silhouette of Bora Bora, closing in on a recording of Sylvie and Luc standing and waving in their new clinic building, Sylvie wishing him a Happy Birthday and thanking him again for designing, building, and equipping her clinic, then walking into the other rooms, crowded with their Tahitian friends, waving and shouting Happy Birthday.

A new video began, catching the men at their dawn work out, Katya doing her one arm pushups, Sasha and Katya emerging from snorkeling, from scuba diving, Sasha doing somersaults on horseback, Sasha in an especially virtuosic moment of *Gaspard,* then on solo violin, with a quartet, an octet, Katya at the piano then singing as Edith Piaf, Katya and Sasha caught in several kisses and embraces, then ending with Sasha and Katya in feather headdresses and leis receiving leaf bracelets at the Tahitian wedding ceremony, Katya wearing the same dress she had on today, the image remaining frozen on the screen. This wasn't Hau's work – this could only have been Jake.

Katya looked over the gathering of civilian guests. They would certainly have formed a better opinion of her Sasha after these videos, even without any knowledge of his secret career as an inventor and innovator. They looked suitably impressed, and she smiled to herself that she cared so much. Sasha deserved some accolades. He was always so busy avoiding them. At least until recently. He was looking rather proud of himself, she had to admit.

She was surprised Peter had included the video from the President's office in the Philippines. The *Trib*'s work chasing criminals was almost as sacred a secret as his inventive genius. The videos with his prostheses also came a bit too close to implying Sasha was more than just a neurosurgeon working with the innovations of others. Peter must have trusted that the five civilians on board would never talk to the press. She laughed to herself that she would have to ask David if Peter had made them all sign non-disclosure agreements. But Peter was not finished. He pushed a button and a new image appeared on the screen, another live feed, a man in a suit, a familiar face to Katya.

"Friends, we have another well-wisher for Sasha," Peter said, smiling. "This is John Howard, the Prime Minister of Australia. He also has some important news for our Sasha. And I have some for him. Mr. Howard, Sasha has just surprised me with a New Year's Eve wedding to our Katya."

"Sasha, there you are! Am I hearing this right? Then I need to double my congratulations! Or triple them! Happy New Year on your time, happy birthday, and best wishes to the two of you! Katya, I hope I have the pleasure of meeting you soon. I cannot thank you enough for what you have done for Sasha, and therefore for our country. I wish I could make you an honorary Australian! Now that you're married to one, I hope you *do* choose to become a citizen! But here's what I can do. Peter had me look into the matter of your not being paid. You are as much a member of the crew as any man there. You are now an official assistant to Dr. Borodin, with a paycheck retroactive to the beginning of your service in July. How does that grab you, as they say in the States?"

"I am overwhelmed, Mr. Howard. Like Sasha, you will find me giving most of it away. My house, my former house, is a sanctuary for Central American refugees and the money will go a long way towards resettling them. Thank you."

Peter leaned over to whisper the sum to both of them. She didn't say how unfair such a generous salary of sixty thousand Australian dollars would be, almost fifteen thousand more than any of the doctors on the crew, more than she now knew Sasha made as captain.

"A woman after Sasha's heart indeed! And Sasha, Peter also had me look into the fact that despite all you do for your country, you accept no pay besides your captain's salary, and that you refuse all promotions. You have served your country tirelessly for over forty-two years. I know I cannot reveal what else you do for us, but we owe you. We know there are other projects to help the poor and improve our planet you would like to see happen. We're creating a fund for you. It will be your money to do with as you wish, yours to monitor and control, in fact, a good portion of it is your own money, profits set aside for you from your work for…"

"Sir! A reminder we have civilians aboard," Peter interrupted.

"Ah yes, I'll let Peter explain where the money comes from, Sasha," Mr. Howard sighed. "Your fund will start with…"

"Again, sir, a reminder."

"… a whole lot of money, and we'll add a substantial salary to handle it, that's in addition to your captain's salary, a bargain considering what you've done for our economy. We'll let you do most of our foreign aid this year! That's your birthday present from your country, Sasha!"

"Mr. Howard, you really have left me speechless. I can't even fathom having a fund of my own. The first idea that came to my mind was a fleet of boats like the *Retribution*, then there's free medical clinics around the globe, ocean clean-up, housing…" Sasha said, his head spinning such that he thought he'd better stop talking. So much for being speechless. "Thank you, Mr. Howard."

"Careful there, Sasha, you'll find even the amount of money I'm talking about will disappear quickly given your lofty goals! Congratulations again to the two of you!"

The screen faded. Peter leaned over again to Sasha and Katya and whispered the sums Mr. Howard had been forbidden to say. Three billion for the fund, a half million in salary. Katya and Sasha looked at each other. Katya suddenly started laughing and couldn't stop herself. Sasha and Peter tried to calm her down, but she kept on laughing for a long while, then dried her eyes and shook her head.

"I'm so sorry. That was just too, too much. Are you sure this isn't April Fool's Day and not New Year's? Did you just become one of the wealthiest men on the planet, my poor knight, my not so humble Sasha?"

"It won't be my money for long," Sasha whispered back. shaking his head. "That fund is getting spent. As for my salary, I'm starting by adding thirty thousand a year to each of the crew's salaries out of my own to continue until my government pays them what they deserve." He looked over at Katya, who smiled and nodded to him. He then turned to Aashir and spoke aloud. "Aashir, you're in need of a job when you leave with Tuan, who will be making very little in his residency. I'm naming you two co-directors of my fund, for whatever

374

you want to be paid. I'm going to need a whole lot of help." Sasha addressed their civilian guests. "Please, I cannot, will not, have my name openly associated with this fund, well, for lots of reasons. I know you will all respect my wishes."

Everyone began excitedly talking at once. The air of celebration on the boat grew more and more wild as the reality of all that had just happened sank in. David finally found a moment to speak to Katya alone.

"So, you're back to being Kat the Hero," he said, only half in jest. "Now that I've learned what you did for Sandra and those captive women, I am truly blown away, but I wish you wouldn't take such risks. You might get yourself killed. But what you're doing is really quite amazing. And I had no idea who Sasha was before now, though I still feel I only know the half of it. How could you not love him? Take care, Kat. I can't accept the gift of your house, you know that. I promise to keep it in good shape for you... I don't know when I'll see you again after this."

"I don't know either. Things have gotten more complicated than I can tell you. I do know we're headed to straight to Australia, not Hawaii as we will announce, and we'll be safe there. It will make me very happy to give you all the money you need for the house and the sanctuary program now."

David didn't seem to relax at her reassurance of her safety, but felt the need to lighten the mood. "Behave yourself, dear Kat. I thought I was hopelessly jealous of how handsome Sasha was, but good God, each of these men is more striking than the next! I... I will be thinking of you every day."

David gave her one more hug and moved off to find Sonya before Katya could see how worried he was about her. Katya collapsed onto a bench, overwhelmed by all that had just happened: their near death, the videos, her new income, Sasha's sudden fortune. The wedding itself seemed a fantasy, already forgotten.

Sasha took the opportunity to speak privately with Peter while Katya and David were talking.

"Why didn't I know about this money?" Sasha demanded. "All these years I could have been affecting real change..."

"You made it quite clear on numerous occasions that you were satisfied with just your captain's salary," Peter replied. "I myself had no idea how much your account had accumulated. It was your dear

Katya who pushed me to look into your finances. The decision was made long before my time to put aside ten percent of the labs' annual profits into a special account for you. The money was invested and the profits reinvested in ways S-Branch thought you would approve of and, I must admit, ways that would benefit the government as well. I've been working to untangle it all for months now. It was Mr. Howard's decision to add additional money. He began by doubling the sum. He also thought ten percent seemed rather low since there would be no money at all without you. Australogic Labs will be donating twenty percent of their profits annually to your fund from now on."

"I'm just overwhelmed, Peter, overwhelmed. You wait and see how fast I can give it all away."

The *Retribution* was already back off her hydrofoils before she entered the calmer waters of the bay, the crew rotating quickly through the single man helm/watch duties, as no one wanted to leave the main cabin for long. Sasha looked over at Katya sitting alone and gave her his near smile.

"But you've managed to completely overshadow our wedding, Peter. We weren't finished."

Taking Katya's hand, Sasha pulled her to her feet and nodded to Maxim, then kicked off his sandals so he was barefoot like Katya. Maxim hurried back to his violin, Dima, Hiro, Sonthi, and Keung quickly taking up their instruments as well. Everyone else moved to the benches as Sasha and Katya stood holding hands in the small open space once again. Katya didn't know what Sasha had in mind until the quintet began playing the transcendent Allegretto from Beethoven's Symphony Number Seven. She wondered at the choice – she'd always found the opening dark and fateful... perhaps because of its theme of triumph over adversity. Sasha placed a hand on her lower back and swept her into a dance. Sasha had never danced with her. He was as smooth and graceful as the ballet student he had once been. Katya couldn't take her eyes off of his, couldn't stop smiling. Sasha the romantic was back. But Sasha the rational was there as well. Knowing the Beethoven was eight minutes long, in precisely three minutes Sasha swept Katya over towards David and the two old friends took a spin together laughing, the fears of just minutes ago swept aside.

Sasha nodded for Carlos, then Fujio to dance with Katya next, then Peter, grinning from ear to ear, took a turn, whispering to her how lovely she looked, then reluctantly passing her to Aashir, as the quintet switched to play one famous waltz after another. Small as he was, Aashir was an excellent dancer. Looking up into her face, he told her how thrilled he was with Sasha's offer to head the new fund with Tuan, how he knew he would be working closely with both of them, was so happy he wouldn't be saying goodbye to her. With a kiss he handed her smoothly off to Tuan, who managed a few fast spins and a dip before Kiko stepped in. Smiling shyly, Kiko thanked her for making his Sasha such a happier man, and promised he would do anything in the world for her.

Embarrassed by his own emotions, Kiko quickly moved to take a hand-off of Dima's viola and join the quintet while Chen took his turn dancing with Katya, holding her awkwardly but smiling too broadly to speak. Dima, waiting impatiently, took her from Chen, enveloping her in his loving bear hug, as overcome with emotion as Kiko. He, too, was speechless as they danced. Tuan took over Keung's cello, and he rushed to steal Katya from Dima, who then bounded up the steps towards the pilothouse to relieve Hau, tears pouring down his cheeks.

Handsome, handsome Keung, Katya thought as he swirled her around the small space – she'd never imagined being swept into his arms. He'd let down his top knot and his long black hair waved sensuously around his face. Keung oozed sexual magnetism – she'd learned from Chen that women flocked to Keung at each port. Katya admonished herself for her attraction to him, on her wedding day to the man she worshiped. She found it difficult to think of these men as her colleagues, her brothers, while dancing with them. What was her attraction to Asian men... then she laughed to herself thinking Sasha shared the same attraction, even if just subconsciously. Hell, they didn't have to be Asian, just muscular and good-looking.

Hiro abandoned his cello to be next, but was frustrated that Keung kept purposely dancing Katya away from him. Placing himself in their path, he commandeered her into his own arms and proved he was just as good a dancer as Keung. Hiro told her what a lucky man Sasha was to have discovered her first; she was everything he could imagine wanting in a woman. He then made her laugh by teasing that he'd only ever loved Japanese women, that her ancestry had to be part Japanese, not Chinese, after all.

Hau stepped in, his perfect white teeth gleaming in his movie-star face, declaring himself to be her devoted servant for giving Sasha a sense of humor, and for bringing new life to the *Trib*. Sonthi handed him his violin and Hau replaced him in what was now a quartet, after first giving Katya a dramatic low bow. Katya was surprised what a terrible dancer Sonthi was. For being so musical, he couldn't find the rhythm with his feet. When had Sonthi ever danced in his life, she mused. Maxim was last to have a turn dancing with his Katya, Chen standing by with his own violin, ready to take over in the quartet. Sonthi looked relieved when Maxim cut in, but stopped to plant a kiss on Katya's forehead before retreating.

Maxim was almost as smooth a dancer as Sasha. He expressed his love and admiration as they moved, apologizing for his first moments of doubt. He would be her big brother, now and always, watching out for her, but expressed the hope that he would never have to choose between loyalty to Sasha and to her.

Sasha had to tap Maxim several times on the shoulder to get him to release Katya back to him for the final dance. Katya hugged Maxim closer, kissed him on the cheek, then pushed him away, laughing, as she returned to Sasha. The quartet sped up the tempo of another waltz as they twirled in the small space, then the music took a short break.

Dropping onto a bench, Sasha enveloped Katya in his arms and they melted into a long kiss. Leaning over to his ear, she whispered how thankful she was no one had stepped on her bare feet, then how grateful she was to him for surprising her. She declared she couldn't have been happier.

"Promise me this won't be the only time we ever dance," Katya entreated.

"I will dance with you on your birthday next month, on every holiday, birthday and anniversary, Katya." *If we survive*, Sasha said to himself, squeezing her tighter. *If we survive*.

"I will make you keep that promise! You dance divinely, Sasha. Did you and Le dance together? I hope that you did!"

Sasha caught his breath. How could she ask that question, but then, how could she not... He was moved by her understanding of his undying love for his first wife, that Le would be in his thoughts at this moment. Sasha felt Le's approval of his decision to open himself to love again. To dance again.

"Yes, yes we did, Katya," he finally answered. *Every night of our life together,* he didn't add.

As soon as the music started up again, David pulled Sonya out onto the newly opened space for a long dance, then ceded the floor to Fujio and Umi. When the music ended, everyone cheered and applauded. The celebration resumed for another hour in a new mood of joy.

Katya knew it was time to bring the celebration to a close. The *Retribution* was nearing the end of her sailing, the crew rotating quickly through the helm/watch duties, as no one wanted to leave the main cabin for long. She sidled up to Sasha and whispered in his ear. He nodded, walking over to pick up Hiro's cello. Katya retrieved her guitar, and by the time they'd arranged two chairs in the music area, the small group had quieted and found places to listen.

"Sasha and I have one last musical selection for you tonight, or this morning I should say," Katya told her tired, attentive friends. "We will be furling the headsail and motoring back to the dock soon. I recommend putting on your coats and going out on deck to enjoy the view of the city as we return. Chen and Hiro have arranged a few last snacks for anyone still hungry, and I thank them for the delicious food they worked so hard to prepare. This has been an emotional night for us all, with an ending as surprising to Sasha and me as it has been for you. Thank you, Peter, for all that you've done, for the videos, and for making this incredible, and I do mean incredible, change in our fortunes possible through your advocacy. I've just learned we'll be departing for Hawaii later today, on our way back to Sydney, which will complete an around the world trip for our *Trib*. This last piece of music was written for singer and piano, and I have found an arrangement for cello and guitar that will allow Sasha and me to perform together for you. I knew I wouldn't be able to sing at the end of this celebration! This is 'Siete Canciones Populares Españolas,' Seven Popular Spanish Songs, by Manual de Falla."

Katya and Sasha gazed at each other for a long moment before they began. Sasha could have played an arrangement with his violin instead, but he liked the deeper, richer tone on the cello for this piece. Besides, with the cello, it would be easier to look at her while he played. They were both ready to be alone in their cabin, their bed telescoped out, making love. Only five people on board, four if you discounted David, were unaware of the dangers they would be facing

379

every day from now on. Their new-found fortune would be worth nothing if they didn't live to make sure the money was put to good use. This Cutter had come as close as any enemy ever to blowing the *Trib* to oblivion. He would not stop.

Chapter 49

Twelve hours later, the *Trib* sailed under the Golden Gate Bridge once again, heading to the open sea. Sasha waited until they were far from sight of land before having the sails furled and engaging the hydrofoil wings and motors at one-quarter maximum speed. The air of celebration on board morphed into one of gloom. The threat against them had been determined to be ongoing and imminent. They'd been ordered to return to Sydney with all haste, their leisurely tour of Hawaii, Japan, Korea, mainland China, and Taiwan put off indefinitely. S-Branch made sure the *Trib* was expected in Hawaii in just over four days and had a dozen agents in place to trap any attackers.

Sensing the mood of the crew, Sasha devised a plan to cheer them up. They would make an unexpected stop back in Bora Bora and be off again before either S-Branch or their enemy could catch up with them. Katya reminded him they were surely under S-Branch's constant satellite surveillance, but he didn't care. As long as Cyrus Cutter was looking for them in Hawaii, they would be safe. Maxim was the only other person who knew. Sasha would make an announcement over dinner.

Katya's brain was racing to create a plan that would save them from Cutter's threat of extermination. Additional information still being decrypted from Markus Cutter's computer files by the FBI was proving helpful, along with testimony from two of the men captured from the attacking speedboat. The new information also sealed Mason's fate. He was as corrupt as Katya had imagined, and as cruel. Mason had said enough to Dima to have him taken off the *Trib* in handcuffs by the FBI, after their guests had departed. The FBI had been quietly building a case against him over the last five months. To save himself, Bill had turned against Mason and had spilled a decade of secrets going back to their years together in the CIA. Jake, a recent hire, was determined to be innocent.

Faced with irrefutable evidence, Mason confessed to having discovered Markus Cutter's plan to abduct Sasha in New York and allowing it to happen, knowing Sasha would suffer, could well be tortured or killed before he might be rescued. Mason had thought he would make himself a hero by eliminating Markus, who had been blackmailing him for years, guaranteeing his advancement in Interpol. The timing of Mason's raid on Markus's compound had been no fluke. Sasha's arrival in the van was to have been the distraction, like Katya's fight with Gunner. Successfully rescuing Sasha would just have been a well-rewarded bonus.

Since Katya had gotten the van to arrive several hours earlier than expected, since she had so boldly engineered Sasha's escape, Mason's original plans for the raid had been scrapped. She had no doubt his raid would have failed without her, that Sasha and the federal agents would have all died. The responsibility for Derek's death was on Mason's head as well. Thanks to Katya's work inside the compound, the raid had worked, and Mason had received the accolades and promotion he'd desired... until his arrest. Katya enjoyed picturing Mason in a federal prison somewhere but hoped he wasn't making deals to procure his freedom or early release. The arresting FBI agents had informed her Mason was spewing hatred for her. She already knew Markus Cutter's man Gunner, safely in prison for now, wanted her dead.

Pieces of a plan against Cyrus Cutter began to grow clearer in Katya's mind. Without telling Sasha what they were, she convinced him to use some of his new funds to have construction begun immediately on three duplicates of the *Trib*, even before their arrival in Sydney, part of Sasha's envisioned new fleet. Katya also casually asked where the submarine they'd liberated in the Philippines was now located. She was thrilled to discover it was already in the secret boat harbor at S-Branch's Sydney headquarters, their destination. All her hopes were on the War Room session that would take place upon their arrival. She prayed her ideas would be listened to, that the S-Branch leadership wasn't a bunch of testosterone-crazed old Aussie males, as Sasha had intimated.

At least Sasha hadn't been too beset with concern to pay attention to her needs. They made love when they finally arrived in their berth at three in the morning, then he'd let her sleep in, along with rest of the crew not on duty. When she awoke, Sasha had already finished his dawn workout alone in the main cabin and had put in an hour with his laboratory. The long talk midmorning with the FBI agents carting Mason away had dampened any last celebratory mood. To cheer her,

Sasha promised her a tour of his Australogic Research and Development laboratories while they were in Sydney. She would finally see the hidden component of his life, the part that made him a national treasure worthy of special governmental protection. Or a cash cow under constant watch, as Sasha bluntly put it.

The glum faces at dinner perked up considerably with Sasha's announcement; they would have exactly fifteen hours in Bora Bora, with an expected arrival time of 7 a.m. and a nighttime departure. Sasha was almost too embarrassed to get the words out, but he managed to inform the men that all cabins, even his own, would be available during their stay for any last chance trysts with the natives, and to not forget the lanyards. The men laughed and planned how they would spend their precious hours, looking forward to not thinking about Cyrus Cutter and the possibility of death for a short time, and started plotting a goodbye celebration for Tuan and Aashir while they were there. The two would stay in Sydney with them long enough to help create a survival plan but would then head on to Ho Chi Minh City to start their new lives together. The rest of the trip passed quickly, with music keeping their spirits high.

Sasha didn't forget his wedding day promise: he declared the crossing of the equator a holiday this time. He and his quartet played her the Borodin first string quartet, then Maxim took over first violin, and joined by Sonthi, the quartet performed Borodin's second quartet while Sasha danced with her. This time, however, none of the crew were given a turn. Sasha kept her all to himself.

The *Trib* motored quietly into the Bora Bora harbor and tied up at le Hédonisme's dock about the same time that she was expected in Hawaii. S-Branch was able to intercept not one, but two torpedo-loaded boats and diffused a bomb at the landing dock in Honolulu. No one breathed any easier on the *Trib*. Their foe was determined and well-armed and would keep trying. It hadn't taken long for a Cutter to find Katya on Bora Bora the last time, so they knew they couldn't linger any longer than planned. S-Branch had been furious with Sasha's contradiction of direct orders, but not surprised. Satellite surveillance would continue 24/7 and the small airport would be carefully monitored.

Sasha and Katya were first off the boat and hurried to see Luc and Sylvie. Hiro had already hit the island with a communications disrupter that would put all internet and cell phone reception on their

383

portion of the island out of commission for the length of their stay. They would be asking Luc and Sylvie to not let any of their guests leave for the day, and to not let in any deliveries or even visitors, unless they were checking in to the resort.

Despite the early hour, the Roussels were overjoyed to see Sasha and Katya and learn of the *Retribution*'s return. As soon as they learned the *Trib* was under threat, they were more than happy to agree to the conditions of her visit. The Roussels would make excuses to their clients and promise all communication would be restored by the next day. Word of their arrival spread quickly among the staff, and the crew found themselves mobbed by their Tahitian friends and admirers as they departed the *Trib*. Maxim put the two-man watch duty at two and a half hours per shift, with Dima and Hiro replacing Aashir and Tuan for first watch. Katya and Sasha would take a shift as well.

Katya, Sasha, Sylvie, and Luc had just settled on the front porch when Sylvie took notice of Katya's ring, then Sasha's.

"Mon Dieu, tell me you two decided to marry after all!" she cried out, taking Katya's ringed hand in hers.

"Right on New Year's Eve, the stroke of midnight, aboard the *Trib*. It was all Sasha's idea. The birthday celebration came right after," Katya answered. "I wore the same dress and we had flower leis specially ordered. It almost didn't happen at all, but we pulled it off," she said, looking over at Sasha, who just shook his head with that near smile she loved so much.

"She never looked more beautiful," he said.

"Congratulations, the both of you!"

"We enjoyed seeing all of you on the video," Katya said. "Thank you for doing that. I can only guess that Jake was the videographer. He took videos of us all over the island, too. Did he really take a video of us at the wedding he was mocking us with?"

"Oh no, we gave him that footage, minus the last few minutes. We would have presented the video to you after the ceremony since it was part of the package you, well whoever, paid for. The dance is on the video, too."

"I never saw anyone filming the dance!" Katya said in surprise.

"No one ever does. I wonder why!" Sylvie laughed.

"I can see why no one would notice," Sasha intoned, completely serious. "The audience would be so distracted by…"

"Sasha…" Katya grinned and took his hand.

384

"Ah…"

Sylvie looked back and forth between them and smiled.

"Well, I think we're ready to take a copy now, especially since it's missing those last few minutes," Katya continued. "And I would like to talk with Jake while we're here."

"He and Atea got married too, about four months ago," Luc said. "Seems there's a baby on the way. He got a job with security at one of the bigger resorts and they're helping him with citizenship. Your disruption of our communications will make it difficult to contact him, but we'll give it a try. I'll send someone over to their house and maybe he can stop by."

"I would appreciate that."

"We've come into a bit of money since we were last here, so we would be happy to pay you for our meals while we're here today, in fact I insist," Sasha said. "That is if we can get our crew out of the water and off the beaches long enough to eat. They're so happy to be back here, if even for such a short time."

"Then off with you, too," Sylvie laughed. "We'll talk over meals, but you should be snorkeling and scuba diving, maybe even hiking up to Alain's horses. The stars have been glorious, and you'll have time to see them before you leave. What am I saying, you see them from the *Trib*! We're so excited to see you, I still can't believe you're here! I know I can't ask about what kind of threat you're facing, but I pray you find a solution soon. Just put Katya on it. If anyone can get out of trouble, it's you, Katya."

"I'm sure she's already working on it," Sasha replied, giving Katya a knowing look.

The hours sped by, crammed with everything one would want to do on a Tahitian island before dying. The crew even found time for snorkeling and visiting their favorite scuba spots. Lanyards were exchanged at least once on each of the five sleeping cabins. Katya was thrilled just to watch Sasha swimming off the white-sand beach again, reveling in the sight of his powerful body doing the butterfly and front crawl through the calm turquoise water against a backdrop of emerald green motos glinting in the warm sun.

Maxim hired a group of muscular male dancers and drummers, wearing nothing but Tahitian buttock-baring g-string loincloths and tattoos, for their goodbye party for Tuan and Aashir after dinner, and the crew spent the evening before departure in a private torchlight

385

bacchanal on the beach under countless stars. Katya didn't mind at all being the only woman. The men presented Tuan and Aashir with colorful g-strings for themselves and they delighted in trying them on. Katya couldn't help thinking how great Sasha would look in one.

The entire crew was soon shirtless and wildly uninhibited. Even usually serene Sonthi and earnest Chen were excitedly pounding drums as the laughing Tahitians attempted to teach the other crewmembers their dances. Katya vehemently refused entreaties to try to dance the fast, swivel-hipped women's dance with them. Her knowledge of storytelling Hawaiian dance would be of little use and she didn't want to slow down the manic tempo. Maybe someday she would share her Hawaiian dances with Sasha and her colleagues, but not this day... Sasha remained seated with her on the sand, but she could sense his arousal. She was aroused as well. A near smile flitted over his face. The frenetic celebration was a fitting conclusion to their island adventure. Katya leaned back against Sasha, watching, satisfied that if their world had to end tomorrow, at least she'd helped him find happiness once again.

Endgame

Chapter 50

The *Trib*'s 10 p.m. departure from Bora Bora had given them no last look this time, and they'd immediately accelerated with the hydrofoil to full speed flight. Now they were just another sailboat traveling slowly along the Australian coast, although one with a not too subtle escort of three patrol boats. Working with his engineering laboratory through the *Trib*'s computer, Sasha had used the information gathered from the captured torpedo-armed speedboats in San Francisco and Honolulu to quickly develop a technology to screen each boat on the water for weaponry, and crew members on the patrol boats were staring intently at their new devices. They approached the entrance to Sydney Harbour, first seen by Captain Cook in 1770, although known and loved by its soon to be displaced native people for centuries. Maxim steered the *Trib* between the dramatic cliffs of North and South Heads and followed the twists of the long, beautiful harbor past beaches, green parks, and low house-covered hills to the heart of the city.

Sasha pulled Katya up the companionway to the deck as the *Trib* approached the iconic opera house and the dark gray arched metal bridge beyond it. The vista was glorious: the water sparkling, the January summer sun lighting up the tall towers of Sydney, the angles of the sails on the Opera House ever changing as they passed. Sasha proudly pointed out Mandelbrot House, perched conspicuously on a hillside overlooking the view. Would he live long enough to bring Katya there to play the piano? He wished they could linger among the innumerable smaller sailboats, ferries, pleasure cruisers, and tour boats, but their orders were to motor directly on, deep into the inner reaches of the harbor, to the hidden, private shipyards that belonged to S-Branch. As they sailed under Sydney Harbour Bridge, the largest steel arch bridge in the world, Sasha directed Katya's attention to the Australogic Laboratories neon sign affixed atop the prominent modernist façade of a tall building on their right. Australogic's headquarters, which included his five Research and Development laboratories, was situated just back from the harbor in North Sydney. So public, so world-famous, unlike him, its impenetrable security completely invisible at this distance.

S-Branch was not wasting any time. As soon as the *Trib* was safely docked, Sasha, Katya, and the entire crew were escorted into the Situation Room. S-Branch had what they called an ace in the hole and Katya was anxious to hear what it was. She was warned that only Sasha and Maxim called it the War Room, and that S-Branch had no sense of humor. One look around the group of seven ancient white males already seated confirmed her concerns. The room reeked of testosterone and privilege. She would be the only female. But she would speak her mind no matter what. She knew Sasha was not cowed by them, so why should she be? Sasha was the reason for S-Branch's existence. One of the men stood to address them.

"Welcome, Katya. You may call me Hugh. We're all on first names only here. No 'sirs', nothing formal. Sasha, welcome back. I would ream you out for giving us the slip like you did, but since you managed to return in one piece and take down three of the Cutter brothers while you were at it, I guess we'll have to forgive you. I understand we really have Katya to thank for the demise of the Cutters, and for the fact that you and your crew are back with us at all and not at the bottom of the ocean. Katya, your work in California and the Philippines was outstanding."

The speaker was tall and rather heavyset, with white hair and a ruddy complexion. His Australian accent was thick, even stronger than Peter's. Despite her misgivings, she liked him. But before she could open her mouth to reply, he sat down and continued.

"And your medical tour was quite the success, Sasha, put our country in a good light indeed. I know how grateful you must be for your renewed status with the University and for your generous funding. I see you're spending it already. We've got your three boats in the beginning stages of construction out there. But until we solve this problem with Cyrus Cutter, you're not going back to sea. I've lost track of how many times we've almost lost you. So let us show you where we are. We have a real opportunity here to end this fatwa once and for all and take down Cyrus for good."

He looked around the room to measure the reaction to his words, then continued.

"In just a few minutes I'm going to introduce you to our best weapon, live on-screen. We have an inside man. Hu'a Quang Minh was a lieutenant in the police force in Hanoi, working anti-crime until eighteen months ago, when he decided to go after Cyrus Cutter. Minh knew he would have to go deep undercover and pretended to quit the force to start up a security business, his cover job, while working for Cyrus. Cyrus runs things in Vietnam quite differently than his brothers did. He operates his own cover as a legitimate businessman with an international import-export company and has close ties to the government. Minh has been moving up steadily in Cutter's ranks, undermining and eliminating the other leaders, until he is now one of Cyrus's top men, his head of security. Only one top brass officer in the Hanoi police force knows he's still on the side of the good guys, biding his time to be able to take down the whole organization from within.

"Minh knows and admires your work, Sasha, and after the attempt on the *Trib*, which he found out about too late, he felt compelled to act. He came to us. Minh thinks he can convince Cyrus to hold off on any more attempts for the time being for one big future splash that will annihilate Sasha emotionally before torturing him to death. Sorry, Sasha, but that's how Minh put it. We will lay our own trap for Cyrus, using you, Sasha, as bait. We can set the timeframe and be ready to stop him."

"You're asking me to put my life in the hands of Cyrus's right-hand man?" Sasha snapped angrily. "How can you possibly know he's not a double agent? Even if he was once a heroic police officer, you cannot trust that he hasn't been corrupted. A year and a half! Once you start doing the unthinkable day after day, you lose who you once were!"

Sasha was used to short-sighted stupidity from the S-Branch leadership, but this was beyond anything remotely reasonable. This was a story straight from the mind of master manipulator Cyrus Cutter: too good to be true, so therefore S-Branch would believe it because it sounded too obvious to be false.

"Sasha, I know it sounds impossible," said another of the S-Branch members, a plump white-haired gentleman in a tweed jacket and bow tie, looking a bit too much like a dull university professor.

389

"We have vetted this Hu'a Quang Minh every way imaginable, even used your best truth detector technology on him. He's real, he's truthful, and he wants to help,"

"I'm sorry, Ian, you haven't convinced me. You cannot convince me," Sasha stated firmly.

"Let me have Minh try to convince you himself. He's sitting in a secure location ready to talk with us. We can't make him wait any longer," Hugh said, as he touched a few buttons on a pad.

A large screen in front of them flickered, and the clear image appeared of a handsome man in his early thirties, impeccably dressed in a tight-fitting black silk shirt, perfectly creased black slacks and black tassel loafers, with stylishly long dark brown hair and slightly Eurasian features. He was relaxed and calm, leaning back in his chair, one leg crossed over the other at the knee. He sat forward immediately, forearms on his knees, looking them over, smiling when he saw Sasha. But then his dark brown eyes settled onto Katya's face and froze there. He remained staring at her for such a long time, Hugh had to cough to attract his attention. The camera zoomed in on his face.

"Minh, welcome. We appreciate that you are taking a great risk in meeting with us. Let me introduce you to Dr. Sasha Borodin, his new partner and wife Katya, and to his crew."

"I know who they are already." Minh spoke in softly accented but excellent English. "It is my honor to meet you. I am a great admirer of your work, Sasha. I know everything the Cutters have learned about you. I will do anything to protect you; I cannot let Cyrus Cutter destroy any one of you. We need to come up with a plan together, and I don't have much time. Let me tell you one more extremely important piece of information that might convince you to trust me, Sasha. I haven't even told it to your S-Branch."

So he'd been listening in on Sasha's arguments before his image was put on the screen, Katya thought. It unnerved her, the way his eyes kept darting back to hers. She didn't know what to make of him. Minh stared at her again, then continued, looking at Sasha, coming straight to his astounding announcement.

"I know that Cyrus has located your son, right here in northern Vietnam. He is, like you, a genius, a scientist, and working for a secret government laboratory not unlike your own, but he is far less free. He is well-protected and isolated, but not enough to keep him from being reached and killed. I can get Cyrus to put off his destruction to a future date if you will work with me to choose that date and help make a plan to outwit him."

Sasha blanched, and Katya reached for his hand. He didn't look like he could speak, so she spoke for him. "Tell us how you know this. Tell us what you know about Sasha's son," she demanded.

Minh smiled at her, which she found even more unnerving. His attraction to her was all too clear, but she was disconcerted to feel an attraction on her side as well, a purely sexual one. Maybe because he was staring at her with the same look of deep desire she remembered on Sasha's face as they first stood naked across from each other. This man wanted her, but how could he know her? She'd never seen him before. She prayed she was the only one who was noticing his attraction to her. The oddness of the situation gave her a new idea.

"His name is Nguyen Van Khai. That was the name given to him as an 'orphaned' Eurasian," Minh finally continued, turning his full attention to Sasha. "I'm sorry, Sasha, but his youth, I have learned, was not quite a happy one as a half-breed. My mother's wasn't either. Although he had no public schooling, he mastered physics and advanced math on his own, and his abilities came to the attention of a secret branch of the government. They set him up to work in a hidden facility. I don't know the nature of his projects other than that they are considered vital, are ongoing, and do not deal with weaponry. I know you have been searching for him all these years, but even the top officials you spoke with didn't know about him. They were not lying to you. I have only recently learned this information myself from Cyrus Cutter. Cyrus's bribery finally paid off and he was able to intercept and decode an encrypted transmission about him. I learned that he too has been looking for your son for years, but not for good reasons."

Katya knew now they had no choice but to trust him. She couldn't explain why, but she found she did trust him. Sasha was about to lose the one chance he had to keep his son alive, to ever meet him. She stood up and looked over at her friends, her mates, her beloved new husband, Sasha, the old men of S-Branch, and up at the young man staring intently at her from the big screen and chose her words carefully.

"Hugh, gentlemen. I believe we must all be ready to work with Minh. Let me give you the plan I've been working on. I only had the first step in mind before Minh. Now I can see it to the end. Sasha, you are not going to like any part of this but hear me out. Cyrus has to think he has won, that he has crushed Sasha emotionally, as Minh put it. Sasha must be seen to anguish over my betrayal with another, have his heart broken. Cyrus must see Sasha witness the *Trib* and its entire crew, including me, blown to bits. And he must see Sasha learning of the nearly simultaneous explosion that kills his son and destroys his life's work. Sasha will go into a deep depression, and escaping from his guards, turn himself in to Cyrus. He will watch his violin be destroyed before his eyes and see proof of my betrayal. He will be prepared to face his terrible death."

Katya heard the gasps all around her and felt Sasha's eyes boring into her. She waited a beat before she continued.

"And it will all be an illusion."

Chapter 51

Everyone started talking at once, the crew to each other, Sasha to Hugh, the other S-Branch members among themselves. Katya stood looking at Minh on the screen and he stared back. He nodded his head and smiled.

"I knew you would get it," he said quietly, to her alone. "You trust me. I'm the only one who can save your Sasha, and you."

"Who are you?" Katya asked, just as quietly. "You seem to know me."

"Right now, I'm the best friend you have. Help me convince the others."

"You know I'm trying."

Katya was still standing. The room was in an uproar and she had to get everyone's attention. She put her two fingers in her mouth and gave a loud whistle, glaring around the room until all was quiet. No one, not even Sasha, looked ready to listen to what she was going to say, but that wasn't going to stop her.

"Sasha, if Minh is telling us the truth, your son will be dead before you can meet him. Contact whoever you trust most in the Vietnamese government again, now. Tell him, or her, you have unimpeachable intelligence that your son is in a secret facility in the north and that his life is in imminent danger. You will exchange information that will save his life and save the projects he's working on for an immediate visit with him. I can guarantee you, your conversation will be overheard, word will get to the right person, and you will hear back from them with an explanation for his sudden discovery and your invitation. Go, go now, Sasha. You don't have to believe Minh to try this, but you will believe him afterwards. Hau, go with him. Take one of the S-Branch members with you."

Sasha didn't hesitate. Her words made perfect sense. There was nothing to lose and everything to gain by trying. He and Hau and one of the gray-haired men rushed out of the room. Sasha looked back at her with a new sense of hope.

"Katya, you're not in a position to dictate what happens in this room," declared another S-Branch member, looking exasperated.

"You need to sit down and let us all talk this through. It takes time to create a plan. This is far too important. Sit down, I said."

"Excuse me, Arthur, she is saying exactly what I hoped someone in your room would say," Minh called down from the screen. "It's obvious to me from the heated discussions that not everyone there believes or trusts me. You would not have set up this meeting if you didn't trust me. Let her speak."

"Maxim, Hiro, you listened to me when we were planning the rescue in the Philippines. Please listen to me now," Katya pleaded. "Let me lay out my ideas and then everyone can add their input or suggest alternatives. Hugh, how long will it take to make an outwardly perfect copy of the *Retribution* from one of those boats under construction? We won't need the hydrofoil wings. Any fast engines will do. Minimal material inside. This one is just going to be blown up, quite publicly, but it has to get from here to Vietnam."

"My God, woman. Arthur told you to sit down!" shouted another one of the old men.

"I'm waiting for an answer," Katya insisted.

"With every hand working around the clock, we can get you that boat in two weeks," a different gray-haired men replied.

"Thank you! Minh, how much time can you get from Cyrus? How long would he be willing to wait for his spectacular set of explosions and a docile, captive Sasha?"

"I would have no problem getting two or even three weeks, if I make him some juicy promises. You could just as easily be sitting there in safe harbor, untouchable for months."

"And you're sure you can keep Sasha's son safe until then?"

"Cyrus will not be able to resist hitting Sasha with everything all at once," Minh answered with a smile. "I know how that man's mind works by now."

Katya smiled back at him. Minh reminded her of Angel and the submarine. An unexpected gift from heaven sent to rescue them. Or so she hoped.

"Minh, where would Cutter take Sasha, if he's picked up in Vietnam?"

"I have no doubt to his cave system near the coast in central Vietnam. About fifty-five kilometers from Da Nang, the port he uses. He likes to do his dirty work there. I'll make sure that he does. And I'll make sure Sasha stays safe."

"Then, gentlemen, we're going to need an invitation from the Vietnamese government to honor Sasha in Da Nang in just under three weeks. Bleacher seats with lots of dignitaries to watch the arrival of the *Retribution* into the Da Nang harbor from Sydney, with her full complement of crew and his wife Katya. Plenty of advanced notice to let him send out his torpedo boats to greet us."

"And where will we be?" asked Maxim.

"On the boat, of course. Until right before we enter the harbor."

"Then how do we get off without being seen?" Kiko inquired anxiously.

"I'll get to that. I think I see Sasha returning already. That didn't take long, Minh."

Sasha was flushed with excitement, Hau smiling broadly behind him. The S-Branch member had not come back with them. Sasha returned to his seat but stopped to grab Katya and embrace her, then they both sat, arms around each other.

"Only minutes after my call, we received a call back," Sasha said, breathlessly to the group. "It seems that an old colleague of the late General's had just passed a letter on to them, detailing my son's name and history, and that they would be honored to have me escorted to a visit with him two days from now. Although it would be as one scientist visiting another. I'm not to say who I am. And I must come alone. Barton stayed behind to work out the details."

"Will that be enough for you?" asked Katya.

"It will have to do," Sasha answered, his mind already far away.

Minh smiled his enigmatic smile at the two of them. Katya wanted nothing more than to share this long-awaited moment with Sasha, but she was concerned that the longer Minh was away from Cyrus, the more he would be endangering his position of trust. She outlined the rest of her complicated plan to the men in the room. This time they all listened carefully and did not interrupt. The discussion and questions afterwards lasted another hour before Minh signed off and his image disappeared from the screen. Cyrus Cutter would hear Minh's plan for Sasha's demise immediately. Then   Minh would meet Sasha and Katya at the Hanoi military airport in two days in his new roles as head of their private bodyguard detail, Katya's pretend seducer, and Cyrus Cutter's supposed weapon to trap and destroy Sasha utterly.

Chapter 52

Sasha was so lost in his own thoughts and memories he hardly noticed the Situation Room emptying out. Only Katya stayed by his side, remaining in her seat, running her fingers through his hair. He was grateful for her silence. Once again, he'd been overwhelmed by her uncanny ability to create a complete and daring plan in such a short period of time. She had thought of every contingency, countered every argument, answered every question in detail. This was going to work if, and only if, they were not betrayed by this Minh. Who knew what lay in his heart, what his true motivation was? He couldn't help but notice how Minh had looked at Katya. Why the necessity of the illusion of a seduction, of his broken heart? The idea hadn't even been Minh's, it had been Katya's, and only thought of after she'd met Minh on screen. He tried to push a tinge of jealousy aside and think of Le, how beautiful she had been, heavy with child, her shining black hair even thicker and more radiant than before. How they were still carefully, gently, making love in her eighth month.

With a start, Sasha realized that Minh could be the same age as his son. Minh had implied that his mother was also the fruit of a Vietnamese and Caucasian union. It was clear that Minh's features were more Vietnamese than not. He could well have only one Caucasian grandparent, like Katya with her Chinese grandmother. Maybe that's what had attracted Minh, her similar Eurasian background. He wished it could be so simple.

Sasha shuddered: the idea passed through his mind that Minh could be his son, that a tortured childhood had led him to become a corrupt police officer, then a criminal. Perhaps his son hated him and wanted revenge. But no, this was not the face of his son. Minh had told the truth. He now had a name, Khai, if not a face. There were several meanings for Khai, but the ones that leapt to Sasha's mind were strong, brave, a warrior. That sounded like a son of his. One who was self-taught, brilliant, now a scientist. Sasha might already have his answer about his extraordinary intelligence being passed down to the next generation. The Vietnamese official he'd talked with had confirmed that his son was in the north, and the rapidity with which he'd agreed to Sasha's demand to see his son confirmed his importance to some branch of the government. This was real, this was happening. He would know all, meet Khai, in a matter of days.

Sasha tried to imagine the kind of life his young son had faced. Not quite a happy childhood, Minh had said. Perhaps born prematurely, but at least thirty-six weeks gestational age, rejected by his grandfather, a shunned half-breed. He must already have been taken from Le as an infant. She would never have left her newborn, even to get back to him, Sasha was certain. So many half-breed children had been abandoned to live on the streets during the war, taunted and abused, many more had been turned over to orphanages. He could not imagine General An completely abandoning his infant grandson. Perhaps he'd been placed with a poor family in the country. Sasha had also heard of unofficial group homes for the forgotten and the unwanted, for physically and mentally disabled children, placed there by parents of means. These were corrupt, poorly funded places, often cruelly managed.

He pulled himself back into the present moment and squeezed Katya's hand. How could he have imagined she could be seduced away from him, after all they'd been through? He knew she would give her life for him. They stood up and walked out together hand in hand. The rest of the crew had waited patiently for them in the hall. Maxim, Hiro, Sonthi, and Dima had long known of Sasha's search for his son, but this had been news to the others. Somehow congratulations didn't seem in order with the threat hanging over them all, and they stayed quiet. Sasha imagined that thoughts of the events to come crowded their minds. None of them seemed as hopeful as Sasha that Katya's plan could come off without a major hitch.

A meal had been prepared for them, and afterwards they had the choice of wandering the small headquarters, helping with boat construction, or returning to the *Trib* at the secure dock. They wouldn't be allowed to leave the area before hearing back from Minh. At worst, they would have to stay until the decoy boat was finished, until they were to sail to Vietnam in two weeks. Sasha promised he would get clearance for them all to visit his extensive laboratories the next day. He was going to give Katya a short private tour now, clearance or no, then throw himself into a few hours of work to settle his mind. Katya wanted to return to the labs again with the crew.

The security for Australogic Laboratories, already strict, had been tightened even further since the attack on the *Trib*. S-Branch considered shutting all the laboratories down entirely until the threat had passed, but Sasha insisted there were far too many ongoing experiments that could be ruined by delays. Now it seemed that everyone might be able to breathe a little easier if word came from Minh that Cutter had agreed to his special date. D-Day, the crew started calling it. Destruction Day, but never around Sasha or Katya.

But nothing was going to stop Sasha from flying to Hanoi and on, by two separate helicopter links, to visit Khai. S-Branch would be sending two bodyguards, but they would not be allowed on the final helicopter segment. He would see Khai late morning just days from now. Sasha absolutely refused Katya's offer to come with him as far as she would be allowed. She would stay in Hanoi under the watchful eye of Minh, but now he was beginning to regret that choice. He was also displeased that he could take only a small shoulder bag, that his violin and laptop would have to stay with Katya.

It surprised Sasha how much he enjoyed showing Katya and his crew around his realm. The crew was as astounded as Katya had been by the private entrance and elevator to the Research and Development top floors of the public Australogic building in North Sydney, by Sasha's futuristic, high-tech laboratories. They loved scrubbing up and donning lab coats, masks, foot and head coverings. Sasha apologized in advance that they couldn't enter the various clean rooms, but promised there would be plenty to see.

Just over sixty employees worked with Sasha closely in person the one month a year he spent in the labs, and over computer live feed interactions the rest of the year. He knew all their names and positions, and where they were on which experiments. Even casually walking by, Sasha called out changes or new ideas and they were welcomed with grateful smiles. Everything happening here was the result of his creativity and his staff respected his ownership. Katya noticed that fully fifty percent of the staff were women, and almost a quarter of all the employees were Aboriginal, black or South Asian.

They toured the physics and engineering lab first, with its amazing array of large and small devices under construction, like security systems and drones. Some of the work still appeared to be military, but nothing lethal. Katya knew Sasha had foresworn creating lethal weaponry a few years back. Hiro pointed out dart pistols and rifles.

399

More improvements, Sasha informed him, giving him his near smile. He was close to achieving his goal of instant unconsciousness, without the consequent severe headache caused by his current models.

They moved on to the computer section, which included robotic creations and A.I. in every state of experimentation, then the chemistry and pharmaceutical lab, followed by the medical devices lab. On this second visit, Katya saw Priya, back to a day shift, and they gave each other a warm hug. Sasha introduced Dr. Priya Anand to his crew as the long-time head of the Chemistry Lab. He moaned and blushed as she told a few jokes at his expense. Katya was sorry there would be no opportunity to get together with her. She was sure Priya had many tales to share from their forty year history of working together.

Sasha saved the prosthetics laboratory for last. Looking around at Katya and his crew, Sasha felt a small degree of satisfaction that he could share his accomplishments with at least this small group. Other than S-Branch, Australogic's CEO, the Prime Minister, and the lab staff, sworn to secrecy, no one else knew who he was, and in all his years as a captain, he'd never invited crew to his laboratories. He'd purposefully kept these two worlds separate. Would there ever come a time when he could let the world know these labs were all his? His handlers' refusal to allow him to at least claim the prostheses and the tiny computer and neural implants that connected them to the patients' brains remained a source of frustration, growing worse now that he planned to rejoin the University of Sydney Prosthetics Department after a thirty-five-year absence. If he survived Cutter's threat of annihilation.

Over two dozen employees were testing or piecing together the robotic frameworks for hands, arms, feet, and legs that had been ordered by the University of Sydney Prosthetics Department, along with orders taken during the *Trib*'s world medical expedition. Australogic was still offering these prostheses free of charge to the impoverished patients Sasha and the local hospitals selected to receive them, financed by the profits generated by Sasha's other inventions. Sasha displayed the completed framework of a forearm and hand, just in the process of receiving a covering of realistic, highly sensitive electronic skin, the tone matched carefully to photos taken of the patient. He told Katya this prosthesis was for a twenty-year-old Cambodian, Chhay Kosal, who had lost his arm to a land mine while reaching into the dirt for a sweet potato on his family's farm. Holding up the robotic framework for a child's leg and arm, Sasha demonstrated the telescoping parts that allowed the prosthesis to "grow" with the child, extending its usefulness over several years.

Sasha invited Katya and his crew to look through the glass walls of a separate unit, a Class One clean room, where his finest, most advanced developments, the delicate artificial eyes and minuscule computers and other neural implants that operated them and all his prostheses, were being constructed. He couldn't bring himself to try to explain the science to his crew. Sasha took a moment to acknowledge to himself that he might not be alive to personally insert the implants that would activate his most recently ordered prostheses. He needed to think like Katya and never visualize failure. Her plan would work.

The first night aboard the docked *Trib* was an anxious one for the crew. Sasha tried to lighten their mood with music, but he could tell their hearts weren't in it. Katya then played one of her instruments after the other, starting with her guitar, then her mandolin, Chinese pipa, and koto, and the novelty distracted the crew for a while. Her instruments, while precious to her, did not require the same kind of climate-controlled cabinetry as did the crew's superb violins, cellos, and violas, and were now stored in the bow. She wished she'd brought more of her instruments from Berkeley. Sasha allowed Katya's optimism to keep him buoyed up. Then there was the excitement of knowing he would soon be meeting his son.

Sasha expressed concern about the two helicopter trips they would be making. After touring the labs with Katya and his crew, Sasha insisted on learning how to fly the S-Branch helicopter, although he was disappointed he was only allowed to fly it straight up and down and just over the compound. After five landings, he declared himself ready to fly in Vietnam if need be. He promised Katya that airplanes would be next, and she laughed when he told her he had ideas on how to improve them. They made long and passionate love together multiple times per day. Sasha hoped that Katya couldn't tell that he was thinking of Le.

The evening of the second day brought the good news they were hoping for. Minh claimed Cyrus Cutter was ecstatic about the plan and timetable Minh had outlined, the plan that Katya, Sasha, and the

401

crew had so carefully worked out. Everyone was prepared to be "dead" for three days after the explosion. Now it was up to Sasha to convince Khai and his government handlers that Khai would have to do the same. S-Branch insisted Sasha and Katya fly immediately from Sydney to Hanoi overnight on a military cargo plane for a mid-morning arrival, four bodyguards accompanying them. They must continue to act as if they were taking all precautions against a new attack from Cyrus. The crewmembers were free to enjoy Sydney, escorted by their new bodyguards. Sasha and Katya would part in Hanoi. For Sasha, thirty-three years of searching and waiting were about to come to an end.

Chapter 53

Sasha half expected to be blindfolded during the second leg of the helicopter trip. The cloak and dagger maneuvers were beginning to grow tiresome. They'd left the gray, polluted skies of Hanoi behind, then stopped briefly at an unknown location to change helicopters. His two bodyguards could accompany him no further, leaving him with one Vietnamese escort. After nearly an hour of flight time, passing over steep granite mountains in rich greens and blues, the helicopter swerved down a valley. Here the sun was shining brightly. They swept low over tall hills covered in palm forest, then green, lush farm fields and rice paddies, until they were above a circular settlement of neat bamboo thatched-roofed houses, each with its own garden.

A large circular structure, also skillfully constructed of bamboo, stood in its center. Sasha counted only fourteen houses. He found it strange that there were no roads visible into or leading away from the village, and none anywhere nearby. There were no other settlements for miles. The helicopter landed in an empty space that would have held another house on the symmetrical grid. His escort was a young man with an expressionless face, who was dressed in casual civilian clothes, yet looked like a soldier. He hadn't spoken a word during the flight and didn't introduce himself. They had no more than ducked under the wash of the rotors before the helicopter was away.

Sasha found the village charming by any standards. The few women, children, and old men visible were simply dressed and healthy looking; everything was spotless and tidy. There were a few chickens and ducks roaming freely, and he could see a solitary water buffalo grazing in a field, along with two ordinary looking small white horses. The thatched-roof houses, although built in traditional style on stilts, were sturdier and larger than they had appeared from the air, with spacious open-air porches and shaded work spaces underneath. The surrounding blue-green hills and open areas in the village were thick with thriving vegetation. Tall, dramatic granite mountains backed the hills. A clear stream ran through the village from the hills, and a small fish pond was dammed off to the side of it. The word that came to Sasha's mind was scenic. The village did not seem artificial, just thoughtfully created and cared for, which left him utterly confused. His son was supposed to be working in a top-secret laboratory of some sort, and here Sasha was, standing in a tiny idealized Vietnamese village.

His guide motioned for him to follow as he made his way down a stone path to the circular structure. It was, as he imagined, an open sided community center. A woman sat weaving in one area, a few children were being taught math in another, a group of three elderly men and women practiced Tai Chi in yet a third. The guide walked on to the solid bamboo walls of another circular structure in the center of the building. He opened a barely visible door and invited Sasha to join him. Sasha could have sworn the young man was stifling a grin.

As soon as the door closed behind him, Sasha felt the floor begin to drop slowly down. He was in some sort of elevator, and he counted a full minute before it stopped. His now smiling guide opened another door and Sasha found himself looking at a most outlandishly futuristic subway, a long gleaming silver car waiting for him, a single track leading off into the darkness of the tunnel ahead. The subway car reminded him of a pneumatic tube, but the inside was again done in bamboo laminate and held two dozen comfortably padded seats equipped with plug-in outlets for laptops. Sasha and his guide sat down, and the car sped forward with enough g-force to press Sasha deep into the back of his seat. The car rode smoothly and was remarkably quiet inside. Sasha counted the time and attempted to calculate the speed and distance they traveled. By the end of the journey he was astounded to come up with the estimated figure of around 220 kilometers in thirty minutes, around 440 kph, or over 273 miles per hour.

The subway car slowed and came to a stop, and Sasha's guide motioned him forward. Sasha found himself in the courtyard of a large, handsome underground complex, well-lit and ventilated. Carved wooden posts of Vietnamese mythic animal figures framed concrete doorways and a number of contemporary sculptures decorated comfortable seating areas. Verdant exotic plants grew under artificial sun lamps. A few young and early middle-aged men and women in white lab coats could be seen walking purposefully through the courtyard. Hallways and entryways screened by elaborately carved and painted wooden panels led away in several directions.

Sasha was entranced. The mind behind the design of the village, subway, and complex was phenomenally creative, a genius.

His guide led him down a few stairs to what appeared to be a small cafeteria. The aroma of spicy cooking wafted through the room, although he couldn't see a kitchen or serving area. The guide motioned for the two young men finishing their meals to take their food with them and leave. They stared in surprise at Sasha's blond hair as they departed. When his escort spoke for the first time in halting Vietnamese, Sasha detected evidence of a traumatic throat injury.

"Please be seated... Khai will be here shortly... Sorry, he doesn't pay much attention to time."

"Thank you," Sasha answered, wondering at the casual apology.

The escort bowed and departed. Sasha was left waiting for twenty minutes. He had time to admire the carefully constructed bamboo laminate covering the concrete walls and floors that made the place inviting, less austere. He examined the room from his seat, discovering a wall with built-in key pads, perhaps used to order food, and a grid of closed woven panels that might pop open to retrieve each order.

Sasha heard fast footsteps on the stairs and watched a young man in his early thirties rush into the room. He was dressed casually and holding a white lab coat over his arm. Sasha caught his breath. This could only be his son. He was of average height, his height, but tall for a Vietnamese, with a build like his own – powerful shoulders, well-muscled arms, narrow waist, although much less sculpted by exercise. In fact, the man had a bit of a soft paunch. Unkempt medium brown, slightly curly hair, grey eyes, and a handsome face with strong Eurasian features that was achingly an echo of Le's. Eyes and nose that were not Vietnamese. They were his. The lips, ears, and shape of face, his delicacy, were Le's. His air was decidedly distracted, serious, like he was thinking of a dozen things at once, a look Sasha knew all too well. He stood by Sasha's table.

"Thank you for coming," Khai said, with no inflection in his voice, looking just past Sasha's left ear. "Okay to speak English? I like to practice... and nobody here speaks perfect English."

"Of course. I'm happy to meet you, Khai. Do you know who I am?" Sasha asked. He was surprised by Khai's monotone voice and strangely clipped phrasing.

Khai's eyes darted to meet Sasha's then back past his ear. He nodded his head vigorously.

"You are the scientist from Australia... I am supposed to talk to. And you're my father," he added without emotion.

Sasha was so taken aback he couldn't reply for a moment. What he felt was anything but emotionless. He was glad their relationship would be out in the open from the start.

"I am. I was told not to tell you."

"You didn't have to. It was easy. You look like me. No non-Asian has ever been invited here. They told me you're smart like me."

"Did you design this complex, the subway?"

"And the village, and the laboratory. You haven't seen the laboratory yet."

"I would like to see it, Khai."

"Follow me."

Walking fast, Khai led him back up the stairs and across the courtyard. Everyone they passed greeted Khai warmly but gave Sasha a surprised and curious stare. Sasha noticed several half-Vietnamese/half-Caucasians and several half-Koreans, a blind man with a cane who still greeted Khai by name, and a woman with one arm among them. As they walked, Khai turned to look back at Sasha and spoke in a near whisper, like he was telling a secret.

"I forgot to tell you... Please don't touch me... I don't like to be touched. New people get into trouble sometimes... if I don't tell them and they touch me... I get all hot and cold... and start to sweat. If somebody grabs me, I might even pass out... I don't like that."

This news almost undid him, as tight as he was holding in his emotions. Sasha knew that the tendency to develop phobias could be hereditary, and here they were, suffering from the same one. Surely Khai had suffered abuse too in his youth to develop this particular one.

"Do you want to know something funny, Khai?" Sasha replied, when he felt able to speak. "I'm the same way. And I don't like to pass out either."

Khai stopped for just a moment and turned around, this time looking Sasha straight in the eye.

"That's not at all funny," he said. "I'm really sorry for you... It's made my life... difficult."

Sasha didn't know if there was going to be a right time or place to talk, so he decided to just take the opportunities as they arose. He wished Khai would remain stopped, let him look at him longer. There was so much to say, so much to learn.

"It's made my life difficult, too," Sasha sighed. "Until I met your mother. She could touch me. She was the first person who could, and I liked it. I liked it a lot. We were married in Ho Chi Minh City, Saigon back then."

Khai didn't react. Sasha knew he had to resist reaching out to him, trying to put a hand on his shoulder. Here was his son, standing right in front of him, as untouchable as he was. Himself, before Le, before Katya, and still untouchable by every other person on Earth. Seemingly emotionless. No curiosity about his father at all. For a moment, Sasha wished he could go back to being without emotion. What he was feeling was far too painful. His son was on the spectrum. Khai turned away and strode on, talking over his shoulder.

"I didn't know my mother."

"I didn't know my mother either," Sasha replied, increasing his stride to keep up. The emotional pain was becoming too great. He would swallow it down, ignore it.

"We should really talk to each other. After the laboratory. They told me to take the day off... and I have never taken a day off... I have so much work to do."

"I do want to see your laboratory, Khai. Let's go on."

"What should I call you? They told me... Dr. Borodin was coming."

"You can call me Sasha."

The tour of the huge laboratory took over an hour. Khai had focused his efforts on applied physics and a staff of ten who seemed to adore him were hard at work at black surfaced tables. Again, Sasha noted several half-Vietnamese among them, all in their thirties. Amerasian offspring from the war, he surmised. The floor held a dozen car and truck engines in various stages of completion, and like in Sasha's laboratory, dozens of small devices were spread out in pieces across the tables. Just walking by, Khai would pick out seemingly random parts and place them or hand them to an assistant, offering instructions. *So much like me,* Sasha thought. He noted that, like himself, Khai was left-handed. From the kinds of projects now in the works, Sasha was sure the secret government branch had been earning a great deal of money from Khai's inventions over the years.

407

He wondered where the profits went, since the regular government seemed to have no knowledge of any of this.

All the walls were covered in white board, most of the space filled with equations and graphs. Khai would suddenly dart over to a blank wall and fill half of it with mathematical symbols, then move on. Sasha could see from the writing that Khai was deep into fundamental physics, String Theory, quantum computing for artificial intelligence, the Core Theory, entanglement, and the proposed unification of forces. Khai seemed to regard theoretical and applied physics with equal importance. Sasha's interest in the theoretical had never gone much beyond quantum computing.

Sasha took a closer look at one of the largest engine models in the room. Something about it seemed familiar.

"Are you working on Mandelbrot's fuelless engine?" Sasha asked, growing more excited as he walked around the giant model.

This must be what was most interesting to his government handlers. The commercial prospects were enormous. Work towards a clean, free source of energy had been Sasha's goal as well, and he reflected how saddened he still was that his own process had been sold by his adoptive father to fossil fuel interests and never pursued commercially as he had hoped. He'd concentrated his efforts on solar energy ever since.

"I'm almost there," Khai explained, nodding. "I know that was Mandelbrot's lifework... He was from Australia, too. Just imagine... every car, truck, motorcycle, generator, and every factory, being noiseless... pollution free, self-dependent."

Khai showed Sasha a single large skylight, sunshine streaming to the floor from a great distance. Free fuel from the sun, Sasha remembered well. Nikola Tesla's idea of using radiant energy, never yet commercialized, awaiting a catalyst a thousand times more conductive than copper, among other missing pieces.

"I have a workplace above ground too... at the army border station... in the sun... but radiant energy is always there... out of doors... whether sun is shining or not. I was told I can't take you there... But I'll show you here what progress I've made... from Mandelbrot's time."

"You would be proud to know Mandelbrot was something like your grandfather, Khai," Sasha said, reeling from the coincidence. He stopped himself. This couldn't be a coincidence. Someone had to have

408

set Khai on this path of inquiry. The idea excited him even more. "Mandelbrot adopted me when I was five, almost six, and raised me. I worked on this motor with him all during my youth. I moved on after he died and never got back to it. I'm glad you're continuing his work. Our work. Mandelbrot's major advances, the ones he's famous for... were all my ideas."

"My grandfather? Harrison Mandelbrot? You are an inventor too, Sasha?"

"Very much so, Khai. In many fields, but I do love applied physics and robotics best of all. You have gone beyond me with your work in theoretical physics, I can see that. I also became a doctor, a surgeon, and that is an important part of my life. I too have a laboratory, four or five, depending on how you look at them, but they are not kept secret like yours. The laboratories are known throughout the world. Still, I can't tell anyone about my work there. What is kept a secret is who I am. Almost no one knows that I am an inventor, that all of the work the laboratories produce is mine."

"Are your labs underground too?"

"No, and I can travel and do my work by computer with audio and visual connection to every part of my labs. I used to work much of the day inside my labs when I was younger, nearly every moment I wasn't involved with medicine, until I was twenty-five and came here, to Vietnam, as a surgeon with the army during the War, although the labs came with me. I found there was more to life."

"Like my mother."

"Yes, in Vietnam I found your mother, Lê, 'Lee' she called herself to her English-speaking friends, although 'Lay' would have been closer. She loved you, Khai, was excited about your pending birth. As was I. She was only a month away from her due date when she was taken away from me. You were stolen from her, from us, and I was devastated I couldn't stop that from happening. Then I couldn't find you."

"I remember very bad people... when I was young, ones who hurt me... but I also remember good people. I had friends."

"That is good. I had no friends growing up. I first had friends when I knew your mother."

"Where is my mother now?"

"I'm so sorry, Khai. She died shortly after you were born. It's taken me decades to recover from losing her. I just remarried recently.

409

I found someone else who could touch me, who can love me as I am. But I think of your mother every day."

"Do you have a picture? I have no picture in my head."

"I did bring one, knowing I would see you. Here it is. You can keep this copy, Khai."

Khai stared at the photo for a long time, then put it in his pocket.

"Do you think I can ever find someone... who I can allow to touch me?" he asked, his face clouding over. Not waiting for an answer, he swerved over to the whiteboard and wrote down a long equation, concentrating hard. Khai's mood brightened after a moment and he smiled, the first smile Sasha had seen on his face.

"You haven't visited... my two favorite rooms yet," he said, as he abruptly walked out of the lab, Sasha hurrying to keep up.

They entered the next work space in the complex, and again, Sasha was astounded. Dozens of computers and computer parts filled the room, interspersed with simulations of human heads and robotic upper bodies, connected to computers with thick cables. The staff working there turned to stare at Sasha. There were half-Vietnamese workers in this room as well, including three who were half-black, some who looked half-Korean. The grown children of war. Khai had a childish, delighted look on his face as he made entries on a computer keyboard, demonstrating how the heads could move their eyes, talk, and turn different directions, and how one half-body could move its arms and hands in life-like motions. Sasha could see applications to his own work immediately. He and Khai were going to have to have a long talk. But before he could ask a first question, Khai hurried on, motioning for him to follow.

They moved quickly down a long concrete hallway and Khai stopped before what looked like a solid wall. Just down the hall Sasha could make out a door labeled maintenance in Vietnamese, but he could see no opening where they had stopped. Khai looked up at a small light on the ceiling and a hidden door slid open. Sasha found himself in a large room, with a kitchen, living room, shelves of books, and three narrow beds built into niches, each with a heavy cloth privacy curtain.

Sasha stopped and caught his breath. In the center of the room sat a single chair with a cello leaning against it, a bow propped against the back.

410

A gray-haired man in his late sixties with a wispy gray and white beard stepped into view. He looked alarmed at the sight of Sasha with Khai.

"Bao! I brought you a visitor," Khai said in Vietnamese. "This is my father... Dr. Sasha Borodin. Call him Sasha."

Sasha didn't know who was more surprised, himself that Khai would introduce him this way, or Bao. He did know that Khai had the biggest, brightest smile imaginable, as he looked around his special room. If only he himself could smile like that, just once, Sasha thought. Sasha bowed, and Bao gave a deep bow in return.

"Please pardon the intrusion," Sasha said in Vietnamese. "I am pleased to make your acquaintance. You cannot imagine how thrilled I am to be allowed to meet my son."

Bao seemed startled by Sasha's perfect Vietnamese. He stared intently at Sasha's face, then he too smiled. Sasha could see the scars of napalm burns across half of the man's face and down his arms. He was dressed in blue-gray maintenance worker's coveralls with the sleeves rolled up, and socks with no shoes.

"Sasha doesn't like to be touched either," Khai blurted out in his monotone, continuing in Vietnamese. "He gave me a picture of my mother... Her name was Le... Do you want to see it?"

Khai pulled the picture out of his pocket and showed it to Bao. Bao took the picture gingerly and Sasha saw a tear glisten in the man's eye as he nodded his head over and over. He handed the picture back to Khai.

"This is where I come to talk... and to play the cello," Khai continued, his voice growing more expressive. "The walls are soundproofed... I hid this room in the designs... no one knows about it but me... and Bao and Lan. Bao works at night, cleaning, and likes to be here... with me during the day. Sometimes I stay all night. Bao lives with Lan in the village... when he's not here. Bao and Lan are my best friends."

"Khai, you shouldn't have brought your father here," Bao said to him, gently. You know this place is our secret."

"But he's my father. And he's a scientist too... and an inventor, and a doctor. He's got his own laboratories... like mine... but it's a secret that he's so smart."

Sasha wanted more than anything to be able to embrace his son. Now he knew how his crewmates felt all these years. For a brief

411

moment, he wondered if perhaps he was only a little less far out on the autistic spectrum than this beautiful, brilliant man that was his son. Perhaps many of the eccentric mannerisms of his youth, his inability to make friends, his literalism, had been caused by more than his experiences in the camp. Over time he'd learned how to talk to people, how to look people in the eye. His time in Europe with the Roma had been a fluke, a game. He'd played a role. His Romani mates had humored him, protected him.

Since then he'd been in society, unlike Khai. College, medical school, his residencies, the Prosthetic Department. Always with a minder living with him. The army. Then he'd had Le to help him. But no, the horrors of the camp would have been sufficient. He was merely damaged and eccentric, he decided. His son's temperament was so different from his own. He had known few people with autism or Asperger Syndrome who seemed as happy and beloved as Khai, though he appeared to share his own sudden mood swings. And now, he saw that they shared a love of music. The sight of the cello was almost too much for him to bear.

"May I?" Sasha asked, and he picked up and tightened the bow, rubbed on some rosin, and sat down with the cello between his knees. He began playing one of his favorite Bach cello suites. The world has come full circle, he thought, watching the broad smile on Khai's face, the surprise on Bao's. The cello was not bad, just mediocre, but it would do. He wondered if Khai's handlers would allow him to send his son a finer instrument as a gift.

As he played, the door opened and shut quickly behind a young woman, whose smile changed to shock when she saw it was not Khai on the cello. Sasha observed her as he continued playing: an attractive but plain woman about Khai's age, with gold wire-rim glasses, her long black hair pulled into a simple ponytail down her back. Napalm scars were also visible on her hands and neck. She wore a white lab coat. This would have to be Lan, who must be Bao's daughter. It didn't take Sasha but a moment to note her love for Khai, and Khai's total indifference to that love. Sasha wondered if he would have ever noticed such a thing just six months ago. He finished playing the sixth suite, then carefully replaced the cello and bow exactly as he had found them and spoke, again in Vietnamese.

"Hello, Lan. My name is Sasha, Dr. Sasha Borodin. I'm Khai's father. Before he tells you himself, I also cannot allow myself to be touched. I'm afraid he may have gotten that from me, in addition to good things like brains and musical talent. I think we should all sit down before I tell you why I was allowed to come here."

They sat at the small dining table, Bao bringing over an additional chair. Khai was still smiling, but Bao and Lan sensed the seriousness of the situation and looked anxious.

"I have been searching for Khai his whole life," Sasha began, addressing them both without preamble, "but I have enemies and they have been searching for him as well. Just three days ago I learned they had discovered where he was, and I was able to find out too. His life, and his laboratory will be forfeited unless we act. I know you think you are invincible here, but these are ruthless, clever people. They will find a way. You have to have deliveries of materials made, there will be a soldier or a guard or official bribed or blackmailed. I need to let these evil people think they have succeeded. We will soon learn the exact time and date of the attack. It will be in less than three weeks. You can move out Khai's experiments, his work, put in dummy pieces. I imagine there will be an explosion – your concrete walls will survive, you can move your material back in afterwards. But these people need to think that Khai is dead. We will need three days, then, if all goes well, you can resume your life as if nothing had happened. This hidden room is perfect. Khai can stay in here."

"What about you?" asked Lan, wide-eyed with terror.

"I am the bait to catch and end this threat forever. We have a plan to rescue me when the time comes. All the people close to me are going to be doing the same thing as Khai, pretending to be dead. I'm sorry that my life has put you in such danger."

"I can move some of my work in here," Khai said, looking excited instead of worried. "I'll have three whole days... to work uninterrupted, Lan!"

Lan and Bao looked over at him and shook their heads, smiling. Sasha felt an extreme relief. This was going to be much easier than he'd anticipated.

413

Chapter 54

Katya found the noisy, bustling streets of Hanoi difficult to get used to. January was Hanoi's coldest month and the air was chilly, and nearly solid with fumes from the heavy traffic. She stood staring at the vast tangles of electrical wires, as messy as eagles' nests and nearly as large, barely clinging to the top and sides of each pole, individual strands snaking dangerously into connectors on every floor of the buildings around her. Parked motorcycles, men playing checkers or selling individual cigarettes, and street food sellers with small grills, their short colorful stools crowded with loudly chatting customers, filled the sidewalks, forcing her to step into the busy street to get around them. An old woman squatted at a curb, burning a small pile of rubbish. Crossing the street would take an enormous amount of courage, facing a nonstop flood of bell-ringing bicycles, beeping motorcycles, often bearing two or even three helmetless passengers or huge loads behind their helmeted driver, and honking, diesel-fuming mini trucks coming at her from both directions. Minh laughed at her consternation and took her hand.

"The trick is to not stop walking. Look them in the eye and forge ahead," he said, holding on even after they were safely on the other side.

Katya had been most displeased when Minh dismissed her bodyguards as soon as Sasha departed to meet his son; his own security firm would take over. He told her he had his assurance from Cyrus Cutter that he would wait for the *Trib* to arrive in Da Nang harbor Minh was doing his best to introduce Katya to the joys of Hanoi, which in his mind seemed to be mainly the delicious, dirt cheap street food. She finally demanded a seat where she could sit without squatting and enjoy a hopefully cold, not lukewarm, drink. He led her up some stairs to a decent café overlooking the street. Minh was even better looking in person, if just a little too flirtatious, and again, impeccably dressed. Still, his forceful masculinity was a change of pace from the drama and emotionality of the *Trib*'s crew, their brotherly sweetness, and the unpredictability of Sasha's mercurial temperament, his calm, logical, imperturbable constancy alternating with his manic-depressive cycles, his needy jealousy. She loved Sasha madly but he could be exhausting to keep up with. Katya thought of Keung, how attracted she was to handsome Asian men; this man was nothing like Keung. She couldn't begin to explain the physical attraction she felt for this preening, over-dressed stranger in front of her, Sasha's very opposite. But she also believed Minh's story and couldn't deny his courage. Sasha was with his son because of Minh. Their fate was in his hands.

"So, tell me about yourself, Minh. I'm sure there's nothing you don't already know about me," Katya said in Vietnamese, wanting to blend in with the café crowd, as she drank her cold soda. She breathed deeply of the somewhat cleaner air, glad to be out from under the damp, gray skies.

"On the contrary, Katya, I want to know so much more about you. What you like, what you don't like," he replied in his good English, not taking his eyes off her. He suddenly appeared to have even less of an accent now that they were alone.

"I don't like flirting. Or avoidance. Or machismo."

"Ouch. One day together and already I'm in trouble. All right. I am a man of honor. What I am doing right now is incredibly difficult. I hope to come out the other side unscathed and alive."

"Yes, I know Cyrus Cutter is extremely dangerous. I'm sorry you've had to put yourself at such risk for us."

"Shh. Don't say his name. I mean spending time with you and not trying to steal you from Sasha."

"You simply must stop this, Minh."

"I have to say you started it. Poor Sasha and his broken heart, proof of your betrayal. Exactly what did you have in mind?"

"Don't make it about you. I just thought it would be something to excite what's-his-name, help get him to agree."

"You were right. He was practically salivating over the plan. And I know just how we're going to pull it off. You will really have to trust me, though."

"You're making that more difficult by the moment. Let's pay and get back to the safe house. I need to know if Sasha is ready to come back. They said he could have a few hours with his son."

"If you insist. I am at your command."

Katya couldn't have been more disappointed at the news waiting for her at the safe house. Sasha had gotten permission to spend the night, all the next day and maybe the next night as well. Although she was happy for him, that left her alone with Minh in a difficult, noisy city. Minh did give her some peace for a couple of hours but returned with a mischievous smile and tales of great plans for the next day. Katya hoped it included some sightseeing, despite the dreariness of the damp, polluted air. She had seen a colorful temple on a small lake that looked like an attractive destination.

That evening, Minh took her to one of Hanoi's many French restaurants for a leisurely dinner, flirting outrageously the entire time. Katya played along, sure that Cutter's men would be watching. She indulged in meat dishes and fine wine but then excused herself early, feeling guilty. Her bed was cold and lonely that night without Sasha. This was her first day and night without lovemaking since their first time in Tahiti. Dawn brought an immediate horrendous cacophony of honking and beeping horns from the street.

At breakfast, Minh was closemouthed about his plans. He tried to take her hand as they crossed the busy streets, but she followed his advice and walked steadily, if not quite fearlessly, through the traffic, then negotiated her way carefully around the sidewalk blockages. He used a key to open the door to a large room on the second floor of a nondescript building in the city center. The shades were drawn but she could make out a variety of vague shapes in the gloom. Next to her stood a camera on a tripod and she noticed several other cameras set up nearby. Minh flicked on the lights with a flourish, and she backed towards the door. The room was designed for filming pornography, with a large hanging bottomless basket, a bed and couch, handcuffs high on a wall, and myriad sex toys she couldn't begin to name the purpose of. Minh stood smiling in front of the exit.

"Open that door now or I'll break both your arms," Katya said steadily.

"I know you're quite capable of doing just that. I've heard the Gunner story. But hear me out," Minh said soothingly. "I know I've been flirting with you, but I just wanted to get you in the mood sexually. I really need you to trust that I'm not going to lay a finger on you. We are going to make some really great pornography, to prove your betrayal of Sasha to Cyrus Cutter. Cyrus is going to love this, and it will keep him moving towards our goal. We will take some great photos that will make it look like we're having fabulous sex. It will be an illusion, like all your other illusions. I know you can kick my ass,

417

so I would be a fool to try something. Are you following me?" he asked, somehow looking serious and innocent at the same time.

"And do I get to break your arms if you do try something?" Katya asked, reeling from the implications of Minh's plan.

"I'm going to be behind the camera most of the time. There will be enough shots with me in them to leave no doubt, but I'm going to concentrate on close ups of your face in ecstasy, having orgasms. I know you're an excellent actress, but I bet I can get you hot without even touching you."

"You bet your arms?"

"As I just said, without touching you. Are you game?"

"And you get to watch me squirming around naked?"

"Well, that's not a very sexy way to put it, but yes. Remember you're doing this for Sasha. Think of him to get yourself going."

"I thought you were a cop, not a pornographer."

"I am a man of many talents."

"Is this your studio?"

"No, no, I just rent some time here on occasion. For my personal enjoyment. I like photography. Policemen know where all the fun, illicit stuff is."

Katya needed a few minutes to decide. Minh was right, she had started this. But she had more in mind a discovered love letter, not photos of her having sex, even pretend sex. And what was pretend sex? How could she not feel she really was betraying Sasha? But she was intrigued and felt confident in her martial arts skills. *Just let him try to go too far*, she thought.

"All right. But I get to stop this any time," she finally said, startled by her own recklessness.

"Deal. Let's start with some pretend oral sex."

"Oral sex? You mean like putting a tongue in someone's mouth?"

Minh smiled. "I mean pictures of your mouth reaching to suck a cock, you looking like you're about to have your pussy licked."

"Don't be disgusting, Minh. I've never done those things," Katya replied, genuinely shocked.

"Oh my, this is just too rich." Minh looked incredulous but highly amused. "Story chapter title, 'In which Katya learns about the joys of oral sex.' You have to be kidding me. Really? Never? In six months with Sasha? In all your twenty-nine years? Please tell me you're joking."

Katya's face turned red. Of course she knew what Minh was talking about, but she was being truthful – she just hadn't put that name to it, had never experienced either kind. In her mind she found herself making excuses: she didn't watch pornography, she had pretended to know what other people were talking about, but she'd never visualized herself doing it, she'd been a virgin. And Le – Sasha and Le had both been virgins, too. Le might not have known to offer... Katya still didn't fully understand oral sex on a woman, must have known that's how women lovers pleasured each other, was a little frightened of the idea, but it probably would have been as unknown to Le as it was to Sasha. And Sasha was so obsessively clean... Katya loved sex with Sasha, had never felt something was lacking in their lovemaking, but what did she know. If she was missing some exciting aspect of sex, she wanted to learn about it, share it with Sasha. But why was she so sure she could trust this man? Or that she could stay in control? This Minh was no bigger than she was, in fact, she was taller. She'd made her threat clear. She would be cautious. She would continue.

"I am sorry, I've embarrassed you. I guess you can tell I honed my English skills reading American pornography," Minh said, looking like he was trying hard not to laugh. "But you *are* joking, aren't you?"

"I'm not joking. I guess I'm an oral sex virgin."

"That must mean Saint Sasha is too. God, he's sixty! You poor children. Let me say you are going to make each other very happy if you survive once you figure this out."

"When we survive this, Minh. And please don't ever call him that. I've only ever heard the Cutters call him that."

"Yes, *when* this is all over. And sorry, Saint Sasha just suits him. How often do you two have sex, anyhow? You must not have experimented much."

"You know that's none of your business," Katya objected.

"It is my business now. I am trying to determine what we need to do first."

"Then, never less than once, almost always twice," she answered, looking him in the eye. "Three times when we can."

"Per week? That's pathetic," Minh laughed. "You're practically still newlyweds. Maybe he's just too old."

"No, sessions per day," Katya answered, taking offence for Sasha's sake. "Sometimes multiple times per session. Every day until yesterday. Sasha never tires and I'm insatiable."

Minh caught his breath, and Katya swore she saw his knees start to buckle. He looked like he'd been punched in the gut. She had thought to put him in his place, but her words seemed to be having quite a different effect. She watched him trying to control his breathing, composing himself.

"Let's start with a dildo, then," he finally sighed. "The room is full of them. I'll find one that looks like me, unless you want to try the real thing."

"Don't get cute. This whole thing is getting very unsexy." Katya wished she wasn't feeling so desperately curious. She couldn't resist. "All right, show me what you mean."

"Here, I've just sterilized this one," Minh braved. "The camera isn't on, give it a try. Take your shirt off so your neck will be bare. You can leave your bra on. Sit here, right next to the camera."

The next half-hour was a comedy of learning how not to choke, of trying to imagine Sasha not being repelled, of trying not to be repelled herself. Katya suddenly thought of the sexual abuse Sasha had suffered as a child and all humor went out of her. Minh kept shaking his head and laughing, giving instructions, not sensing her new hesitation.

Katya was appalled. She'd only been thinking about herself. Sasha would know all too well what oral sex was – between males... She thought what he, a small child, must have had to do to satisfy his abuser... And he'd been raped, beaten, tortured... the trauma remained unresolved, was part of his memory attacks... No wonder he'd never asked her to put her mouth on his cock, that there was a place on his body she could never touch him, that loving gay sex was unthinkable to him.

Poor Sasha... having been forced to give pleasure to a sadistic man, he'd never been able to experience the pleasure for himself as an adult, untouchable as he was... Katya made a decision. She would give him this gift. She would do this for Sasha.

"Good! You're back!" Minh said. "I thought you'd changed your mind for a minute. Imagine you are giving Sasha the most blissful kiss possible, you are going to put him in heaven. Put the damn thing down and use your imagination! Lean forward. Close your eyes, there, that's

420

it, hold your hands out, facing each other, as if they are on either side of it, about to touch it, about to hold it, about to stroke it. Keep your eyes closed, don't you dare open them, this is perfect, perfect. Don't move."

Katya began to feel turned on, like she was doing something sexy after all, that she could imagine Sasha's pleasure. She felt movement in front of her and something warm near her hands.

"I said keep your eyes closed. Open your mouth a little more. Wait, Wait."

Katya heard a number of clicks. The warmth disappeared and there was another quick movement. When she opened her eyes, Minh was looking in the camera, a remote shutter release in his hand.

"Got it!" he shouted. "I'd better have, because I'll never get you to do that again."

"Can I see?"

"No. And that's final."

Then Katya noticed that his shirt was untucked. He was looking hot and flushed himself. She imagined the shirttails also hid the bulge in his hastily zipped slacks.

"Tell me you didn't," she gasped.

"All for a good cause," Minh answered, breathless but unapologetic. "The dildo looked like a dildo to the camera. You are going to make me have to take a cold shower."

Katya glared at him but did not retreat. Each of the rest of the shots had its own difficulties. Minh cajoled and smooth talked her into taking off her bra for a shot with his face clearly in the frame, both with their eyes closed in pretend ecstasy, his tongue reaching out for her nipple, her breast dripping with water from a spray bottle. He undressed completely while her back was turned and arranged several additional less contested poses.

Getting her bottoms off was harder, this time for photos that would look like he was performing oral sex on her. Not being able to kiss or tongue her was already driving him crazy, now trying to demonstrate oral sex without touching her was proving nearly impossible. Minh kept up a steady stream of highly descriptive, pornographic language detailing what he could be doing, his face   only centimeters away from that which he so wished to possess, using the remote to snap his pictures from behind his head. Katya tried to stifle her desire, barely able to keep her hands from grabbing his hair and pulling his head onto her. Regaining self-control, she quickly scooted away from him and crossed her legs. She breathed in and out slowly, then nodded for him to set up another pose.

While he finally had her unclothed, he had her stretch out on her side, and knelt behind her, leaning on one arm, his other hand hovering over her hip, his head bending towards her shoulder as if about to kiss it, her face a study in aroused anticipation as he clicked a series of photos. They were both trembling with unreleased sexual tension, Minh the more so. He kept his promise and did not so much as touch her skin, but Katya felt Minh's desire for her becoming undeniable.

"This would be a lot easier if you just allowed us to have sex," he said, breathing heavily.

"Good try," she answered, her arousal never diminishing, and sorry for his obvious state, "but it's not going to happen and you know it."

Katya found the last pose she was asked to do the hardest. Minh had her get on all fours facing the camera and moved behind her, kneeling. She imagined the scene from Minh's view and flushed deeply. She and Sasha had never had sex in this position. Guilt and pleasure washed over her in equal measure.

"You even come close with your dick and I'll break it in two," she called over her shoulder. She was far too vulnerable in this position, although incredibly aroused. Katya felt protected as much by Minh's hope for real sex in the future as by her own threats. If he tried to force himself on her, that would be the end. She knew she couldn't really carry out her arm-breaking threats. They needed Minh too much. But she would be quick to twist an arm painfully behind his back or put him in a choke hold.

Katya heard several clicks of the shutter, then Minh's footsteps as he hurried away. Good man, no doubt beating off, isn't that what David told her it was called, in the bathroom, she mused. Katya dropped to her stomach with one knee forward and brought herself to a lengthy orgasm and climax. When she sat up, Minh was sitting on the floor near her, one hand resting on a camera. He tossed her a towel and she covered herself. Minh had a towel wrapped around his own waist and his head was wet, like he'd splashed himself with water. From his tender look, Katya could tell he had been taking great pleasure in watching her.

They dressed, not even pretending to look away. There were twelve shots Minh called perfect and said they would be even better when he got through with them, softening the focus, giving them a slight sepia tone. The only one he let her see in the camera was of their two faces, turned from different directions to each other, lips parted, eyes downcast, faces and hair dripping with water, looking like they were just about to kiss. She had to admit it looked convincing and quite sexy. Minh put the room back together the way it had been and made sure he had removed all film and memory cards out of the four cameras.

Katya wanted to thank him, give him some sort of gift for his work and all she had put him through with her protests and arguments, and especially for his remarkable self-control. A chaste kiss would not do, a long, deep passionate one out of the question. She turned him to her as they were leaving and took his face in her hands. She kissed with a pressure she hoped was not too demeaning, not too promising. When their lips separated, Minh leaned back against the door, his back arched, his face a sea of emotions.

"That was a mistake, Katya. A very big mistake."

Chapter 55

Sasha had no real hope of being able to stay longer. They found Sasha's escort in his security office, and Khai ordered him to convey his demand that Sasha stay, or else he would stop working.

"Dahn will make it happen," Khai said, as they watched Dahn typing on a keyboard. "They always give me what I want... if I say I'll stop working," and he surprised Sasha with a laugh.

A response came back immediately. Dahn turned the computer so they could read: "Need Dr. Borodin's information and plan."

Sasha asked if he could respond on Dahn's computer and he nodded. He corresponded back and forth for several minutes and won the approval he needed for his plan, along with permission to stay as long as he wished. Pleased and appreciative, he returned with Khai to the laboratory and had him explain just about everything in his artificial intelligence room. The two men took no notice of the passage of time. A pleasant but insistent chime sounded at 6 p.m. and Khai looked up, annoyed.

"They want us to go home to the village now."

"We have all day tomorrow," Sasha said, though he too was reluctant to leave. "We have as long as we want. I haven't eaten all day, so maybe we should go."

Since he hadn't been allowed to bring his own laptop, he didn't know how he would fill the hours until dawn. He convinced Khai to return to Bao's room to get the cello, although Khai protested that the cello would be hard to hold onto on the subway.

They joined the twenty-three other workers heading home, all of them staring with disbelief at Sasha's presence. They were one too many for the twenty-four seats in the car. Khai was strict in his rule that no one was allowed to stand during the half-hour ride. Lan stopped when she saw their situation and volunteered to stay with her father or take the subway in an hour. Khai promised her he and Sasha would stay the next night and that she could return with the group. Only Sasha caught the disappointment on her face.

Sasha was amused that the subway seats cleverly flipped around so they would be facing forward in both directions. Before he could stop him, Khai was telling everyone that Sasha was his father. Expressions of mistrust turned to surprise and joy. Khai also blurted out that his father must not be touched. Khai introduced Sasha to the laboratory staff, all doctors of physics, computer technicians, programmers, and mechanical engineers. Danh was also there, a well-trained nurse who ran the one-person infirmary, plus a cook and a kitchen helper.

Since Khai had only been speaking English with Sasha, his colleagues were amazed by Sasha's fluent Vietnamese. Sasha met the staff member with one arm he had noted earlier, Dr. Kim, and discussed the possibility of creating a new arm and hand for her. Everyone was excited by the cello, which Khai had never brought to the village in all these years. Khai happily informed them both he and his father would play it for them. When they learned that Sasha was also a violinist, one of the physicists, Tuyen, offered to take out his old violin for him. By the time they reached the village, the workers had cheerfully committed to a communal feast and celebration.

Khai, carrying the cello, hurried on ahead of his father towards the bamboo house he called home. Built on stilts, the roof covered in thatch, Khai's house looked for all the world like a typical Vietnamese village abode. Work and play areas were set up underneath. Chickens scratched in the dirt. All fourteen houses were identical and widely spaced on their circular grid, but Sasha noted personal touches of art and beauty on each that set them apart, such as woven and carved wall hangings and flower boxes or plantings in front. The fifteenth space, used as the helicopter pad, was lined with large and small rocks in a pattern.

Sasha found the interior of Khai's house impressively designed, with bamboo laminate flooring and walls like he'd seen in the café, and bamboo built-in shelving and cabinetry throughout the kitchen, bathroom, and living room. There were three bedrooms, two with double beds, one with twins, and one bathroom. The design would be easy and inexpensive to build in any country where bamboo was abundant, and Sasha was already imagining using some of his new fund money to create housing where most needed. The rooms were comfortably furnished, and the cushions and drapes, sheets and towels, even the throw rugs were all fabricated using bamboo cloth. Sasha looked for a label on a cushion. Someone did indeed know who he was, knew he was Khai's father. The cushion, and surely all the bamboo fabrics and much of the clothing he'd seen on the staff had been manufactured at one of Sasha's rehabilitation and refugee centers. The same fabrics he used inside his boat and for his own clothing.

Khai proudly pointed out the independent water recycling and purification system he had designed and placed in each home, and the toilet waste recovery system that dropped packages of clean compost under the house ready for use in the gardens. Sasha mentally added two more items to his world-wide funding checklist. He was pleased to see the village was using his own solar panels. They would provide more than sufficient power.

"Do you live here alone?" Sasha asked, thinking that three bedrooms was rather an extravagance for a frugal, single man.

"Oh no, Lan and Bao live here with me. You can have Bao's bed tonight... or Lan's if she stays with her father. Or the extra twin bed."

Interesting, thought Sasha. Poor Lan. He wondered if Khai was capable of the sort of revelation that happened to him when his fingers touched Le's. Lan was waiting for him.

"What about the other houses? Does everyone share space?"

"Single women and men... like me... share a house... or have a room in a house. Some even get married... to each other. We have seven children here now. They're lots of fun... I like children. Several of my staff brought their older parents. We still have eight empty rooms... space to grow."

Khai was bustling in the surprisingly modern kitchen while he talked, putting together a communal dish for the celebration. He seemed quite adept at cooking, checking seasoning, tasting as he worked. Sasha thought with a start that he hadn't cooked in decades, and badly then. He was thankful the dish Khai was preparing was vegetarian. Sasha imagined meat was a rare treat here in the village. They would have plenty of fish from their stocked pond. He looked forward to exploring the gardens and fields in the morning. More ideas for his fund checklist, he was sure. Sasha noted that Khai's use of language, although still eccentric, seemed to improve when he was away from the many distractions of his laboratory. He found himself enjoying the peace and harmony here immensely.

"When did you design this village, Khai?"

"Eighteen years, two months, and four days ago. They brought me to that underground place... when I was about fourteen. I don't know my birthday. Very boring here then. Had been a military place. I redesigned the inside... but I missed the sky and fresh air. I grew up on a farm. I had them fly me around... until I found where I wanted to live... then I had them build the subway there. I designed and built the tunnel borer, too... I built the village around where we came up... lots of soldiers helping. Finished seventeen years, ten months and three days ago. Everybody loved it. Much easier to get people... to come work with me."

"Tell me about where you grew up," Sasha asked, not quite sure he was ready to hear.

"Big farm, rice fields to work in... lots of kids. Most not like me... something wrong with them... but we were all friends. All of us orphans. I called one woman my mother... although I knew she wasn't. She was very young... Her son was my best friend... the same age... we grew from infants together, she told me. She was like me... a half-breed, they called us. There were other half-breeds there... the half-American, and the half-Korean. They called them the Lai Dai Han... mixed bloods. I don't know why everyone was so mean to them. She loved me... even though I didn't like to be held. Tried to protect me... from the mean men who ran the place... and she taught me to read and write French and English... as well as Vietnamese... taught me math... I was always in trouble. The men beat me a lot... but I still got in trouble... me and Minh... especially when someone called us bastards," Khai said. "Then they beat me so much I got sick... if anyone touched me. That was bad."

"Wait, Minh?" Sasha asked, startled by the name.

"Lots of Minhs there. Don't know why."

"What happened to your special friend Minh, the one that was your age?"

"My brother Minh? Someone paid to send him to school... when he was still young... and he never came back. But he sent me books... and a Walkman... and lots of music cassettes... with violins and cellos and such. Lots and lots of books... Math, science. Some were physics books... That got me started."

Sasha's mind was reeling. His brother, he'd called him. This had to be their Minh, with his half-Caucasian mother, his knowledge of Khai's childhood. Minh had discovered Cyrus Cutter was about to kill his childhood friend, and then who his friend's father was and had to intervene. Minh had made Khai's future possible. Sasha owed everything, finding his son, finding a way to save all their lives, to Minh. He wondered if Minh knew who his sponsor was, and why he would support Khai as well. The gifts of books and music hadn't been chosen by a child.

"How old was Minh when he left?"

"He knew his birthday... unlike me. He was eight years, three months and thirty days old. His mother got sick... and then she died after he left. I got books for six more years... I especially liked the books on Tesla and Mandelbrot. Then mean men left... new men came. Talked to me about all the books... asked lots of questions. Then a man came... and talked to me about physics. I'd never been able to talk about physics... and engineering and math and robotics... with anybody. One day some officers came... and took me with them. Then I was here where the lab is now. They gave me fun jobs to do. Making things. Designing things. They found smart people to work with me. Many were half-breeds... like me."

"Did you ever see Minh again?"

"No, never. I missed my best friend... my brother. A new box of books that got sent to the farm... got sent on to me... but not again."

Sasha found it difficult to enjoy the celebration the village put on for him. His mind was completely occupied by thoughts of his son and Minh, and then of Katya and Minh. He tried to sit back and observe the gaiety, but kept getting requests to talk about his life, his past, his music. He was pleased Lan appeared, and spoke with her for quite a while. She asked him all the questions Khai would never think to ask, especially about his mother, and how Sasha had made the connection with Le, and now with his new wife, those magic moments of touching. Sasha felt odd telling Lan how passionate he and Katya had become, that he hadn't believed he could ever be passionate again after Le.

Lan told him a little about her life, that she and her father had lived with Khai since she and Khai were fifteen and sixteen, that her mother and two older brothers were killed in the napalm bombing that left her and her father so badly burned, that Khai had taught her to be a computer coder and she'd gotten quite good at it. She also unabashedly asked Sasha how old he was and was surprised that he was sixty. He looked so much younger than her father, who was only eight years older. Sasha stayed close to Khai to try to prevent him from talking about his laboratories. He already wished he had said nothing about them. He could imagine Khai boasting about his father's secret work to his government handlers, but there was nothing to be done about it now, and he decided he wouldn't care. Besides, it seemed likely they already knew who, and what, he was.

The old violin Tuyen provided him was playable, and he performed with enough spirit to more than satisfy his listeners. Sasha knew dozens of original works or transcriptions for violin and cello. He was able to download a few for Khai and they played duets together, thrilling the staff, then he played the cello himself.

All the villagers, from a child of four to the oldest grandparent, seemed to be tech-savvy, and computers were everywhere. Sasha noted satellite dishes discreetly placed in many locations. Khai had taught himself to play the cello with a lesson book that came with it and computer programs. Sasha found him to be a fine musician with a delicate touch and a good ear.

Khai told his father he liked the sound of the cello in the music Minh sent him. One day, sixteen years, four months and two days ago, he decided he wanted a cello and asked for one. It arrived without a bow and he had to wait a month for it, learning the notes by playing pizzicato. Tuyen gave him lessons when he arrived to work in the laboratory the next year.

The celebration wound down, family members leaving first, then the staff wandering off to their own houses to sleep before beginning work again in the morning. Sasha found Khai to be in as little need of sleep as he was and they talked until late in the night. Explaining his life to Khai was more difficult than he thought. He skipped over Bergen-Belsen and the more negative memories of his life with Harrison Mandelbrot, preferring to describe practicing medicine and playing music on the *Trib*, his crew, his love for Katya. Khai asked few questions, offered little information about his own life, and especially didn't seem to want to talk more about his mother.

Dawn found Sasha outside finishing his workout. Since the sun rose so late in January, he had started in his room an hour before, not knowing when Khai and the others would be leaving for the laboratory. He shivered in the morning chill in this northern mountain zone. The garden was still lush and productive, the views towards the blue-cast hills and granite mountains heavenly. This was the Vietnam he had always dreamed of living in, not the war-ravaged country of his memories or the still poor, if not quite as poor as before, coastal villages and cities he visited on his medical missions, with their floating islands of plastic trash. The drop in population with his One Pill had not seemed to have affected Vietnam much, but at least there weren't the scores of unwanted children he remembered during the War. Children were wanted and cherished, like they were here in Khai's village.

Sasha was determined to be more successful in clearing his mind and enjoying this gift of time with his son. He would spend one more day and night here, return to Katya in Hanoi and fly back with her to Sydney, then travel on without her to Da Nang to begin the terrible endgame. The rest of his second day was spent in the laboratory working with Khai. They didn't return to Khai's house until 8 p.m., the only passengers on the subway. He and Khai talked for hours about their work before they both went to bed. Sasha found he didn't mind continuing to break S-Branch's rules of secrecy, proudly claiming his work in all his fields, but especially in robotics and prosthetics, happy for Khai's brilliant input. After a difficult night of strange visions and partially glimpsed memories, Sasha was up again before dawn to work out, finishing in the yard at first light.

Khai, looking downcast, watched his father exercising from the doorway, then came down the steps to join him when he finished. Sasha had been observing him as well, surprised that his departure today was apparently going to be as hard on Khai as it was for him. Sasha wanted to put his hands on Khai's shoulders and touch heads like he did with the crew, but he knew that wouldn't work. How do two people who cannot abide touch reach out to each other? He thought about the progress he'd made the day of New Year's Eve, tolerating physical contact with Aashir, Tuan, and Kiko. He had not yet dared with any of the rest of the crew. He did a few breathing exercises and decided to try.

"Khai, I've been working on something. You can help me."

Khai quickly dropped his sad demeanor and nodded eagerly, happy to oblige, as was his nature. Sasha stood close and took a few more deep breaths. He loved the way Khai could turn on a smile like a light bulb.

"Listen, Khai, I want you to try putting your hands on my shoulders," he said, speaking in a calm and reassuring voice. "I promise I won't pass out."

"Are you sure? I know how bad I feel... if someone does that to me."

"I'm sure. Just don't take them away if I cringe or shudder. Hold them there."

Khai did as he was asked, and Sasha let a strong shudder move through his body and away. He then felt such a connection with his son standing there before him he didn't want to move, such inner peace that he didn't want it to end. He couldn't tell if Khai felt the same way.

"Now touch your forehead to mine, Khai. Don't move your hands."

Khai moved his head forward awkwardly and they stayed in that position for a full minute. The sense of connection was even stronger, memories of his time with Le washing over him like waves over sand. Sasha could tell Khai was getting restless, and he reluctantly stepped back, breaking the connection. He looked into Khai's face. It was expressionless.

"Well?" Khai asked.

"That was wonderful. Thank you, Khai. I hope someday you will experience something like what I just did. I felt it with your mother for the first time in my life."

"I hope for that, too, Sasha..." Khai jumped to another thought altogether. "We still have time... before work... Let's ride the horses."

Sasha gave his son his near smile.

"There's nothing I would like better."

The ride to the laboratory on the subway was boisterous, the staff still excited by Sasha's presence. Sasha worked alongside his son on dozens of ongoing projects, making suggestions and finding solutions, taking copious mental notes on Khai's robotics and artificial intelligence research. Khai helped him figure out how to order food in the little café and they took it outside to eat in the courtyard, surrounded by Khai's admiring staff members.

Sasha watched as his son separated all the food on his bamboo plate, eating one kind at a time, fish, vegetables, and rice, the same way he had eaten his food as a child in Sydney. Like father, like son. Perhaps also like father, Khai would be able to grow and change the way he had, first because of Le, then because of Katya. Perhaps Khai would discover Lan. Sasha felt he'd changed more in the last six months than he ever could have imagined. Because of Katya. But his son was happy and successful, he could smile and laugh. What father could wish for more. He couldn't have been more pleased with his son's life, especially since he'd imagined a dreary existence for him in a soul-less industrial complex as a protected government scientist. Now he had to ensure that it would continue.

"There's one more room... I want to show you," Khai said, the monotone of his voice belying his obvious excitement.

Sasha headed after Khai as he rushed down a different set of stairs. Sasha found himself in a large store, not unlike the strange drug store he'd discovered in San Francisco, but with more groceries, clothing, and household items as well as a pharmacy. He heard laughter and saw Mai, a computer coder, sitting next to Van, the blind former physics professor, at a pair of computers.

"They are ordering new shoes for Van," Khai explained. "We can go online... and choose anything we want. The order goes to Dahn. And if we can't find what we like... he'll try to find it for us. He keeps the store stocked too."

"How do you pay for things?" Sasha asked.

"Pay? We just take what we need... or order what we want and it comes. Dahn gives it to us."

"Is anything refused? Does anybody order more than they need?"

"Why would we?" Khai asked, genuinely confused.

"Why indeed," Sasha replied, smiling his near smile. "Tell me more about Van."

"Van is so smart. We work on projects together. He was the only one who could talk at my level... about physics, before you. He inspires me. Makes me think harder. He was a theoretical physics professor... in Hanoi. So sad... lost his vision... his family... his job in the bombings during the War."

"I hope I get a chance to get to know him. I might even be able to help him see again. I'm so sorry I have to leave today."

Once they were back in Bao's room, Khai was eager to share his plans, his voice rising out of its monotone in excited bursts.

"I'm going to start right now... building a special tube... to place inside our fake engine model. I'll let the bad guy... see me run inside. When he blows it up... I'll be untouched in the tube!"

"Khai, I hope we can do something safer than that," Sasha replied, shaking his head.

"No, Sasha, this is perfect. I can wear a bullet-proof vest... in case he tries to shoot me first. I bet the soldiers have one they can loan me. From the base... way above the laboratory. We're right on the border with China... but I've never been there."

"Your schedule is so predictable, Khai. Your staff tells me you always work on that model first thing in the morning, and that might be right before the explosion in Da Nang. I bet the explosion here will be on a timer and he'll be long gone."

"That will still work! I'll just stay in the tube... for a long time... waiting. I could take a laptop with me. No one... will be able to ask me a question for hours."

"We will know the approximate time of the explosion but we're only guessing it will be your model that they blow up."

"Your job... is to make sure that it is. Tell them it's my most important work. Let me demonstrate my tube for you. In an hour. I'll make a little model. You'll love it."

Sasha could see there was no arguing with him. He hoped the would-be killer would be gone and that a body would not be needed as proof. Khai's clothes and a bloody mangled mannequin from the robotics lab under a sheet would have to suffice. Bao would see to it. Khai showed him a design he'd drawn for a morgue-style cart with space to hide him underneath. Bao would take the "body" away to prepare it, and their government handlers would collect it. Sasha was sorry for the emotional pain he would be causing the staff, but then they would have their moment of joy when Khai was returned to them after three days. He hoped he would be alive to celebrate with them from afar.

434

Chapter 56

Katya sat impatiently waiting at the Hanoi heliport for Sasha's flight to arrive. It was already 7 p.m. and dark. Sasha had postponed his return so many times. She'd spent an uncomfortable rest of the day with Minh, an all too quiet dinner, and another day of half-hearted sightseeing after a nearly sleepless night in her cold and lonely bed. Minh had tried to carry on with his wit and flirting, but Katya could see the pain in his eyes. He wanted her, that was clear, and she was now certain he loved her as well. She'd insisted on waiting alone for Sasha, although she noted two of Minh's security men lurking nearby. Minh looked far less capable of hiding his attraction for her now than he did when he first saw her in the Situation Room.

Sasha would never have noticed just six months ago, but now things were quite different. Sasha's life would be in Minh's hands once he was Cyrus Cutter's captive and it was her fault Minh might now be unmotivated to save him. She would have to explain it best she could to Sasha immediately. Maybe they would have to rethink their plan, take out Cutter while Sasha remained safely hidden somewhere. She would let him decide. It worried her to think that Minh might use the photos to blackmail her or show them to Sasha now and destroy his trust, even his love for her. The photo shoot had been a huge mistake.

She threw herself into Sasha's arms when he arrived. He looked tired and disheveled but pleased, and despite the crowd around them and the two Australian bodyguards who had met him at the last helicopter landing, they shared a long and passionate kiss. She wondered how much time they would have together before she would have to tell him. They had no more turned to leave when Minh appeared, an innocent smile on his face.

"Welcome back, Sasha," Minh said, "I can tell your trip was a successful one since you kept extending it. I'm sorry you have to wait until the morning for a flight to Sydney with Katya, but that gives us a chance to get to know each other."

Sasha surprised Katya by putting both his hands on Minh's shoulders in greeting.

"We have much to talk about, Minh. I'm glad that you're here. Let's head out, Katya." He and Khai owed this man so much, he thought.

He kept a hand on Minh's shoulder as they walked, something Katya had never seen him do with any man. She brought up the rear, confused. Minh had a van and driver waiting, and they traveled in near silence to the safe house. As much as Minh trusted his security staff, Cyrus Cutter could have a listening ear anywhere. Sasha knew well that Minh could not let his connection to Khai get back to Cyrus Cutter. All the bodyguards disappeared when they arrived and were safely inside.

Food was brought in so they could talk while they ate. Katya had not had a moment alone with Sasha. Minh gave Sasha his full attention, and she began to wonder if, in her mind, she had exaggerated the threat.

"Katya, I have a story to tell you that will rival any I've told so far," Sasha began. "First, Minh, why didn't you tell me your mother raised you and Khai together? You're like his brother."

Minh didn't reply for a long moment. He didn't even glance over at Katya when he heard her gasp in surprise.

"I really didn't think you would find out," Minh finally answered. "It didn't make any difference to the plan to save you and him. I haven't seen Khai in twenty-five years, but I recognized his name and put it together. I wasn't even absolutely sure it was him, although Cutter's certainty was good proof. The man would die whether he was Khai or not. I knew you would be able to verify him. How is he?"

"Amazingly successful and happy, thanks to you. Your gift of books allowed him to educate himself and his genius for physics, engineering, and robotics became recognized by his government. He has built quite the world around himself, with an adoring laboratory staff that he lives with in a remarkably harmonious village he created. I have a lot of new ideas from examining his work. He's the same happy, uncomplicated autistic child you knew, but now thirty-three years old."

"Still can't be touched?"

"Like me, though Katya's helping me make some progress. I made a physical connection with him that was amazing while it lasted. Nothing from his side, though. But he did know who I was right away and seemed pleased to meet me. I can't thank you enough, Minh. I owe you his happiness, and now his life, if this all works out as planned."

Mentioning Katya's name brought her back to his attention. Sasha looked over at her for the first time since they sat down to eat. She was staring back and forth between the two of them, smiling broadly. He reached over and touched her cheek.

"I'm sorry, I'm still excited," he apologized. "I will fill you in on every detail later, Katya."

"I would like to hear every detail, too," Minh insisted. "He is very much like my brother. My mother told me we both nursed from her breast. She said Khai arrived when I was only a few weeks old, he a tiny newborn. I guess that makes him more like my twin."

"Then let me be like your father, Minh. I am more of a fellow scientist than a father to Khai and I don't know when I'll get to see him again. Plus I want to hear what kind of mischief you and Khai got into as boys."

Katya stole a glance at Minh and he looked back at her with resignation.

After a long night of talking, Sasha told Katya to head on upstairs, that he needed to talk to Minh for a moment. Once she and Sasha were alone in bed that night, she debated telling him about the photos and Minh's attraction to her. How was there ever a right time, she wondered. Certainly not before they had a chance to make love again. She decided it might be too suspicious to try anything new she had learned. She sat across his lap and leaned down to kiss his lips, his face, his neck, sliding her fingers over every inch of his upper body, tracing his lines of scars. He pulled her down close and their mouths touched, then he did that thing with his tongue that drove her wild. She moaned with pleasure as he moved down her body, kissing her from throat to just above her pubic hair.

She could imagine now how it would feel if he were to kiss further down, and she came just at the thought of it. Sasha moved up, kissing her breasts while she let the orgasms continue on and on. Then he was inside her and they rocked up and down for as long as he could hold back, her continuous orgasms melting into his. At last, he lay still on top of her, certain that she could hold his weight, her hands stroking his back until he fell asleep. Katya lay for a long time thinking before she rolled him onto his side, curled up against his familiar warmth and slept.

Katya awoke to the dreaded cacophony of horns from the street that almost drowned out the footfalls coming from the far side of the room where Sasha was doing his morning workout. She sat up and smiled at him. She'd decided she would wait until they got to Sydney to talk about Minh and the photo shoot. She couldn't face a confrontation between the two of them, not when Sasha was so happy with him. Sasha the father figure. The idea was hard to get used to. Sasha's enthusiastic description of his visit with his son was worthy of a short story, or even a novella. She was relieved that he'd worked out a coded signal system with Bao to confirm that his son was alive and well after the supposed catastrophe would occur. The signal would work both ways. Bao would get an immediate notification that would tell him Sasha was out of danger or that the Cutter threat had ended, that Khai could be resurrected. Bao insisted on staying hidden and on guard to protect Khai. If he had to, he would kill any intruder before he would let Khai be killed.

Sweaty and unshowered, Sasha came over and sat on the bed next to Katya. He ran a hand through her hair and kissed her, then held the back of her head gently but firmly and looked into her eyes.

"What is it that you're not telling me?" he asked, careful not to sound accusatory.

"For someone not terribly intuitive about people's emotions just six months ago, you're doing extremely well. It's Minh," she answered, feeling guilty.

"What about him?"

"I'm afraid he has a real crush on me. He's been overly attentive, shall we say."

"Well, I would hope so," Sasha said, again keeping emotion out of his voice. "He's supposed to be seen having an affair with you."

"But I think he's serious. What if he changes his mind about protecting you?"

"You're worrying needlessly. If you've been giving him the cold shoulder, Cyrus Cutter's spies will see it. You have time to see him this morning before we go, someplace public. Or maybe we should stay longer."

"I thought you'd be jealous, Sasha. Now I'm just confused."

Sasha bent over more and pulled her face to his and kissed her again, then sat up straight, trying not to look as agitated as he was. He had his poker face on, his eyes gave nothing away.

"You should trust me more since I trust you. And if Minh has fallen in love with you, all I can say is, how could he not?"

"So, what are you asking me to do?"

"Put on a show, look like you're sneaking behind my back, go to him. Get dressed. I bet he's downstairs already."

"Don't make me do this, Sasha. It will be a mistake."

Sasha leaned over and kissed her again, then took her hands and gave a teasing pull.

"I'm going to take a shower. Be back in a half-hour or so."

Katya felt trapped. How could she be sure Sasha wasn't testing her, hoping she would refuse? She finally pulled on some clothes, ran a brush through her hair, then opened the shower curtain and kissed his shoulder before leaving. Minh was downstairs standing in the open doorway, watching the insane traffic of early morning motorcycles and trucks that never ceased their beeping, choking fumes wafting into the room. She put her arms around his waist and pushed him gently forward with her body.

He didn't turn around but reached for a hand and pulled her carefully through the traffic to the entryway of a still closed storefront on the other side of the street, out of view of the safe house. He turned toward her slowly and drew her close. His hands were suddenly everywhere, his lips crushed hers. Minh's forceful pressure was painfully unpleasant. Katya hadn't taken him for such a terrible kisser. Despite the discomfort, she did her best to look like she was returning his passion, and although she was just pretending, her body couldn't help responding to his wild touch. It was evident to her Minh was aroused as well. Once again, she wondered what she was thinking when she started all this. Minh finally released her lips and spoke in her ear, his hands still roving her body.

"You smell deliciously like sex. I have to say thank you for this. I know it's not real, but I don't care. Now trust me."

Minh took her hand, turned, and stuck a key into the store's lock. Opening the door quickly he pulled her inside. He gave her a much less passionate kiss, then led her to a table and chairs near the back. There were two mineral water bottles waiting for them. He hunched over the table, breathing deeply. Then he picked up a bottle and handed her the other, clinking his against hers in a pretend toast. Katya was overcome with guilt. She could hardly believe that what she felt

439

was disappointment. She too breathed through her arousal, looking down at the table.

"We'll give our watchers about twenty more minutes," Minh said. "We don't want them to get bored looking at a closed door. Listen, Katya, things are going to look really bad next time I see you. I know what Cyrus Cutter has in mind for Sasha. Just know I'm not going to let it happen."

"Thank you, Minh," Katya sighed, looking up, grateful once again for Minh's self-control, for his promise. "But tell me, did Sasha set this up with you?"

"What do you think?" Minh said, a sad half-smile on his face, nodding towards a security camera pointed their direction.

In the shower, Sasha let his head and hands rest against the front wall as the lukewarm water streamed down his back. Telling Katya to go had been harder than he thought. He wanted to trust her, and he trusted Minh to control himself, to a certain degree. Katya was right. Even he could tell Minh was in love with her. Minh had told him briefly about the photo shoot, but what bothered Sasha was what Minh was leaving out in the telling. And the fact Katya didn't tell him anything at all. Nobody knew better than he what a sexual creature Katya was, how irresistible. How easily aroused.

Sasha dressed, pulled a watch cap low over his blond hair, put on sunglasses and headed out to the street. He ordered a vegetarian dish from a sidewalk vender not too far away and sat on the low stool, his back to the pork sizzling on the grill, watching the front door of the supposedly safe house. He was only acting, playing the just enlightened cuckolded fool for Cutter's watchers, as he stared forlornly at Minh and Katya when they returned, and as they shared a lingering last embrace and quick kiss before entering the house. Only acting... Or so he told himself.

Once back in Sydney, Sasha felt his love life with Katya was not the same, despite three long sessions per day in their cabin on the *Trib*. He couldn't stay away from her, returning midday from the labs. Katya seemed to need something more from him, had some urge that he had no idea how to fulfill. She didn't speak of it and he didn't ask. Katya had tried to inform him about the photo shoot, but he'd been curt in answering that Minh had told him all about it, that her concerns were baseless.

Strange dreams continued to disturb Sasha's sleep, apparently triggered by his new relationship with his son. The same question kept repeating itself – would he take a bullet for Khai, for Katya even? Katya had already taken two for him and he had no doubt she would take any conceivable risk again. Maybe he was more worried about the coming endgame than he thought. There were no guarantees that anything would work as planned, no guarantee of anyone's survival.

On the fourth night, Sasha awakened Katya with his loud shouting. He found himself sitting on the side of their berth, drenched in sweat, shaking uncontrollably. He had no memory of getting half out of bed. But the memory he'd recalled in his sleep was clear and horrifying. Katya moved quickly to him, kneeling behind him, massaging his shoulders. Hiro and Maxim heard his shouts as well, and she called to them that she was handling the situation.

"Sasha, talk to me," she spoke soothingly in his ear.

"I've been seeing images in my dreams," Sasha replied, continuing to shake. "Bits and pieces of what must be a repressed memory. It started after I met Khai, when after all these years I was truly a father myself. And just now, Katya, I saw my own father, and an image of my mother... I saw them at the moment of their deaths."

Sasha felt Katya's hands cease their rhythmic stroking, heard her gasp, felt her arms encircle him.

"Sasha, I'm listening," she whispered. "I'm here for you. Go on."

"I don't know if I can."

"I think you should, Sasha," she said, as she sank lower, leaning her head on his shoulder, holding him tighter.

"I've been obsessing over whether I would sacrifice my life for Khai, or for you, take a bullet to be precise. I couldn't understand why, until now. Katya, I saw my father jump in front of my mother and me, I saw his fear, his sacrificial love. I watched him die."

"Tell me what you saw. Tell me everything," Katya said, repressing her own emotions.

"There was a group of us, maybe seven adults and me... I remember being hauled up from a hiding place under the floorboards, then we were standing in front of a house. I don't remember any talking, I still don't know for certain what nationality we were. I just heard loud shouts in German. There were men with guns, a pair of

441

Nazi SS officers and a number of regular soldiers. The officers were arguing back and forth, one pointing at my mother. I knew enough German to know they were debating whether to shoot her or take her with..." Sasha's voice trailed off, he hesitated to go on. His body continued to shake violently.

"Why wouldn't they want to take her with the others, Sasha?" Katya managed to ask. She could barely speak herself.

"My mother was very far along with child, the child that would have been my sister or brother. I remember she was also terribly ill. As I clung to her skirts, I could feel her trembling, her body swaying with the effort to stay on her feet. One officer finally pushed the other away and raised his pistol towards her head. My father broke away from the soldiers and threw himself in between them, taking the bullet. The officer... the officer began viciously kicking him, over and over again, even as he lay dying, his eyes never leaving my mother's.

"A soldier came forward and knelt down, reaching out for me. His face was grim, but he looked kind, sympathetic. I remember he was blond. Maybe he had a blond son of his own at home. He looked up at my mother and I saw him nod. Maybe she nodded back, I don't know, but she gently pushed me towards him. I couldn't see my mother until he led me away, and even then I still couldn't see her face, just a halo of golden hair. I turned further, looking back over my shoulder, and the face inside the halo turned into Le's face, smiling sadly at me. The soldier picked me up and pressed my face firmly against his uniform. I remember how scratchy it felt, that it smelled sour. I heard the sound of a second gunshot. The rest of us were quickly loaded into the back of a truck. I saw two bodies left on the ground as we drove away. My next memory is of being held by a woman I didn't know in a hot, crowded cattle car, its loud rumble and clacks, its jerky movement, the stunned silence of the people around me, a gruesome smell I now associate with fear... a long, horrific journey..."

Sasha leaned his head against Katya's, held onto her arms and closed his eyes. She moved forward to sit next to him, resuming their embrace, and began to speak. He quickly shushed her. How he had longed to remember his parents, and this horror was all that came back to him. He had a hard time imagining how his father must have looked before being hunted, hounded, starved. Sasha could see his face clearly enough in his mind to think he must have been handsome once,

442

with high cheekbones, light brown hair, dark grey eyes like his. His own blond hair was from his mother, no doubt once beautiful. His heart told him they were both Russian Jews, what else could they be. His mother perhaps ethnic Russian, with that bright blond hair. A convert out of love into a persecuted religion, a religion he had callously walked away from.

What a terrible trick of memory, replacing his mother's face with Le's. Both dead, both shot in front of him. Sasha resolved that he would not lose any more people he loved no matter what the price – his soul, his sanity, his life. He would win this endgame. Cyrus Cutter would go down in permanent defeat. Katya, Khai, and his crew would be safe when it was all over. He would show no mercy. He would waste no more precious time with Katya, no more worrying about Minh. He would seize every moment with her as if it were their last.

Chapter 57

Sasha sat down in his place of honor on an improvised grandstand directly in front of the swankiest hotel on the Han riverfront, near the mouth of the harbor. His two bodyguards were seated directly in front. Minh took the seat next to him and three of Minh's security men sat behind them. Almost two weeks had passed since he had returned to Australia, and everything was going according to plan. A week ago, Sasha had made his farewells to his crew and kissed Katya goodbye in Sydney, watching the boat motor away from the safe harbor, heading towards Vietnam. Aashir and Tuan had departed quietly for Ho Chi Minh City earlier that morning. Five days later, Sasha traveled to Da Nang by military plane with two Australian bodyguards.

A large number of Da Nang dignitaries and government officials turned out for the ceremony, along with scores of local businessmen and doctors, and a dozen local and national reporters. The international press had not been notified. Sasha tried hard to look animated and excited but had to depend on Minh to provide the smiles and laughs. Sasha also tried hard not to look in the direction of Cyrus Cutter, who was seated not three meters away, just two rows behind them to the side. Minh had no such compunction, openly smiling at him in greeting. After all, Cyrus Cutter was a well-known and respected businessman, friend and supporter to half the politicians in Da Nang and Hanoi. And his employer.

The *Retribution* could already be seen just outside the harbor, unfurling her sails for a glorious entry after motoring her way from Sydney. The mayor of Da Nang was ready with a commendation for Sasha and the crew of the *Retribution* for their years of service to the medical needs of the country of Vietnam. The President and Prime Minister, while protesting their exclusion, had been convinced to stay away. Minh nodded to Cyrus and received a nod in return. Minh watched Cyrus lift his high-powered binoculars to observe the *Retribution* and raised his own to the boat as well. He could see the crew moving around the deck, even Katya, and spied Maxim at the helm, accompanied by Hiro and Dima in the pilothouse, barely visible through the tinted glass windows. This can't be right, he thought. He forced himself to stay calm. Why were they all still on the boat?

With all her sails unfurled, the Retribution was a beautiful sight as she made her way quickly towards the harbor. Her sails filled with wind on this warm and sunny day, the incessant rain of the past week thankfully past. The crew disappeared into the main cabin and the *Retribution* sailed on.

A young official moved through the grandstand, apologizing to each person he stepped around. He held a piece of paper in his hands, an urgent message, and the look of sorrow and dismay on his face showed that he knew what was written on it – Sasha's son had been killed in an accidental explosion. He was stopped and questioned by a bodyguard, then allowed to continue. He reached Sasha and handed him the paper with an apologetic bow, and quickly retreated. Sasha and Minh appeared annoyed at the untimely interruption, and Sasha seemed reluctant to take his eyes off of his glorious sailboat to read it. Minh glanced over at Cyrus to make sure he was watching and nodded again. Sasha finally glanced down at the paper and seemed to collapse into himself. He stood up and stared out at his boat with a look of terrible and fearful anticipation.

The *Retribution* was fast approaching the space between two large motorboats, one on either side of the wide bay, the only boats that far out in the harbor. When she was even with them, two nearly simultaneous booms split the air and the *Retribution* exploded in a massive fireball, flaming pieces flying in all directions, billowing smoke filling the space left by the boat, then clearing almost instantly in the wind, leaving nothing visible but a wildly rocking ocean covered in burning debris. A shock wave moved out in a fast-growing circle, splashing the observers closest to the seawall.

The terror-struck crowd stood up as one, screaming and shouting. Only one man was not staring at the horrific scene on the water. Cyrus Cutter was looking straight at Sasha, smiling at the look of utter devastation and loss on his face. Sasha fell to his knees, then collapsed further to the boards of the grandstand, his eyes remaining fixed on the place where the *Retribution* had been. Minh, his face displaying horror and panic, reached for him, as did the official standing on his other side, but Sasha fought them off wildly, his eyes unmoved from the scene of destruction. He clutched at his heart, sweat dampened his body, his hair, and he began to shake and tremble violently. Minh

446

stayed by him, holding his shoulders tightly although he continued to resist, and the shaking became much worse. The crowd stampeded off the grandstand around them; guards rushed to secure the safety of the dignitaries and officials. Military patrol boats zoomed towards the debris on the water, but the two motorboats had vanished in opposite directions.

Minh, his security service men, and Sasha's bodyguards were finally able to load a nearly catatonic Sasha into Minh's van, and he had his driver take off quickly towards a secure safe house in a Da Nang suburb, far from the city center, riverside hotels, and docks. Minh listened with increasing genuine horror to the first reports from the harbor investigation on his police scanner and decided to give Sasha a strong sedative. He knew Sasha would never have agreed, but now he wanted him asleep as long as possible. His men carried Sasha in and placed him on a bed in an upstairs room, and Minh covered his damp body with blankets. Fighting down his own fears, Minh sat with him for a while, watching his unconscious sleep, then got a pitcher of water and a glass ready for when he awoke.

Local news reports were full of the disaster, and international reporters were quick to pick up the story when they learned an American had been on board. Minh and Katya had been sure the story would have stayed local. The government didn't want to cause a panic among the populace and tourists about torpedoes in their harbors and put out a story that the two powerful motors on the sailboat must not have been properly shut down or had malfunctioned after the long voyage from Australia, had exploded. Bits of bodies were discovered among the wreckage, along with pieces of clothing that had been seen on the crew. Film images of Sasha's collapse, though from a distance, were all over the news.

Over the next two days, condolences issued from around the world. The Australian government demanded an immediate investigation. Katya's friends in California talked about planning a memorial service. Fujio and Umi mourned. David was inconsolable.

Not in the news was the explosion in an underground science laboratory in northern Vietnam that claimed the life of the lead scientist. The government officials handling the facility informed the stunned staff that Khai had been running an experiment alone in the laboratory when the large engine he was testing malfunctioned and exploded, killing him instantly, destroying almost all of the ongoing

447

projects in the room. The deeply saddened staff gathered together to mourn. No one knew how they could possibly continue. The physics laboratory was closed until further notice, absolutely no admittance. Only the robotics laboratory would remain operational. In addition, until further notice, the officials were shutting down all internet access to the staff, both in the underground facility and in the village. Many of the tech-savvy staff noted quietly that internet service had been shut down nearly an hour before the explosion.

Sasha awoke dry-mouthed and exhausted. The sedative had kept him unconscious for hours. Minh helped him drink several glasses of water and encouraged him to think about taking a long shower, but he didn't move.

"Did it all work as planned? Have you heard from Bao?" Sasha was barely able to ask, as he lay back on the bed. He hated the crushing sense of nameless guilt that overwhelmed him, would sink him into an unavoidable, dark, post-attack depression.

"Bao sent his message, so everything worked out well there," Minh answered quietly. "Khai is safe. No word yet from the crew or Katya. Just rest now."

Minh didn't want to tell him yet about the body parts found in the water. He felt sick enough himself knowing that it was all in vain, that some, or all, had not been able to get off the *Trib* replica in time, that Katya might be dead. Sasha looked far from recovered from his forced panic attack. Minh and his unwitting accomplice, the official sitting on Sasha's other side, had accomplished that by seizing tight hold of him in the guise of trying to help a stricken man. Minh could have warned Sasha what he was going to do, but he'd chosen not to. He'd already heard from Cyrus that he couldn't have been more thrilled with Sasha's suffering and what he saw as the public humiliation of his blackout. Minh knew well the world only saw a man collapsing in unbearable sorrow and loss. For his boat, his crew. For his wife Katya.

Oh, Katya, Minh mourned. How could one fall in love with a voice?

Nearly seven months ago, a short time after the first report of Markus's death, Minh had been at Cyrus's side when he'd called his brother William. Gunner's lawyer had just called Cyrus filling him in on as many details as he'd been able to discover, including news of

Sasha's and especially this unknown Katya's involvement in the fatal FBI/Interpol raid on their brother Markus's compound. And then, such a surprise, Cyrus continued, Sasha's name turning up on a flight list, first class no less, San Francisco to Bora Bora, with that same meddlesome minx, the one who had allowed Sasha to escape the van and slip from Markus's clutches in the first place. The man had never flown in his life. Cyrus had to share it with William, it was just too strange.

Cyrus had to know what this Katya was up to now, redoubling his efforts to hack into the transmissions between Sasha's tracker and S-Branch. This time his specialists were successful. Everything said by or near Sasha was coming in loud and clear, starting with Sasha's arrival in Papeete.

William blamed Katya for Markus's death. But neither Minh nor and Cyrus had any idea William, the reckless fool, would take the next flight out of Jakarta to Bora Bora, would be there before Sasha and Katya even arrived, before S-Branch could put in security. William had taken Markus's death hard, although he'd been quick to commandeer what was left of his criminal businesses, as Cyrus had now taken over Williams's.

Cyrus followed Sasha's and Katya's conversations, and replayed their first night of lovemaking multiple times, taking perverse sexual pleasure in every moan and sigh. Minh listened too, he'd had no choice. "Saint Sasha," Cyrus had laughed, "and a bride half his age." Then they heard about William's attempt at revenge and news of his death at Katya's hand. Cyrus was angry but thought William had deserved his fate. And then nothing, the transmission ending abruptly.

But Minh kept a copy of the transmissions, listening to the tapes of Katya's voice over and over ever since. He felt he knew her, fell in love with her cleverness, her boldness, her sensuality... the wild sounds she made during sex, her first sex. He could hardly believe his ears as she and Sasha talked afterwards. A twenty-nine-year-old virgin. Minh swore he'd discovered the exact moment Sasha first entered her. That gasp. She'd become his obsession, he couldn't stop wanting her.

Then came the death of Jack Cutter in the Philippines. Cyrus was beyond fury. The *Trib* embarked on her long medical expedition and Cyrus didn't discover the involvement of Sasha's crew until shortly before New Year's. A Filipino sailor had talked too much to the wrong man in a bar. Minh was careful to hide his horror when Cyrus told him about his attempts to blow up the *Trib*. Then Cyrus had taken off for Da Nang, ordering Minh to stay in Hanoi. He returned more excited than Minh had ever seen him. He would get his hands on Saint Sasha now, he'd crowed, showing Minh the intercepted and decoded transmissions about Sasha's son Khai. Minh recognized the name immediately. His Khai. Cyrus would kill them all, Khai, too. And Katya.

Minh wasted no time in finding a way to contact the Australian government, and thus S-Branch. Then seeing Katya on his video screen, hearing her voice again, conversing with her alone... The unexpected opportunity of her pretend betrayal of Sasha becoming part of her plan... Katya being even more beautiful than he'd imagined. There was no way this woman was only a quarter Chinese... The only pictures Cyrus had of her were from her passport and driver's licenses, hardly flattering images.

Meeting Sasha in person at the Hanoi military airport had been a shock for him. Saint Sasha was even more handsome and youthful looking than he had appeared on his video screen – muscular, graceful, and surprisingly gracious, Sasha's love for Katya, and hers for him, all too evident. Minh had to swallow his envy, his jealousy. He concentrated hard to keep his face neutral when he took Katya's hand, hoping she wouldn't notice he was trembling. His fantasy Katya, in the flesh. He was wildly looking forward to having her to himself for the next ten hours or so. The unexpected joy of additional time when Sasha extended his trip.

Then the miraculous photo shoot. Katya was such a delicious package of naiveté, danger, and surprising sexual adventurousness. That he could get her naked, get his own naked skin within centimeters of hers, was far more than he'd dared to hope for. Minh had thought more than once about just taking her in his arms and kissing her passionately. She was so totally aroused at times, he was sure she could not help but respond... and then she would break both his arms just as she threatened. That last pose. He had nearly lost his mind with desire. Sitting there watching her afterwards, so beautiful, so sensual as she touched herself, he'd quietly snapped a dozen photos that would be his alone. He would be patient, win her with superhuman restraint and persistence. Sasha might not survive what was coming next. And then she'd kissed him. He'd been a moonstruck idiot ever since.

450

Touching and kissing her in the doorway, he could feel her arousal. Promises of the future, he wanted to believe, despite the whole charade being orchestrated. He would wait. He stared up at the S-Branch security camera above Sasha's bed.

Minh's thoughts were interrupted by a moan from Sasha.

"Minh, I need to tell you," Sasha said quietly in a dry voice from the bed. "I will have some strong mood swings for the next few hours. If I seem deep in depression, I won't be acting, but it will pass. Just talk to me."

"Let's talk about anything but the next few days, then," Minh answered, helping him drink another glass of water. His rival lay helpless and totally in his power.

They had seemed to grow close, without Katya between them, since Sasha's return to Vietnam. Sasha brought his violin and Minh heard him play live for the first time. Sasha would never know he'd heard him play in Bora Bora that first morning through his tracker. Minh was surprised to learn that Khai had been able to take up the cello and that he and Sasha had even played duets together in the village.

"What was your mother's name, Minh," Sasha asked, falling back on the pillow. "Tell me about her."

"Mui. Her name was Mui. She was a remarkable young woman, looking back at her life. She had enough strength for the both of us, and we were a fearsome pair, Khai and me. She couldn't have been more than twenty-four when she died of a fever, or so I was told. It's amazing that Khai survived without her. I surmised from things my mother said that her father was a French officer. He supported her mother and Mui, sent her to school. My mother told me she'd been an exceptional student in French, English, and math, but then her father disappeared from their lives and the money stopped. Mother and daughter managed to carry on somehow and the school let my mother stay through the end of the year, but they grew more and more destitute. I learned my mother was only about fifteen or sixteen when she was raped by Vietnamese soldiers and became pregnant with me. My grandmother sent her with much difficulty to her sister's in the North. I guess the sister didn't realize Mui was a half-breed, and pregnant, and sent her on to the farm. She stayed there as a poorly paid employee after we were weaned, but I always suspected she was abused by the men who ran the farm. She did her best to keep her troubles from me and Khai. As an adult, I tried to locate my grandmother and her sister, but neither survived the war."

"What did Khai look like as a child? Anything unusual about his body?" Sasha asked, hoping he knew the answer. Khai had his build. Sasha didn't know the cause of his infant musculature, but if Khai had it too, it would help rule out his lifelong fear of being the product of a Nazi experiment and would be a tremendous relief. On the other hand, Khai's strange appearance might have been too much for a grandfather already willing to overlook the stigma of a half-Caucasian grandchild.

"How did you know? Most unusual. A baby with adult muscles, my mother said. Khai was always bulging with muscle. He still hadn't grown into them when I last saw him."

Sasha accepted the information with a sigh and decided to deal with its emotional impact later. If his recovered memory of his parents was real, this and Khai's brilliance should be proof enough. "Did you help decide what to put in the boxes of books and music for Khai?"

"What? No, but I did examine them when they came. They were sent to me with instructions and the teachers at my boarding school helped me relabel the boxes and send them on. After my last box was sent, the farm wrote to the school and told them Khai wasn't there anymore. I assumed he'd been sent out to work and try to live on his own. They wouldn't say and I had no way to find out."

"Did you know who your sponsor was?"

"The school wouldn't tell me, and they might not have known either. I was grateful, but I missed Khai and I missed my mother. They wouldn't even let me return for her funeral. That was as devastating as anything. I wasn't quite nine years old."

Sasha tried to sit up. Minh caught himself wanting to help and remembered to keep his hands off him. He was going to get as depressed as Sasha, thinking about his young mother and her short, tragic life. Sasha managed to prop himself on his own.

"Did you ever see anyone at the farm, a visitor, checking you and Khai out?"

"Yes, now that I think about it. It was a couple of months before I got sent away to school. There was a big black car with tinted windows that sat in our rutted dirt drive for a couple of hours. None of us kids had ever seen a car like that, so we were playing all around it, trying to look in the windows. I remember Khai and I were making faces. One of the men who ran the farm dragged us off and berated us, but he didn't beat us like he usually did. I remember the car had a military license plate."

"That's what I thought. It's only logical. That had to be Khai's grandfather, General An, who'd kidnapped my wife, his own pregnant daughter, and tried to kill me. General An's only son was killed in battle near the end of the war. The General probably spent months in deep depression, then got desperate. He was checking out his grandson, to determine if he might reclaim him. But once he actually saw him for himself, looking more like me than a Vietnamese, with his strange body and behavior, he knew he couldn't, or wouldn't. I'm sure he gave you the schooling he would have given his grandson, so you could act as a layer in between them. The gift boxes would be coming from you, not him."

"Then he probably never learned what happened to Khai when he left the farm."

"I'm sure he didn't. The men General An knew were long gone, the new ones were forced to stay silent, and I'm certain now that the regular government and military officials I talked to knew nothing about the secret laboratory program. It served the old man right to die not knowing his grandson was a successful scientist and living a happy life."

"But at least give him credit for sending the boxes, and for educating me. When I think about what he put in those boxes, I can tell he was thinking about you, Sasha. Why else the music, the physics, the math, why else would he have thought of robotics? And I remember a book on the Mandelbrot fuelless engine project, another on Tesla's work. Yes, I've done my research on you, Sasha. Obviously, the General did too, at least what was public knowledge. He would have known of your history with Mandelbrot, of your brilliant youthful work with the University of Sydney, that you were a neurosurgeon, had been on the staff of the Prosthetic Department before coming to Vietnam, would have known of your musical talent, from Le, or from his spies."

They both sat quietly for a moment, lost in thought and memories. Minh cleared his throat. He knew there would never be a good time to tell Sasha about the deaths from the *"Trib"* explosion, so he decided to hit him with it now. He braced himself for a violent reaction.

453

"Sasha, I don't know how to tell you this gently. There were parts of human bodies and clothing from the crew in the debris."

"There were supposed to be," Sasha answered calmly.

"I don't understand!"

"We didn't share everything with you. Hau came up with the idea of getting three unclaimed bodies from the morgue. S-Branch had no trouble making that happen. We made masks of Hiro, Dima, and Maxim, added wigs and their clothes. The crew pulled up the corpses from a cold storage unit we'd installed on the boat, just before they sighted land, and dressed them. Kiko was to crawl on the floor and turn them once or twice as they neared the harbor."

"So the figures we saw in the pilothouse were dead men?"

"I take it they were convincing. The tinted glass we put in the new boat helped too. We needed them to be seen, but not clearly."

"My God, they convinced me, and Cyrus! But you wouldn't tell me how the crew were getting off the boat in the harbor. I saw five of them, Katya, too, on the deck just minutes before the explosion. The sight had me terrified!"

Sasha grew more animated, almost manic, as he talked. "We learned a trick from Jack Cutter. The replica *Trib* was built with a chute right in the middle of the main cabin and out the bottom to an attached submarine, also courtesy of Jack. S-Branch had the sub brought back to their headquarters after Katya and the crew escaped in it. We even employed the same sub commander Jack had used and Katya protected. He lives in Sydney now – S-Branch hired him. That's another story you can't have known about, but you do know Katya's taking down of Jack Cutter is what got us into this mess with Cyrus. He didn't seem to be as fond of his other two brothers, or maybe three was just too much.

"The sub was powered the whole way so as not to slow the replica *Trib* down with drag. The new boat's outward appearance copied the *Trib*'s as exactly as possible and crew members moved around on her deck as they motored down Sydney Harbour for the benefit of Cutter's spies."

"The replica certainly passed Cutter's inspection. He never suspected a thing. I could hardly believe it wasn't the real *Trib* myself."

"We had not one but three boats under construction at S-Branch headquarters, and left the *Trib* disguised as one of them. Despite all

454

my technical skills, we haven't found a way to communicate when the sub is under water. Jack Cutter had it constructed that way. The crew and Katya were going to wait until dark to pop up and get over to a safe house for the duration, then S-Branch will get a signal."

"So you're confident they all survived," Minh exclaimed, with tremendous relief and wonder at their ingenuity. Katya was alive.

"I would know if Katya was hurt or killed. We have a connection you will never begin to understand. I couldn't feel her in the sub the first time, but now I can. And Katya is a force of nature – she's an entire U.S. Marine Corps. She would be the last one down the chute."

Sasha's look of confidence quickly faded. Minh could see that Sasha's concern about his own fate was pulling him back down into depression. Minh tried not to look guilty. He would reassure Sasha, he couldn't help himself. Even if his words were all lies.

"I appreciate your love for her. You will stay safe as well, Sasha, until your rescuers come. I have a comfortable cell waiting for you. I won't let Cyrus Cutter get near you."

Sasha only nodded.

By midday, Sasha's mood had sunk to rock bottom. Minh tried to get him to eat, but he wouldn't touch his food. The illusion of Sasha's depression was far too easy to maintain, Minh thought. He brought Sasha's untouched plate downstairs, making sure the Cutter spy he'd purposely hired to help in the kitchen saw it. He had the man come clean Sasha's room as well so there would be more corroboration of his reports.

When he returned in the evening, however, Sasha had showered and was finishing his workout as silently as he could. Minh brought up two covered plates from the kitchen, his own piled up double, fixing it himself. Sasha ate ravenously off the shared plate, and Minh made a show of returning the untouched plate to the kitchen. By nightfall, Minh forced a reluctant Sasha to sit outside for a while. He sat doubled over, wrapped in a blanket, unspeaking and unmoving. Minh didn't even try to determine whether this depression was real or faked. It didn't matter. The signal from the crew didn't come until eleven. All were alive and well. Katya was alive and well. Minh relaxed for the first time and it was all he could do to keep Sasha from getting out his violin. Minh hadn't allowed him to open the case since the evening before the explosion and Sasha's frustration was

455

threatening to undermine everything. Minh decided he preferred dealing with a depressed Sasha than a manic one.

Normalcy returned by morning, but Sasha maintained the illusion of depression and deepening despair. At nightfall of the final day, Sasha eluded his protectors and escaped out the window, fleeing across the rooftops of the compound, crossing the back streets of the Da Nang suburbs. His violin remained in the room. He arrived in near darkness at the river's edge, where, at the dead end of a cul-de-sac, lights softly glowed from the houses on either side.

Minh made a show of turning out his entire security team to look for Sasha, sending them in the opposite direction. He arrived at the agreed on location in one of Cyrus Cutter's long black cars with three of Cutter's men and had them park and turn off the engine. Motioning the men to stay behind him, he quietly approached. Sasha was seated in a cross-legged pose on the edge of the steep riverbank, staring down at the roiling black river below him.

"I guessed I would find you here," Minh said, speaking softly in Vietnamese but loud enough for the men behind him to hear clearly. "You could go that way. Or you could come with me. We'll get through this."

Sasha didn't answer or move. Minh walked slowly up to him. He looked down for a moment at his head of blond hair, shining in the glimmer of the house lights, then hit him hard with the butt of his gun. He quickly grabbed Sasha's shoulders and roughly pulled him back so he didn't tumble forwards into the black water. One of Cutter's men gave Sasha a vicious kick before he was picked up and thrown into the trunk of the car.

456

Chapter 58

Sasha awoke in a cold place, the back of his head throbbing with pain. He could feel the sticky half-dried blood on his neck and down his back and tried to estimate how long he'd been out. His arms and shoulders ached. He looked around and saw he was hanging by his wrists, his feet touching rough rock, but barely. Some sort of complicated system of ropes led out of sight above him and to the sides. He was shirtless and seemed to be wearing nothing but a pair of white shorts. The Cutters and their religious mockeries, he groaned to himself. Where was Minh's promised safe cell... Sasha tried to control the wave of terror that washed over him. Had he been betrayed – by the man in love with Katya... He tested the ropes holding his hands.

Flame torches lit the large cave, which was elevated in front where he was strung up. Four steps led down to a larger lower space. The firelight flickered over a sea of cruel-looking, eager faces crowding the lower level. He counted twenty-five men of a dozen nationalities, Cyrus Cutter's top men, brought in from the far reaches of his criminal holdings for the show. Sasha looked to his right and saw a low metal barrel on the same level as he was, flames licking its edges. He wished some of its warmth could reach him.

"Ah, the sacrificial lamb awakens," said a voice he didn't recognize, speaking in English with an accent he couldn't trace. "Saint Sasha is ready for his martyrdom."

Sasha heard quiet guffawing and snickers from the assemblage. He turned his head painfully further to the right and saw a broad-shouldered older man, tall and thick-bodied but quite fit, with a distinguished head of graying hair, standing behind the burning barrel. He was warmly dressed, his thick coat collared in fur. He remembered Cyrus Cutter from his surreptitious glance behind him from the grandstand in Da Nang. He'd been surprised Cyrus wasn't overweight like his middle two brothers, as he knew he'd once been.

"I see someone else has had the pleasure of carving you up before me! I like his handiwork. It's a good look on you. I can tell Saint Sasha likes my new look as well. I have Minh to thank for that. He got me on a fitness routine as soon as he started with me. Said he couldn't have me dying of a heart attack on him. How I needed to look more like a businessman. I couldn't be more grateful to him. Isn't that right, Minh?"

Sasha turned his head a bit more, trying not to show how much it pained him. Minh was sitting on a tall stool against a wall of the cave, as relaxed as he'd first seen him on the video screen in the Situation Room. He wore a stylish black leather jacket, padded black trousers, and black dress boots. Minh was holding an open laptop connected by a cable that snaked into darkness. There were cables and wires draped all over the cave floor, exiting the room in bundles via two openings, one behind Minh and one in the front wall, leading to a long curving rock tunnel illuminated with more flaming torches. A small wooden podium stood next to him. Minh didn't answer Cutter, just stared at his laptop, punching its keys. Cyrus seemed determined to get him to talk.

"How does our perimeter look, Minh? All clear?" Minh just nodded. Cyrus frowned and continued. "Oh, I forgot to tell you, Sasha. Minh is my head of security. And he did a fine job of stringing you up for me. I'm sorry if you thought he was your ally, your colleague, your friend. Seems like he's your rival in love instead. I have something to share with you."

Cyrus pulled out a packet of photographs from his breast pocket and made a show of looking through them, making obscene faces.

"I've been enjoying these for days now, and so have my men. Makes me sorry I didn't take the time to do her myself."

Cyrus walked over and carefully placed twelve photos on the floor in a half circle in front of Sasha, leering up at his face when he was finished. Sasha stared down at each of the photos in turn, writhing on his ropes, then hung his head and brought his knees up towards his chest, hanging there by his arms, gasping and twisting back and forth. Cyrus appeared pleased and stepped back to where Minh was sitting. Minh reached down and handed him Sasha's violin case. Cyrus opened the case and took out the worn and nicked violin and one of its bows. He walked over and used the bow to touch Sasha's chin. Sasha lowered his feet back to the ground, staring wild-eyed at the violin in Cyrus's hands.

"Why don't you play it for him?" Minh said, finally speaking. "Give him the pleasure of hearing its tone for the last time."

"Minh, what an excellent idea," Cyrus answered. "If only I played the violin. I'm afraid the last sounds it will make will be rather scratchy ones, my apologies."

"Hand me the bow. Let me tighten the screw or you'll get no sound at all," Minh said, holding out a hand to Cyrus.

"Ha, I wouldn't have thought of that," he laughed, watching Minh work.

Cyrus took back the bow, placed it on the strings, and made a half-dozen screeching strokes that were so terrible a burst of laughter arose from the assembled men.

"At least it will make good fuel," he said as he placed the bow in the fire. The horsehair singed, then burst into flame, and the bow bent and smoked before catching fire.

"No!" shouted Sasha, sounding desperate. "There's no need to destroy her!... please. You have me. Destroy me…"

"Ah, now he speaks! Oh, I will destroy you, Sasha. I have a syringe ready for you. You will not bleed or die before I have cut off every finger one by one, every finger you played this violin with. Every toe you moved with so gracefully, then I will work up your body, your feet, genitals, hands, ears, nose, all into the fire. I will leave you faceless, hung on a cross by the river where Minh picked you up, a warning to all those who dare oppose me, vengeance for my dead brothers."

With a quick motion, he tossed the violin into the flames. The violin took a while to begin to burn, but then one by one the four strings popped, each with its own last note. Sasha twisted away on his ropes from the sight, moaning.

"Not the hands," Minh said calmly.

"What? Why not the hands?" replied Cyrus, studying Sasha and looking satisfied.

"That will ruin the effect. How will you attach him to the cross?"

"You're right as usual, Minh. I'll leave the hands, but not the fingers. Let me show you what I mean, Sasha."

Cyrus pulled a bar on the block and tackle closest to him and Sasha's arms were pulled violently straight out to the sides, his feet yanked off the cave floor. The men roared their approval and Cyrus smiled as he lowered him back down to the floor.

"Are you prepared to meet your fate?" Cyrus asked, hoping to get another rise out of Sasha, and looking disappointed when he remained

459

silent and still. "I'm ready for the syringe, now, Minh. My men didn't come here to watch violins burn."

Murmurs of agreement echoed around the cave. Cyrus's men were thirsty for torture, for dismemberment. Minh bent over to pick up a filled syringe off of a black cloth on the stand. Before he could reach it, a loud alarm sounded. He quickly examined his laptop, pressing keys, looking worried.

"Perimeter breach in sector two. Dispatching guards to check it out. Probably just a wild animal... perimeter breach in sectors one, three and four. This is real. Dispatching all guards."

Cyrus was suddenly frantic. He turned away from Sasha and shouted out to his men, who were anxiously looking around.

"Get out there, all of you! Take care of this and bring me anyone you don't kill!"

"Cyrus, you need to leave some men here to guard you," Minh admonished, putting his laptop down on the podium. Jumping to his feet, he drew his Magnum from his thigh holster. "Keep at least ten of your best behind. Sending them all is not a good choice."

"Then you ten will stay," he shouted, quickly pointing. "The rest divide up and check each sector, now!"

The men raced down the front tunnel and disappeared from Minh's view. He looked over at Sasha. He was hanging even more limply, head down, eyes closed, as if he had given up. Cyrus paced back and forth, listening, but there was no sound from outside. He motioned for eight more of the remaining men to go, and the last two to come closer. A long flurry of distant gunshots echoed through the cave, followed by an even longer ominous silence, then several dozen single shots, one after the other. Minh looked down at his laptop and smiled.

"They got them all. And one captured. Bringing her in now. The rest are staying out to make sure no one else is coming."

"Her? Who have we got here?" wondered Cyrus aloud.

Two of the bulkiest of the men returned, half dragging a woman between them, holding her arms tightly. The creature was a pathetic sight, her dark hair half singed off to her scalp, part of her face, throat, and neck a raw mess of three-day-old burns. Minh stood up from his stool in horror.

"Katya. There's absolutely no way you could have survived that explosion!" Cyrus exclaimed.

460

"Luck was with me," Katya was barely able to croak. "I was reaching into the cold storage unit and was blown into it. I have fifty men outside, Cyrus."

"Minh? Ah, Minh is shaking his head no, but mostly it looks like he's just shaking. Your sweetheart looks a little worse for wear, Minh. What do you think, Sasha?"

Sasha lifted his head a moment to look at her, then collapsed again, motionless.

"Sasha!" Katya called out, but he did not respond. She looked down at the photos on the floor in front of him. "Oh God, Minh, you traitor, you monster!" she shouted.

"Oh, this is a different kind of fun," Cyrus said, relaxed and smiling again. "But I don't have time to torture you both. Maybe I'll just have to settle for you dying a second time, this time right in front of him, like his first wife. Fate just won't give you a break, Sasha. Minh, show them who's side you're on. Put the little bitch out of her misery."

Minh stepped forward, his gun in front of him, and aimed down at Katya's ruined head. She stared up at him, pleading with her eyes. Minh hesitated, then took another step closer. Katya started to panic.

"Just shoot her, Minh. Or were you foolish enough to really fall in love with her?" Cyrus asked, looking highly amused by Minh's hesitation.

Minh stepped to the ledge, his gun barrel less than two meters from Katya. There was no hesitation now. He calmly fired four times, hitting all four of Cyrus's men in the head. They collapsed onto the cave floor. Then he turned and just as calmly shot the astounded Cyrus in the chest. Thrown backwards, Cyrus hit the cave wall and slid down, his legs splayed in front of him. Katya stared in disbelief and alarm but didn't dare move.

Sasha grabbed his ropes, pulled himself up by his arms like a gymnast, and flipped over in a slow, deliberate somersault, releasing his unbound hands as he landed nearly soundlessly among the photos. He strode over to Cyrus's body. Minh's and Katya's eyes watched his every move, both unsure whether he had lost his mind. He bent down and took Cyrus's head in his hands, and gave it a hard, powerful twist, breaking his neck with an audible snap. Then he stood looking back and forth between the two of them.

461

Katya slowly pulled off her wig and face mask, rubbing at the remaining make-up. Minh's total surprise showed on his face as he looked at both of them, but he stayed where he was as he pointed his gun now at Sasha. Sasha jumped lightly down from the raised area, Minh's aim following him, and approached Katya. He held his hands up and out to the side as if surrendering and gave her a quick kiss on the forehead, then just as slowly turned, lowering his arms, to see Minh's gun still pointed at him.

"We're done here, Minh," he said quietly. "Thank you. Especially for having him play the violin. I needed to hear for certain it wasn't mine."

Minh lowered, then holstered his gun. Sasha's mind was definitely all there. Minh was a little disheartened to think he hadn't been completely trusted after all. Katya was too horrified at both men's actions to find words and stood mutely staring at them. Minh stepped into the back tunnel and fetched some warm clothes and shoes, handing them down to Sasha. Sasha rubbed his arms and wrists, then dressed hurriedly. He invited Katya to come close and help warm him, wrapping his arms around her.

"Minh, what did you do?" she finally managed to say. "They were all supposed to be captured, not killed. That was the purpose of my disguise, so I'd look weak! I would have taken these men and Cyrus down with your help. You just executed five men... And you, Sasha!" Katya said, still incredulous, looking around her at the bodies, at Cyrus Cutter's broken neck.

"My own trusted men have killed the rest of them," Minh said, unapologetically. "There will be no one left alive to keep on seeking revenge."

"But we dropped them with dart guns, Minh, they were down!" Katya didn't want to believe what Minh was telling her. She'd had it all carefully planned. No one was going to die this night.

"When your crew moved out, my security men and trusted police officers came behind them and finished the job. I'm sorry to have lied to you, Katya. But I wanted them all gone. We, Sasha and I, needed them all gone. This has to be the end of it. The police will be raiding all of Cutter's businesses in several countries tonight and tomorrow, and those at the lower end will go to jail, but the heads will be gone and won't grow back. And you're lucky I didn't shoot you, too. For a moment, putting you out of your misery seemed like the right move to make. Your fake injuries were another thing you didn't tell me about. But then I thought Sasha would love you no matter what you looked like."

"You, probably not," Katya said, her voice cold.

"No, me probably not," he said, smiling for the first time. He walked over to the photos on the cave floor, picked them all up and dropped them into the fire.

"Don't!" Sasha called out, but the photos had burst into flame. "I hope you have copies," he said, as he watched the flames rise and then quiet down.

"I don't," Minh lied. "I thought it best. But why…?"

"I liked them. In fact, I got quite aroused looking at them. I had to hide it."

"Saint Sasha enjoys my photographic talents," Minh laughed, recalling the moment when Sasha pulled up his knees. "Just use your photographic memory. They'll always be there in your head now."

"It's just not the same," Sasha replied, looking disappointed.

"I don't understand either of you," Katya said shaking her head, still traumatized, growing angrier with both Minh and Sasha for their cavalier attitudes, for the slaughter.

The sound of many footsteps echoed from the entrance tunnel, and Maxim, Hiro, Sonthi, Aashir, and Tuan appeared, guns drawn.

"It's over," Sasha said. "Time to contact Bao, time to go home. And what are you two doing here," he said to Aashir and Tuan, affectionately. "You were supposed to leave before all this for Ho Chi Minh City."

"Not until you were free, Sasha," Tuan said. "We came with Angel on the sub."

"Good to see you safe, Sasha. Thank you, Minh." Maxim looked around at the dead on the cave floor and Cyrus's corpse. "But what the hell happened here? Katya had a plan…"

"Change of plan, Maxim, Hiro, all of you," Sasha said, his voice steady. "You're going to have to accept what we've done. I couldn't go through this again, couldn't risk losing any of you. We've taken them all out, even those you darted. These men were powerful. They could have ordered retaliation from prison, even gotten out on bail and attacked us personally."

Maxim hesitated, looking over at Hiro and Sonthi, then nodded, then Aashir and Tuan nodded too.

463

Chapter 59

Katya could tell Sasha had plans he wouldn't share with her. He was excited, manic even. She still hadn't forgiven him for the execution of Cyrus Cutter and his men. The state of affairs was exceedingly tense between them.

Sasha thought he really would go mad soon if she didn't come back to him. She had not let him touch her or put a hand on him since they left the cave and he was more desperate for her touch than he could ever remember. He had wanted to enjoy the anonymity of her being considered dead for one more day before facing the public, to have her all to himself. It was now three in the morning, but the night's terrors were still fresh and both their adrenaline levels far too high to consider crashing. They sat drinking water in the safe house kitchen in Da Nang, not talking, the crew tucked into a second safe house nearby. They'd both managed a shower and a change of clothes.

"I have someplace I want to take you," Sasha blurted out, unable to contain himself any longer.

"At this hour?" she asked suspiciously.

"Especially at this hour!" Sasha insisted.

"Do I have a choice?" Katya objected, her voice angry, cold.

"This time you don't. I really need you to come with me."

He grabbed both her hands and half pulled her to the door. She had never seen him so giddy. He practically pushed her into a waiting car and the driver sped off into the darkness. They stopped at what looked like a row of neon-lit low-rise hotels, and he hurried her inside. The lobby was plush with red velour, and an older Vietnamese woman, beautifully gowned in a red silk traditional ao dai, let their way to a second-floor room. She turned on the low wattage lights and left. Katya couldn't believe her eyes. She found herself in an extremely lavish sex hotel, surely not on the socialist government's list of approved businesses. A giant bed took up most of the space, with mirrors on the ceiling above it, and full-length mirrors on all the walls. When she angrily turned around, Sasha was on bended knee.

"Forgive me my betrayal of your plan, for the necessary killing, Katya, and I'll forgive you Minh," he said, as he held out a small silk box.

She wanted to retort that nothing had happened with Minh, but she knew something had. The two were far from equivalent, but she kept quiet. Katya couldn't imagine Sasha presenting her with any kind of jewelry, it just wasn't in his character, and he knew that she didn't wear anything but her wedding band and a cheap watch. Clueless, she took the box gingerly from his hand and opened it. Inside was a single small exotic flower, similar to the ones their wedding leis had been made from.

"It may seem a bit early to renew our vows, but this has been an extraordinary month," Sasha pleaded. "I cannot live without your love, Katya. And after these many days without you, and this terrible night, I can't go on another moment without making love with you. I'm aroused beyond all self-control and I need you back. I love you, Katya Zhang Kaplan."

"That has to be the weirdest and most self-serving vow renewal ever uttered," Katya declared sternly, trying to be serious, but she found her anger melting in the face of his desperation, his sincerity.

She loved him too much to continue punishing him. She missed having sex with him. Sasha was right. The men that Minh and his security forces and police had killed were evil and the cycle of violence would surely have continued, against them, against more innocent victims, before they were tried and convicted. Death sentences would have awaited most, some would have faced torture in their own countries, she rationalized. She had become a killer of killers herself. And she had long known of the violence hiding in Sasha's soul. That he had killed before. Krüger was in his head, and the horrors of Bergen-Belsen... the Vietnam War, Le shot in front of him... his decades-long battles with murderous human traffickers, pirates, and other criminals... Katya thought of what these men had been planning to do to Sasha and resolved to forgive him for wanting them dead. She hated her rationalizations, but gave in to them.

"I hear you, I apologize, and I forgive you. Sasha Borodin, I forsake all others and want to have hot, dirty sex with you and just you until we're too old to try. I've turned you into a sex maniac and I love you all the more for it. And if we're being charged by the hour, we'd better get started. Just tell me one thing first. Are there cameras here?"

"Yes. Guilty. Lots of cameras. But automatic cameras, no one peeking. I can make my selection quite discreetly later. I want pictures of you and me, not of you and Minh, in my head, and in my hand."

Katya wanted to say these photos would never compare to the quality of Minh's, but she knew to keep quiet here, too. She sank down to the floor next to him and they kissed more passionately than she thought possible after over a half year of passionate kissing. Sasha started pulling off her clothes and she pulled off his, throwing them wildly around the room. They stumbled over to the bed locked in an embrace and kiss, and Katya tried not to laugh as she caught their tangled reflection in the overhead mirror.

Sasha was eager to recreate all the photographs he'd stared at on the floor of the cave. The pleasures of oral sex were no longer an unknown mystery to either of them and the actual performance was so far beyond their imagining, so sublimely enjoyable, they both thought they would lose their minds.

Katya could feel Sasha's inhibitions fall away; what he'd been forced to do as a sexually abused child was forgotten as he found himself on the receiving end of ecstasies. Only one taboo remained, and Katya fully understood. She knew Sasha would always love men, would continue to love looking at them, but he would remain incapable of any sexual connection with them.

They made love in every new way Katya had learned until they felt they couldn't be any more aroused, and then they would find another position and start over. All the tension, all the fear they had experienced since the attack on the *Trib*, since the destruction of the duplicate *Trib*, melted away and they finally lay on the bed more spent than they had ever been after sex.

"I hope they have a shower here," Katya mumbled, barely able to speak.

"Double shower, jacuzzi with rose petals, the whole works," Sasha answered. "Just don't let us fall asleep. Even with our new fortunes we'll be broke again."

"Tell me, how on Earth did you know about this place?" Katya asked casually, then sat up abruptly, pulling the sheet to her neck, as the obvious answer came to her. "Oh God, Minh set this up for you, didn't he?"

467

"By way of apology maybe." Sasha sounded totally relaxed and unconcerned. "I think he understood how much we both needed sex after this week, after this night. And he knows now he doesn't have a chance with you."

It was Sasha's turn to be naïve, Katya thought. She knew Minh wouldn't give up so easily. He was obsessed. They would just have to keep their distance from him. She imagined Minh making his own selections of photographs from the automatic cameras, and then panicked momentarily that he might be here himself, watching them, taking more photographs, or even worse, videos. Any or all of these mirrors could hide a secret room with one-way glass. On second thought, let him have his fantasies, she mused, relaxing. Minh had been more than honorable and they owed him their lives. But she would never let him touch her again.

"Let me prove one more time that you're the only one I'll ever have sex with, Sasha," she avowed, eager to put Minh out of her thoughts. With that, she pulled him off the bed and into the jacuzzi, already steaming and ready, closing the bathroom door behind them. With her second wind, she proved it there and again in the double shower.

An hour later, sitting over hot tea back in the safe house, even more exhausted and still unslept, Katya wondered again how she and the crew were going to be resurrected. Why had she not paid much attention to that part of the plan, she thought, wearily. Sasha had told her he had it covered. She thought of Fujio and Umi, her sifu, David and her other housemates, who were mourning her death. She'd badly miscalculated the interest the world would take in the destruction of one boat in a Vietnamese harbor. Sasha was out of bed somewhere, no doubt exercising. He bounced into the room a few minutes later, manic again, with more news.

"You're staying dead for another day," he called out. "I've gotten us both an invitation to see Khai. Something momentous has happened, besides his not being dead, and his handlers are eager to share the excitement. I'm working on getting the whole crew invited, Minh, too. Minh deserves to see what became of his friend, his twin."

"Doesn't he have a lot to clean up here and in Hanoi? Bodies to dispose of? Reinstatement with the police to work out?" Katya asked, too tired to even pretend enthusiasm. She was not thrilled at the prospect of being in Minh's company again so soon.

468

"The police here will write up all the bodies like there were multiple power plays with those gang leaders in one space, that they shot each other, and a police raid killed the rest in a shoot-out. They're so happy to have them gone, they will cover it up. I'm sure they were all being blackmailed. Minh's reinstatement with the police will take longer. He will come out a hero when this settles."

"Good for him," she snapped. That should keep him happy and busy, she thought, and away from her. "Now tell me how the crew and I come back to life," Katya said a bit more eagerly, starting to recover.

"I had all this worked out in my head before we left the Situation Room," Sasha stated, speaking rapidly. "Tuan and Aashir were supposedly never on the boat, so they're fine. The submarine concealed beneath the *Trib* was going to be a surprise gift to the Vietnamese government. The double engine failure on the *Trib* became evident just a few minutes before they blew up, and you were all able to evacuate to the sub, swimming into its underwater diving entrance, but the sub was crippled in the explosion and sank to the bottom. There was sufficient air and food for three or four days, but no communication was possible, and the underwater exit hatch was now jammed. Heroic efforts on the crew's part got the sub to rise. That's when rescue boats rushed out to you. A great survival story for the media. You will all have to get yourselves dirty and sweaty to make it look real. Can't have you smelling deliciously of shampoo like you do right now," he said, burying his nose in her hair and kissing the back of her neck.

"Not bad," Katya said, thinking fast. "But even better, the sub stays down. Let's have investigators arranged by Khai's handlers send divers looking for more evidence, and they'll hear pings bouncing off the sides of the sub, or us banging on the inside walls. The divers go deeper and find us; they get the diving hatch open, and we all swim to the surface with assistance. The water's not too deep to make it work, I checked earlier. We'll be too wet to see how clean we are."

"You're right, much better. Khai's government handlers will make sure that all happens, then they'll raise the sub for the media and take it away without a public inspection."

"We left out explaining the body parts in the water, since we're all alive."

"Don't forget our three corpses. You'd taken on three extra passengers, guards, in Australia. S-Branch has already gotten us fake names and identities, and they unfortunately didn't make it to the sub."

Katya visualized the scene, her hair still wet as she stood draped in a blanket talking to reporters after their rescue, sadly recalling how the three men had panicked and tried to swim for shore, explaining how the rest of them had survived, running low on oxygen, the desperate banging on the sides of the sub. She would have Sasha arrive in his white mourning clothes, calling out her name, rushing to the front of the room, kissing her in feigned relief in front of all the cameras. The kiss seen around the world... Or maybe not that last part with Sasha. She smiled and brought herself back to the present moment.

"And how are we getting to Khai's laboratory and back to the sub without anyone seeing us?" she queried. "We're a rather large number of mostly supposedly dead people."

"Minh's security employees will get us to a private heliport. We'll be flown by helicopter to the second location, where we'll meet two smaller government choppers that will drop us off at the village. We have a particularly trustworthy pilot for the first leg," he said, looking mischievous. "Whole thing in reverse for the way back, but most of you will be driven to the bay where the sub is hidden. How about a late afternoon resurrection for you?"

"So how much time do I have before we go?"

"Just enough to finish your tea, if you drink fast," Sasha sighed happily, checking his new encrypted cell phone, foisted on him by S-Branch as soon as they arrived back in the safe house. "I just got the go ahead."

It was still quiet and empty at the heliport when they arrived for their first flight at dawn, but they made sure to dash from the van to the large military helicopter in order to remain unrecognized. The crew was euphoric over the successful conclusion of the endgame and excited at the prospect of meeting Sasha's son. Katya glanced around for Sasha as they buckled in, but he had disappeared. She looked over at Maxim and Hiro but they just shrugged. Katya studiously ignored Minh's longing stare. She unbuckled and moved up to the cockpit on a hunch. There was Sasha, getting ready to take off, and he motioned for her to take the jump seat. The pilot, moved to the co-pilot's seat, turned and gave her a grin and a thumb's up. Shaking her head, she buckled herself in; she had no concerns about Sasha's flying skills. Sasha announced their takeoff to the crew over the speaker system and she could hear the muted sound of their laughter even over the rotor noise. She put on her headphones so they could talk.

"Please don't tell me you're redesigning this helicopter in your head while you're flying it," Katya pretended to admonish him.

"That and nine other projects. Plus enjoying the printed pictures from the hotel in my memory and re-experiencing our time there. Plus thinking about what we're going to do to top our performance tonight."

"You are so back to normal."

Sasha landed at the isolated transfer point where two smaller helicopters awaited them, taking off the instant they were loaded. The sight of the village from the air was as impressive as Sasha had described, but nothing prepared Katya for the quiet beauty of the village itself. Sasha let them wander for a half-hour, then gave a tour of Khai's house, pointing out each unique architectural and design feature, before leading them through the empty community center to the hidden elevator. Katya felt like she was caught in a strange moment in time between an idealized past and an idealized future. All the village residents must already be at the underground laboratory, she surmised. If Sasha knew the reason for the double celebration, he kept his thoughts to himself. Was it Fate that had brought Sasha to his son, or was it destiny?

Katya found the subway a mind-blowing technological wonder and she could see Minh and the crew marveling as well. Pretty good work for an abused, autistic, farm-raised, self-educated boy of fifteen, she thought. What might Khai have accomplished if he'd had Sasha's upbringing in Australia, or even better, if Sasha had been able to raise him? He was definitely his father's son. Katya was sure Sasha would have been a wonderful father. She'd watched him interact with children of all ages on Bora Bora and on their medical expedition, although he carefully avoided their physical contact. That would have to be her next goal: getting Sasha to accept the gentle and innocent touch of children.

When they emerged in the beautiful underground courtyard, they were greeted by a crowd. Khai, his staff, Lan and Bao, Dahn, two dozen or so family members, and five of the government handlers,

471

their version of S-Branch, Katya mused, were all talking excitedly. There seemed to be a happy smile on every face.

Khai stepped forward and he and his father nodded to each other awkwardly. Sasha took some deep breaths and allowed Khai to place his hands on his shoulders as they'd done in the village, but this time Khai touched his head to Sasha's without hesitation. Khai spoke some words that no one else could hear. Sasha nodded. The crew and the crowd cheered as Sasha put his hands on Khai's shoulders, then to everyone's surprise, they both lowered their arms into a loose embrace. Katya tried but could not hold back a tear. After a moment they broke apart, Khai with a huge smile, Sasha with a beatific look that made her instantly think of Minh's moniker, Saint Sasha. Khai had only begun his surprises. He reached out to Lan, and pulling her forward, raised her hand up for all to see their intertwined fingers. Then he took her face in both his hands and kissed her. Lan put her arms around him and returned the kiss. Katya and all the crew lost their composure now; the tears began to flow in earnest.

"It wasn't one touch, like with you," Lan said to Sasha in Vietnamese, smiling. "We were both willing to try and it took a lot of trying, a lot of practice. But I stayed with my father and Khai the whole time Khai was in hiding. We started with the shoulder and head touch like you, and then at the end of the second day he just kissed me."

"And I'm going to marry her. Now I have to, we've had sex!" Khai shouted out, smiling broadly. Lan flushed and hid her face behind her hands. Katya quickly embraced her to help hide her embarrassment. Yes, his father's son, all right, she thought. Sasha had told her he'd had few self-filters before he met Khai's mother.

Sasha made introductions, starting with Katya, then Minh. Khai and Minh smiled at each other and nodded, each trying to see the child of eight in the grown face before him. Sasha described the relationship between them to the assembled Vietnamese, their near twin-ship and brotherhood, Minh's sponsorship by Khai's remorseful grandfather, the boxes of books and music, Minh's fateful courageous warning that had saved them all. The crowd cheered, and Minh found himself mobbed by his thankful countrymen. Sasha introduced his crew, and Katya, Hau, Tuan, Aashir, and Maxim dove into the crowd, offering greetings in Vietnamese and shaking hands. A number of the English-speaking staff and handlers shook hands and chatted with the rest of the crew.

Khai raised both of his hands for quiet and said the real reason for the celebration was about to be unveiled for the guests. He turned and walked briskly out of the courtyard. Katya was confused, but Sasha took her hand. She could see the look of proud anticipation on his face and on all of the Vietnamese faces. She was as impressed as Sasha had been at the number of fellow war survivors and children of the war who had found their way to a permanent home in Khai's village and laboratory: the half-Vietnamese, the war scarred. None of that mattered here. She saw the crowd turning as one to look and followed their gaze. A small car was silently approaching down a ramp from the left, looking out of place in the underground pedestrian courtyard. The Vietnamese crowd cheered again, and Khai stepped out and opened the hood.

"I've done it!" he said, addressing himself to his father in English, his voice loud and excited instead of monotone. "It came to me... while I was hiding in Bao's room... From ideas about using nanotechnology for coolants you gave me, Sasha. Bao brought me what I needed and I finished it... He even set up the car... I installed it this morning... They will begin production immediately! Small cars, motorcycles, mopeds and generators first...vans and trucks later. They are already working on planning the factories... using the same power!"

"What is he talking about?" Katya whispered.

"The Fuelless Engine," Sasha answered in English loud enough for Minh and all his crew to hear. "Free radiant power, based on, but far beyond, Nikola Tesla's model and dream, my ideas, and Harrison Mandelbrot's lifelong project. Free radiant energy from the sun to produce free electricity. It's here, not in a model but in a completely realized motor. The future is here, and the Vietnamese will have the patent. Soon there will be no more need for gas or diesel for engines or generators, there will be free electricity for lights and power, and I bet no more Avgas or jet fuel needed for airplanes soon, knowing my son. No more pollution from fossil fuels. A motor that operates on free clean energy, Katya, self-dependent."

Sasha started a slow, rhythmic clapping that was then joined by everyone in the courtyard. Sasha knew the true Vietnamese government would soon be apprised of the windfall to come. He knew

473

he would be using his influence with them to get a stake in this, that he would use some of his new fortune to help build factories and promote sales. This would be just the beginning. Together he and Khai would change the world.

Afterwards...

October 2003

San Francisco was experiencing a typical sunny fall day, the air crisp and clean, just warm enough not to need a jacket. Sasha held Katya's hand, Khai held Lan's as they headed over to Davies Symphony Hall, walking the short distance from the new Civic Center location of the Asian Arts Museum. They had enjoyed a lengthy visit and lunch, having been dropped off earlier in the day by the private car and guard Peter had arranged for them at the Australian Consulate where they were staying.

Katya found the sidewalks empty of homeless, Sasha's One World Fund having helped build supportive housing for nearly the entire population. She'd been doubtful there would be an afternoon performance of the Symphony on a Tuesday, but Sasha was insistent. As they walked, Katya noted how the bright sunlight made the new gray strands in his still blond hair more visible. He was aging well, she mused, still nearly as fit and definitely as handsome as when she first laid eyes on him.

There were no crowds around the lower entrance doors to Davies and Katya saw no one milling upstairs through the glass walls. Sasha pulled her gently past the box office doors and on around two left corners to the opposite side of the building. They were heading to the musician's entrance, she realized. They entered and walked up the stairs. Sasha gave his name to the laid-back guard at the desk and they were ushered in. Katya was surprised they weren't handed the usual visitor stickers, then even more surprised to see another Consulate guard waiting for Sasha. He handed Sasha his violin case.

Giving Katya a kiss and nodding to his son and Lan, Sasha said he would see them soon and disappeared. A Symphony employee asked them to follow him down a hallway to the backstage entrance into the main hall. They were told they could sit anywhere they pleased, which was obvious, since they were the only ones in the entire hall. A few musicians were on stage warming up, everyone dressed casually. Katya found the row she and Sasha had sat in so many years ago, a lifetime, it seemed, but moved in towards the center. At six months pregnant, both she and Lan were just starting to feel a little uncomfortable with long walks and it was a pleasure to sit down. Touring the Asian Arts Museum had kept them on their feet for hours. Khai was smiling as usual, but Lan looked confused. Katya told her to be patient, that Sasha evidently had a surprise for them. Katya smiled as well. She now knew for certain what was about to happen. More musicians wandered in, chatting among themselves. Katya thought they looked a little uncertain, curious. Only her old friend Vladimir recognized her and waved.

The musicians took their places and the concertmaster led them in a final tuning. They started chatting again but they all stood when the conductor stepped out and walked toward the rostrum... behind Sasha, carrying his Artemisia and bow. Sasha looked out at his audience of three and nodded. Lan put her hands to her mouth and Khai waved happily. The conductor smiled over at Sasha, then raised his baton. The opening four soft timpani beats of Beethoven's Violin Concerto sounded through the hall, followed by quiet woodwinds and increasingly dramatic strings stating the theme. The Beethoven seemed fitting: glorious, passionate, and German in the best sense. It might be a warhorse, Katya thought, but Sasha had never tired of playing it, since this was his first time ever playing with an orchestra. He had played the cadenzas and his favorite moments a thousand times.

Over four years had passed since the Symphony conductor made Sasha the astounding offer to have him perform as stand-in for a soloist at a special rehearsal just for him. They'd communicated often online since then, discussing music, and had formed an interesting friendship. Katya never understood Sasha's reluctance to perform publicly, or with an orchestra; it had seemed to be his greatest wish. Sasha must have connected his training sessions and lecture-demonstrations of his prostheses at San Francisco hospitals, and this trip, with the Symphony schedule; his latest prostheses had only recently received FDA approval in the United States. Katya was last "home" at the end of their voyage most of the way around the world, when she and Sasha married on the *Trib*, in international waters off San Francisco Bay. In these last years, Katya, Sasha, and the *Trib* had continued their clinics in Southeast Asia and traveled entirely around the world on medical expeditions two more times, but had never returned to California.

After a thirty-five-year absence, Sasha had returned to work part-time for the Sydney University Prosthetics Department, while still living on the *Trib*, working in-house only one month a year, working in person at Australogic as well that month, as he had for decades. Sasha was just one of three talented neurosurgeons among a staff of seven, his unique creations still only known as products of the renowned Australogic Laboratories. Training neurosurgeons in the use of the neural implants for his – Australogic's – prostheses had Sasha traveling internationally by air, but he'd only managed to complete four trips a year these last three years.

His feet were firmly on the ground now, Katya thought, his first time on the sacred concert stage of Davies Symphony Hall. He swayed slightly, eyes closed, waiting for his entrance, then his Artemisia was quickly up to his shoulder. Sasha's violin soared up to the concerto's sweet, quiet first notes. Katya thrilled to the sound. She had heard many famous violinists perform the Beethoven concerto, but she found Sasha's lyrical interpretation equal to any of them. His first movement cadenza was emotional, bold, musically powerful, technically flawless, breathtakingly beautiful.

The musicians looked around at each other in appreciation of what they were hearing; few in the orchestra besides Vladimir and the conductor had heard Sasha play backstage on Vladimir's borrowed violin. Now the trusting conductor and his orchestra members were hearing Sasha's incomparable Stradivari and the full force of his virtuosic power for the first time. Katya had no doubt it would not be the last time. She was soon lost in her memories of their recent weeks together while she listened.

Katya thought of her last sight of Maxim, Dima, and Keung on the *Trib*, waving from outside the pilothouse as she and Sasha disembarked in Pho My, just over a month ago, near the end of August. Hau, Kiko, Chen and the four newer crew members had already said their farewells. Sasha and Katya headed right into Ho Chi Minh City to visit with Aashir and Tuan. The *Trib* would head on to Sydney for her dry dock month and the crew would scatter for loves and adventures of their own.

It was a bittersweet parting; Sasha's last mission as Captain of the *Trib* was over. The *Trib* had been his only home for thirty-four years; this was an end to thirty-seven years of nearly constant shipboard life. Katya knew the *Trib* hadn't been the same for him since first Tuan and Aashir departed, then more devastating, Hiro and Sonthi just over a year ago, but Sasha's sudden decision was a total surprise. Katya was still in shock over his retirement. She assumed they would raise their son on board, that life would continue as before. Maxim and the crew were as upset as she was. Sasha's decision was final. No one could convince him to change his mind.

Sasha had spent his last evening playing his last performances with his quartet, or what was left of it. The loss of Hiro and his cello had been almost too much for him to bear. Sasha's quartet would continue without him, with Maxim, Hau, Dima, and Keung. Hiro had turned his duties as Chief Communications Officer over to Hau; Chen was the new First Officer. Sasha was eager to see Hiro in just a few days from now. Hiro would meet them in Japan to continue the family three-country tour, then they were on to Sydney.

Maxim had become not only sole Captain and Chief Medical Officer of the *Trib*, but also commander of the eleven new boats in the fleet, all identical replicas, all hydrogen-powered and hydrofoil-equipped, and their eleven captains, two of whom were Hiro and Sonthi. The twelve boats each had a dry dock month; Sasha had chosen September, spring in Australia, for the crew's new free month; Hiro's boat, the *Fūjin*, had an October dry dock. The medical world was convinced the "*Retribution II*" was itself a replica, the original destroyed in that spectacular accident in Vietnam.

The reputation of the *Trib* after their around the world medical expeditions ensured that there was never any shortage of adventuresome doctors eager to sign on, if only for a two-year stint. Four temporary doctors were assigned to each new boat in the fleet. The Australian government provided a more permanent crew of four medically-trained sailors, along with two officers and a captain, who were also doctors or surgeons. Only Sonthi insisted on choosing his own crew. Nearly four dozen nationalities from six continents were now represented by the crews and doctors. Katya was proud that four of the boats, including Hiro's and Sonthi's, had taken on four female doctors each, and one of those boats had an all-female crew and captain as well. Only three of the twelve captains cared if their officers and temporary doctors were also musicians.

Katya remembered how hard it had been to convince Sasha to let her share his history of abuse and the horror of Bergen-Belsen with the rest of his crew. He had steadfastly refused to ever speak of it again

480

and had finally left it to her and Kiko to tell his story in his absence. Katya had chosen to tell them a year ago when the *Trib* had just arrived in Sydney for her annual maintenance and Sasha had hurried away to his laboratories. Hiro and Sonthi had flown in to join them. Everyone wished they'd known years before. No one cried more than Maxim.

Afterwards, one by one, Sasha had been able to let his long-time crew members make physical contact with him, hands on his shoulders like Khai, and even embrace him, starting with Maxim, his oldest friend, although the shudders continued each time. Katya imagined Sasha could now shake anyone's hand with no more than that shudder, but Sasha stubbornly refused to attempt it. He had not suffered a haphephobia panic blackout since Da Nang, thanks to Katya's touch. It took another month for him to allow the four newest crew members to make physical contact with him.

Katya was pleased Sasha had added Lan and Peter Hammond to the number of people he would let touch him on this trip. Sasha had still not learned to tolerate small children touching his face and hands during examinations, but Katya was certain having a child and grandchild of his own would change everything for him. The List of Bergen-Belsen dead no longer haunted him, but horrific images of the camp recurred occasionally, quelled by the playing of his violin, or by Katya's touch. The manic-depressive cycles that followed each episode continued unabated. There was still a long road ahead, more repressed memories to recover. It concerned her that Sasha had been acting strangely secretive since he began traveling for the Prosthetics Department. She was devastated when Sasha began traveling without her, although appreciative of his growing self-confidence and independence. She hoped the arrival of the baby would bring them closer together.

Katya and Lan had made the decision simultaneously to start families during Katya's last visit. Khai had enthusiastically agreed, Sasha much less enthusiastically. She and Lan were due just a week apart, and Katya often thought of Khai and Minh. The babies' relationship would be a complicated one. Maybe they could call themselves cousins rather than uncle and nephew. Like Khai and Minh, they might feel more like fraternal twins. Katya decided to raise her son Jewish with a Zen Buddhist mindset. He could decide for himself where to go from there when he was thirteen. Her son's childhood would be so unlike his father's, or his brother's, no matter how brilliant he was. Khai's son would be the first in three generations to have a peaceful, happy childhood, with a loving village to help raise him – the first to know his mother's face, and his father's, as well as both his grandfathers', the first to know the date and exact place of his birth, the first to know the birth name chosen by his parents.

Artemisia's quarter-sized companion was waiting for one or both of the boys to learn on. Sasha and Katya had no doubt his new son and grandson would be excellent musicians. Sasha would gladly pay for additional instruments, or for whatever his son's family might need, though Khai's and Lan's needs would be few. Money meant nothing to Khai, and he was happy to continue to let his government and Sasha's fund enjoy the earnings from his inventions. He had never received a salary in his life.

Still lost in Sasha's masterful playing, Katya wondered when they were going to decide where to live. They only had a few months left at most, and still Sasha hesitated. He wanted to be near Khai and his grandson, but the isolation was problematical. They had been able to rent Sasha's former home, Mandelbrot House, for only five and a half months, after their Japan trip. The baby would be born in Sydney; Sasha wanted Katya to be near a first-rate hospital. But Australia was almost as far from the rest of the world as the village in Vietnam. Now there was the lure of California and the possibility of more Symphony rehearsals like this one. Then Thailand seemed to be very much on his mind recently. This trip with Lan and Khai would be a welcome respite from her worries.

She smiled to herself as she recalled telling Sasha three years ago that he just needed to invent a personal flying machine that would take him anywhere almost instantly. She could see the gears turning in his head and laughed that he was probably half way to a solution before she'd finished her sentence.

Katya had enjoyed her and Sasha's week with Aashir and Tuan in their stylish Ho Chi Minh City home, discussing the distribution of Sasha's foundation money, now titled the One World Fund. Young as he was, Aashir was handling his new responsibilities well and was only now asking for help; Tuan was increasingly busy with his neurosurgery residency. Peter Hammond would be joining them the January after this one as the new CEO of the Fund. So far, Sasha had been able to remain quietly in the background, a complete unknown.

482

Katya was impressed how Aashir spoke English like an Australian now, with barely a trace of his Malaysian accent. He'd become quite famous not only as the head of the One World Fund, but as a fashion designer as well, promoting his line of bamboo-fiber Unisex clothing. Sasha's centers were constantly having to ramp up production.

In addition to funding the fleet, Aashir and Tuan had whittled the fund down with projects such as the creation of hundreds of thousands of bamboo-wood housing units in conjunction with Habitat for Humanity International, complete with Khai's recycled water and waste systems, and the launch of One World Medical Outreach, constructing hundreds of free preventative-healthcare-based, high-tech medical centers in areas of greatest need.

The Fund financed groups dedicated to land-mine clearance and a massive world-wide ocean clean-up, providing them with Sasha's latest technology. Both tasks seemed overwhelming. Sasha put a priority on new research. He added his personal money to the Fund's to complete a major expansion and improvement of his four refugee and rehabilitation centers, and to finance four more green-tech factories building radiant energy Fuelless Motors and vehicles, joining the one built by Vietnam. The Fund purchased the first rugged vans with Fuelless Motors produced by the Ho Chi Minh City factory and put them to use transporting patients to medical facilities in isolated areas, especially in Africa. The Fund provided basic EMT training and salaries for the drivers as well.

The One World Fund also promoted Khai's and Sasha's joint ventures: their compostable tires, A.I, and state-of-the-art robotics gained more worldwide acclaim for Vietnam's government-run research centers. As Sasha had predicted, Khai finished designing jet engines based on his Fuelless model within a year. Katya knew Sasha had aeronautic engineers working on some sort of new jet. Sasha's love of flying was no secret to those who knew him. He'd been taking flying lessons for the past four years and had achieved licenses for every kind of aircraft.

A major car manufacturer and another motorcycle company had signed on to buy Fuelless Motors in just the last year and more car manufacturers were producing electric cars. The oil and gas industry was beginning to get hit hard. On Katya's urging, Sasha had Australogic contact the company holding his hydrogen fuel cell process and they were eager to join forces, beginning production on

483

motors for all kinds of boats, from small outboards to cruise ships and cargo vessels. The One World Fund promoted the boat motors as well, even sending representatives down waterways to exchange free hydrogen motors for polluting gas and diesel ones for small watercraft.

Numerous small factories and power plants in developing countries switched to the new generators, using one or the other of the innovative technologies. One World funded the manufacture and distribution of a million Fuelless generator/stoves for personal use. Sasha's and Khai's names remained unconnected to any of the developments. Katya wished Sasha was happier with the progress. In his mind, too much remained to be done. Most large companies and governments still didn't want to address climate change and pollution. Coal and nuclear energy plants continued to function. The world was still far from having an equitable distribution of clean water, food, decent housing, or medical care.

During their week together, Sasha argued with Aashir and Tuan that all the money needed to be distributed where it was most needed in the world, that the One World Fund should be nearly empty by now. Katya had been amused by their counter argument that the fund was earning so much money in interest, payments from Sasha's unused salary portion, from Australogic's ever-increasing profits, and income from his stake in their Fuelless Motor businesses that they were funding their projects without touching the remaining principal. They insisted that the principal was not sitting in a bank but was invested in a variety of profit-making, world-changing green tech companies and in global microfinancing.

Sasha reminded them that there were still tens of millions of refugees and homeless, that two and a half billion people were still breathing smoke from wood fires and chopping down trees for cooking fuel. Aashir countered again that mothers-in-law preferred the old wood flavors. Katya laughed when Sasha said he would have wood-flavored Fuelless generator/stoves designed by the next week. He told them again to get to work thinking up new projects, though he knew he would be handing them a detailed plan of his own.

Katya reflected on how much of Sasha's work in the laboratories had centered on defense systems and intelligence gathering equipment after 9/11. Security had been tightened once again by S-Branch. Sasha reluctantly followed their new protocols but remained unconcerned

484

about his own safety. This threat wasn't personal, like the Cutter brothers' had been. He was doing all that he could to help provide decent housing, good health care, a clean environment, an end to poverty. Fewer desperate people might translate into fewer criminals and fanatics, but Sasha knew he could do nothing about greed, political injustice, and religious extremism.

Sasha and Katya had also shared a dinner with Minh, now the head of the Hanoi Major Crime Task Force. Minh had flown down to Ho Chi Minh City, Katya having no desire to spend any more time in Hanoi, even though the new power systems and influx of money were transforming the city. Quiet intimidation seemed like the best course of action to keep him at a distance, so she had asked Sasha's two bodyguards to join them at their table in a restaurant of her choosing. She smiled recalling the way Minh had stared at her baby bump and encouraged him yet again to find his own wife instead of trying to steal another's.

Her happiest memories were of the weeks they'd spent with Khai and Lan in their village, enjoying the peace and quiet. Khai and Sasha rode the horses when not immersed in making music or in the laboratory. It still excited Katya to see them bouncing physics ideas off each other at a stratospheric level, the blond and the brown-haired heads nearly touching, the rest of the world forgotten as they tackled a new project in Khai's laboratory.

The Vietnamese government handlers had been so impressed by the increase in creativity and productivity of all the staff, not just Khai, due to Sasha's visits, that they finally lifted their ban on travel, though any requests would be carefully vetted. It took a bit of doing to get Khai to leave his laboratory for this family trip. Sasha promised to let him work with him in his laboratories in Sydney. To encourage him, Sasha presented Khai with a laptop computer identical to his own and set up his entire laboratory and his village for secure live communication. Khai was as thrilled as a child with a new toy.

A plan worked itself out in Katya's brain while she listened to the Beethoven. She now knew what she wanted: to be with Lan and Khai in their village for at least six months after the birth of her baby, after Sydney. Bao had already agreed to move next door so Lan could create a nursery in the middle bedroom. There would be plenty of space for both families, even though there was only the one bathroom...

Afterwards, she could imagine most of the year in California during the concert season, Sasha playing rehearsals with the Symphony. Fall, especially September, was beautiful, like now. Winters were mild and the brown hills turned green. Sasha had never seen California in the winter and spring when the wildflowers and fruit and nut trees were in bloom. Katya's old Berkeley house with its safe, enclosed yard would be a great place to raise a child. Her Steinway was there; music would fill their lives. They would have built-in babysitters with her housemates, Sasha would enjoy working with the Central American refugees who filtered through her home and with the anti-human trafficking organization she belonged to. He could train neurosurgeons in San Francisco as well as in Sydney. Again, they would be sharing the house, a bathroom...

Octobers and Novembers in Sydney, spring again, for his work with the University Prosthetics Department and for Australogic Laboratories. They'd already lived in Sydney every September, in cheap hotels, when the *Trib* was in her new dry dock month – much better than their original schedule of July, Australia's winter. They could find a small, decent house to rent. Perhaps a week here and there visiting on the *Trib*, Sasha playing a few quartets. They could leave the baby with Lan and Khai, or maybe they could take the baby on board before he could crawl, with ten loving uncles to dote on him, spending time with the men who meant so much to them both. If they avoided dangerous missions... They could spend summers back at Khai's in Vietnam. The weather would be fine there in the mountains, in the north, Sasha could stay put for that length of time and not teach... Katya sighed. She would live wherever Sasha decided.

The glorious final notes of the Beethoven brought Katya back to the present moment. Sasha had finally fulfilled his dream and there promised to be more such opportunities. Lan, Khai, and Katya applauded wildly, their clapping echoing in the empty hall, joined by the waving of bows by the string players and the applause of the rest of the musicians. The conductor stepped down to shake Sasha's hand but remembered at the last moment, bowing instead. Sasha bowed back deeply and bowed multiple times to the still applauding orchestra. Katya swore she saw a first ever tear glistening in his eye as he looked over at them, but perhaps it was just an illusion after all, a trick of the light.

486

Coming soon

Fate's Far Winds

Second Novel in the *Fate* Series

By Stephany Cavalier Houghton

Excerpt from Chapter One

The winding Hakone Turnpike out of Tokyo had just offered the first breathtaking view of Mt. Fuji when Sasha and Katya both noted their driver, Hiro, checking his side and rear view mirrors frequently, concern clearly etched on his face. Turning in their seats, they spotted an immense black van traveling a discreet distance behind them. It was still there when they checked again.

Hiro sped up slightly and the van did the same. All conversation ceased. Sonthi took his eyes off Mt. Fuji to size up the situation. Lan and Khai didn't seem to notice the tension. Lan was staring open-mouthed at the sight of the iconic volcano, the peak and slopes of its perfect cone white with snow; her husband Khai, Sasha's son, only glanced nonchalantly out his window, nodding to the music in his headphones. Looking back again, Katya saw the van close on their tail. Her eyes met Sasha's. Their hands reached for each other.

"Did you arrange a security escort after all?" Katya asked Hiro. S-Branch had offered security for the vacation part of their Japan trip, but Sasha had refused. He'd told them he had Hiro. And Katya. Sasha had felt even more secure with the surprise addition of Sonthi.

"Not one of ours," Hiro answered.

Sonthi took out his cell phone and looked back to read the van's license plate number, then texted. They would have an answer soon from S-Branch.

"Ah, not what I hoped to hear," Sonthi sighed, a few moments later. "Yakuza."

"Yakuza?" Sasha sounded skeptical. As if in answer, the man in the black van's front passenger seat placed his bare elbow out the open window. Elaborate tattoos covered the beefy arm to the wrist. "What do Japanese gangsters want with us?"

"What they always want," Hiro growled in response, as he gripped the steering wheel tighter. "They must think we're rich tourists, must have pegged us at the airport."

"Rich tourists, two of us pregnant, one of us sort of Caucasian looking," Katya added. "I bet they're looking for women and babies to sell."

"Don't scare Lan," Sasha warned her. "We don't know what they want yet. The Yakuza are organized crime. It's not like them to try a daytime assault on what they think are tourists."

"Then you think someone sent them?" Sonthi asked.

"If they were sent, the men in the van behind us don't know who we are!" Katya replied. "If they confront us, they'll be making a huge mistake." Katya had no doubt they could take care of themselves, but any situation that might arise was going to need some fast talking and trickery. Her specialty. "Let's make them believe we're something else altogether. Let me think."

"At least they're probably not armed. Even the Yakuza are terrified of Japan's gun laws," Sasha stated, staying cool, but concerned for his son and daughter-in-law. This was supposed to be an ordinary family trip. Nothing ever stayed ordinary in his life.

"I suppose that means we're not armed either, Hiro?" Katya inquired.

"No guns. Not even one of Sasha's dart pistols."

"What about a tire iron? And is it within reach?"

"Yes, but I don't see..."

The big black van moved up to ride their bumper, it's hostile intentions unmistakable. No one in Katya's vehicle was still admiring the view of Mt. Fuji.

"Speed up, Hiro, then stop at the top of that far hill," Katya demanded. "We're a long way from anywhere and I doubt we can outrace them. And tell me where to find that tire iron."

"Behind you, there's a tool kit buried somewhere on the bottom," Hiro answered, frowning.

"Katya, what are you thinking?" Sasha asked, his sense of alarm growing.

490

"Let me tell you what I'm thinking! I'll need you three to play along. Khai and Lan need to stay in the van." Katya carefully leaned her pregnant belly over the back seat and rummaged under the luggage until she found the tool kit. Placing the tire iron on the seat, she started taking off her slacks. While the men were gaping, she told them her plan. "Park the car so they'll see my legs when I get out, Hiro. And tell me the word for 'mistress' and the name of a Yakuza clan headquartered far from here."

Hiro answered her reluctantly. Katya repeated the words to herself. She felt ready.

"Katya, we men are too old for a fight," Sasha insisted. "Who knows what they want! We don't know how many men they have. And you're too pregnant. You're staying in the van!"

"Not happening, Captain. You're officially retired now, Sasha, so insubordination rules!" Katya called out, as she slipped back on her flats. Not very sexy, but pregnant women wouldn't be expected to be wearing heels. She put on her coat and buttoned it up. The coat was loose and fell half-way to her knees. She'd look like she was wearing a short dress underneath, wouldn't look quite so pregnant. Taking the belt from her slacks, she cinched it around her coat, then sat quietly waiting for action, the tire iron in her lap.

"We need a better plan," Sasha declared, shaking his head as he watched her prepare. "Help is too far away and we have no defenses."

"Alternatives then?" Katya asked. "Either they'll back down with my story, or they'll be put off guard and we hit them hard. And then they'll believe my story. We are anything but defenseless. If there's a fight, I'll even the odds with the tire iron. Take off your jackets and roll up your sleeves. You're all professional bodyguards now."

Just then a shot rang out. They felt their van swerve as one tire blew. So much for no guns. Hiro pulled to the side, positioning the car as Katya had requested. He could think of no alternatives. Katya's quick-thinking had never failed them. But the gun changed everything.

The black van stopped four meters behind them. Five powerful-looking tattooed young men emerged and walked purposefully towards them. Katya recognized the tough man she'd seen watching them at the airport. Only one of them, surely their leader, was pointing a gun.

Sonthi exited first and opened the door for Katya. Holding the tire iron tight in her left hand behind her back, she swung her legs out where the Yakuza could get a clear view, then took Sonthi's hand to stand up gracefully. She strode to the back of their van, stopped not two meters from the Yakuza leader, and stood glaring at him, her right hand on her hip. Sasha and Hiro, glaring as well, emerged from the other side of the van and rushed to stand near Katya. Sonthi came closer too, shoulders back, rubbing his knuckles threateningly. Katya began speaking angrily to the Yakuza leader in informal Japanese.

"What is the meaning of this? What do you want? Do you have any idea who I am?"

The Yakuza leader looked surprised by this Japanese speaking tourist, but answered her in a rough, guttural voice, using street slang she could barely comprehend. Katya responded in a long, loud blast of deeply offensive Japanese profanity. All the Yakuza looked startled, their leader shocked. Now that she had their attention, Katya continued, snarling in Japanese.

"I am the mistress of the leader of the Yamaken-gumi clan in Kobe! I am carrying his baby. Drive away and this ends now or he'll cut off all your fingers. Do not mess with me!"

The Yakuza leader gave a short bow but did not back down.

"Then give me the other woman," he demanded, speaking more clearly in standard Japanese. "We will not leave empty-handed. The woman, your money, and the violin. And the two laptops."

Katya continued glaring at him for a long moment, apparently mulling over the offer. They'd been observed leaving the plane, but how would the Yakuza know for certain what was inside the cases they carried? The violin case was rectangular and the computers were stowed in laptop backpacks. Who had sent them? The leader was negotiating to save face. What did he really want, the laptops?

"How about a few minutes with me and you let the other woman go," Katya said, suddenly sexy. "You can have the rest of the items you requested."

Quickly approaching the leader, she held out her empty hand, smiling, entreating. The man lowered his gun and motioned for his men to stay where they were.

Katya swung the tire iron from behind her back and cracked it down hard against the leader's gun hand, then whacked his head with a forceful backhand, knocking him senseless to the ground. Sonthi,

492

Hiro, and Sasha rushed at the remaining four men and the fight was on. Katya scooped up the gun and slipped it under the belt around her coat, turned, and bashed the tire iron carefully against the back of the head of one of the two men engaging Sonthi. Ah yes, they've made a big mistake indeed, Katya thought, swiveling around to check how her Sasha was holding out. Looked like about time to lend another hand.

Made in the USA
Las Vegas, NV
30 January 2024

85108794R00270